## Acclaim for the works of Michael Asher

'It is Asher's achievement to have diagnosed both the complexity and naïvety in Thesiger, yet to have evoked his hero's intransigent grandeur ... A work of unmistakable stature and commitment ... it is hard to see how *Thesiger* will be superseded' – Colin Thubron in the *Independent on Sunday*

'Excellent ... He writes with a true expertise without abandoning independence' – Basil Davidson in the *Spectator*

'Gripping narrative ... [*Shoot To Kill*] is a tale of physical endurance, endless drudgery and frequent humiliation. It will bring home to many what life in our armed forces is actually like ... Michael Asher has a fine, observant eye and a keen writing style' – Paddy Ashdown in the *Scotsman*

'An account of maybe the last great journey man had still to make and it is honestly, magnificently told ... [*Impossible Journey*] is destined to become as great a classic as Thesiger's *Arabian Sands* – and for the same reasons' – Geoffrey Moorhouse in the *Daily Telegraph*

'In the tradition of Doughty, Lawrence and Wilfred Thesiger ... [*In Search of the Forty Days Road*] stands, not as a requiem for this way of life, but as a salute to it' – *Sunday Times*

## ABOUT THE AUTHOR

Michael Asher was born in Stamford. He is a graduate of the University of Leeds, and has served in both the Parachute Regiment and the SAS. Called 'one of Britain's greatest living desert explorers', he has covered over 16,000 miles by camel, and has lived for three years with a Bedouin tribe in the Sudan. In 1986–7, with Arabist Mariantonietta Peru, he made the first ever west–east crossing of the Sahara on foot and with camels, a total of 4,500 miles in nine months. He has won the Ness Award of the Royal Geographical Society and the Mungo Park Medal of the Royal Scottish Geographical Society for his travels, and is a Fellow of the Royal Society of Literature.

His books about the desert and its people include *In Search of the Forty Days Road*, *A Desert Dies* and *Impossible Journey*, an account of his history-making trek across the Sahara. He has also written *Thesiger*, a highly acclaimed biography of the explorer Wilfred Thesiger, which was selected as one of the *Daily Telegraph*'s books of the year, and *Shoot To Kill*, a controversial account of his military experiences. He is currently at work on a new biography of *Lawrence of Arabia*, and recently presented a television documentary about Lawrence for Channel 4.

# THE LAST OF THE BEDU

*In Search of the Myth*

## MICHAEL ASHER

With colour photographs by
Mariantonietta Peru

PENGUIN BOOKS

PENGUIN BOOKS

Published by the Penguin Group
Penguin Books Ltd, 27 Wrights Lane, London W8 5TZ, England
Penguin Books USA Inc., 375 Hudson Street, New York, New York 10014, USA
Penguin Books Australia Ltd, Ringwood, Victoria, Australia
Penguin Books Canada Ltd, 10 Alcorn Avenue, Toronto, Ontario, Canada M4V 3B2
Penguin Books (NZ) Ltd, 182–190 Wairau Road, Auckland 10, New Zealand

Penguin Books Ltd, Registered Offices: Harmondsworth, Middlesex, England

First published by Viking 1996
Published in Penguin Books 1997
1 3 5 7 9 10 8 6 4 2

Copyright © Michael Asher, 1996
Photographs copyright © Mariantonietta Peru, 1996
All rights reserved

The moral right of the author has been asserted

Printed in England by Clays Ltd, St Ives plc

This book is dedicated to my son Burton,
who made me aware of the future.

And to Mariantonietta, again.

*Future Prospects.* The Arabian Desert, until about 1940, had remained practically unaffected by other cultures, and particularly Western culture. In the future one may anticipate change . . . The desert, nevertheless, will remain the desert, although it will become less isolated, more comfortable, and possibly more productive. The question that remains to be answered, however, is whether or not the Arab individuality will become merged into an urban anonymity.

*(Encyclopaedia Britannica)*

A myth is a kind of story told in public, which people tell one another; they wear an air of ancient wisdom, but that is part of their seductive charm. Not all antiques are better than a modern design – especially if they are needed in ordinary, daily use. But myth's own secret cunning means that it pretends to present the matter as it is and always must be . . . But, contrary to this understanding, myths aren't writ in stone, they're not fixed, but often, telling the story of the same figures – of Medea or of dinosaurs change dramatically both in context and meaning. Myths can lock us up in stock reactions, bigotry and fear, but they're not immutable, and by unpicking them, the stories can lead to others. Myths convey values and expectations which are always evolving, in the process of being formed . . . but never set so hard they cannot be changed again . . .

(MARINA WARNER, *Managing Monsters: The Reith Lectures*, 1994)

# CONTENTS

# LIST OF ILLUSTRATIONS

All the photographs were taken by Mariantonietta Peru with the exception of no. 28, which was taken by the author.

# AUTHOR'S NOTE

Most of the journeys recorded in this book took place over a period of about three years, but formed part of a single quest. Several other experiences, from an earlier era, have been brought into the text because of their relevance to the development of ideas about the Bedu over a period of fifteen years. The events recounted are all factual, but the chronological order has occasionally been changed to give continuity to the text. The names of several individuals have been changed in the interests of privacy, and sometimes to prevent confusion.

I have spelled Arabic words according to my own phonetic system, though there is inevitable friction between this and some accepted spellings of Arabic words in English. The ancient Sheban capital, generally spelt Marib, has been rendered Ma'rib – the ' representing the consonant 'ain, not found in English but familiar to Arabic speakers. The same consonant occurs in the word Sa'udi Arabia, but since an Anglicized version of this is in common use, I have excluded it here as unnecessary. The oasis I refer to as Palmyra is generally called Tadmor by Syrians, though both names are known to locals. When in doubt I have followed the spelling in Nigel Groom's excellent *Dictionary of Arabic Topography and Place Names* (1983).

I have thanked all those who played a part in the creation of this book separately, but I would like to record here my debt of deep gratitude to both the Bedu and the Hadr of whatever tribe, who gave me unstinting friendship and hospitality.

MICHAEL ASHER
Stamford and Edinburgh, UK,
Sanur, Bali,
and Frazione Agnata, Sardinia,
7 April 1992–31 March 1995

# ACKNOWLEDGEMENTS

I am deeply grateful to the following:

Dr Steven Simms, Associate Professor of Anthropology,
University of Utah; C. Vance Haynes, Professor of Earth Sciences,
University of Arizona; Donald Powell-Cole, Professor of
Anthropology, American University of Cairo; Dr Darius
Campbell and Alan Rowe of the joint Royal Geographical
Society–Royal Jordanian Government Badiya Project, Jordan; Dr
Edward Allonby and Dr Jane Allonby, Amman; The American
Centre for Oriental Research, Amman; The London Library; The
Library of the School of Oriental and African Studies, University
of London; Edinburgh City Library; Faber and Faber Ltd for
permission to use an extract from T. S. Eliot's *Four Quartets* on
page 54; The Royal Geographical Society; Janet Williamson and
Mbarak bin Musallim ash Shahri; John and Jo Crowther, British
Council, Salalah, Sultanate of Oman; Eleo Gordon, of the
Penguin Group; Anthony Goff, of David Higham Associates,
Literary Agents; Mariantonietta and Burton.

# A Colony of Sphinxes Moulded by the Winds

In Cairo, I booked into a hotel on the third floor of a crumbling Corniche tenement, with a Bedouin called Selmi. The hotel had a vast vacant hall beneath, like an ancient Egyptian temple, its dome festooned with spider-webs and its walls with flaps of peeling paint like sloughing snakeskin. A statuesque Egyptian girl with an elaborate coiffure of black curls watched our toings and froings suspiciously from behind the reception desk. Yes, she had said it was all right to put our luggage in the store, but she had hardly been expecting filthy sackcloth camel-saddles and palm-fibre panniers that leaked chaff all over the lobby. Selmi handed her his identity card apprehensively. 'Aren't you going to fill in the registration form?' she asked.

'I can't write,' Selmi said, gruffly. 'My father never thought it important in our profession.'

Selmi's profession was indeed a time-hallowed one. He was a rock-salt gatherer – an occupation listed on a tomb-inscription on Elephantine Island, Aswan, dating from the time of the Pharaoh Ramses II. He was one of the last group of Bedu – perhaps no more than two dozen in all – who still used camels to transport rock-salt long distances in the deserts of Egypt.

Selmi and I planned to trek with camels across the Western Desert from the Mediterranean to Upper Egypt – a journey of 1,000 miles. Both of us knew that it was a formidable undertaking.

Our path lay through the Great Erg or Sand Sea, a desert-within-a-desert that was smaller but more treacherous than Arabia's Empty Quarter. Its dunes rose to 500 feet and in places formed an impenetrable labyrinth that could be crossed by neither camels nor motor-cars. The Sand Sea itself lay within the frame of a much larger region, known – variously and confusingly – as the Egyptian Sahara, the Libyan desert, the Western Desert and the eastern Sahara. Whatever you chose to call it, it remained one of the least inviting, least hospitable, least familiar areas in all Africa. No major routes passed through it, no friendly Bedui pitched his tent there, no veiled Tuareg grazed his flocks. Outside its oases it had supported no human population in modern times, and in places no plants, no mammals, no birds, and no insects. In much of it there was no accessible source of water, no ancient wadi-systems carrying run-off, no rain-tapping massifs. Its Nubian sandstone core sucked down into deep aquifers the rain that fell in places once every forty years. Its temperatures were ferocious, its evaporation rate the world's highest, its surface grilled by the sun for exactly 96 per cent of daylight hours. In its southern part the sun stood so high in its zenith that at the summer solstice a man had virtually no shadow. In winter Siberian winds lashed it from the north and the water in goatskins had been known to freeze solid. In early summer came the dreaded Ghibli, the hot southern wind that was still regarded with superstitious awe. So alien was the Egyptian Sahara that even the geologists had likened it to the surface of Mars.

It had been difficult to explain to Selmi why I wanted to travel in this alien place, and why, to me, the journey would have no meaning without a Bedouin companion. The Great Sand Sea was the true desert of Western imagination, and Selmi belonged to the only group of Bedu I had heard of who still clung tenaciously to their camels when they might have used motor-cars instead – the only ones to take on this desert-of-deserts in the traditional way purely out of choice. My true object was to discover the Bedu, and all they had become in the last decade of the twentieth century. To know them fully, I knew, I had to travel in the environment that had moulded them, that was familiar to them as it was to no one else.

Although Selmi had not actually crossed the Sand Sea before, the prospect of its dangers did not daunt him. He had been travelling with his family's salt-caravans into the deepest deserts since the age of twelve, and his apprenticeship had been a rude one. On his very first trip his companion had simply dropped dead while cooking the evening meal. Selmi had been watering the camels at the time, and had come back to find him lying against a saddle. At first he had thought the man had been stung by a snake or a scorpion. Then he realized that he was dead, and started to cry from fear. He was twelve years old and had never seen anyone die before. When he arrived back home he swore that he would never go with the salt-caravans again, but within six months he had been off with the camels, and after that had made two or even three journeys to the salt-oasis every year – except for his three years of military service, of course. Now, at thirty-one, he had covered more than 40,000 miles by camel, making him the most experienced caravaneer I had ever known.

I had met Selmi a week earlier in Baghdad, a village in the Kharja oasis. It lay at the base of a crescent-shaped mound where – since Persian times at least – a spring had watered gardens of date-palms, *fuul*-beans and clover. The palm groves were a brilliant halo of green against the pastel wastes of the sands: beyond this haven of moisture the Sahara stretched on and on like an endless ocean – 3,000 miles from here to the Atlantic coast.

It had been mid-morning when my car pulled up by the colony of mud-brick houses where a dozen camels stamped and snorted in a tight alley paved with a decade's camel-dung. Energetic piebald doves squabbled continuously on the cab of a rotting tractor, and around it barefoot urchins performed acrobatics in the dry manure. A slim man in an ankle-length jallabiyya and high-rise turban came out to welcome me. He had a face as grave as a Ramessid statue, and the tan-line at his neck showed that his

3

complexion had been acquired from an outdoor life. His skin was prematurely wrinkled around the eyes, adding several unwarranted years to his age, but his broad, gleaming smile made him a rakish youth again. He was tall and lightly built with a spindly, camelline stride. This was Selmi walad 'Eid.

He drew me into a mud-brick room, where a handful of Bedu with pickled-walnut faces were sitting on the floor. Each one of them stood up to shake my hand. They were dressed in jallabiyyas of striped pyjama cloth with turbans like squashed white doughnuts. Their hands had the feel of wizened buckskin, and they had a way of gripping your palm and grunting 'Welcome!' as if they really meant it. They looked like a colony of sphinxes carved and moulded by the Ghibli winds.

'Eid, an old Bedui with a nose like a purple onion and a mouthful of chiselled teeth, was Selmi's father. The other Bedu were Selmi's brothers, cousins and uncles, all recognizably out of the same mould as Selmi himself. 'Eid had been born in a black tent at Sohaj in the Nile Valley, and as a young man had walked 1,000 miles to Kassala in the Sudan, to visit relatives. He had stayed there long enough to watch British bombers pounding the Italian garrison, and had thriftily exchanged a goatskin of water for the rifle of a parched Italian trooper. Returning home to Sohaj by boat and train, he had later submitted to family pressure and married his cousin – then a little girl of nine. At thirteen she had produced the first of six strong, graceful sons. The third of these was Selmi.

A fat ewe had been slaughtered in my honour: 'Every guest must get his due!' 'Eid said. I hunkered down with the others at a calf-high table on which Selmi's youngest brother laid a tray of roasted meat, stew, intestines, a salad of tomatoes, green onions and white radishes, flaps of bread, and gooey Jew's mallow. After we had eaten the table was cleared, and a boy came round with a pitcher of hot water, a bar of soap, and a steel basin from which we washed our hands. He carried a white towel on his arm like a wine-waiter. Selmi, his father and a couple of brothers sat cross-legged on a rug opposite me. Flies settled on their faces and they flicked them away with ease. Outside, the camels puffed and rumbled as they chewed the cud. A squall of wind-borne grit scratched at the shutters on the door.

For a moment there was silence. Then 'Eid asked: 'How can we help you?'

When I explained that I wished to cross the Great Sand Sea, 'Eid and his sons looked at each other perplexed. 'You aren't looking for antiquities, are you?' one of the boys inquired. 'They put you in prison for that.'

I assured them that I was not looking for antiquities.

'But how will you find your way?' 'Eid asked. 'That is dangerous country, and none of us here has ever crossed it. The worst sin in the desert is thinking that it's easy to find the way! Why, there are plenty of Bedu born and raised in the desert who lose the way and die! Remember that man who went with us once to the salt place, boys? When he came back he said, "Now I know the way, I'll go there with my own camels." We tried to stop him, but he was so cocksure! He took a caravan of camels with him and his son, who was just a boy. They never came back. They're probably still out there somewhere – what's left of them!'

'But I *can* find my way,' I said, holding up my flat Silva compass, 'with this?'

'Let me see that thing!' 'Eid said, chortling through his sharp teeth. He examined it carefully, tapped it and screwed round the bevel, then put it down bemused. I explained that the red needle always pointed north, and that you would thus always know the other directions. 'I don't need a needle to show me north!' 'Eid shrugged. 'I wouldn't put my trust in that machine, any day!'

'I doubt if you'll get anyone to go with you across the Sand Sea,' Selmi said. 'Too far! Too far!'

I felt my spirits sink. It had taken me months – actually years – to trace these Bedu. Now, it seemed, they were not even interested in the journey I proposed. I was just about to get up and beat an ignominious retreat, when 'Eid said, almost casually, 'A journey across the Sand Sea would need a tough companion. Now what would you be willing to pay for a man like that?'

I hesitated for a moment. 'I reckon it'd be worth a hundred Egyptian pounds a day,' I said.

For an instant – and only for an instant – the sphinx-like faces lost their inscrutability and registered decided interest. In Egypt £E100 was a good monthly wage. 'Boy!' 'Eid bawled to one of his sons. 'Where's that tea, by God!'

Selmi's younger brother, a slightly less weathered, more clean-cut version of Selmi, strode in balancing a brass tray that bore glasses and an aluminium teapot. He poured out glassfuls of tea and held one out to me, but I declined. It was time to leave them to discuss my offer in private. While Selmi and the others sipped tea, I walked through dung-carpeted streets to the edge of the village where the unfettered desert wind held the spicy scent of dust. Far off to the west I could see the fringe of a dune-belt – dunes that had not existed at all in Roman times – where the folds and counterfolds of soft sand fell along the sparse cultivation and tiny dust-demons unreeled across the dune-crests like smoke. In their path stood a picket of drunken palms nursing palm-doves, postage-stamp patches of wheat, furry pencil-cedars, sprouts of tamarisk on the sandy hillocks. A battle was being fought there – the old battle between the desert and the sown. Often, the desert won. There was an abandoned village called Arba' – now reduced to a roofless maze of melted mud-brick and belly sand. The creeping dryness had turned the soil to dust long ago, and the wind had threshed it away leaving only a griddle of lines that had once been irrigation canals.

Suddenly, someone touched my arm. Selmi stood there, regarding me with a basilisk stare. 'It has been decided,' he told me with simple gravity. 'I will go.'

It was New Year's Eve in Cairo, and the Corniche was choked with honking taxis and expansive holiday crowds. In Tahrir Square gangs of young people in silver witch-hats were shooting off firecrackers and clapping hands around musicians playing lutes and tablas. Selmi and I spent a fruitless hour trying to navigate through the Metro subways: 'It's a lot easier finding your way in the desert,' he grumbled. A group of excited schoolboys made a circle round him hand in hand, chanting 'Saʿidi! Saʿidi! Man from the south!' Selmi broke out of the circle scornfully. 'Just because we wear jallabiyyas and turbans they think we're stupid!' he said. It was one of the few times I saw him angry.

We sat at the tables outside the Hilton and ordered tea and hookah pipes. The waiter, done up in bottle-green mess-tunic and dicky-bow, sniffed at Selmi superciliously, but made no comment. We puffed gratefully at our hubble-bubbles. 'The pipes are wonderful but the tea is rubbish!' Selmi said. Gazing wistfully at parties of immaculately dressed Egyptian girls with sparkling eyes and red mouths, he said: 'I'd like to marry one of those girls. My wife is a good woman – but she's my cousin and we've been friends since we were small. We've got four children – we had five but one died – and she gets very tired. When I come home she's always asleep these days.'

Next morning we took a taxi to the camel-market at Imbaba. A freezing wind had blown up from the Delta, bringing with it the winter rains. At Imbaba the streets had become liquid chocolate, and portly ladies tiptoed through the mire with their skirts tucked up. The camel-market was a swamp of mud and manure – three great intersecting yards where Arabs sat under awnings and camels shivered in miserable gaggles in the corners. Most of them had come down from the small markets in Upper Egypt, where they had arrived after a 1,000-mile trek on the hoof from the Sudan. They were not accustomed to this winter dampness, for the rains in the Sudan came in summer.

As we walked through the gate, a beefy, beaming Arab threw his wrestler's bulk on Selmi, bawling, 'Welcome! Welcome!' This was ʿAlaysh, a steward of the market and an acquaintance of Selmi's one previous visit. He had a pumpkin-sized face with a moustache like a bramble-bush, and his head was lapped up in a mottled shawl against the rain. His green wellingtons looked as though they pinched his large feet. 'Welcome, Selmi!' he roared. 'Welcome, friend!' Flinging bear-like arms around us, he marched us to the nearest teashop.

An Arab boy brought three small tumblers of tea on a tray and ʿAlaysh doled them out officiously. 'Drink! Drink! By God, you are my guests here!' he thundered.

Selmi told him that we would need five good camels – strong beasts capable of lugging the immense quantity of food and water we should require on our trek.

'You will have the *very best* camels!' ʿAlaysh declared. 'Oh, the *very best*! Selmi knows me, Omar! My heart is white! I will find for you the *most perfect* camels and I don't want anything in return! Nothing at all! I will do this for you because you are a foreigner and Selmi is my good friend. Of course, any little thing you should want to give me – any trifle – would be acceptable. My heart is completely white!'

'How much do you want?'

'Nothing! The very idea of it! Nothing at all!'

'How much?'

'Only a mere trifle – the merest of trifles would suffice!'

'Which would be?'

'Only – let's say – twenty pounds commission on each camel. A mere trifle. It's nothing, really. My heart is like snow!'

'Ten pounds.'

'Make it fifteen.'

'Done!'

All morning we wandered around the yards looking at camels, prodding camels, poking camels, feeling humps and haunches, putting camels through their paces, chatting with camel-merchants and men who were buying camels for rides at the Pyramids. By the end of the morning I had bought Shaylan, a great off-white Bishari reared by the Beja in the Red Sea hills. 'This is a *most perfect* camel, Omar!' ʿAlaysh declared. 'Been to the

Sudan and back twice that camel has!' He leaned over and raised a whiskery eyebrow. *'Smuggling!'* he growled.

It took us eight days to assemble five camels and all our provisions and equipment, and half-way through Selmi took to sleeping at the camel-market to protect our investment. One morning I strolled into the market to find him deep in conversation with two Saudi Arabs in expensively cut dishdashas and speckled red headcloths. One of them wore a drooping Sancho Panza moustache, and the other a pair of reflecting sunglasses. The one with the sunglasses struck me as being familiar.

'We want to offer Selmi a job,' one of them said. 'A permanent job in Saudi Arabia, looking after our camels.'

'But he won't go,' added the other. 'He says he's working for you.'

'Why don't you let him go? We're giving him a really good chance. A good wage and all found.'

'I can't go,' Selmi said. 'I've already agreed with Omar!'

I called him aside and explained that I was prepared to let him go. 'It's a good chance,' I said, 'and I'm only giving you temporary work. We could send a message to Kharja and get your brother Ahmad to come with me instead.'

'No, my word is my word. All is written. If those Saudis had come to me first I would have agreed with them and kept my promise. But God brought you first, and a Bedui never changes his word. I am your man.'

I had often heard the Bedu dismissed as grasping, and occasionally I had found them so myself. But I knew this was as fine a display of personal integrity as I was ever likely to see.

Before the Saudis left, I remembered where I had seen Sunglasses before. I had seen him at Shepheard's Hotel on the Corniche, drinking beer and dining with a pretty Egyptian girl. I mentioned this to Selmi. 'Yes,' he said, 'last night he had a celebration in the market for his new marriage.'

'He has just married an Egyptian girl?'

'Yes. He married her yesterday, and in a few days, when he goes back to Saudi Arabia, he'll divorce her. That way it's all legal you see!'

The next morning a four-ton truck pulled up at the loading-ramp at Imbaba. The driver, a lanky Cairene with a truculent look, jumped out and leaned on the bonnet smoking a Cleopatra cigarette. 'Alaysh and a few brawny friends helped Selmi and me to coax our camels up the ramp, then cajole, heave and shove them into the truck, until they were wedged and trussed up like chickens. Then we humped aboard our mounds of gear – saddles, panniers, 300 kilos of sorghum for camel-feed, bags of sardines and bully-beef, packets of tea and pokes of sugar, ropes, rugs, blankets, hobbles and nose-bags, five kilos of olives, ten packs of cheese, a sack of flour, twenty plastic jerrycans, twenty kilos of pasta and two large waterskins. When all had been squeezed in and lashed down, I paid off 'Alaysh's crew, while 'Alaysh leaned panting on his stick. 'Well, Omar,' he said, 'I got you the camels. I haven't fallen short, have I?'

'No, you haven't,' I said, and handed him exactly twice what we had agreed.

His lower lip quivered. 'Only a hundred and fifty. After all the work I've done!'

Selmi fixed the big Bedui with a piercing stare. I had never seen him look so intimidating. 'You agreed to fifteen pounds a camel, and Omar has given you twice as much. It is twice as much as you deserve, judging by this display. Put it away and don't make a further disgrace!'

The giant wadded the money into his pocket with ham-like fists and stalked away. I looked at Selmi: 'A Bedui never breaks his word?' I said, grinning at the retreating figure.

'The Arabs say, "Never trust a man who talks too much",' Selmi answered sternly. 'There are Bedu and Bedu, like anyone else!'

# I

## Cain and Abel

It was far from Egypt, but in another desert country – the Sultanate of Oman – that I first conceived of the idea of seeking out the last of the world's Bedu, the nomadic Arabs who have played such a dramatic part in the history of Western imagination. I was in Mughshin, a grille of ornate buildings in space-age Moresco set in the midst of sweltering, featureless sands, as a guest of an old Bedui called Musallim bin Tafl, once the companion of Wilfred Thesiger, the British explorer whose biography I was then researching.

In the early morning I accompanied the old man on his rounds, padding the periphery of his small kingdom as he always did, carrying the rifle presented to him by the Sultan of Oman's Special Forces. The wind was drifting off the desert, uncorking scents of salt and dust, and though the opal sky held a pledge of baking heat, at that early hour the air was cold across the naked sands. Among the salt-bush Musallim happened upon the spoor of a young gazelle. He crouched down to examine the V-shaped nicks, cut cleanly into the sand, and smiled. 'Allah is truly great!' he muttered. 'For He has brought back even the beasts of the wilderness!'

The old man never ceased to marvel how water had worked its magic on a land that had known nothing but aridness and drought for 10,000 years. Where the Bedu not long ago had licked parched, cracked lips as they searched desperately for a single, sulphur-smelling spring, gallons of groundwater now gushed from steel cocks, sousing the sand and coaxing it to life. Here, in the deserts of southern Arabia, where for generations the Bedu had eked out a precarious living from the barren soil, feeder-canals carried bubbling water amid new forests of palm-trees that dappled the earth with their shade.

Musallim paused often to listen to the magical sound of water flowing in the desert. He breathed in the bittersweet smells of leaf-mould, humus and moss, the perfumes of oleander and jasmine, that now toned the chalk smell of the sands he had known from childhood. With the trees had come the shrubs, and with the shrubs the grasses. With the grasses had come the darkling beetles, the lizards, the skinks, the butterflies, the spiders, the ants and the moths, the kangaroo-rat, the gerbil, the fennec and the Ruppell's sand fox. Now the greater animals were returning too. One day, perhaps, even the oryx would come back just as it had reappeared on the bitter plains of Jiddat al Harasis, where it had been extinct for a generation.

Following the slim path beaten by the passage of his bare feet each morning and evening for years through the mesquite and the camel-thorn, we reached the garden of melons, cucumbers and tomatoes Musallim himself had had planted. He called his Punjabi gardener, a gaunt brown man named Mohammad, from his tiny thatched hut in the garden, to have him start the fresh-water pump that fed the crop. Mohammad, clad only in a chequered loincloth, but carrying his bean-pole body with assurance, stepped out of his house and stared at us. He knew that there was no need to irrigate the garden now, but Musallim never grew tired of watching the pump work – of seeing before his eyes the miracle of water where all his life there had been only sand. The Punjabi climbed down to the oily lump of machinery and jerked the starter until, with a gunshot crack, the exhaust-pipe spat a single guff of smoke, and the cogs and ratchets rattled suddenly into action. A few moments later, clear water surged in a foaming torrent out of the conduit and into the feeder-canals. Musallim laid down his rifle and dabbled both hands in the stream, beaming, and splashing it over his face. 'Praise be to God!' he intoned. 'This is what I dreamed of when I was a boy. Water and green trees where there was only desert! Running streams where men used to die of thirst! No God but God, we live in a wondrous world!'

Despite his pleasure in the gardens and the palm-groves, though, it was evidently Musallim's discovery of gazelle-tracks that excited him the most. He had been a hunter since he could hold a rifle, and by the time he was twenty had become one of the most renowned marksmen in the Sultanate of Oman. So famous was his shooting, indeed, that small-arms instructors in the Sultan's Armed Forces would ask their best shots, 'Are you trying to equal Musallim bin Tafl?'

Not that Musallim had any further ambitions in the hunting line: his eyesight had been so poor for the past few years that he would, he admitted freely, have been lucky to have hit a camel at twenty metres. Still, he yearned for the game as he yearned for an old friend — it was something that had always been there in the old days when the larder was empty. 'In those days there *was* game, by God!' he told me. 'There were Barbary sheep in the canyons at Mughsayl, there were oryx in the steppes, and you saw gazelles in hundreds — as many as goats! I find the track of one baby gazelle in the wadi today, and I am as thrilled as a little boy!'

Even at seventy-odd, Musallim was an impressive figure. Small, squat, barrel-chested, and slightly bow-legged, his head was squarely symmetrical, his face a complex of wrinkles that formed and broke like rivers on the map of a drainage-system, his nose crooked, his eyes slightly blank — more from the ocular problems that had beset him in recent years than from nature. The features which defined him most, though, were his feet. They were wide and leathery, the toes hard-grafted and splayed, the heels cracked into clints and grykes by the interchange of heat and cold. These were not the feet of a townsman: together with his scarred and calloused hands, they looked out of place against the milk-white dishdasha, the multi-coloured headcloth, the silver cartridge-belt and the bone-handled dagger in its filigree scabbard that befitted his rank of Sheikh and Vice-Wali of the Government Administration Centre here at Mughshin on the edge of the great Empty Quarter, the Rubʿ al Khali.

The dream of creating a town out of this wilderness had come to Musallim, he said, when, during a border crisis between Saudi Arabia and Oman, Sultan Qaboos had sent word to Dhofar that Mughshin must be occupied at all costs, lest it fall into the hands of the Saudis. He had gathered a dozen Bedu tribesmen who bolted up to Mughshin on their camels, and waved an Omani flag facetiously whenever the Saudi spotter-plane hummed over. Thereafter, at his own expense, Musallim had built an Arab-style castle not far from the spring, which he had manned faithfully until the government disbursed two million dollars for the modern centre, which was sited a couple of kilometres away.

The dazzling new centre struck you at first like a mirage from the *Arabian Nights* – an enclave of quaint zinc-white houses sealed against the heat, their crenellated roofs giving them the look of miniature forts; a mosque with a marble dome of delicate jade-green; a modern hospital, a school, a generating plant, water-towers, guard-posts, all disguised as a sort of kasbah. It didn't take you long to notice that there was something missing, though: the centre had few inhabitants. Mughshin lay in no man's land on the edge of the world's largest single expanse of land, the Empty Quarter, 300 kilometres from Salalah and 600 from Muscat. Few people, at present, anyway, cared to live there. 'But the people will come,' Musallim assured me. '*Inshallah* they will come!' He was sitting in his *majlis*, a room of staggering dimensions – ice-box cool from purring air-conditioners – in which moisture-seals on the outer doors went 'Shooosh' as they closed. It was a gaudy palace that might have been dreamed up in Bedu imagination. The reception room was carpeted wall to wall with electric-blue deep pile, its main furnishings a score of gilt baroque chairs, padded with blood-coloured velvet and standing with their backs to the four walls. There was a glass-lined bookcase containing leather-bound volumes, and on the wall blown-up, out-of-focus photographs of Musallim mounting a horse and Musallim shaking hands with the Sultan. An entire platoon of retainers and relatives – mostly young men with earnest, bearded faces in working dishdashas – occupied the plush chairs, passing around tea in a giant vacuum-flask and listening to our conversation intently, like a tribunal.

Musallim had been born around 1920 in the Wadi Mughsayl, west of the town of Salalah, among gorges that, for half the year, were swathed in soupy sea-mist. The gorges were now traversed by a multi-million-dollar highway of switchback hairpins that spanned sheer cliff-faces where protruding rocks had simply been shaved away by the construction teams. Such a thing had been as undreamt of in Musallim's youth as a camel-race on the moon: his was a poor family of a poor Bedouin tribe. 'We had about twenty goats and no camels,' he told me. 'We lived on our goats, what we could shoot, a bit of trading with the towns in butter, wool, and skins. Apart from our goats, we had waterskins, a leather well-bucket, ropes and hobbles we made out of palmetto-fibre, cooking-pots, a coffee-set, fibre mats and goatskins for sleeping on, rifles, cartridge-belts and daggers and the clothes we stood up in. That was about the total of our possessions. Some Bedu would tend the incense trees that grow on the north side of the mountains, but our family didn't.'

'Then what are the Bedu?'

'The Bedu are those who live in the desert. They are tribesmen, and are loyal to their blood-relatives. They are strong, they can fight and they carry weapons. Not all Bedu are Arabs, and not all speak Arabic. But those who are permanently settled – the people of the towns and villages who never move from their dwellings, are not Bedu. They are called Hadr or Fellahin. Bedu and Hadr are different, but like two branches of a tree. Some tribes, like the Murrah in the north, have both Bedu and Hadr sections.'

'What distinguishes the Bedu from the Hadr?'

'The Bedui is more generous and more hospitable. Those are his most important qualities. He is also brave, but then bravery and generosity are almost the same thing, because when you are poor you have to be very brave to give away even what little you have. If your family depends for its livelihoood on twenty goats, it is very hard to kill one to feed to a guest, but that is what the Bedui would do. No one would be turned away from his camp, not even an enemy. If anyone stole from the guest or did him any injury under the host's roof, the host would avenge the insult for the sake of his reputation. Among the Bedu reputation counts for everything. A man *is* his reputation.'

I could see that the old man was growing restless, looking around him and inching nervously forward on his seat. Soon he was buckling on his cartridge-belt and dagger and calling for his rifle. We were going on a tour of the hospital and the school, I was informed. We marched across the hot sandstone of the square in a horde, Musallim at point, striding fast and furious, hardly pausing in his endless commentary, with myself struggling to keep up, and the rest lagging behind, armed to the teeth as if on a foraging raid. The hospital was spotlessly clean: six beds, well-stocked drugs cabinet, laboratory with microscopes, emergency clinic, operating theatre with state-of-the-art accessories. A friendly Indian doctor turned out to accompany us. 'We haven't got any patients at the moment,' he said, apologetically. 'In fact, we've never actually had any.' I had to admit that the lack of patients did tend to spoil the effect of it all.

'I was only three years old when my mother died giving birth,' Musallim said. 'There were no hospitals then. The Bedu had a hard life. A woman used to go on working until she felt the birth-pains coming on, then she would just sit in the shade under a tree and if there was no one there she would deliver the baby herself. My people never had any tents anyway. In the rains we would live in caves in the wadi sides, and the rest of the time we just lived under the trees. The Bedu were tough in those days, tougher than they are now. But being tough and being strong are not the same thing, because knowledge is strength also, and in those days the Bedu were completely ignorant of anything but their own lives. What good is toughness when your mother dies under a tree? We saw our children dying of sickness in front of us and had nothing to give them but a cup of camel's piss! We couldn't even read the Holy Quran or write our own names! What good is toughness when you have a dagger and a rifle and the others have tanks and aircraft? To be tough is a good thing, but – God have mercy on her – it wasn't enough to save my mother. Of course, it was Fate, and we all die when it is time for us to die. But Allah helps those who help themselves, and I wanted to have a hospital and a proper doctor here at Mughshin, so that our daughters would no longer die in childbirth under a tree!'

The school was a little more active than the hospital: it boasted three classes, three Moroccan teachers, and about eight pupils. The classrooms were air-conditioned and fully equipped with brand new desks, tape-recorders, videos, and every modern teaching aid. The pupils, intimate cabals in the front row, were all boys. And, I learned quickly, all were the sons of Musallim's relatives or his guards. 'I never learned to read or write,' Musallim commented. 'In those days no one thought it was important for a Bedui. Your school was the desert. You learned to look after goats and water camels, to shoot and to ride, to read the tracks of men and animals. You might be sent to herd the goats from when you were very small and you had to guard them against wolves and leopards – and you had to be on the lookout for raiders too. If you saw raiders coming you would just mount your camel – if you had one – and run away. There was no honour to be gained in fighting ten or twenty men, when all you had was probably a dagger and a stick. Then the families would band together and pursue the raiders on camels. Sometimes they would catch up, and there'd be a tremendous battle and people would be killed on both sides. Anyway, before I reached manhood, my uncle – who brought me up after my father died – was shot by Mahra raiders in one of those battles, and the wound festered and he died. I swore that I'd get revenge on his head from the Mahra, and by God that's what I did! Years later I went into Mahra country, and found a man from the section of the Mahra who had killed my uncle, and shot him. I didn't feel guilty about it at the time, because after all they had robbed me of my uncle, and that was the law of the blood-feud, a life for a life. Now I realize how futile it all was and what a waste of life, but I didn't then. When we had the opening festival here at Mughshin, with feasts and camel-races, I recognized the son of the man I had shot among the crowd. He was my guest. I saw that he had fallen on hard times. I felt sorry for him, so I gave him a sum of money. It was then that I realized how pointless it had all been. Things are far, far better now that Sultan Qaboos has brought peace. At least you can travel anywhere you want without being afraid that someone will put a bullet through your head!'

Back in the cool interior of his house, two great platters of mutton – whole joints of roasted sheep set on a bed of rice moist with fat – were brought in and placed before us on the floor. Musallim fussed about, directing the Indian servants to bring water, soap and towels, supervising the hand-washing, distributing various members of his guard around the trays. The Bedu knelt around the food, assuming the prayer-like posture they had grown accustomed to since childhood, with both feet tucked beneath them. Musallim busied himself in breaking open leg-joints and rib-cage and handing succulent titbits out to various people: pieces of liver and heart ended up on my side of the tray. 'In the name of God,' he said, 'let's eat!' Hands began scooping rice, moulding it delicately into round pellets which were popped into the mouth by a single finger; then began the tearing of the meat, the deft, carefully calculated selection of a joint, the daggers coming out of their scabbards to part flesh from bone.

I felt strangely ambivalent. All this was very different from the Arabia of which Thesiger and the other Western travellers had written: the land in which a herdsboy would lie down naked in a trench on a freezing winter night with only his shirt to cover him, in which a man would ride 300 miles by camel just to obtain news, in which travellers would make fire by striking a flint against a dagger-blade, kindling the spark with a strip of their own clothing. The Bedu Thesiger travelled with in the 1940s – bin Tafl among them – had known no other world but their own, and accepted the hardships of their lives as a small price for their freedom. They met every challenge, he wrote, with the proud boast, 'We are Bedu!'

For centuries the desert Arab had haunted the Western psyche as the epitome of all things chivalrous. He was the quintessential warrior archetype, lusting for deeds of glory and heroism, enduring incredible hardship for trivial gain, competing for personal distinction through fantastic acts of hospitality and generosity. He was famous for his individualism and natural democracy, for his pride of race and the purity of his blood, but above all for a spiritual perfection which accrued from his lack of attachment to material things. All that was best about the Bedouin, the Orientalists believed, came to him from his poverty and from the utter hardship of his life. Always, the Bedouin character was expressed through a polarity which compared it favourably with that of the settled farmer. As early as the fourteenth century AD, the Arab historian Ibn Khaldun wrote of the Bedouin that 'they were closer to the first natural state and more remote from the evil habits that have been impressed upon the souls of sedentary people . . . sedentary life constitutes the last stage of civilization and the point where it begins to decay. It also constitutes the last stage of evil and remoteness from goodness. Clearly the Bedouins were closer to being good than sedentary people . . .'

This polarity, with its overtones of Cain and Abel – the eternal conflict between the nomad and the settler – seemed so perfectly natural to the Western colonialists that it became an unquestioned part of their picture of the East: 'The two professions . . . stock-breeder and agriculturist never became united,' wrote John Bagot Glubb. 'The inhabitants of these countries remained, for thousands of years, divided into two distinct halves, the graziers and the cultivators, the nomadic and the settled. These two distinct manners of life produced entirely different characters and entirely different communities, often at bitter enmity, and regarding one another with contempt and aversion.' The distinction between nomad and farmer was useful, because by any other terms the definition of a Bedouin was hazy. Glubb wrote that a Bedouin must be a nomad who bred and kept camels, and must be able to trace his descent back from certain recognized pure-bred tribes. This definition might have suited the region of northern Arabia in which Glubb operated, but it was clearly unsuitable in other parts of the Arab world. In southern Arabia, for instance, men could have goats, cattle, camels and even cultivation and still be called Bedu, and as for having 'noble blood', in the Yemen even Somalis – an African people – were regarded as 'Bedouin'. In North Africa, where the term 'Bedu' was rarely used, nomadic tribes – even those who bred camels exclusively – were known simply as 'Arabs', a term which in Glubb's scheme of things meant 'shepherds'.

Wilfred Thesiger defined the Bedu as 'the nomadic camel-breeding tribes of the Arabian deserts', and wrote of them passionately: 'I knew I should never meet their like again. I had witnessed their loyalty . . . I knew their pride in themselves and their tribe; their regard for the dignity of others; their hospitality when they went short to feed chance-met strangers; their generosity with money they so badly needed . . . their absolute honesty; their courage, patience, endurance and their thoughtfulness. Constant raids and counter-raids with the blood-feud dominating their existence made them careless of human life as such, but no matter how bitter a feud, torture was inconceivable.' Thesiger bewailed the nascent modernization and settlement of the nomads as a tragedy: 'I realized that the Bedu with whom I had lived and travelled . . . were doomed,' he wrote. 'Some people maintain that they will be better off when they have exchanged the hardship and poverty of the desert for the security of a materialistic world. This I do not believe.' Later he added, 'I have encountered individuals among many races with high standards of conduct, but only among the Bedu were such standards generally observed. I was fortunate enough to know them before the discovery of oil in southern Arabia destroyed forever the pattern of their lives. The years I spent with them were the most memorable of my life.'

Taking Thesiger's as the definitive Western statement about the fate of the Bedu in modern times, I had come to Mughshin convinced that I would find the dull monotony of a desert suburbia, a once proud people now condemned to the humdrum of modern life. I had found instead something different – a traditional culture in the actual process of change, and, though I regretted the passing of the old life, I had to admit that the transformation had its fascinating aspects. Thesiger and the Orientalists had condemned the apparent acquiescence of the Bedu in their own modernization and settlement as a 'betrayal'. Now I found myself wondering who or what had been betrayed. It occurred to me that Ibn Khaldun had a lot to answer for: it was the notion of 'distinction', of 'polarity' – Cain against Abel, the 'pure' nomad against the 'corrupt' settler – which was to blame for this sense of moral outrage. I wondered if the terms Bedouin and cultivator had ever really been as mutually exclusive as some liked to believe. The celebrated Israeli scholar Emanuel Marx recorded in 1967, for example, that 16,000 Bedu still living in the Negev were 'primarily farmers' who also reared camels, sheep, and goats and worked for wages, yet considered themselves and were considered by the settled population 'true' Bedu. There was, in fact, an almost infinite variety of definitions of Bedu and 'true' Bedu, even among the Arabs.

Viewed in a different light – a light in which nomads and settlers were not polarities, but merely alternating stages of organization that the same groups used in response to changing conditions – the settlement of these Bedu at Mughshin looked less like 'betrayal' than flexibility. For centuries they had wandered across the harsh landscape of southern Arabia, from the hills of the Yemen to the soaring heights of inner Oman. For centuries they had fought a running battle with the wilderness. Here at Mughshin the wanderers had come home. Here, for a time anyway, the great battle had been won.

I asked Musallim whether it was true that the Bedu had lost their traditional qualities since adopting a more affluent life. He laughed dryly. 'Of course, something is lost when the old ways change. There are advantages and disadvantages. The Bedu certainly aren't as tough or enduring as they were. I don't suppose many of these boys could ride a camel for even a day without getting tired. The Bedu are not so hospitable or generous as they used to be, but then people are not so poor. When I was born the Bedu were unbelievably poor and anyone who wants to go back to being poor must be absolutely crazy! Old Bedu today will tell you that some things about the old days were better – and they were. But you won't find one of them who really wants to go back to those old days. Where do you think we would be today if we were still riding about on camels carrying our mother-of-ten-shots rifles, when our neighbours were flying aeroplanes? They would take our country from us as easily as raiders with rifles used to take the camels from an unarmed herdsboy. The world belongs to the survivors. Those who do not change with it will simply be destroyed.'

It was difficult to resist Musallim's rhetoric. I had assumed that the Bedu either did not want change or were naïvely unable to cope with its pitfalls. But my meeting with Musallim had shown me just how little they shared the Western vision of their future: by the very nature of where and how they lived, they were pragmatists rather than romantics. In the 1950s, Thesiger had written that they were 'doomed'. Now I questioned how much and in what ways that was really true. Had the skills and qualities that had made the Bedu famous – their bravery, endurance, hospitality, generosity, honesty and loyalty; their ability to read tracks, to handle camels, to live in the desert – survived into the last decade of the twentieth century? As we sped back to Salalah on the desert highway the next day, I resolved to travel in as many Arab countries as possible on a quest for the last of the Bedu – and what remained of their traditional way of life.

# 2

# Snow upon the Desert

It was midwinter, and the tribes had descended from the mountains to graze their sheep on the plains of Palmyra.

A famished wind was prowling the Baadiyat ash Sham – the Syrian desert. The plains were packing out in umber and ochre, spreading to infinity and reducing our vehicle to a mote under the great crystal dome of light that was the sky. Nomad tents – segmented like immense black caterpillars – were pitched in the lee of the barren hills, and sheep advanced everywhere in close columns that speckled the landscape with their colours.

'But God, it's cold!' Ahmad said, dragging deeply on his cigarette. 'I think it's going to snow.'

This was the first time I remembered hearing a Muslim predict the weather.

It was two hours since we had left Palmyra, and Ahmad was nursing the pick-up across a surface as brittle as pack-ice. It was Ahmad who saw the camels first. He took the cigarette from his mouth and gestured towards them casually, as if he had known where to find them all along. They were flowing slowly in open formation across the range, not less than 100 of them, their behemoth bodies picked out and magnified by the crystalline light. Among them – almost under their feet – was a flock of sheep whose fleeces glowed like molten gold. I could also see the dark perpendicular shapes of humans – a boy riding a camel, a girl at his feet, an old man among the sheep by a donkey wadded with a blanket. As we drew near, the girl peered timidly at our city-white faces. Suddenly she made off in terror, sprinting helter-skelter through the ranks of placid camels, her layers of ragged clothing flying and her plastic flip-flops going slap, slap, slap on the hard earth. The boy, clinging on to the hump of a pot-bellied bull-camel, steered carefully away. Ahmad pulled up near the old man, a bone-thin, leathery figure, cackling through the gold fangs that were all that remained of his teeth. 'Ha! Ha! Frightened the life out of them!' he chortled. He had a jutting chin and a sliver of beard, and his knuckles were tattooed with wandering blue squiggles. Though he wore a heavy fleece-lined coat against the cold, he was on the move constantly, weaving and ducking as if to avoid the blows of an imaginary opponent. The Siberian wind seared across the frozen landscape with the sound of rending cloth, and in our shirtsleeves we were immediately quivering breathlessly. We plunged back into the car for our jackets and headcloths. The old man shook hands with us and jerked his head towards the donkey. 'Come and share my food!' he said. 'Come on!' The donkey was hobbled to a stake in the ground, and she wheezed, stamped and shuffled as the spider shadows of the camels floated by. 'Afraid of camels, this donkey!' the old man announced, jiggling bundles of dirty cloth from the animal's saddle-bags. 'Bought her from the Kurds. Kurds don't have any camels. She's a good beast, but she's not used to camels.'

He crouched down and unwrapped some flaps of thin bread, a pot of yoghurt and a bowl of fat. 'Only simple shepherd's fare,' he said. 'It's simple, but it's good!' He remained crouching, but his head assumed the task of movement, nodding and jerking from side to side. He broke off a piece of bread and dipped it in the yoghurt. 'Come on!' he said again. I followed his example, but Ahmad hung back and lit another cigarette. 'I'm not hungry,' he said.

I asked the old man if the camels belonged to him.

'God bless you, they aren't mine!' he said. 'No, no, I don't have any camels! Not me! Only Bedu keep camels. Those camels belong to the Bedu!'

'Aren't you from the Bedu, then?'

'No, not me, no never! I am an Arab, not a Bedui. The Bedu keep camels. The Arabs keep only sheep.'

After we had finished eating, he stood up and waltzed about in the wind. He pointed out a black tent, standing alone on a bleak ridge far in the distance. 'That's where you'll find the Bedu!' he said. Then, as a sort of parting gesture, he jumped up and down making a warbling sound from his throat. Instantly the sheep halted in their tracks, swerved around and came pelting towards us, led by a ferocious, shaggy belwether with broad horns, looking like the incarnation of the Pharaonic god Khnum. The belwether hurled itself at the shepherd's legs with such gusto that he was obliged to fight it off, laughing and cackling. He evidently took this as a sign of affection: 'See!' he said. 'You wouldn't get camels to do that!'

A little later we halted at the Bedu tent. In this pristine light, each detail of the tableau was highlighted perfectly: the long shank of fraying black wool with its peaks and troughs, tightly guyed and shuddering in the wind; a thick-bodied woman in a black dress dragging a heavy sack from a pile; a fluffy white sheepdog baring her fangs at us over a nest of puppies; small children with gold streaks in their hair, playing around a stack of basins made out of rubber tyres; two tractors in day-glo orange; a pair of Bedu boys tinkering under the engine-farings, who grinned at us through teeth that were stained dark with grease. A tall man wearing a fine camel-hair cloak and a shamagh was coming to meet us. His face was parched hide-brown with heavy features: high brow-ridges, deep eye-sockets, sad eyes, pursed lips, a moustache that was completely grey. He did not smile as he shook hands, but held himself grave and aloof as he sized us up. 'Welcome!' he said. 'Come into my tent! You will be my guests for the night!' The magic words, I thought. There might be tractors outside the tents, but the old code of hospitality still reigned supreme.

Inside the guest-section of the tent, neatly cordoned off by wool hangings, a fire of camel-droppings was smouldering dismally in a hearth. The stout woman bustled in and greeted us without shaking hands, shouting, 'Rest! Rest! Make yourselves comfortable!' She pulled out rugs and hard woven cushions, and arranged them around the fire. Although her thick dress covered her body from neck to ankle, her face was bare, displaying a mandala of woad-blue tattoos. We sat down at the hearth and our host – Salim – brought in a pile of spiky brushwood, arranged it over the camel-dung, and added a nip of kerosene. 'Watch your feet!' he roared, as he stabbed a tongue of flame at it from a disposable cigarette-lighter. A mushroom cloud of smoke belched up in our midst, and when it had died down we sat with our freezing hands outspread across the welcoming flames. 'Allah alone is all-knowing, but it is cold enough for snow,' Salim said. 'This *rimth* doesn't give out much heat, but it's better than camel-dung, and it's all there is at this time of year!'

He sat down on a rug, and a horde of small children in pyjama-cloth jallabiyyas rushed in and bounced upon him, chattering. Salim made tea methodically and poured the amber liquid out into small glasses. He refilled them every time one of us set a glass down. At last he asked Ahmad, 'Where is this foreigner from?'

'He is from England.'

'Where?'

'England . . . you know, Britain!'

'Where's that?'

'Haven't you ever heard of London?'

'Yes, I've heard London on the BBC. Do they speak Arabic in London? All the people I hear on the BBC speak Arabic perfectly!'

'What is your tribe?' I asked diffidently.

'Syria.'

'No, I mean your *tribe*.'

'We are Bedu. What can a foreigner know of tribes?'

'I know a little.'

'Very well, then. We are ʿAnaza. Do you know the ʿAnaza?'

Indeed I did. My 'handbook' to the tribes of Arabia – *Notes on Bedouins and Wahabys*, compiled by John Lewis Burckhardt in 1831 – listed the ʿAnaza as 'the most powerful nation in the vicinity of Syria, and . . . one of the most considerable bodies of Bedouins in the Arabian deserts'.

I was in the tent of one of the last families to rear camels in the Syrian desert – in the company of perhaps the most authentic and most aristocratic Bedouin tribe of all.

When I stepped off the Damascus bus in Palmyra only two days earlier I had despaired of finding any Bedu in Syria. The first thing I noticed was a chipboard sign nailed to a tree, with a straggling arrow pointing to some unknown object beyond: 'TOYRISTS WELCOME!' it read.

Chuckling, I humped my rucksack to the Zenobia Hotel, a French Colonial style oblong the colour of Gruyère cheese, which had been built when privileged tourists first began motoring to Palmyra across the desert in the 1920s. It stood right in the middle of the most impressive classical ruins in the Eastern world. The size and scale of the ancient town was breathtaking. The architecture spoke of fabulous wealth and deliberate ostentation: the vast entrance portals of the temples and the great arches suggested that they had been built to admit giants. There was nothing cowering to be glimpsed in Palmyrene style: power and confidence were writ large in wide expanses, towering tombs, dozens upon dozens of Corinthian pillars. As I walked through the fields of fallen masonry later, I was able to savour the same privilege that the exclusive tourists of the 1920s must have experienced: there were no other visitors in the ruins – I had the place completely to myself.

Except, of course, for the Arabs. Inside the perfectly preserved Roman-style theatre, there were two round-faced tribesmen warming their hands over a blazing wood fire, and in the colonnaded street outside there was a lanky boy in a full-length jallabiyya who tore after a clutter of fat-tailed sheep, vaulting over fractured pilasters and skimming stones calculated to miss them by inches. It was clear that the shepherds had been at home among the ruins for centuries: in the inner sanctum of the temple of Bel Shamim – the largest and most interesting section of the ruins – the ceiling was black with the smoke of their cooking-fires. By the time Islam arrived, Palmyra's expansive, confident civilization had long since shrivelled to a fearful defensiveness and suspicion. The Muslim Arabs had torn down the carefully crafted stones and pillars and turned the temple of Bel Shamim into a makeshift fort. The ancient caravan-city of Palmyra might have boasted a population of hundreds of thousands, yet the first Westerners to investigate the ruins thoroughly – a group of English merchants from the Aleppo trading colony, who arrived here in 1691 – found them inhabited by only thirty or forty families: 'poor, miserable people', whose 'little huts made of dirt' were installed inside the temple compound.

Freezing sleet began to sift down as I left the Bel Shamim temple. A Bedui – his face a diamond of chapped flesh between the folds of his shamagh – was sheltering against the wall near two very hypothermic camels. The man squared his shoulders expectantly as I passed. 'You ride camel, mister? Very nice!'

'Not the weather for camel-riding!' I said, in Arabic.

He shrugged, abandoning his hustling tone. 'It's going to snow. We haven't had weather this cold for two or three years. God is generous, but it's bad for the tourists!' Then he sank back with resignation into the shelter of his wall.

I took refuge from the rain in the Ethnological Museum, housed nearby in a fortified villa that had once been the residence of the Ottoman governor. A guide called Marwan, a gangling man who wore a permanent grin, ushered me around rooms filled with Fellahin tools, jewellery, and carpets, delivering a set speech in Arabic with English footnotes on each item. In the 'Bedu Room', two full-sized plaster models of camels displayed the traditional north Arabian riding-saddle, the *shadad*, and the ceremonial women's litter – the *markab* – which, with its great bow-shaped wings, had once been used to transport the new bride. Known as the 'Ark of Ishmael', after the father of one branch of the Arabs, the litter had traditionally been occupied in battle by the Sheikh's daughter – her hair flowing like a standard – and was the tribe's rallying-point, beyond which the warriors were not supposed to retreat. Burckhardt recounted the tale of Jedwa ibn Ghayan, notorious for having slain thirty Bedu in a single encounter, who sacrificed his life by charging through the enemy ranks to fell the camel carrying their *markab* with a blow from his scimitar. He was shot dead by a Bedui with a firelock only moments later, but, heartened by the fall of the standard, his own side rushed forward and routed their foes, leaving 500 enemy warriors dead on the field.

Marwan told me that the Bedu no longer used these artefacts: 'The bride is carried by car, now,' he said. 'They have forgotten how to make camel-saddles. The only real riding-saddles you will see are on the camels they use for tourists.' Marwan told me that no Bedu families reared camels now, anyway. 'I don't suppose there are more than two thousand camels in all Syria,' he said. 'In my father's day the 'Anaza alone had hundreds of thousands of them – probably millions. In the 1930s the bottom dropped out of the camel-market, because the Egyptians – who used to import thousands of camels for meat – could get them more cheaply from the Sudan. The camel-tribes were rich, but started to become poor: they had these masses of camels, but no one would buy them. The money was in sheep, so most of the Bedu went over to raising them instead. In fact, if you think of the Bedu as camel-rearing nomads, you can say that there are no Bedu left at all.'

When the rain had eased, I walked disconsolately through a date-market that occupied a stretch of the main road. Syria had seemed the obvious starting-point for my quest for the last of the Bedu, yet apart from the tribesmen in the ruins and the man hiring out camels to tourists, I had encountered none at all. I walked slowly past the stalls of sackcloth and nylon fibre erected around racks of peach- and wine-coloured dates cut freshly in bunches from the tree, noticing that they were not the hard dates of Bedu tradition, but the squishy ones eaten by Westerners at Christmas. Palmyra had been a ruin for more than seventeen centuries, I reflected, yet the date-palms for which the Romans had named the oasis 'Place of Palms' still flourished today. Indeed, it occurred to me that the great tousle-headed columns which I had taken to be Corinthian were not Corinthian at all: they were the architectural equivalent of the palm-trees which had always surrounded this settlement on the desert floor. Some of the vendors were lighting brushwood fires with kerosene, and one of them waved a kettle at me. 'Welcome!' he bawled in a voice set some decibels too high. 'Arab *hospitalité!*' Nearby was a large sign on which was painted in English, 'DATSES FOR SALE HERE.'

The Ottoman citadel lurked on a pinnacle above the town, dark and brooding like a single crushed molar. Later, I climbed up to it by the steep and shaly pathway. After the lightness and feeling of space in the ancient city, the keep seemed wretchedly claustrophobic. If the Muslim Arabs had dined in the ruins, the Turks had withdrawn from them entirely to the peak of this natural spire. They had lived in more dangerous times than the ancient Semites – times of muskets and artillery – during which they sat astride this desert place uneasily as a foreign ruling élite. Whatever it was that the Turks had feared, they had gone to great pains to protect themselves from it: the castle itself stood on an island of rock completely surrounded by a deep, sheer-sided fosse which had been quarried out of the belly of the hill. The only means of entry was by a perilous wooden bridge to a heavily fortified doorway. As I approached the bridge, I met a big-bodied, grey-bearded man coming the opposite way. He was the custodian of the ruins. 'I've just closed,' he told me. 'There aren't many tourists about today. Because it's so cold. But I'll open it up for you if you like.' The interior was dank and crumbling, but from the parapet above there was a lovely view of the oasis. The ruins, their pieces laid out like bits of a gigantic jigsaw, were vast, but their scale was humbled by the sheer wild immensity of the desert. The wind up here had an arctic chill to it, and the sky was trawled by a stream of dark clouds which cast the Baadiya into a patchwork of light and shade. To the west lay the mirror-sheen of the Wadi al Ma salt-lake, and to the east, desert and sky mingled along the rim of a horizon that hid the distant Euphrates.

The forbidding yet fertile steppeland I could see from the parapet might well have been the birthplace of the Bedu. The word *baadiya* itself provides an important clue, since while in one sense it means merely 'desert' or 'desert steppe', in another it implies 'the beginning of life'. 'Bedu' is derived from the same root, and means 'the people of the *baadiya*', though the word cannot be traced back to any great antiquity.

Forty centuries ago, a people called the Amorites lived on the fringes of the cultivated land. Although they possessed neither camels nor horses, their lives were similar to those of later Bedu, for they herded sheep, cattle and goats and used donkeys as pack-animals. While some of them remained close to the cultivation, others roamed farther afield. A thousand years later a tribe known as the Aribi or Aribu, perhaps the descendants of the Amorites, appears on the Kurkh Monolith – an account of the battle of Qarqar in 853 BC – as one of a number of Syrian peoples that were defeated by the Assyrian king Shalmaneser III. The Aribi were led by a chief called Gindibu – the first individual Arab in history – and though it might never be known whether in fact the Amorites and the Aribi were one and the same, it is certain that, by the time of Shalmaneser, the people of the Baadiya had acquired the camel.

The idea of the Baadiya as the cradle of the Bedu is supported by Arab legend. Tradition has it that there were two main branches of the Arab family: the sons of Ishmael – Abraham's eldest son – and the sons of Qahtan, a descendant of Shem, son of Noah. The division was originally a distinction between southerners and northerners, for while the Ishmaelites settled around

Mecca and the Hejaz, the Qahtanites were based in the Yemen. According to a lesser-known legend, though, neither of these branches were 'true' Arabs but acquired their language and culture from a third group, the 'lost Arabs' or 'Arabizing Arabs' who originated in the semi-fertile steppes of the Baadiyat ash Sham. If they were originally the people of the Syrian desert – where the camel was hardly known before about 1000 BC – then the 'true' Bedu were originally humble shepherds, and not camel-men at all.

It was only from the vantage-point of this high keep that I began to understand the drama of Palmyra's history, the romance of the caravan-road on which its fabulous wealth was built. Through this place the ivory, ebony, spices, pearls and jewels of Persia and India were freighted on the backs of camels. Over these horizons had marched caravans laden with Cathay's silks and jade. Palmyra's burghers had grown fat on the caravan trade, and the public coffers overflowed with gold from the duty charged on every commodity brought through the town. The most telling monument to old Palmyra, indeed, was not the great temple of Bel Shamim, but the Palmyrene Tariff – a stone slab one and three-quarter metres high – which had once stood at the main gate. Dating from AD 137, and inscribed in both Greek and Aramaic, the Tariff listed the duty payable on slaves, dry goods, purple, cloth, cattle, water and salt. No trade was too shameful to escape the scrutiny of the Tariff-maker, as a fascinating clause of the tablet showed:

Also, the publican will collect from prostitutes, from the one who charges 1d or more he will collect 1d [per month], from the one who charges 8 As he will collect 8 As [per month]. As for the one who charges 6 As he will collect 6 As [per month] etc.

Of such significance was the Tariff that it bequeathed a new word to the languages of Europe.

The name Zenobia is inextricably linked with the history of Palmyra. Her story was of a drive for power which led ineluctably to the downfall of the Palmyrene state. Zenobia was both beautiful and ruthless. She was intelligent, cultured, and as fluent in Greek and Persian as in Aramaic. A superb military strategist, she was the Diana of her time, excelling in the hunt and marching on foot with her regiments during her campaigns. She came to prominence as the second wife of Odaynath, doyen of Palmyra's leading family, who took the part of the Romans in their war against Persia, and was recognized by them for his partisanship with the title *dux* or viceroy of the east. Zenobia almost certainly arranged her husband's murder, and declared herself regent in the name of her son, Wahb Allah.

After her successful *coup d'état*, she rebelled against Rome, smashing the Roman legions sent against her and bringing the entire Province of Syria under Palmyrene control. She then marched to the Hauran and razed the town of Bosra, adding to her orbit the Province of Arabia. To the astonishment of the world, she went on to lead her army to Alexandria and actually succeeded in wresting Egypt from Roman grasp. By AD 270 this tiny palm-oasis in the Syrian desert had acquired an empire that stretched from Asia Minor to the Nile. A year later she renamed her son 'Augustus', in direct challenge to the Roman Emperor, Aurelian. This was too much for the dignity of Rome. Aurelian dispatched a punitive expedition which engaged the Palmyrene army near Homs, and for the first time the Semitic forces were soundly whipped. Zenobia fell back on Palmyra with Aurelian's legions in hot pursuit, but the town's defences could not sustain a determined siege. Aurelian quickly seized it and put a number of prominent citizens to the sword. Zenobia herself escaped, but was taken while attempting to cross the Euphrates. She was deported to Rome and paraded through the streets at Aurelian's triumph, shackled in chains of gold. Palmyra never recovered from this blow. In the following centuries the trade routes were diverted to the north, and its halcyon days forgotten. Only the olive-groves and date-palms remained.

What lessons did the rise and fall of Palmyra have to teach me about the Bedu, I wondered? Though classical Palmyrene culture incorporated Greek and Persian elements, it was essentially indigenous and Semitic – as Philip Hitti has put it, 'an illustration of the cultural heights which the Arabians of the desert are capable of attaining when the opportunities present themselves'. If the Bedu really did lay the foundations of Palmyra – and traces of them have been found here dating back as far as 2000 BC – then it is an illuminating example of the way in which nomadic and settled life were continuously fluid and interchangeable, and by no means fixed in eternal opposition as traditional authors maintained. In this case, clearly, the nomads had not remained poor out of preference for the freedom of the desert, neither had their ways been immutable. Here was an unmistakable parallel with what was happening in Arabia at the end of the twentieth century: a situation in which the Bedu had taken advantage of new opportunities, and adapted to a different mode of existence in order to survive.

The wind dropped as the day bowed towards sunset. Blue ribbons of smoke from among the palm-groves now curled up vertically to the darkening sky. The hills glowed like firecoals in the clear, cold, midwinter light. The custodian was growing impatient, shuffling and coughing on the parapet. As I finally followed him down the broken stairs, he said, 'There is no entrance fee. You can give me anything you like.' I took out my wallet and handed him a fifty-lire note. The old man crinkled it in his palm and regarded it mournfully. 'The last person here gave me a hundred,' he said.

I was walking back through the date-market, wondering what my next move should be, when I met Ahmad, sitting patiently in his new, polished Toyota pick-up, waiting for tourists. He was a shy, thoughtful young man of about twenty-four with a bristly red face, not handsome, but trim and athletic. I learned later that he had just finished his three years of national service in the army, and had bought the pick-up out of his savings.

'Where do you want to go?' he inquired.

I explained that I was looking for traditional Bedu – nomads who still bred camels in the Syrian desert. 'But they told me there aren't any left!' I said.

'Nonsense!' Ahmad said. 'I know where there is a family who still rear camels – real Bedu. Their tents are pitched near the oil-pumping station, T4.'

I arranged for Ahmad to meet me at the Zenobia the next morning. When he arrived I slung my rucksack into the back of the pick-up, and we followed the route of the old silk caravans, heading east. At first the way wound ponderously through the sandstone crags, as if wary of the infinite space beyond, but soon it turned arrow-straight and raced on over the ochre plains with a sense of uplift to the boundless sky. Suddenly, as the hills fell away behind us, a wonderful sight met my eyes: the desert was smothered by sheep in massed battalions, and black tents lay along the spreading skirts of the hills. 'The tribes have gathered here from everywhere this year,' Ahmad said. 'For ten years we had no rain, and this year there was a deluge! Look at that pasture! Just look at it!'

The pumping-station popped up out of the desert like a tiny oasis – shining industrial plant, ringed in mesquite trees and stone pines. Outside a tin shack full of automobile parts, an Arab in an overall was prising the tyre off a rusty wheel. We asked for directions to the camels, and he waved a spanner vaguely towards the north: 'That way!' he said.

I was excited to meet the ʿAnaza because they were one of the seven or eight great tribal entities of the Syrian desert, and traditionally regarded themselves and were regarded by other tribes as 'true' Bedu. They were a vast family of Ishmaelite clans which had migrated to Syria tent by tent, lineage by lineage, over a century and a half, building their power, attracting clients from other tribes, until, in 1860, they had expelled their Qahtani rivals – the Shammar – and chased them back into Iraq and the deserts of the Nejd. The multitude of their tents and the great quantity of their animals was a byword, and was explained among them by a story about their ancestor, Wayl. He had happened on the correct instant, they said, on the Night of Destiny – the twenty-seventh of the fasting month of Ramadan – when God was bound to answer men's prayers. Placing one hand on his she-camel and the other on his phallus, Wayl prayed that both her seed and his own should multiply and prosper, with the result that, by the 1940s, the ʿAnaza numbered 37,000 men and owned over a million camels.

My first surprise in the ʿAnaza tent was to learn that these 'noble' Bedu owned cultivation. 'We've got quite a few hectares,' Salim said. 'The barley's about knee-high now and coming on well. But heavens, it is hard work! Most days I am working there from dawn to sunset.'

They moved only a few kilometres a year, since their herds were no longer dependent for survival on the grazing. 'I can remember what it was like before we had motor-cars and tractors,' Salim said wistfully. 'We had no cultivation then and we used to go off scouting on *dheluls* (trained riding-camels) and then moved the tent to wherever the pasture was. We still have some *dheluls*, but we don't have any saddles. In the past we moved farther than we move now. It used to take five camels to carry the tent and everything. In those days we ate less bread and more dates and milk, but we bought flour and we sold our animals in the towns. It must have been a good diet, because then there was no disease.'

Ahmad sniffed doubtfully. 'There's always disease!' he said.

'Well, what I mean is that whoever was going to die, died, and whoever was going to live, lived, and there was no lingering on with medicines. We did have our own treatments. We used to give people the branding-iron. You can't beat the branding-iron when someone is sick, but if we use it today the doctors refuse to treat us. Then we had our own doctors too. They belonged to the Solubba, who were a weak people and so terrified of us that if a Bedui arrived they would run away. But they knew a lot of secrets. They knew more about sickness, about plants and animals and tracks, than any Bedui, by God!'

'Are there still Solubba living in the desert today?'

'No, none at all! They all went off to Saudi Arabia and Kuwait and became rich men!'

The wind was whipping the fabric of the tent above us and wafting the acrid smoke into our eyes. Salim's wife hurried back from the women's side and began to adjust the poles and guy-ropes expertly. In a moment she had sealed off the open side of the tent against the wind and opened the other side, giving us a view across a blasted expanse of *rimth* humps and ground gouged and scored by the feet of camels. It suddenly came home to me how beautifully adapted the tent was to the desert: it was architecture at its most mobile – in itself a symbol of the no-madic way of life. Because of the impermanence of its material, perhaps, little is known about the antiquity of the black tent, the use of which is spread from the shores of the Atlantic to the highlands of Tibet. Certainly it is not man's most primitive struc-ture, for it is highly sophisticated in comparison with the wind-break or the grass-and-timber hut. If the Old Testament may be relied upon, then the tent existed in the time of Abraham – about 4,000 years ago – when the Patriarch left the city to tend flocks with his nephew, Lot, and pitched his tents in the land of Canaan.

A little later the woman returned carrying a tray laden with dishes, which she set at our feet: melting butter, yoghurt, and balls of sheep's cheese. She opened an old coat which contained flaps of moist bread. I expected her to return to her own part of the tent, but instead she sat down on the rug and began stitching a sheepskin coat, watching us eat.

'Was the old life of the Bedu better than the new?' I inquired.

Salim considered the question. 'It was better in some ways. It's true that in those days there was no peace, no security. The strong used to take from the weak: that was the only law. There was slaughter between the tribes. Of course, the Bedu were the bosses then, and it didn't bother us that the strong took from the weak, because we were the strong.'

'It was a hard life, because we had no water,' Salim's wife cut in. 'The water was far away, and we had to bring it on camels in waterskins – it tasted horrible. That was the hardest thing – no water, and never enough to eat. Now we have plenty.'

'But in those days, we had freedom,' Salim continued. 'There were no borders then – we could go to Iraq or Saudi Arabia or Jordan – we could move where we liked. We were free.'

'We were free, but we were hungry and thirsty,' the woman said. 'We could go where we wanted, but we only moved because we had to find grazing for the animals. Now we spend most of the year here: if only there was a school, our children could learn to read and write.'

Salim sent an irritated glance in her direction: 'Yes, and who would look after the camels if the children went to school? They don't need to read and write. The desert is their school!'

'Every Fellah's child can read and write. Why should their children have schools and not the Bedu?'

I asked if there was any fundamental difference between the Bedu and the Fellahin.

'In the past we had nothing to do with the Fellahin, and they had nothing to do with us,' Salim said. 'The ʿAnaza are of noble blood, and we looked down on them, and all the other tribes.'

'What does "noble blood" mean?'

'It means power. The ʿAnaza were the most numerous tribe, and had the most tents and the most livestock – tens of thousands of tents and hundreds of thousands of sheep and camels. Once we were so strong that all the villages near the desert, and all the weak tribes paid us *khuwwa* – "brotherhood tax". That's gone now, of course. Most of the ʿAnaza moved to Saudi Arabia because of the oil money. Now only the government is strong, but there are still tribes that we would never give our girls to, and never take wives from – like the ʿAwazim and the Shararat and the Solubba. They are just like slaves – white slaves. We still wouldn't marry into them, no matter how rich they were. That's a matter of blood! It is true that we aren't nomads like we used to be, but we still live in black tents. We could easily have a house in Palmyra if we wanted, but we prefer it in the desert.'

It was almost sunset, and the cold had become more intense. When I stepped outside the tent for a minute, it was like walking into a freezer. The sun was lodged on terraces of cloud above the horizon, sending vapour trails of brilliant colour along the frozen ground. Ghost figures were migrating across the periphery of my vision, and I turned to see the camels coming towards me, loping madly in twos and threes, pursued by the herdsboy's shrill cries. Soon they were gliding in from all directions, converging on the water-tank that stood on a farm-cart behind the tent. Salim tramped out and opened the water-tap, and the camels began to roar and tussle, entwining their great necks. 'We water them every day now,' he told me on his way back. 'In the old days we had to take them to the wells. Now we bring them water with the tractor and trailer.' He advised me to fetch my things in from the car and make myself at home, and as I was collecting my rucksack, Ahmad appeared. 'I'd better be going now,' he said.

'Wait a minute! I thought we were staying the night here.'

'It's perfectly all right for you, but I'm not used to it. I've never slept in a tent before.'

'Not even in the army?'

'No. I was an ambulance-driver. I've never slept in a tent in my life!'

I could see that there was no changing his mind, and I let him go with instructions to pick me up soon after sunrise in the morning.

It was dark in the tent now, except for the flickering light of the fire. As soon as the sound of Ahmad's pick-up had petered out in the night, there was an ominous silence – the harbinger of a distinct sea-change. After a while, Salim asked, 'What exactly do you want in the tents of the Bedu?'

'Only experience.'

'Who was that man who came with you?'

'A driver. A townsman from Palmyra.'

'Are you sure he doesn't belong to the government?'

'I don't think so.'

'How much are you paying him?'

'That's my business.'

'What profit do you make from staying here?'

'Directly – none.'

My rucksack had been laid in the corner of the tent and while Salim was grilling me the children started to open the straps and examine the contents – my sleeping-bag, my water-bottle, my small tent. Salim looked on, interested but unconcerned: 'What have you got in there?' he inquired.

'Just my sleeping and washing things.'

'Have you got any spare shoes? I could do with a new pair of shoes.'

'Sorry.'

The boys were unrolling my sleeping-bag, and unscrewing my torch. I watched, trying to conceal my concern. 'Don't worry,' Salim said, making no effort to stop them, 'your things are safe in a Bedui's tent. Much safer than you would be in a hotel. How much did you pay for your hotel in Palmyra? See, you are getting a bed here free! No one is as hospitable as the Arabs! Tell me, in *your* country could you just turn up at someone's house and unroll your blanket?'

I had to smile, assailed by visions of a Bedui arriving at a semi in suburban England and bedding down happily on the lawn. 'Look, it's not that my people are inhospitable,' I told him, 'it's just that we don't live in the desert. It's a different way of life!'

We were joined by Salim's eldest son, a lad of eighteen with an inquisitive face, who was on leave from his military service in Damascus. He seemed friendly when he shook hands, but as soon as he had sat down at the hearth, he asked his father: 'Who is this man? What does he want here?'

'He is a Christian.'

'Perhaps he is a spy!'

His opinion obviously weighed heavily on his father, for afterwards Salim seemed to fall into a kind of lethargy, sinking back upon his cushions and answering my attempts at conversation with monosyllables. Instead I tried to strike a rapport with his son. 'I was a soldier once,' I said. 'Parachutist. In some ways it's a good life. What unit are you in?'

'I'm the servant of an officer.'

'Oh. Do they give you plenty of leave in the army?'

'You should know, if you were really a soldier once!'

Salim and his son began rolling stubby cigarettes from a pouch of tobacco: 'Don't you smoke?' Salim asked.

'Yes, I smoke a pipe.'

'Smoke it! Smoke it! I want you to be at ease here!'

When I did, though, it caused consternation. 'What's that stuff he's smoking?' Salim demanded.

'It could be hashish and you wouldn't know!'

The children had left off sorting through the contents of my rucksack and had gathered around me, giggling and chattering too fast for me to understand. When I got up to go outside I tripped over a box hidden in the darkness, and they roared with laughter. Some of them even followed me outside to watch me pee.

Back inside the tent, Salim's son said, 'Aren't you afraid to sleep in the desert?'

'No. Why should I be?'

'Well, there are wolves and hyenas here,' he said. 'There are some bad people too!'

I suspected that this was a rather puerile attempt to frighten me, for even Salim roused himself from his doze long enough to say, 'That's nonsense! In a Bedu tent you are completely safe! Just think of what you would have to pay in a hotel! In the tents of the Arabs it's free!'

This was the last sentence he uttered all evening, and before long his wife entered with a sheaf of heavy blankets and allowed me, thankfully, to retire.

I was awoken by the sound of camels being hustled out of the camp to the clicks and shrieks of the herdsboys. A little later came the roar of tractor-engines being fired. The sun was up bleary-eyed, swathed in cotton cloud: the bell-clear brightness of yesterday was gone. Salim peeled back his covers and built up the fire, warming his hands until his wife entered with a pot of fresh tea. We sipped in silence, until Salim said, 'God knows all, but there might be snow today. Last time it snowed our tent was almost buried. The shepherds had to bring their sheep inside their tents and light big fires until help came: sheep can't stand the cold, but camels can resist it well enough.' Later, he watched me packing my things away in my rucksack, scrutinizing each item carefully. Quite nonchalantly he said, 'I need a new pair of shoes, size eight. If you come again, you must bring me a pair!'

His wife surfaced again with yoghurt and bread for breakfast, but after I had taken two mouthfuls the dish was mysteriously whipped away.

I took it that they were waiting for me to go.

Almost at once I heard the buzzing of an engine, and Ahmad's pick-up came bumping into view. We watched it through a gap in the tent, increasing in size until I saw his whiskery face smiling through the windscreen. I was very glad he was here. I loaded my rucksack into the back, and as I shook hands with Salim, I asked him, 'Since no one rides camels any more, and people don't eat them, why do you bother raising them anyway?'

'People buy the *dheluls* to give rides to tourists!' he said.

Much later I discovered that some small items had disappeared from my rucksack: trifling things such as my razor, some soap, and the toggle-rope for my shamagh — and I was sure that the small Bedu children had taken them. It didn't bother me, but when I thought of Salim saying, 'Your things are completely safe,' and the huge investment the myth-makers had made in the sacred inviolability of a Bedui's guest, I could not suppress a wry smile. I had achieved what few travellers before me had achieved: I had been robbed in the tents of the ʿAnaza – the noblest Bedu tribe of all!

I refused to be perturbed by my first contact with the 'noble' Bedu of the Syrian desert. Once, I might have explained their less than gracious behaviour by claiming that they had been 'corrupted' by contact with civilization. To the traditional travellers, Bedu who became semi-settled had somehow 'failed' the desert's rigorous selection-test: they were 'rejects of the desert' or nomads for whom the nomadic life had been too much. These 'failures' were considered to have little moral worth, and indeed were 'reputed to be thievish, treacherous and untrustworthy; whereas there were few known instances of travellers receiving anything but good treatment from Syrian nomads . . .'

Now, it occurred to me that the 'corrupting' influence of civilization was an illusion. The 'freedom' travellers had claimed to find among the Bedu was surely the projection of their own delight in being freed from the constricting demands of European society. The 'true' nomad – clinging to the remote desert, shunning all contact with the outside world – has probably never existed. There were never any nomads who lived exclusively in remote deserts – oscillation between the fertile or semi-fertile steppes in summer and the desert in winter had always been the nomadic way. Burckhardt noted, a century and a half ago, that the ʿAnaza – the *crème de la crème* of the Bedu – did not stray far from the settled country in spring and summer: 'Their principal residence . . . during that time,' he wrote, 'is the Hauran and its neighbourhood, where they encamp *near and among the villages.*' In fact, the nomad who lived entirely on his own animal products was another figment of the romantic imagination. On the contrary, it is well known that the Bedu ate little meat. Apart from milk, their main diet was always bread and dates, obtained in one way or another from the 'despised' but vital Fellahin.

The conversion of 'noble' Bedu to 'morally worthless' semi-nomads or settled farmers was lamented by the traditionalists, because they wanted to believe that the East had always been static. The life of the Bedu had, they imagined, remained unchanged since the beginning of time, until they were rudely forced out of their ancient ways by technological and economic development, and obliged to settle down. In fact, there was absolutely nothing new in the process of settlement: the various means of livelihood which travellers observed in the Arab world were actually part of a sliding scale of survival along which lineages and households had moved backwards and forwards throughout the millennia. Men do not willingly look for a 'death in life' – as T. E. Lawrence described the nomad's lot. They seek always the best means of survival the ecological and political conditions can provide.

Many cultivators, semi-nomads and shepherds were once camel-breeding Bedu, and settled, not because they had 'failed', but because conditions were favourable for a more settled way of life. Conversely, when conditions became unfavourable for cultivation, due to drought, disease, disaster, or high taxes, for instance, these families would make for the desert – perhaps after decades or even centuries as farmers – and take on the mantle of the Bedu once again. There may not have been – as T. E. Lawrence claimed – a single settled Arab unmarked by the brand of the nomad, but neither was there a single Bedui, no matter how 'blue-blooded', who did not have a Fellah's planting-stick in his saddle-bag.

Not long after we had regained the asphalt road that led east to the Euphrates, the snow began, drifting down across the gaunt plains. The sky was pregnant with white and soft purple, and the distant hills dissolved into mist. 'It's snowing!' Ahmad said, 'Let's go back to Palmyra!'

'Not unless it gets really bad!'

We were heading for Qasr al Hayr ash Shariqi – a brace of desert fortresses built during the Ummayyad era – near the ruins of which there was supposed to be a large Bedu encampment. All along the road the Bedu had lit fires from discarded tractor-tyres, whose smoke wreathed up among the snow in coal-coloured spirals. Men in sheepskin coats and headcloths congregated around the pyres shoulder to shoulder, hands outspread, while others lay on the ground beneath the falling snow, transforming their sheepskins into miniature tents. The sheep stood in miserable wedges head to tail and flank to flank. Tractors came drumming up the wet road carrying Bedu swathed tightly in cloaks, scarves and headcloths. We hummed through Sukhna – once a caravanserai on the Silk Road, now a mean town of deserted streets. In the open door of a breeze-block store a cluster of boys and men stared at us from the comforting glow of a brazier. Beyond the town we left the road and headed once more across the desert. A bleak weirding wind gusted against us, and fizzles of snow fell upon the windscreen like cold volcanic ash. Ahmad had lost the way. He had been to Qasr al Hayr many times before, but never in such white-out conditions as these. The country pitched and yawed under the blizzard. There was a billiard-table green in the surface, and shortly there was an armada of long-coated sheep, brown-and-white and red-and-white, led by a bare-headed man in a cloak. Ahmad jumped out to talk to him: the air seeped in and it was unbelievably cold. In a moment he was back, saying, 'It's only two kilometres from here!'

Fifteen kilometres on, we were still searching for Qasr al Hayr, and Ahmad was cursing silently. 'The Bedu have no idea of distance!' he said. 'They'll tell you it's two kilometres when it's twenty, and twenty when it's two!'

The snow seemed to be easing, the sky clearing, and for a moment we glimpsed in the distance feldspar hills veined in blue like Stilton cheese. Then, very suddenly, a great edge of masonry sprang out of the desert – an L-shaped wall, many feet thick. I stepped out into the burning cold to inspect it, while Ahmad warmed himself with yet another cigarette. My guidebook said that this was a 'khan' or caravanserai, associated with the two sister-fortresses of Qasr al Hayr which stood four kilometres away. It was easy to observe how that conclusion had been reached: the wall was so perforated by Moorish arches along its length that it could not possibly have been a defensive structure. Standing on the Silk Road as it did, in proximity to two forts, it might therefore have been a halting-place for caravans.

In fact, the entire distance from here to the fortresses was marked by traces of a mud wall whose external and internal buttresses show that it was no military bulwark, but the boundary of an immense area of cultivated land. *Qasr al Hayr* means 'fortress of the enclosed garden', and in the period Westerners call 'the Dark Ages' the Arabs actually created a man-made oasis here in the remote ranges of the Syrian desert. The crops were fed – perhaps – by a rain-harvesting system from which the collected liquid was funnelled along feeder-canals. These arches were sluicegates put in place to drain off the excess water.

It was too cold to linger, but as we rattled along the remnants of the boundary-wall, I reflected that the garden planted here as early as the eighth century AD marked yet another triumph of adaptability for the nomadic Bedu, and yet another indication that the Syrian desert was not the utterly inhospitable wasteland it was often supposed to be.

The snow had stopped, and we had a clear view of the ruined castles standing in a perfect hollow on the desert surface. From a distance the desert's vast scale reduced them to models, and it was only when we pulled up between them that their true size became apparent. They were squarish, built of two-metre-thick blocks of peach-coloured stone, with bulging turrets topped with brick domes. The easternmost and smaller of the structures had but one gate, which directly faced the entrance to the larger castle across a corridor no more than 100 metres wide, marked by a square watch-tower. The iron grille across this gate was locked, and of its interior we were able to glimpse only some fine Corinthian pillars of the same style as those found in Palmyra. We wrapped our shamaghs around our heads against the biting cold, and walked through the gateway into the larger citadel, where great vaulted arches seemed to be perched tentatively on the most fragile of supports, and top-heavy slabs of masonry hung out of the walls at perilous angles. There were the remains of mud buildings inside, but their structure had been obscured by the quarryings of Bedu, intent on buried treasure.

Constructed by the Caliph Hisham in AD 728–9, Qasr al Hayr is the oldest fortified structure in the Islamic world yet dated. This, and the man-made oasis it helped to guard, were products of the so-called 'Golden Age' of the Ummayyads, when Islam still remained firmly in the hands of the Arabs from whom it had derived. The Ummayyads were one branch of the Quraysh, the settled townsmen from Mecca whose ancestors had once been Bedu, and among whom the Prophet Mohammad had been born. Drawing their support partly from the Bedu tribes of Syria, they presided over an era in which tribesmen were settling in urban centres such as Damascus in great numbers. Nevertheless, Hisham and his brothers – three of whom also ruled as Caliphs – retained an affection for the Baadiya, where several of them had been sent as children to hunt, ride, shoot, drink wine, and compose oral poetry in the tents of the Bedu. Their affection manifested itself in the foundation of many such estates, hunting-lodges, and country residences in the Syrian desert.

We emerged from the far gate to see a pair of Bedu boys grazing their sheep among the *rimth* bushes. They were wearing heavy sheepskin coats with stiff empty sleeves that stuck up like vestigial wings, giving them the appearance of amiable penguins as they hopped about in the cold. 'Who used to live here?' I asked the boys, after we had shaken hands. 'We don't know!' one of them answered. He pointed north, to where I could see a village of mud-brick houses and black tents, about a kilometre away. 'That's where *we* live!' he said.

The Bedu village might have been less monumental than the Ummayyad ruins in whose sight it stood, but it was a fascinating illustration of the successful integration of desert and sown. The houses were plain, windowless boxes of mud-brick, centred on sheepfolds of twisted thorn and low walls. For each house, though, there were one or two battered black tents, and despite the cold it was in the tents that the life of the settlement seemed to be going on. To the north I noticed an elliptical pool of burgeoning wheat, bottle-green like the waters of a deep and placid lake. Goats and long-haired sheep skulked around the houses, and flocks of turkeys grazed the stony ground beyond. We halted outside one of the houses to inspect some baked-mud monoliths that looked like traditional grain-silos, but were in fact sealed stores of firewood. A woman whose face was a horoscope of spiralling tattoos bustled out of the nearby tent to call us in for tea.

In the smoky recesses of the tent another woman sat cross-legged on a mat, working with a Singer sewing-machine. A younger woman and a girl of no more than five were sitting by a fire, both contentedly smoking cigarettes. The women were strikingly nun-like in their enveloping black dresses tied at the waist with rope, and their pointed, wimple-like headcloths. They wore only narrow kerchiefs to provide the hint of a veil when drawn across the mouth. Our presence seemed of insufficient weight to urge them into a show of respectability, though, which was fortunate, as the younger woman was remarkably beautiful, despite a mouthful of gold teeth. Ahmad sat down next to her on the rug, and his rubicund face blushed yet more redly when she smiled at him and said, 'You are from Palmyra. You look exactly like our teacher here. Perhaps you are his brother!'

'You have a school here?' he asked.

'Yes. All our children can read and write.'

As the older lady poured out tea, she told us that, like the Bedu I had stayed with last night, the people here belonged to various branches of the 'Anaza. 'We have our fields, and our sheep,' she said, 'but we don't have any camels. We got rid of them thirty years ago, because they were no good any more. Cars are more comfortable. In the wet season we take our tents out into the desert, and we carry the sheep in trucks. Sometimes we go as far as Homs.'

I asked about the *markab* – the traditional camel-litter for brides with its curious sweeping arms. The young woman

49

giggled. 'The bride is carried by car now,' she said. 'No one has used the *markab* for a very long time!'

'But are you still Bedu now you have houses?' I asked.

'Of course,' the old woman replied with a touch of indignation. 'Houses don't make any difference. We are still Bedu, just the same!'

The woman with the sewing-machine worked away silently during our conversation, hunching uncomfortably over the device, turning the handle with terrible concentration. I watched her with interest for a moment, and realized suddenly that this Singer was a genuine antique. 'That's an old machine,' I commented.

The old lady paused and glanced up at me, her face a pattern of tattoos on tanned leather. 'It certainly is!' she said. 'It belonged to my mother. It's a *Sanja*, by God! A foreigner like yourself once came here – an Italian he said he was – and offered me four thousand lire for it. "I won't sell, by God!" I said. "This *Sanja* belonged to my mother! I wouldn't exchange it even for a hundred goats! And besides, if you are ready to give me four thousand lire, it must be something very special indeed!"'

As we drove back along the wall which, 1,000 years ago, had marked the boundary of gardens which the Bedu created out of the desert, I wondered if indeed very much had changed. Nomads who reared camels exclusively had always been a tiny minority even among the pastoral population of the Arab world. In the Baadiya, with its oscillation between fertility and barrenness, it had always been those who combined agriculture with livestock-rearing who had been most in evidence. If there was a norm in the Arab way of life, it was surely this, for in a changing environment it was those who were the least specialized who had the greatest chance of success.

On the way back to the road, we halted at a modest tent made of jute sacks, where 500 head of sheep were guzzling grain from dozens of rubber bowls. Two white-haired sheep-dogs bounced towards us, snapping, as we left the car, but they were called off by a young man in a jallabiyya, with a mop of tousled black hair. He bade us sit down at the hearth inside the tent, while his wife – a dark, lively gypsy of a woman – made tea on a spirit stove.

His name was Habib, and he too belonged to the ʿAnaza, though he worked as a professional herdsman for a merchant from the town. 'These sheep belong to him,' Habib said, 'and they're all rams – no ewes at all!'

'How do the flocks increase?' I asked.

'They don't. We buy the lambs from other shepherds and rear them here. Then we sell the lot for meat in Damascus, and buy another lot. The government gives us barley to feed them on, but when there is good grazing, like there was this year, the price of sheep goes up.'

'Goes up? Surely, if conditions are better the price will go down. Isn't it the law of supply and demand?'

'It doesn't work like that. If the grazing is poor we have to buy more grain, and to do that we have to sell more sheep in the market, so the market is flooded and the price of sheep goes down. For us a year of poor grazing means poor prices.'

Habib had only recently been married and had just acquired his first tent. 'I haven't made enough to buy a proper tent of goats' wool,' he explained. 'They cost about thirty thousand lire to make. The women still make them, but we have to buy the goats' wool because the Bedu don't have goats these days. Sheep's wool is no use for making tents. The women can only work in the summer and it takes months just to weave one section of the tent. Unless you buy bits of it from other people, making a full tent is the work of years!'

There was a gas-lamp attached to a cylinder in the tent, and a chest of drawers, upon which Habib's wife was unscrewing plastic jars. She produced a tray loaded with balls of cheese, black olives, bread, and a delicious pickle called *fetr* made from local mushrooms. We crouched around the meal together. Habib looked at his wife with the affection of a newly-wed. 'In your country, do you get married for love?' he inquired.

'Usually, yes.'

'We got married for love. My wife belongs to a different tribe. I was herding the sheep near her family's tent, and we fell in love at first sight.' The girl grinned and laughed uncomfortably. 'What I want now is to earn enough money to get my own tent, and to have children. As many as God sends. I would like them to go to school, because I never learnt to read and write. I have spent my whole life in the desert, except for the two years of military service, which I did at Homs – a dirty, noisy place! You feel trapped in the city. Give me the desert any day!'

Within minutes after we left the tent it was snowing again, and this time the snow was coming down in large, flat flakes like feathers. The plains were transmuted from ochre to alabaster, under a sky that was grey and so low that it caressed the ragged peaks of the hills. There were drifts along the edges of the highway, and the pyres of the Bedu had been soused, the tractor-tyres spluttering and choking for air. The only living things moving in the desolate landscape were the dark figures of shepherds and their flocks, but as we whizzed past, they too were frozen for an infinite moment in our memories, as they plodded at snail's pace towards black tents that were already sagging under massed white wedges of snow.

# 3

# The Land of Edom

Sunset in Damascus was the tramp of grey-robed men out of streets smeared with the day's drizzle. It was the sun like a wan eye blinking feebly through the last shreds of flaccid cloud. On the Avenue of the Revolution the traffic was an endless scream of brakes and tyres, jostling and jerking forward in a roil of benzene and burned rubber smells. The crowds in Martyrs' Square were a tide ebbing out into the main arteries, mingling with the traffic like stragglers across a raging torrent. From the grid of alleys behind the Hejaz railway station emerged a three-wheeled refuse truck. A man leaned out of his cab, honking a brass horn like some prehistoric trumpet, miraculously clearing a swath through the fevered cars. Below the Avenue, the Barada river issued unnoticed from a cloaca, a grey surge of foam running shallow over stones, weaving and writhing beneath the decrepit buildings that hung over it on tenterhooks. It was difficult to believe that this shallow froth was the inspiration for the sacred river Alph in Coleridge's *Xanadu*, or indeed that without the Barada this city would not be here at all.

This was the hour I chose to lose myself in the warren of Old Damascus – the Ummayyad town that lay along the Barada's banks. I watched the rags of the day rinse away into the scurrying waters, and turned into the covered market, where the night-globes were already firing up, brindling the flow of humanity with bars of sulphur-coloured light. Disconnected faces floated before me: Arab, Sudanese, Mediterranean; men in shamaghs and hats and heavy turbans, women wearing masks and veils and coloured *hejabs*. Along the walls of the Ummayyad mosque, men were sitting around glowing braziers on little stools. The Street Called Straight was a dark conduit where vehicles were shooshing past, scarcely visible but for blazing headlamps and an aura of petrol fumes. I hurried through pools of light cast out from the doors and windows of shops, each one a glimpse of a self-contained planet: a man sharpening a knife on a grinding-wheel in a shower of sparks; another shaping a coffee-pot on a press; three cross-legged boys in white skull-caps embroidering carpets; a butcher shaving strips of flesh from a loin of hanging meat; a barber enveloped for an instant in a halo of cigarette-smoke as he rested from shaving his client. This street would always be associated for me with the figure of Charles Montagu Doughty, one of the greatest of Western explorers in Arabia. He had been here almost a century before, yet I could sense his presence. I had this irrational feeling that if I hurried I could somehow catch him up. It was as if Doughty and I were linked by this street on a level where the barriers of measured time no longer constrained us:

> Time present and time past
> Are both perhaps present in time future,
> And time future contained in time past . . .
> What might have been and what has been
> Point to one end, which is always present.

I savoured these thoughts for a moment as I marched, for I knew that time and change were the central themes in Western ideas about the Bedu and the East in general. Doughty and three other nineteenth-century British travellers in Arabia – Palgrave, Burton and Blunt – had done more than anyone else to generate the idea of the Bedu as a race which had preserved the primeval innocence of mankind, a people who, it seemed, were impervious to the normal process of history. The Bedu were 'static while the world moved', Rana Kabbani has written, 'pure of all corrupting influences, a purity that greatly endeared [them] to a Western eye so appreciative of symbolic horoes'.

In Doughty's time, Europe was undergoing a period of change so rapid that it was difficult to comprehend: in the East there remained to artists, travellers and philosophers a vision of the immutable – the unchanging landscape of the biblical era. 'As for the nomad Arabs,' Doughty wrote, 'we may see in them that desert life, which was followed by their ancestors, in the Biblical tents of Kedar . . . we almost feel ourselves carried back to the days of the nomad Hebrew Patriarchs . . . And we were better able to read the bulk of the Old Testament books, with that further insight and understanding, which comes of a living experience.' So enticingly unimpeachable was this concept that Doughty's words were still being paraphrased uncritically a century later: 'The Bedu . . .' wrote the naturalist Bryan Nelson in 1973, 'practise a specialized and demanding way of life almost exactly as they did in pre-biblical times.'

But no culture truly remains outside the process of history, not even the camel-rearing Bedu of Arabia. Indeed, the biblical scholar W. F. Albright says that there is little archaeological evidence that camels actually existed in the region during the time of Abraham – the nineteenth century BC – nor are there any references to camels in the records of Mesopotamia from that epoch. Albright claims that biblical references to Abraham's camels were added to the scriptures later by scribes attempting to bring them up to date. If the camel existed at all in those times, it must have been in such small numbers that it had no impact on the economy of the day. If Doughty had indeed been transported back to the biblical tents of Kedar, he would have been surprised to find that the way of life he believed so timeless simply did not exist.

Yet as I dashed through the darkness on the Street Called Straight that night, I could not restrain a sense of empathy with Doughty, as one who went before, who risked all to live and travel among the Bedu. Nor could I deny the dewdrops in my eyes when I recalled his encounter – after all his privations in the desert – with an old friend, on this very street: 'Tell me (said he) since thou art here again in the peace and assurance of Ullah, and whilst we walk as in former years, towards the new blossoming orchards, full of sweet spring as the gardens of God, what moved thee, or how couldst thou take such journeys into the fanatic Arabia?'

Next morning I was at the taxi-station behind the Hejaz railway terminus, where rows of cabs were parked fender to fender in muddy puddles, and drivers in leather jackets were hustling for passengers. A man called Abdallah agreed to take me to Amman in his taxi, an enormous Chevrolet, originally white, but now almost coral-coloured from the rust. 'Don't worry about the car,' Abdallah said, 'it is highly trustworthy. I do this run from Jordan and back almost every day!' Abdallah was small and carelessly dressed in jeans and biker-jacket: blue chin, cavalry moustache, long black hair swept back in a brylcreamed slick. He said that he was from Amman, but it was not difficult to guess that he was Palestinian. 'I'm originally from the Negev,' he admitted. 'You know the Bedu? I am a Bedui. My tribe is the Tarabin.'

As it happened I had heard of this tribe, because only recently I had read *Bedouin of the Negev* by Emanuel Marx. The Negev Bedu were particularly interesting, because while they were mainly offshoots of the great Bedouin tribes of the Hejaz, they included cultivators and herdsmen under the tribal aegis. 'I understand the Negev Bedu are doing very well,' I said. 'The Israelis have given them tractors and things and they are better off than ever.' Abdallah scowled over the driving-wheel as he piloted the Chevrolet out of the bleak streets of Damascus. 'Maybe they are,' he said, 'but those who remained in the Negev after the Israelis came were not true Bedu!'

Here was yet another definition of 'true' Bedu to weigh against my favourite one – that of the anthropologist Shelagh Weir: 'the Bedouin are pastoral nomads whose traditional way of life is based mainly on herding animals, and partly on small-scale farming, smuggling, protection of trade routes and other activities.'

Abdallah wore modern clothes and drove a taxi, but – according to Weir's definition, at least – he had not abandoned at least one aspect of the 'traditional way of life'. This became evident when he pulled up next to a shop, disappeared, and returned a moment later with 1,000 Marlboro cigarettes in five cartons sealed in plastic covers, which he secreted behind the dashboard and in cavities under the bonnet. We drove off and coasted along in silence for a while, then Abdallah said, casually, 'Taxis normally drop their passengers off at the taxi-station in Amman. But I will take you to wherever you are staying.' He was too discreet to add, 'As long as you don't say anything about the cigarettes,' but we both knew that a bargain had been struck. Since the air had been cleared, I felt free to ask him what he was doing with the cigarettes, anyway. 'Syria is a free market for cigarettes,' he explained. 'They come into Damascus from Beirut. In Jordan they are more expensive. I take some back with me every time I come to Syria, just to make a few dinars extra. Times are hard and petrol is expensive – you know!'

Damascus fell behind us, and we raced through rolling limestone country – red land, shell-white stones as thick as fallen leaves, stands of Aleppo pine, stone pine and peeling eucalypt. There were mountains in the distance trimmed with snow and sombre farms stitched into the contours of the landscape, with fig-trees in rows planted with military precision. At Dara'a, there were interminable queues at immigration. At the last barrier, a rotund Syrian guard in Ruritanian khaki with a woollen hat pulled over his ears turned up his collar to the freezing drizzle. He took a handful of melon seeds from his pocket, and chewed them while he examined our documents. He weighed my oversized passport with exaggerated wonder, and said, 'This is not a passport. This is a *book*! Ha! Ha! Ha! Ha!' Then, with the skins of melon seeds hanging from his upper lip, he waved us on.

Jordan was a bleak stony hillside washed by the rain. At Ramtha we halted in the customs-tunnel, and a man in civilian clothes ordered me to bring my rucksack for inspection. 'Bring your rucksack!' Abdallah bawled. The official laid the contents out along the table, while Abdallah watched me, frowning. 'Have you got a video-camera?' the man asked.

'A video-camera?' Abdallah parroted nervously.

'No.'

'All right. Get moving!'

'Come on!' Abdallah shouted at me, so belligerently that even the customs-man stared at him. 'Are you in a bad temper?' he inquired.

'No! No! Of course not!' Abdallah said, but he looked uneasy and beads of sweat were gathering along the line of his forehead. If I had been the customs-man, I should certainly have suspected him. The official waved us on, however, and as soon as we were through the last barrier Abdallah let out a whoop, and stabbed his foot joyously down on the accelerator: 'Marlboro country!' he yelled.

True to his word, he dropped me at ACOR – the American Centre for Oriental Research – where I had booked a room. It was a place of almost monastic calm, overlooking hills smothered in adobe-block houses. Here, on the outskirts of Amman, country and city coalesced: there were ploughed fields among the flat-blocks, men shepherding goats along the wet roads, and horses tethered on overgrown plots. It was in ACOR's library that I met Steve Sims, a small, reed-slim man who was associate professor of anthropology at the University of Utah. Sims, an expert on Native American culture, was now applying his expertise to the Bedu of Jordan. Over coffee in his tiny room, I asked his opinion of the traditional view of Bedu immutability: 'Anthropologists always like to divide and comprehend,' he said, 'but while we were excavating at Petra, we were constantly coming up with traces of pastoral nomads in the strata. I mean, they have been able to adjust to new political, economic, climatic and technological conditions throughout history. The desert and the sown were never completely distinct. There was always a continuum between them.'

'What do you think of the idea of the Bedu as pure nomads?'

'I prefer to take an ecological view. When you think of it, why should you call certain nomads "pure" just because they herd camels and migrate over long distances rather than herding sheep and migrating over shorter distances? Or because they obtain their grain by trading for it rather than growing it? It's a subjective value-judgement which is totally meaningless. You can't pigeonhole things so neatly, because nomadism is so diverse anyway – it is an adjustment to a set of ecological conditions along a continuum of numerous possibilities. It was never fixed, but dynamic – some people were always dropping out of nomadism and others going in.'

'But it is true,' I said, 'that among some Arabs, only the camel-herding tribes were regarded as being "real" Bedu.'

'Yes, but even the Arabs themselves aren't the final arbiters of the truth. We have to look at the evidence, and the evidence doesn't fit the concept that only the "noble camel-rearing tribes" are "true" Bedu. There are many tribes who regard themselves as Bedu who don't rely on herding camels – even some who are settled, like the Bedu of Petra. In fact, it's possible to say that "Bedouinism" *never* entails a monoculture of camels – even the supposedly "pure" nomads like the ʿAnaza had always interacted with others.'

'What about the idea of "noble blood"?'

'The Bedu liked to preserve genealogies which showed their descent from a noble ancestor, and this seemed to fit in with a Victorian concept which influenced a lot of the writers and travellers of the first half of this century. They were obsessed with the idea of inherited blood and race, and made the fundamental mistake of confusing things like race and culture. People liked to believe that the Bedu had kept their blood "pure" due to isolation in the desert, but it is clear that they were always in contact with the outside world, and in reality their gene-pool must be amazingly diverse if you look at it at the macro-level. The point is that the traditionalists believed that some races were "pure" and therefore superior. They wanted to arrange races in a hierarchy with them-selves at the top.'

Next morning I was in a Mercedes taxi nearing Petra, where Steve Sims had suggested I should start my quest for the last of the Bedu. He had advised me to contact a man called Dakhilallah – a Sheikh of the famous Bedouin tribe called the Bedul, who had until recently lived within the ancient rock city itself. As we drew nearer, the landscape became increasingly mountainous, coarse limestone on which grass grew with the sparseness of receding hair. There were pockets of Aleppo pine here and there, with apple orchards and figs. Suddenly the high ground dropped away beneath us into a great valley – the valley of Petra, in which a shapeless mass of purple and burgundy sandstone seemed to have boiled like confectionery out of the centre of the earth and set hard. You could see nothing of the rock city itself from up here, but the basin in which the sandstone core stood was battened in on all sides by chalky sheep-ridden hills. This was as dramatic as it was unexpected. I had always imagined, somehow, that Petra would be an oasis like Palmyra, surrounded by waterless desert on all sides. But this was not real desert at all: this was the sown land. Wadi Musa – the village standing at the entrance to Petra – was a crescent of white blocks crawling up a fertile mountainside that in Roman times was even more intensely cultivated than it is today. Rather than the 'desert citadel' it had often been called, you could fairly say that Petra was a city on the rim of the sown.

It was noon by the time I reached the Bedul village, and the only thing that seemed to be moving was a mangy camel, trying to insinuate itself into a crack of shade by a cinder-block wall. Dakhilallah's was the penultimate house in the village, a concrete cube notable mainly for its great size and astonishing lack of char-acter. Again, this was unexpected. I had imagined this Bedu tribe living in snug one-roomed houses of mud, like the 'Anaza at Qasr al Hayr in Syria. Instead, this village seemed to have combined so many of the most sterile features of modern design – or lack of it – that one could only believe that it had been done on purpose. There was, at least, a donkey tethered at the back of the house, and – albeit amid a dozen crates of empty cola bottles – a rolled-up black tent on a steel frame. These alone were good signs.

I found Dakhilallah at the front of the house, supervising three Egyptian labourers in baseball caps, who were stripping wood off recently set concrete pillars with chisels and hammers. 'I'm extending the house,' he said, after greeting me. 'It's going to be a new salon. In the summer I'm going to let the whole house to archaeological parties.'

'Where will you go?'

He pointed to the lump of woven wool standing on the steel frame nearby. 'I have my tent!' he said.

He was a wiry man with a grizzled face, wearing what looked like a khaki ranger's uniform and a loose lounge jacket. His black and white checked shamagh and the toggles looped around his crown were his only concession to tribal dress. Later, as we crouched on a hot mattress in the doorway of his house, sipping glasses of tea, oppressed by small, squeaking girls in dungarees, he made an imperious motion towards the valley. 'Have you seen Petra before?' he asked.

'No, this is my first time.'

'That is Petra!'

Thousands of feet below us, across bubbles and stacks of stone and scree, beneath chiselled faces of crimson rock, lay Petra's only free-standing monument. Known to the Bedul as 'The Castle of the Pharaoh's Daughter', it was actually the temple of Dushara – Dionysus to the ancient Nabataeans who had built the rock city of Petra, and whose human remnants – two millennia on – Dakhilallah's people claimed to be.

I wondered that Dakhilallah wanted to extend his house, for it was already a mansion. From the inside it was a curiously asymmetrical amalgam of rooms and passages that blossomed organically out of each other without any suggestion of planning. My room contained two unmade beds crammed close together, and smelt distinctly of human excrement. It was only after a time that I discovered the reason for this: the smell emanated from the upstairs toilet in which a modern pedestal had been fitted without the benefit of modern plumbing.

And there was an explanation, too, Dakhilallah told me later, for the lack of design: 'The government built these houses for us, when they moved us out of Petra,' he said. 'They promised to build us houses with two hundred and forty square metres of floor space but in the end the space was only forty-eight metres square. I've been able to add to mine bit by bit, but many of the others don't have the money.'

Dakhilallah was one of the Bedul who had grown up inside the confines of Petra. In the winter they had lived in the caves that honeycombed the rock city, warmed by fires of brushwood they collected freely from the wadis. There were plenty of caves to choose from – natural as well as man-made – and families would own several – one for the men, another for the goats, a third for the women and a fourth for guests. Some of the caves they occupied lay high up in the valley sides because of the danger of flooding, and they would build dry-stone walls across the cave-mouths to prevent the young children from falling out. In summer, when the caves became unbearably hot, they moved up to the plateaux, and pitched their tents. Traditionally they depended on goats, and grew a little wheat, barley and tobacco, keeping a handful of camels to transport their crops to Ma'an along the Wadi 'Arabah in the pilgrim season. Their possessions were almost ludicrously few: an iron cooking-pot, an iron griddle for making bread, a tin for carrying water, a basin, a chest for clothing, and perhaps a gun. In the past the Bedul would hunt the rabbits and gazelles that abounded in Petra, and kill the hyenas, wolves and leopards that harried their flocks.

As early as 1925, when Thomas Cook built the first tourist camp in Petra, a few Bedul were employed in the seasonal tourist trade, though the tribe remained so poverty-stricken that in the 1930s the archaeologist Margaret Murray had commented of their physical condition: 'The Bedul were not only ignorant but weakly, and were very different from the strong, hard-working Fellahin of Egypt and south Palestine,' she wrote; '. . . the [Liyathna] were better fed and therefore stronger, but they suffered from the disadvantage of extreme bumptiousness, a vice from which the Bedul were free. This was not from a natural virtue on the part of the Bedul, but was probably due to the weakness of malnutrition.' The Liyathna were the settled inhabitants of Wadi Musa – neighbours and age-old rivals of the Bedul. Though considered Fellahin or cultivators, from the 1860s onwards they had dominated the Bedul by force of arms – a situation in contrast to the classic Orientalist concept of Bedu raiders terrorizing settled farmers and disappearing camel-borne back into the desert. Rivalry between the tribes had remained sufficiently fraught by the 1930s, when Margaret Murray began her excavations at Petra, that she was obliged to recruit an equal number of labourers from both tribes, lest the Liyathna murder the Bedul tribesmen out of jealousy. Murray called the Liyathna village – Wadi Musa – 'the most murderous settlement in Transjordan'.

Until the 1960s, visitors to Petra remained a trickle – no more than 100 a day – but with the world-wide boom in tourism afterwards, the numbers swelled to thousands. The Bedul, based within the site, were well placed to serve the new invaders, selling trinkets and snacks, or renting out camels and horses. Bedul tribesmen who had never lived in the caves, but had continued in their traditional means of subsistence, were attracted into Petra to join the bonanza being enjoyed by their clansmen. 'Then, about ten years ago, the government comes along with Unesco and turns the place into a National Park!' Dakhilallah said. 'They said that we were getting too many and that in twenty years' time the place would be full of Bedul. In a way they were right, we saw that – we didn't want to do anything to put off tourism, because that's what we depended on. Anyway, they promised to build us houses here in Umm Sayhun that would be big enough for us and they turned out to be these middens! I think there was some dirty business involved, because I once saw a truckload of baths turn up that must have been meant for our houses, but they disappeared. Who knows what else disappeared too! Anyway, we moved here even though we were happier in our caves, and at least we were near enough Petra to carry on working with the tourists. Well, now they say they are going to move us again, somewhere far away. Umm Sayhun is going to be turned into a tourist village with hotels and local handicrafts, and someone will make a fortune at our expense.'

'Don't these houses belong to you?'

'That's the worst thing: we don't have any written agreement to prove that they're ours. The government won't even let us plant trees! They are just moving us around like baggage, and if the truth be known Petra is rightfully ours, because we lived there before there was a state called Jordan. We were far better off when we were in the caves – everything was free, and we were accustomed to living there: our fathers used them and our fathers' fathers used them right back to the Nabataeans, our ancestors.'

From out of northern Arabia, from the margins of the sown land, the Nabataeans came: some have even called them 'the first Bedu'. Their appearance in the region of Petra – the biblical Land of Edom – was part of an upheaval in the balance of power taking place in the Middle East throughout the last half-millennium BC. The sheep- and goat-herding Bedu tribes of northern Arabia and the Syrian desert had known the camel for centuries as a pack-animal bred and managed by foreign caravaneers from the Yemen. The Assyrians had experimented with the animals as war-beasts, but found them wanting, for the simple reason that the saddle – a pad behind the camel's hump – was too unstable a platform for warriors trying to wield a spear or loose an arrow. The Bedu tribes had learned to rear camels from the Yemenites, though – since wheeled vehicles were still in vogue among the settled peoples – their usefulness was limited to the long-distance carrying-trade. Only by supplying pack-camels for the caravans were the nomads able to benefit from the fabulous wealth in incense and other commodities that had been pouring across the Arabian Peninsula for 2,000 years. The control – and the fat profits – of this trade lay in the hands of foreign city-states too powerful for the desert tribes to challenge with ease. Then, around 500 BC, all this had begun to change. The catalyst was a simple technological innovation – the *shadad*, or double-poled camel saddle – yet the revolution it brought about over the next 600 years has only been paralleled in the modern era by the advent of the motor-car.

*Shadad* means 'the firm one' in Arabic, and the saddle placed the rider over the camel's hump rather than behind it, providing the stability necessary to use a long sword, a lance or a bow without promptly being pitched off. The advantage this conferred on a camel-borne warrior was, in its day, equal to that enjoyed later by the machine-gunner mounted in a light car. The Bedu of the fringe-lands were now more than a match for the heavily defended caravans, and steadily they began to take control of the incense trade. Some tribes exacted tolls on caravans passing through their territory, while others offered them protection against the predatory bandits of the remoter desert. One of these newly powerful Bedu tribes – the Nabataeans – went further: they cut out the middlemen and entered the caravan business for themselves. For 400 years, their capital at Petra dominated the route from the kingdoms of Yemen to the Mediterranean shore.

The Bedul village guarded the rear entrance to Petra, but I preferred to experience it first from the Wadi Musa approach, by which Burckhardt, disguised as a Muslim, had rediscovered the site in 1812. I hitched a ride to Wadi Musa, and the driver dropped me near the ticket office, where I faced the attendant through an iron grille.

*Attendant:* 'Do you want a ticket for one day at twenty dinars, for two days at twenty-five dinars, or for three days at thirty dinars?'

*Self:* 'For three days at thirty dinars.'

*Attendant:* 'You can't, because tomorrow is the King's birthday, and it is free. You will have to buy a ticket for one day at twenty dinars.'

*Self:* 'All right, but what about the day after tomorrow – is that free too?'

*Attendant:* 'No, then you will have to buy another ticket for one day at twenty dinars.'

*Self:* (amazed) 'Wait a minute! That means I have to pay forty dinars for three days, when one of them is free. The free day is costing me ten dinars!'

*Attendant:* (pensively) 'Very well. You will pay for three days at thirty dinars.'

I walked away nursing my ornate ticket, and it was not until I had actually passed through the gate that my mistake dawned on me. If two days cost twenty-five dinars, I was still five dinars short!

Inside the gate dozens of horses belonging to the Bedul and the Liyathna were stamping and whinnying as Arab boys in jeans leapt on and off their backs. The air was redolent of horse-urine and horse-dung. As I walked past the pickets, the boys yelled at me to take a horse. I ignored them and walked down the sandy track that dipped between limestone terraces covered in tamarisk.

The first inkling of what is going to happen to you in Petra comes on this initial approach, when you fall unexpectedly upon the tombs of yellow sandstone that at first sight seem to be elongated storage silos with dark entrances at their bases. You realize with a thrill, however, that they have been deliberately and painstakingly separated from the rock wall by adzes and chisels, and shaped into perfect boxes by craftsmen whose skills were rather those of the sculptor than of the architect or engineer. The next surprise is the 'obelisk temple', whose weathered edifice has the effect of op art. The rock here has been transformed into the recognizable façade of a classical church, with columns and cupolas, but is so eroded that you seem to be looking at an out-of-focus version of something familiar, a building melted out of kilter and warped by time in a way no true building could ever have been warped and remained intact. And then it suddenly strikes you that this is *not* a building at all, but just a cave whose exterior has been ingeniously fashioned to resemble one.

These are overture and beginners – an antipasto for the feast of Petra. The road narrows. You enter a gorge called the Siq – in places almost a tunnel between walls that rise sheer above you to hundreds of feet. Each twist and turn brings you to new wonders. The Siq is a fault-line that bisects the massif, created by surging earth forces that have caused the mountain to swell and rupture. Over aeons it has been polished by water, and there are many fine grades of colour in the rock. In places the sand underfoot is stippled with primary hues, and sunbeams drift along the walls in bars and brindles. At times, the flat echoes and these tricks of light and shade produce the feeling that you are walking in an undersea cavern. Occasionally you find yourself obliged to stop and stare upwards at the soaring walls, sheared into bulbs and peduncles, where the patina has fallen away completely to expose burrows beneath like the lairs of giant worms, or where the wine-coloured rock seems to have trickled down the face like syrup. All these are natural marvels. After about twenty minutes' walk through the tunnel, though, there is a mallow-pink flush of light in the dimness, and you glimpse through the slit in the rocks a miraculous transformation. You step through into the blazing light of an amphitheatre and there before you the stone has been magically refashioned into the vast, elaborate frontage of a cathedral, ten storeys high – the Khuznat al Firun – perhaps the temple of the Nabataean god, She'a al Qum, patron-deity of caravaneers.

It was late afternoon when I reached the Khuzna, and happily the crowds were already dwindling. A troop of Bedul elders in shamaghs and jallabiyyas were sitting in the shade of the rocks, tapping their slender camel-sticks and sniffing the breeze. The air was layered with fine dust and the odour of horses. Cavalry contingents trotted by – aged foreigners on mounts being led by Arabs – and I could not help overhearing one matron with bottle-blonde hair telling her attendant in an unmistakably English accent: 'Actually, you know my father was here in 1918. Of course, it was called Mesopotamia in those days. He was here for eight years and he simply *adored* it. He rode camels and horses. He lived with the Bedouin!' The horse-boy looked singularly unimpressed: yet I was fascinated. Perhaps her father had never really 'lived with the Bedouin' – perhaps he did not even speak Arabic – but her enthusiasm for the myth brought home just how deeply the idea of the Bedouin was etched into our national psyche.

The Khuzna is hewn out of a square fissure in the rock, but gives the impression of having been built inside it. Six Corinthian-style 'pillars' yield the illusion of supporting a grand pediment, above which the complementary halves of another pediment stand like bookends either side of a beautiful, cylindrical cupola, with a domed roof and a great urn on top. The Bedu of Petra traditionally believed that this urn contained gold and jewels hidden out of human reach by 'the Pharaoh', and the bullet-marks which riddle it are testimony to their past attempts to crack it open.

The interior was a cool, square womb sculpted in rigid angles that slashed through the grain of the rock, exposing a shimmering progression of colours – blood, milk, hyacinth, wine-purple – that merged, swelled and ran like those on a hand-made Persian carpet. Lofty portals on each side of the room had lost their sharp edges and the spectrum of colours spread across their ornamented frames. A great fissure in the rock spanned the place from floor to ceiling on both sides, a crack so wide that I was again reminded that this was only the illusion of a man-made structure.

I surfaced into the bright light of day once again and followed the straggle of horses and foot-sloggers around the corner into another narrow chasm, past Bedul boys selling multi-coloured sand in bottles, past minor tombs, past a Roman theatre in marbled colours carved out of a single piece of rock. Above me the shoulder of the gorge had broken out in all manner of gothic façades:

flat gargoyle faces pitched and tilted at uncomfortable angles and flashed back the molten sunlight like polished brass. I stood still beneath them and tried to cradle the whole overwhelming effect of Petra in my thoughts. On one hand it was no more than an incredibly elaborate practical joke – natural rock made to look like tombs and churches, pillars that never supported anything, prodigiously sculpted doorways to what were no more than dark caves: this was form without function, style without content. At the same time, the experience of Petra was not the result of human intervention alone: one wondered at the tombs as one wondered at the Pyramids and temples of Egypt, but there was a difference. Petra would have been an impressive place even without a single human indent – the marbled colours, the textures, the shapes in the sandstone were alive with images before ever the Nabataeans came: the sculptors merely liberated them from their cold sleep in the rock and gave them form according to the highest religious icons of their day.

Near the temple of Dushara, beyond the paved Colonnade Street built in Roman times, I drank a glass of tea at a café with a view of a sloping headland strewn with pebbles and potsherds. It was on this shelf of rock that the actual Nabataean living-quarters were sited, for in fact the people of ancient Petra never inhabited the caves as the Bedul were later to do. Instead they constructed a town of single-storey, flat-roofed stone dwellings, each centred on its own courtyard, with only small windows giving on to the tortuous alleys outside. At its height this town had housed a population of 30,000.

The Nabataean occupation of Petra was less the consequence of invasion and conquest than a leisurely massing of tribesmen who first pitched their tents on the marches of the cultivated land, and in time assimilated themselves completely to the ways of the Edomites. The two tribes claimed common descent through daughters of Ishmael, and since Arab genealogies tended to reflect *de facto* power-relationships, this must at the very least have been an expression of mutual ground. The people of Edom had,

anyway, been decimated in their wars with the Judaeans – spectacularly by King David, whose objective, it seems, was little less
than their genocide. There were also new stars rising in the
firmament of Mesopotamian power. In 587 BC the Babylonians
captured the Judaean capital at Jerusalem, torched Solomon's
Temple and Palace, and led off the Jews into captivity. The rem-
nant Edomites, gleeful over the destruction of their ancient enemies, flocked out of Edom to occupy Judah's green swards. The
vacuum this diaspora created was readily filled by the encroaching
Nabataeans, who by 300 BC had so swamped the remaining
Edomites with their numbers that theirs had become the dominant culture in Petra.

Like the Bedu tribes who were later to create Palmyra – indeed,
like all Bedu – the Nabataeans were exceptionally versatile, with a
talent for commerce and organization. Not only were they remarkably skilled architects and sculptors, they were also engineers
of the highest order, whose farms and settlements have been
discovered in thousands all over the Negev and as far north as
Damascus. In the deserts beyond Petra they developed a sophisticated spreadwater irrigation system, collecting rain whose volume
was too limited to be productive when spread over twenty acres
and directing it via an ingenious network of cisterns and feeders
to a single acre, where it brought forth an abundant crop. The Israelis have estimated that if all the rain falling on the 2½-million-
acre southern Negev were harvested by this system, 125,000 acres
of desert could be turned into productive land. The Nabataeans
constructed reservoirs and aqueducts that are still watertight after
2,000 years, and every drop of rain falling on their villages was
channelled into public catch-basins. Israeli engineers who have
studied Nabataean methods in the Negev have declared that even
with the benefit of modern technology they are still unable to
equal this ancient people's success in greening the desert. If there
is a single conclusion to be drawn from the Nabataean migration
to Petra and their subsequent achievements, it lies once again in
the fluidity rather than the immutability of Bedouin ways.

It was dark by the time I arrived back in Wadi Musa. The taxi-driver who motored me to Umm Sayhun belonged to the Liyathna – the ancient adversaries of the Bedul. When I mentioned that I was staying with Dakhilallah, he said: 'Dakhilallah is an old fox! Don't take a bit of notice about what he says! He'll tell you the Bedul liked it much better when they lived in the caves, but you just try getting them to go back there! They've got the foreigners thinking that they've been unfairly treated, and they are trying to force the government to hand over the sites in Umm Sayhun to them, by acting the aggrieved party. As soon as the sites belong to them they will sell up. Just think of the value of that land to the hotel chains with the new boom in tourism! Overlooking Petra, right near the back entrance: it'd be worth millions!'

There is no direct evidence apart from their own testimony that the Bedul are the descendants of the Nabataeans, or even that they have inhabited Petra for more than 150 years. In 1812 Burckhardt found the ruins of Petra unoccupied, though the fact that his Liyathna guide went in fear of bandits is taken to suggest that he expected some human presence there. Burckhardt did, however, encounter some Bedul outside Petra and recorded that not only were their tents unusually small, but they were too poor to offer him coffee: 'our breakfast or dinner therefore consisted of dry barley cakes, which we dipped in melted goat's grease,' he wrote. The first detailed account of the Bedul comes from the traveller John Wilson, who visited Petra in 1843 and was startled when a Bedul Sheikh claimed that his tribe was descended from the 'Bani Israel' or Hebrews. On closer analysis, though, it appeared that 'Bani Israel' was the name the Bedul gave to the ancient inhabitants of Petra, the Nabataeans, and that far from claiming to be Jewish, the Sheikh was merely asserting his tribe's link with the ancient past. Nevertheless, stories concerning the Bedul relate that they were originally Jews who became Muslims or originally pagans who became Jews, the theme of apostasy being supported by the fact that the name Bedul shares its root with the Arabic word *badala* – to exchange. On the other hand, since the consonants 'l' and 'n' are often interchangeable in Arabic dialects, Bedul may be a corruption of *bdun* – literally 'without', indicating that the tribe were social pariahs in origin – a view supported by the fact that none of the prestigious Bedu tribes they claim to be related to will intermarry with them.

What happened to the Nabataeans after their kingdom was annexed by the Roman Governor of Syria, Cornelius Palma, in March AD 106, remains a mystery. For some time the caravan-trade from the Yemen had been in decline, and many merchants had drifted away to the new hub of commerce at Palmyra. Certainly the Nabataean town of Petra contracted: many of its citizens may have taken to the desert as nomads, spilling into southern Jordan, Egypt and the Hejaz as the famous Bedu tribe of Huwaytat. Others – a handful – may possibly have readopted a semi-nomadic existence in the region of Petra, as the Bedul.

Dakhilallah and his wife – a cheerful, robust woman who chain-smoked cigarettes – were sitting on the floor watching television when I arrived. The programme was a loop showing and reshowing images of King Hussein amid adoring crowds, set to saccharine songs and music. 'Tomorrow is the King's birthday,' Dakhilallah said. 'Everyone loves the King, because he is of the line of the Prophet Mohammad. I'd trust him above any one of his ministers. That's why we're making up a petition to ask him for the deeds to these houses.'

The TV stayed on all evening, and Dakhilallah and his wife were evidently much attached to it.

'No TV in the caves!' I commented.

'We could always get our own generator!' Dakhilallah said, but I wondered about what my Liyathna driver had said. I wondered too about the constant extensions to this house and the profit my host must make from letting it out to tourists during the high season. Despite the rhetoric, he seemed to be doing well in Umm Sayhun. An illiterate Bedui he might be, but he was well versed in the machinations of the wide world.

I remained with Dakhilallah's family for three days. I never tired of the sights of Petra, nor of my conversations with the Bedul. I climbed up to the so-called 'Monastery' on the high plateau, and met Dakhilallah's son, Mohammad, a swarthy, thickly bearded man, who kept a coffee-shop there. He pointed down the precipitous gorge and described the dangers of Petra after heavy rains: 'Only last month a woman was drowned going down from the Monastery,' he said. 'The floods come so quickly that you can't do anything about it. Two women were carried off, but the Bedul managed to save one of them. Nobody realizes how important the Bedul are to the safety of people in Petra.' He also had a fascinating story about the Israeli youths who until recently would undergo a sort of initiation test by racing across the border at night, with the object of reaching Petra and getting back on to Israeli soil by sunrise the next morning. Inevitably many of them got lost, dehydrated or exhausted, only to be rescued by Bedul trackers.

On the last evening of my stay I returned to find Dakhilallah and his wife glued once again to the TV. 'Sit down! Sit down!' Dakhilallah said, without looking up. 'This is about the Bedu!' In fact it was a weekly soap in which ham actors dressed as Bedu made melodramatic speeches and came and went between very clean-looking tents on camels and horses. 'That one is the villain!' Dakhilallah told me breathlessly. 'He is trying to ravish that young girl. And the hero – that one – is trying to stop him!' I dropped the idea of conversation and muttered excuses before retiring. My abiding memory of the 'Last of the Nabataeans' will be of them sitting glued to a TV set watching a soap opera that presented a pale imitation of a life they had left only a decade before, but to which they would never return.

Sombre clouds were massing over the Petra valley. At Wadi Musa a contingent of tourist guides in dungarees and baseball hats was lounging in the lobby of the Rest House, talking of snow. Mas'ud, a Liyathna taxi-driver in a yellow cab, agreed to take me to Wadi

Rum across the mountains: 'But you'd better leave right now,' he said, 'or the passes are going to be blocked and you'll be snowed in for three days!' I took this as sales-talk, but I got in, and as soon as we were above the valley I saw that I had misjudged him. There were rashes of snow on the crests, and below us clouds gyrating in a kaleidoscope, strobing the sunlight into starfish shapes, providing snatched glimpses of the boiled-brain rocks of Petra beneath. As we drove higher freezing cotton-wool mist shrouded the road. Masʿud slowed down to a snail's pace and gripped the wheel till his knuckles turned ashen, but even then I could feel the tyres slipping on the ice. There was silence: the tension was palpable. Suddenly the windscreen was splashed with water that converted it instantly into a freezing blindfold, and the vehicle careered desperately across the road. Masʿud jumped, then threw the wiper-switch. A second later the wipers had clawed a translucent patch on the windscreen just enough for him to steer by, and he brought the car under control, gritting his teeth. 'Thank God there were no other vehicles coming!' he said, his voice shaking slightly. 'I don't want that to happen again!'

We continued to slither along until, almost imperceptibly, we were losing altitude. The snow-drifts cleared and the black ice gave way to wet asphalt road. At Ras al Nagab the sun was exhaling light freely across the valley. Streams of fire snaked along the cool ground, unhitching blurs of mist which distended like smoke rings around massive sandstone polyhedrals. We hauled past breeze-block hamlets, shredded old gunny-bag tents with chimneys, oblong sheepfolds, sheep-dogs, children in cloaks and mufflers, tractors billying smoke. Soon we were turning off the main road and speeding into Wadi Rum.

In Rum a bone-biting wind was blowing out of the Arabian Peninsula. The Rest House was hemmed in on both sides by cliffs so grooved horizontally that they might have been cut by a giant cheese-grater. I paid my entrance fee in a tiny office, where a man dressed as a Bedui answered my Arabic in English and handed me a ticket on which was written 'Genuine Bedouine tea or coffee free with this ticket!' The House was crammed with tourists, and in the dining-room a Jordanian singer with a voice like gravel was retching out a local pop-song to the thrum of a lute, while the audience cheered deliriously and beat time. I asked to see the manager of the House, and as I sipped my genuinely anaemic Bedouine tea, he agreed to fix me up with camels and a guide to take me as far as Aqaba. He led me through the Bedu village, where black tents were pitched inside shanties of timber and cinder-block, and the sand was scattered with rusty machine-parts and bits of dead car frames. An unruly camel shrieked as it dashed down the track, its jaws open and its tongue bulging in a diabolic rictus. Boys in red-specked shamaghs raced after it, screeching. At a one-roomed shop, a man called Sleiman emerged from behind an alp of sardine-cans, a tiny figure with a long Bedouin nose peeking out of his shamagh. 'I will take you to Aqaba,' he said. 'The journey will be four days, and you will pay two days for my return: six days at thirty dinars a day.'

Like all the Bedu in Wadi Rum, Sleiman belonged to the Hu-waytat, the famous tribe of T. E. Lawrence's ally Auda Abu Tayyi, which was spread across Jordan, the Hejaz, and Egypt. If there were ever a 'middle class' in Bedu society, the Huwaytat would fit this niche, for though they looked down upon lesser tribes such as the Bedul, they themselves were shunned by the mighty clans of the 'Anaza, with whom they shared a traditional enmity. Huwaytat history was a fine example of the fluid response of Bedu tribes to changing conditions. Originally they were traders, and settled farmers along the shores of the Red Sea. At the end of the nine-teenth century they acquired the fertile Sherah plain from the Neumat tribe, and began to practise both cultivation and animal husbandry in conjunction. In the days of their warrior-sheikh Auda Abu Tayyi, though, they took to raiding on a large scale, abandoning their farms or renting them out to Fellahin, within a short time gaining a reputation as the most warlike tribe in Arabia. After 1918 many of them reverted once again to cultiva-tion. The Huwaytat were perhaps the second most powerful tribe in Jordan, and in the Rum–Aqaba region alone numbered at least 1,000 tents.

The camels were grazing behind the shop in a field full of old tyres and broken saddles. Sleiman bridled three of them – two for riding, he said, and one, an untrained calf, as a 'spare'. A crowd of little peanut-coloured boys and girls led them out, jumping and shouting piercingly, and couched them by the shop door. Saddle-girths were lapped and buckled, woven saddlebags and my rucksack slung on, a plastic jerrycan was attached. 'Don't worry about food,' Sleiman said, 'all that is taken care of!' Within minutes we were leading three camels out into the great spaces of the Wadi Rum.

The glacial wind had splintered the cloud into quills of smoke, and the sky was radiant. Rum was more than a mile wide here, an imperial boulevard between smelt-coloured stacks that receded from us in diminishing perspective to their vanishing point on the high horizon. There were no dragons and demons in the hills of Rum as there were at Petra: instead there was a grain to them – the grain of old timber, chased and bevelled. They looked like the buttresses of unbelievably large trees whose trunks had snapped off and fallen into the desert behind them. The valley floor was a soft meniscus lapping at the cliffs, brick-dust and burnt umber, a-whiffle with plants whose oilskinned undersides gave the place a feel of wetness. Bedu tents stood along its edges like the abdomens of huge dismembered black scorpions.

We tramped into the eye of the wind, and for an hour I tried to engage Sleiman in meaningful conversation. He was a young man, shoulder-high, no more than twenty, wrinkled up like a prematurely senile turtle into the folds of his shamagh and his camel-hair cloak, stalking on silent and resentful. I sensed that he regretted having to travel to Aqaba by camel when he might have made more money more easily in a motor-car. I felt too that he was taken off guard by my Arabic, accustomed to using a few well-honed foreign phrases to control visitors. Like almost everyone involved in mass tourism, he regarded foreigners as a predictable herd species without the attributes of individual humanity. Tourists were the new flocks of the Huwaytat in Wadi Rum.

He emerged from his shell to ask me: 'Do you want to go to Aqaba itself, or only to the main road?'

'We agreed on Aqaba.'

'It won't matter if it takes less than four days, will it?'

'Yes it will. I'm paying for four days!'

Sleiman fell silent for a few moments, then he asked: 'Do you want to ride?'

'No. Why, do you?'

'No. Of course not!'

Presently, we came to a tent pitched by a well, inevitably called 'Lawrence's Well', below a deep chasm cleft by water running down the rock. Because of its proximity to Rum village, this must have been the most photographed Bedouin tent in the world. Certainly, it was the only one I ever recalled seeing that was surrounded by a fence of rickety plywood. This bespoke a siege mentality that was uncharacteristic of the Bedu: the tent had not been designed originally to close its occupants off from the desert, but to allow them to merge with it. Certainly the place was not picturesque in the romantic sense, for the tent lay within an orbit of mechanical debris: the rusted frames of stripped Land-Cruisers, fractured camshafts, antique cylinders, a cracked engine-block to which an ugly black donkey was moored. Five or six camels were kneebound by the fence, next to a wire coop of squawking chickens. I recalled Steve Sims telling me, 'When you're digging and you get down to what we call the "chicken line", you say, "Aha! This was when they stopped being nomads!"' My feeling of 'siege-mentality' was confirmed when an old woman with a determined jaw marched up to the fence and shouted, 'No photographs! If you want to take photographs you pay me five dinars!'

We passed the tent and struck on into the wadi. 'Are you ready to ride yet?' Sleiman asked.

'No. But you must ride if you want to. Don't wait for me!'

'I do not ride yet. I am a Bedui.'

A little later he pointed out camel-riders like ants, far away across the valley.

'Military patrol!' he said. 'They still use camels. They sometimes stay with the Bedu, but they don't go far.'

'What is their job – I mean, are there any bandits here?'

'Never! There are no dishonest people in Rum. They do it just for show – or to encourage the tourists, to help the Bedu – that sort of thing.'

The wadi walls had lost their grain here, and the buttresses were fractured into abstract entities like piles of jellyfish or columns of parachutes. We moved through the scrawny neck of a pass and into another long bed of apricot sand.

'Do you want to rest for the night here?' Sleiman inquired, 'or to stay with the Bedu?'

'To stay with the Bedu.'

'But they may be a long way ahead.'

'That's no problem. Why, what do you want to do?'

'My only wish is for your comfort.'

We marched on while the clouds rolled over us like liquid splashes, drowning the sun and leaving only a lemon-coloured stain along the hills. The night hid us in its coils, and the dark walls of the wadi receded to a thickening of shadows on the rim of our vision. The night brought no stars, but it brought silence – the aching silence of infinite spaces, ruptured only by the reassuring sound of our own tramping feet. 'Do you want to ride?' Sleiman inquired, more insistently this time. I could feel his frustration when I refused again. Despite his claims to the contrary, I was beginning to suspect that he was more concerned with his own comfort than mine. He wanted to ride but could not bring himself to do so before a foreigner. His continual badgering only made me feel more stubborn, and it was a cool, crisp evening – a wonderful time for a long walk, anyway.

We had been going several hours when two pinpoints of light flickered out of the darkness. 'Bedu!' Sleiman said in a voice full of anticipation. We made for the nearest light, stumbling over loose rocks, until we came upon a canvas tent slung over a make-shift frame, furled in the odours of invisible camels. A thickset man loomed up out of the shadows and shook hands with us grumpily, then turned sharply away. '*Fut! Fut!* Come into my tent!' he said.

Sleiman hung back. 'Are you with your Arabs?' he inquired, meaning, 'Are you with your womenfolk?'

'No. There is only me and my brother.'

Without another word, Sleiman pulled his camels off into the night.

When we were out of earshot, I asked him why.

'He is a crazy man. He did not know a guest!'

'But he invited us into his tent!'

'He didn't mean it. They were just empty words, that's all.'

I recalled the brusque manner and the sharp turning aside. Sleiman had read these nuances much more acutely than I. For him, 'Come into my tent!' might just as well have been 'Clear off!'

We moved towards the second light, which resolved into moonbeam rays of fire dancing upon the flap of a black tent as if upon a screen. As we came within shouting distance, watchdogs began to bark. A Bedui in a cloak appeared in the doorgap, a coal-coloured cameo outlined in light and smoke. He told us to unbelt the camels and come in out of the cold. I had not realized how cold I was until I was toasting my hands and feet before the fire. The brushwood crackled, illuminating the faces of our hosts: Gasim of the Huwaytat, a teenaged boy, and a blind old man with slits for eyes. 'Who is it? Who's come?' the old man whined.

'It is an Englishman, uncle,' Sleiman said.

'The English! I know the English! I am more than ninety years old! I can remember the days of al 'Aurens and Auda Abu Tayyi, by God!'

'Glubb, that was another of the English,' Gasim said, grinning wickedly, dispensing glasses of tea. 'He wanted to be the king. He *was* the king, really – Abdallah was only king in name. But you know, Glubb helped the Israelis by moving the Arabs out of their villages and letting the Israelis in. Then Hussein came. He kicked Glubb out. There was no Jordan before Hussein. I have nothing against the English personally, but we don't want colonialism any more!'

For a man who lived in the desert, it seemed to me, Gasim was extraordinarily well informed, but he soon jarred me out of my prejudiced notion: 'We have a house in Rashdiyya, with a TV,' he said. 'We have our own farm, and I keep a shop in the village. I am a shopkeeper in the morning and a Bedui at night. I prefer to sleep among my goats and camels. No, I don't think cultivation is a disgrace for a Bedui. There is no real difference between a Fellah and a Bedui, and if a Fellah bought goats and lived in a tent, he would be as good as a Bedui any day.'

'But you wouldn't let your daughter marry him.'

'Of course not! There are degrees of blood!'

'Do you think you will live in the tents for ever?'

'Why not? There's nothing wrong with tents. Having a house doesn't change that. We have tents, houses, livestock, crops, a shop, cars and tractors, and our children go to school. Why give up tents? We have the best of everything!'

'Don't cars and tractors mean the end of the Bedu?'

'Pooh! The Bedu are people who herd goats, sheep and camels. Motor-vehicles just make that easier.'

'What about the children? Don't you think they will want to change?'

'The young ones are even more keen on the tents than the old ones. Some of them will always come back to the desert. But if one of them wants to be a doctor or a shopkeeper, he has the chance. The more choices you have the better off you are!'

Later, I asked the old man how long it used to take in the past to travel from Rum to Aqaba by camel. His answer was unequivocal: 'Two days,' he said, 'going slow!'

Sleiman avoided my gaze and poked at the fire listlessly with a stick. His phrase, 'It won't matter if it takes less than four days, will it?' clanged in my mind. 'Ah, but the camels get tired, uncle!' he

1. Mohammad walad ʿEid. One of a small group of Egyptian Bedouin – perhaps no more than a couple of dozen – who still use camels to carry rock-salt from the Sudan.

2. The ruined heart of Shali, Siwa oasis, Egypt. The population of Siwa oasis moved to the village of Shali in AD 1203, and their descendants remained there until recently, when the government condemned the old mud-built houses as dangerous.

3. Ruins of classical Palmyra, Syria. In the third century AD, under Queen Zenobia, this tiny oasis in the Syrian desert had an empire stretching from Asia Minor to the Nile.

4. Bedouin woman of the ʿAnaza, Syrian desert. She wears the traditional gold earrings given to her as part of the bride-price.

5. Bedouin woman with facial tattoos, Syrian desert.

6. Shepherds at Qasr al Hayr ash Shariqi, Syria. For generations shepherds of the ʿAnaza and other Bedu tribes have grazed their flocks in the ruins of this early Islamic fortress, which once guarded a man-made oasis in the Syrian desert.

7. Bedouin girl, Syria. She wears the wimple-like headdress, tight veil and long plaited tresses typical of the Syrian nomads.

8. Shepherd of the Bani Khalid, Syrian desert. In Syria, shepherd tribes like the Bani Khalid are considered Arabs but not Bedu.

9. Petra, Jordan. In the foreground once stood the houses of the Nabataeans, the Bedouin tribe from North Arabia which took over the city from the Edomites in the last centuries BC.

10. Sunset over the palms in the Mahrat, Yemen.

11. Wadi Mahrat. The heartland of the Mahra Bedu, the Mahrat is a well-watered seam of greenery running through arid, rocky deserts in the remotest corner of eastern Yemen.

12. Wigwam tent, Mahra. Perhaps uniquely among the Bedouin tribes of the Arabian Peninsula, the Mahra sometimes use such tents of palm-fibre in place of the more familiar black wool tent.

13. Tribesman of the Rawashid, Wadi Mahrat. Famous in the past as nomads, the Rawashid (Rashid) are a Bedouin tribe living in Yemen, Saudi Arabia and Oman. This man belongs to a sedentary section of the tribe, cultivating dates in the Wadi Mahrat.

14. The Mahra coast, Yemen. It was probably somewhere along this coast that the camel was first domesticated, around 3000 BC. Tribes living in this area continue to use camels today.

15. Mosque at Al Qarn, south Yemen coast.

16. Old fisherman, the Tihama, Yemen. Using rafts made out of driftwood lashed together, such fishermen range into the Red Sea as far as the coast of Eritrea.

17. Ruins of the Ma'rib dam, Yemen. Built perhaps as early as 1800 BC, the dam was the centrepiece of a vast system of irrigation-works which transformed southern Arabia into a rich and fertile land. Arab legend ascribes the diaspora of the Bedouin tribes to the bursting of this dam, which drove the settled farmers into the desert.

said sheepishly. 'Aqaba is a looooong way! It's no good me losing a *dhelul* worth fifteen hundred just for a few dinars!'

'Losing a *dhelul*! No God but Allah, who ever heard of losing a *dhelul* between here and Aqaba!'

'What's the point in rushing? Take it easy, that's what I say. I wanted to make camp back there at the pass, but the Englishman insisted on staying with the Bedu! I keep on asking him to ride, and he says, "Not till you do!" God gave us camels for riding didn't he? He's paying for them but he just wants to walk all the time! What's the matter with the English, I'd like to know?'

Gasim weighed the question for a moment, then he smiled with understanding.

'Did you ever see that film *Lawrence of Arabia* – the one they made here in Wadi Rum? I've seen it many times. Well, that was the way al 'Aurens behaved with the Bedu. This Englishman must be trying to copy him!'

I carried the laughter that followed this to my sleeping-bag, but as I rolled myself up for the night, I realized that Gasim was perfectly right. I must have seen *Lawrence* a dozen times myself, but I had forgotten completely that it was filmed here in Wadi Rum. On reflection, though, I could remember the scene precisely – the one in which Lawrence was travelling by camel with his Bedouin guide on his apprentice journey in the desert:

*Guide:* 'Drink!'
*Lawrence:* 'Do you not drink?'
*Guide:* 'I am Bedu!'
*Lawrence:* 'Then I will drink when you drink!'

I hadn't once thought of the film, but the soundtrack – a distillation of all my culture's notions about the Bedu – must have been playing secretly in my unconscious all day as I travelled with Sleiman.

It took only minutes to load the camels in the morning. The new day unwrinkled from the tatters of darkness in a long procession of hues: quince, Persian red and chrome yellow, riding like beacons on the galleries of cumuli. The sandstone pinnaces were racks of ruby light and purple shadows. A flap of woodsmoke hung over the tents, and as we set off the flocks were already streaming from the nightfolds in the wake of dark-robed women, a procession of soft-edged shapes upon the golden meadows. We had scarcely reached the lip of the gorge when Sleiman asked if I would like to ride. When I refused, he couched his own camel and slid gracefully into the saddle. Today, pride had assumed second place to comfort. We travelled for an hour into rasping cold, until we spied a girl in a scarlet dress herding goats on a scree, and beyond her a Bedouin camp tucked under the hem of the sandstone. 'Bedu!' Sleiman said, gratefully.

We hobbled the camels and approached the tents, where a few plump sheep were penned up next to a Chevrolet pick-up so bashed-in that it was hardly recognizable. An old man with a blade face and a quill of a beard popped up and beckoned us towards the hearth. I asked why he had these few sheep penned up in the camp. 'Those are the ones we sell,' he answered. 'Sheep aren't clever like goats. They're all right in a big flock of their own kind, with dogs to keep them together, but if we let them go off with the goats they'd get lost!'

He told me that his family had no cultivation, but he owned a house in Rashdiyya. 'I don't go to the village much,' he told me. 'We move camp whenever there is some fresh grazing. We drive the flocks on foot and we carry the tent in our car. That old jalopy is no good on the road any more, but it's all right for driving around the desert.'

I asked him my standard question: 'Who are the Bedu?'

'The Bedu are those who live in the desert,' he told me. 'The Bedul? Yes, the Bedul are Bedu, but not *real* Bedu – they are Bani Israel. We Huwaytat wouldn't give a daughter to the Bedul, no indeed!'

Sleiman asked the old man if he would look after the camel-calf we had brought with us from Rum, which had proved a nuisance. 'Just for the night,' he said.

'I can't,' he replied. 'I'm on my own here. I have too much to do. It might die or get lost and I can't take the responsibility. Why on earth did you bring it, anyway?'

'There was no one to feed it in Rum, and I thought there would be plenty of chance to graze on the way to Aqaba. But this Englishman wants to keep moving all the time.' He fell quiet and stared at the fire moodily, displaying no eagerness to leave.

'I think we'd better be going!' I said.

We meandered on for another half hour, then Sleiman said: 'Why don't we halt here? The camels have to eat, you know. Otherwise they will die!'

So mournful was his expression that I almost forgot for a moment that we were talking about the same hardy animals which had given the Arabian Bedu dominance over their Peninsula for more than 1,000 years: which caravaneers in the Sahara still used to carry 300 kilograms of baggage fifty kilometres per day, day in day out: the same animal on which I had crossed the world's greatest desert from west to east through sandstorm, rain and withering cold – a distance of 4,500 miles in nine months. It was scarcely mid-morning, and the camels had been going for an hour and a half. They had covered about seven kilometres, I estimated. Not only were they virtually unladen, but I knew that Sleiman had with him a large bag of barley – the heaviest thing in our baggage – and on this alone the animals could quite easily have survived. Sleiman's ploy came into perspective with devastating clarity: Aqaba was two days' slow journey from Rum, and he hoped to do two days' work and get paid for six.

'Sorry,' I said, 'but I've never heard of a camel dying after one and a half hours' march. I cannot pay you thirty dinars a day to graze your camels. You agreed to take me to Aqaba.'

I led my camel on into the wadi and Sleiman followed reluctantly, letting his camels browse on every tree he passed until I had left him far behind. I realized that this was hopeless, and waited for him to catch up. 'The main highway to Aqaba is very near,' he said. 'Why don't you just pay me the money and go to the road and catch a bus?'

'If the road is so near, then we will go back to Rum, and I'll tell everyone why!'

'No! No! That would be a disgrace! All right, I'll take you to Aqaba. It's just that it's so cold. The camels can't stand the cold. You wait till you see the route to Aqaba – it's really hard going! Real mountains! You'll see!'

When we had climbed the next scarp we came to a valley covered in stones and green shoots, beyond which the landscape curved up towards peaks of biscuit-toned granite, whose sides were jagged and sheer compared with the grooved massifs of Wadi Rum. 'See! See!' Sleiman cried in apparent exoneration, but I saw that the track we were following was not at all steep, undulating gently beneath the peaks. 'That's not difficult going for a camel,' I said. 'You won't even have to get out of the saddle to do that!'

Sure enough, and despite his constant protests, Sleiman didn't bother to descend from his camel on the next climb. The hills opened into a hollow, where Huwaytat tents were pitched, and where rabbles of goats were scurrying after jogging herdsboys. Murky cloud spun in a majestic vortex, striping the ground in a slow carousel of light and shade. 'It's going to rain!' Sleiman announced, swinging down from his saddle at last. 'It will kill the camels, by God! I'm going to stop for the night in those tents!'

'The night! It's only just passed noon!'

'But I'm so cold! Feel my hands! It's no good. You walk too fast! The camels are exhausted!'

'The camels must be very poor animals indeed if they are exhausted so easily, when they are carrying almost nothing. I haven't even ridden mine. And I am hardly the world's fastest walker. You are a young man, half my age. And you are a Bedui.'

'What's the point in going on for hardship's sake?'

I saw that he was right. What was the point, after all? This was a country of cars and buses. Sleiman was twenty years old, born in the 1970s, in an era when motor-cars had already become more familiar than camels. Ironically, I had been riding camels when he was still a small boy. I knew that I had come to Jordan expecting too much. To him, travelling by camel when one could go by car was pointless: here in Jordan, the life of camels and hardship – the old life of the Bedu – was gone.

We couched the camels by a canvas guest-tent some distance from the Huwaytat camp, and a middle-aged, bearded Bedui in an embroidered sheepskin coat appeared and invited us inside. Once we were seated by the fire, I handed Sleiman a crumpled wad of ninety dinars.

'What's this?' he asked.

'Since you insist on stopping the night, I shall be going on alone from here.'

He shrugged with apparent relief, then counted the money. 'But this is only three days' pay!' he said. 'I want four! You were supposed to pay me four days for the journey to Aqaba, and two to return!'

'We only set off yesterday! You've worked one and a half days at the very most. It was your decision to stay here, when we haven't even done half a day's journey!'

Sleiman appealed to our host for support, but the Bedui stroked his beard and declared: 'It is fair.' Then he added in a soft voice: 'You should not let him go alone from here. Don't you know it is forbidden in the sight of God to abandon your travelling-companion when you have agreed to take him somewhere?'

'What does it matter?' Sleiman countered miserably. 'These aren't the old days. The other tourists I've been with only wanted to ride a camel!'

I shook hands with the two of them, and, shouldering my ruck-sack, I strode out into the valley. Not five minutes after leaving the tent, the rain came down in buckets: Sleiman was right about that, anyway.

By sunset it was still raining, and I found a small sheepfold – a square of piled dry stone – and erected the waterproof sheet I was carrying. All night a stiletto wind struck in gusts out of the hills, but by morning the rain had ceased, and I hiked as far as the main road where after an hour's wait I halted a minibus heading for Aqaba.

The town stood at the head of the Rift Valley, on the shores of a sea that was bronze and sparkling. A great cargo ship was spitting black smoke as it banked corpulently in the smooth waters. I walked along the parade of palms on the Corniche, past the foundations of the port that may have stood here in the time of Solomon, when Aqaba was a crucial link in the sea-route to southern Arabia. A camel in gaudy trappings was tied to a palm-tree, next to a horse and gharry, and across the road hung a sign upon which black tents and camels were painted. 'Come and visit!' the sign exhorted me. 'Bedouin Home!'

For a moment I wondered if this was where retired Bedouin went to die.

# 4

## *East of Aden*

Shukri braked the Peugeot in the dry stream-bed that ran through the village of Nabi Hud, and cut the engine. 'Say what you like,' he said, 'but I'm not going any farther!'

Around us block-houses of carved mud were dwarfed by the sheer walls of the Wadi Hadhramaut. The houses were hulking redoubts of several storeys with façades punctured by scores of loophole windows, their surfaces sun-crisped and crinkled like biltong from the furnace heat. Half-way up the cliffs, reached by an expansive alabaster staircase that would not have disgraced a rococo palace, stood the shrine of the Prophet Hud, a white block-building perched under a dome of fragile eggshell brilliance, around which kites swung in silent orbit. Apart from the kites, not a creature moved in the deserted place. Shukri kept his hands on the wheel and stared about glumly. 'This village is inhabited by Jinns,' he said. 'That's why there are no people here. The Jinns have driven them out!'

As I stepped out on to the uneven floor of the wadi, oily heat engulfed me. There was indeed an evil, brooding silence to the village. I looked up uneasily, following the dozens upon dozens of slit windows, wondering if there were hidden eyes watching me. If the houses had been ruined, the absence of people would not have been so disturbing. But they were generally in good repair, as if the population had moved out only the day before. Their heavy wooden doors were barred from the outside by planks, and fenced with branches of thorn-bush against marauding goats. Guffs of dust skimmed along the wadi and spiky tumbleweeds were urged forward by the wind. I leaned through the open window of the car. 'You're not coming then?' I said.

'Not on your life! If you meet any Jinns shout. I'll shout back!'

'What do they look like?'

'Ugly. And they have donkeys' feet!'

I left him in his car and struck off alone to explore the shrine of the Prophet Hud.

Shukri had been recommended to me as a driver by the concierge of the Movenpick – Aden's only good hotel – and it was in the hotel lobby, a week earlier, that I had met him for the first time. He was a podgy, puffy-faced, unfit-looking man in his late twenties, dressed in a clean shirt and *futa* – the wraparound kilt most Yemenis wore. I noticed he was agitated even before he blurted out, 'I'm very nervous! I'm a bloody fool! It's so long since I spoke to a foreigner. My father told me to get dressed up, to put on a tie and look respectable. He made me put on my best *futa*. I bought it in Saudi Arabia. It cost one thousand shillings. What a bloody fool I am!'

I began to wonder if he was entirely sane.

Shukri proposed to drive me to the Hadhramaut in his eight-seater Peugeot. I told him I would think it over, and as soon as he was gone I took a taxi to visit a 'Tourist Agency' at Steamer Point, which the concierge had told me about. The office was entirely vacant except for a table where a forlorn-looking manager in Western clothes sat by a telephone. I spoke to him in Arabic, he replied in French. He had studied tourism in France, he said. 'Yes, I can get you a car,' he told me, 'next month. Maybe next week, I don't know. We don't get many tourists here. I haven't seen a tourist in weeks.' On the way back to the Movenpick, the taxi-driver told me, 'You'll be lucky to hire a car in Aden. Everything here has gone to pot. It was the Russians who ruined us, you know. We got rid of the British and we walked into the hands of the Russians – who were worse. I wouldn't pick up a Russian if one hailed me in the street. They started a car-factory here, making Ladas. By God, you can't drive a Lada ten kilometres before it breaks down! Yet there are Morris Minors that have been going forty years!'

I had desperately wanted a four-wheel-drive vehicle, but I soon realized that in shell-shocked Aden there was no alternative to Shukri and his Peugeot. In the evening I phoned him, and the next morning he was in the lobby at the crack of dawn. 'I had a bad impression of you yesterday,' he told me frankly. 'My father told me not to phone you, but I was very worried that you wouldn't take me. I came up to the hotel twice in the afternoon, but you were out. My father said it was a waste of time: "If he wants you he'll call you!" he said. He was right, of course. See! I'm always talking about my father. Maybe it's because I haven't grown up!'

Before we left, Shukri insisted on giving me a guided tour of the city. Locked around its harbour by the pressure of sweeping mountains, the tranquil aquamarine waters trawled by flamingoes, Aden could easily have been the jewel of the Arabian Sea. Instead it was an urban carcass eviscerated and picked clean. Alps of debris lay in the gaping blind alleys. Street lights had been shot out. Buildings were warped and buckled, riddled with millions of bullet-marks and shell-holes. Only four years earlier, during the uprising against the communists, 10,000 people had died on these streets in a matter of days. Foreign expatriates had been evacuated from the beaches by the Royal Marines. 'I saw communist tanks driving over traffic-jams,' Shukri said, '*on the roofs of the cars!* There were women and children in them who were just crushed to death! I'll never forgive them for that.'

Trade still hadn't recovered – whole streets of shops were shuttered and of the few that were open, none seemed to have much of substance to sell. As we coasted about, motor-vehicles honked and stuttered past – mobile junk-heaps, hammered, scored and held together by rope. We wheeled around Mu'alla, Sheikh Othman, Crater, Steamer Point – names from an Englishman's dream of the Empire – and Shukri pointed out the barracks that had watched scores of British regiments on parade in starched khaki drill, the parade-ground now a no man's land of broken brickbats, the buildings skewed out of true by bombs and bullets, peeling walls scrawled with communist slogans, windows glassless and ringed with the marks of fire. He showed me the famous Crescent and Rock hotels, once the pride of the city, now gloomy, flea-bitten dens with fractured doors and cracked windows, whose view was blocked by the massive Russian memorial to the Unknown Soldier. Mu'alla was a grand canyon between featureless Stalinist-style apartment-blocks, their balconies sealed with chicken-wire, their rows of windows like sightless eye-sockets. Shukri stopped to let me see a poster on the wall displaying the Mu'alla flat-blocks in better days, with the legend, *'Another Product of the Glorious Revolution!'* printed across the picture. 'What a cheek the communists have!' he said, sputtering with laughter. 'It was the British who built those flats. They were the married quarters for the British garrison!'

We drove through 'White City' – formerly the British officers' lines – once-neat villas mildewed and crumpled, their lawns now jungles littered with old bicycle-frames and rusty tin cans. 'The Bedu live there now,' Shukri said. 'People from the countryside. They just break the locks and take the houses for themselves. It's a scandal!' We passed the wreck of the Sheba cinema – still in operation judging by the garish posters of Arabic films pasted outside. 'When I was a kid you had to wear a collar and tie to get in there,' Shukri said. 'Used to be called the "Regal" in those days!'

The only institution which seemed to be flourishing in Aden was the qat-market. At eight o'clock in the morning, crowds of men in kilts and headcloths were milling like ants around the open backs of shiny new Land-Cruisers whose windscreens and side-windows were covered with blankets against the sun, transforming them into sinister black caverns. Inside lurked truculent, bearded qat-traders amid piles of shoots tied into bundles like coiled streamers. Trading was brisk, loud and acrimonious. Many of the men – buyers and sellers – were already chewing, their faces bloated on one side like toothache-sufferers. They chewed furiously, stripping the succulent green leaves from the qat stems with their teeth, simultaneously puffing hungrily on cigarettes. Qat was a way of life in the Yemen: men chewed it, women chewed it. Shukri's mother ground the qat leaves in a machine for his old father who had lost all his teeth and now had to eat it with a spoon. Thousands of acres of fertile ground had been given over to growing it, the fields so valuable that tribes which once specialized in stealing each other's goats and camels now stole each other's qat, and watch-towers had been erected in the qat fields to house armed guards when the qat was ripe. In shattered, burned-out Aden qat seemed the one thing that was keeping the economy going.

Qat was first thing on Shukri's list of equipment for a journey to the Hadhramaut. 'No one here makes a long journey by car without qat,' he said. 'It stops you dozing. Watch the drivers we pass and you'll see their cheeks swollen with it!'

At the open door of a Land-Cruiser, he weighed two wheels of qat in his hands, held them up to the light, picked a strand and sampled it, pronounced it good, and wrangled for ten minutes over the price. As we nursed the two green spirals nervously through the jostling crowd to the safety of Shukri's car, an officer in down-at-heel combats touched my arm. 'Do *you* chew qat?' he inquired in apparent amazement.

'Why shouldn't he?' Shukri answered, tensing with clownish hostility. 'It's legal, isn't it?'

At a stall nearby he bought two clean hand-towels and sprinkled them with water from a plastic bottle: 'Otherwise it will get dry!' he explained. He wrapped each bundle of qat gingerly in a damp towel, then edged the bundles into two plastic bags, knotted them, then made punctures in the bags with a nail: 'To let it breathe,' he said.

He laid the two bundles on the gearbox-faring, and turned his attention to the rest of the provisions: four bottles of Canada Dry Cola, which, sipped while chewing the qat, would sweeten it: six packs of Marlboro cigarettes, to enhance the effect of the narcotic. At a stall near the harbour we bought fifteen bottles of mineral water, which Shukri poured one by one into a plastic cooler, followed by three bagfuls of ice. He replaced the cooler's lid firmly: 'We've got everything we need!' he said.

It was a relief to get past the guards at the roadblock and to hear Shukri running through the gears smoothly as we rolled alongside the ocean: onyx waters, black lava-sand, the occasional palm tree, isolated buildings encircled with barbed wire, camels drawing two-wheeled carts along the water's edge. To the north there were brazen, fluted hills, puddled low dunes, and once we passed a squadron of camels pouring out of a gully, driven on by two Arab boys in tattered check *futas* and tight headcloths. 'Bedu,' Shukri said. 'In the Yemen, anyone who lives outside the city is Bedu. Bedu are tribesmen: they are tough fighters and they lead hard lives. They eat soap and think it's chocolate!'

'The Aden people have no tribes?'

'Everyone has a tribe. My grandfather was a Bedui from the northern desert – the Jauf – but he killed someone in a vendetta and had to run away to Aden. He settled down there and in time forgot about his tribe. We don't keep in contact with any of our people, because of the blood-feud – they would use it as an excuse to attack us. We became city people in two generations. I suppose you could say that we are still Bedu, but once you leave the tribe it doesn't have any meaning. We married townswomen and became townsmen. Adenis are jokers, not fighters. We don't really give much importance to Islam. I mean, we are Muslims like the English are Christians. The Bedu are crude, unsophisticated and superstitious. Adenis are people of the modern world.'

Shukri told me he had been a bright student, top of the class and head boy of the school, but at the age of sixteen he had suddenly lost interest in his studies. Instead, he had gone off to Saudi

Arabia and after working there for a while, he and his friend, flush with cash for the first time in their lives, had booked a vacation in Thailand. 'It was for the women,' he admitted, 'and by God, there was one girl there that I'd have married – she was so shy and modest. But Mahsin, my friend, would have told everyone she was a whore. Anyway, we had girls, we got drunk on whisky, we even ate pork. Mahsin said, "We can't eat that, it's forbidden!" I laughed at him. "We've just been making love to whores and drinking whisky," I said. "We're not going to prove we're good Muslims by not eating pork!"'

Glistering hills passed, a crumbling, powder-dry communist town with paintings of Martyrs to the Revolution, a village where men were loading camels with stacks of firewood. The sea was out of sight, and we were driving across a rocky plain covered in a wild tangle of tamarisk and acacia trees. 'Well, who's going to start?' Shukri asked, placing a plump hand on the qat.

'It'll have to be you,' I said. 'I don't know how to do it.'

Shukri opened the package with one hand, flipped back the moist towel, and broke the fragile string holding the bundle. He selected a twig of qat – green leaves on a stem, almost like privet – and began rubbing the leaves gently between finger and thumb. 'First you clean it like this,' he said, 'then you pluck the leaves off down to the stem. Don't chew it straight away, just store it in your cheek and let the juices flow. The effect of qat depends on the type. Some makes you feel horny. Some makes you feel like walking till you drop. Some makes you feel like sitting on your arse for hours.' I began cleaning the leaves with attention. Shukri guffawed. 'You've got to do it a bit harder. Pretend you're masturbating!' he said.

I plucked the leaves off and began storing them inside my cheek, remembering that the Arabic word for chewing qat actually means 'to store'. The taste was incredibly bitter. Shukri rumbled with laughter as he watched me. Later, he took a bottle of Cola and pierced the cap with a rusty nail. 'Just sip it very, very little at a time,' he said. 'That takes the bitterness away.' At first I tasted only the bitterness, then, slowly, my cheek turned numb. Desert unfolded outside – dustbowls, claws of thorn-trees, palm-groves, clumps of houses, cactusoid Indian figs with fruit like yellow hand-grenades, women in blazing colours carrying great nests of firewood and waggling broad behinds, grinning men on camel-carts laden with sugar-cane, trickles of shorn sheep wrapped in cloaks of gold-dust, methyl-blue sky in which falcons and kites banked with the exquisite slowness of mobiles on strings, great plains opening up into mile after mile of silvery waste. Suddenly we were sailing along uplifted through the sky like clouds, rhythmically chewing, our cheeks bulging balloons, our eyes glittering jewels, and the world seemed a very, very beautiful place indeed. 'This is good qat,' Shukri said. 'It is qat from the south. The qat from the north is big and bushy but a lot of the leaves are dry.'

We stopped for lunch at an open-sided shack, where we spat our gobs of masticated qat unceremoniously into the sand. My jaws ached as Shukri had warned me they would, and as he had bits of green leaf stuck between his teeth, I supposed I did too. A robust, sweating Arab with a protruding paunch and a moustache shaped like a horseshoe brought us fried chicken, fresh bread, and water in a plastic jug. He charged me twenty-five shillings for the meal. 'You are charging him too much because he's a foreigner!' Shukri said. The perspiring man wiped his forehead with a hand. 'No, I'm not,' he said. 'A whole chicken is a hundred shillings, and that is a quarter of a chicken, so it is twenty-five shillings.'

Shukri grinned. 'It's correct,' he said. 'There are no thieves in Yemen. In Sana'a maybe, but not here!'

As soon as we were out of town we began to chew again, floating in gauze across dramatic volcano country. Great orbs of co-agulated stone rose before us, a waste of black lava slates, gullies with dragonflies and hummock-grass.

'Why do you want to go to the Hadhramaut?' Shukri inquired.

'I want to meet the Bedu,' I told him.

A playful smile quivered on his lips. 'You are one of those Englishmen like Lawrence,' he smirked. 'I have seen the film. But most of those who were interested in the Bedu preferred men to women.' He let this sink in for a moment, then inquired with a mischievous grin, 'Are you married?'

'Yes. And I have a son.'

He heaved a false sigh of relief. 'That's got *that* out of the way!' he said. 'I've got a son too. I'll be seeing him when I get back from this journey with you. I see him once a week, but he won't play with me. Sometimes I think my ex-wife shows him a photo of me and says, "Woo! Woo!" to put him off me. But no, really, we'd both like to get married again, only we can't. You see, in Islam if you divorce your wife three times you can't remarry her unless she has married someone else in between and been divorced by *him*. And they have to have slept together, so you can't fake it. We've been divorced three times, so we're stuck!'

I looked at him aghast. 'How on earth can you divorce a woman three times?'

'You'll think I'm terrible if I tell you why.'

'Go on.'

'The first time I just told her: "I'm going to sleep and if you wake me up I'll divorce you!" She woke me up so I divorced her. Just like that. Then someone told me I shouldn't have done it, and I thought, "Hey, this is something really big!" and I wanted her back. I felt guilty. In a day or two I fixed things up. You see, in Islam you only have to say, "You are my wife!" to get married and "I divorce you!" to get divorced. It's easy!'

I chewed my qat, thinking this was the most flippantly ir-responsible view of marriage I had ever heard. 'What about the other two times?' I asked.

'Well, that was because of a dispute with her family.'

'You don't have to tell me unless you want to.'

'No, I want to.' He took a deep breath. 'All right,' he said, 'let me start right at the beginning. There I was in Saudi Arabia. I wanted to get married, but no Saudi family would have given me a girl, and my own family would only really have accepted a girl from Aden. I couldn't cope with the idea of going home, marrying, and then migrating back to Saudi Arabia again with all the bureaucracy that entailed. Then a colleague of mine, an Adeni, solved the problem. He suggested that I should marry his sister. "She's staying with me here in Saudi," the brother told me. It was so convenient that I didn't bother to consider why the girl should be with her brother rather than at home with her parents in Aden. Anyway, I agreed to marry her right out. I never met the girl before our engagement day. I never even saw her in a photo. You may think it's odd, but I didn't want to see her because I knew I'd change my mind then, and I wanted to get married. The brother said she was neither ugly nor beautiful, which at least was the truth. When I removed the veil on our engagement day, she stood modestly, eyes downcast, which was suitable. "Do you agree to marry this girl?" the *qadi* asked. I said yes and the girl agreed and nominated her brother to speak for her. We agreed on the bride-price and made a contract, the brother specifying that, if I divorced her, I would have to pay twenty thousand riyals compensation. He left me alone in the room, and then he pushed the girl in. She was very nervous. "You realize I'm now your husband?" I asked. She didn't answer. That was good – if she'd been too forward it would have been a bad sign. We stood there in silence for a minute, and then I asked, "Is there any tea?" She said "Yes!" and almost ran out. That was a good sign too.'

'The second time I went, I asked her to remove the veil. Then we talked for a bit, but she always took any opportunity to leave the room. After a few visits, though, I managed to persuade her to sit on my knee. I stroked her hair. At last, I kissed her on the head. Then in the ear. Then I began to kiss her on the mouth. I wanted to make love, but she said, "Wait till we're properly married." Everything went all right, until the night of the actual wedding. Then I realized that she was a woman, not a girl, you see what I mean?'

'She wasn't a virgin?'

'That's it. I discovered it on our wedding night. We made love, then I put the light on. "Where's the blood?" I asked her. "I don't know!" she said. She looked so surprised – I mean it didn't seem like an act. She swore that she'd never been with a man before – that she'd lost it by . . . well, by playing with herself, you know. I said, "I believe you. But I'd better take you to the hospital tomorrow to make sure. If you have anything to tell me you'd better do it now, because at the hospital they will certainly tell me the truth." She said nothing, but in the morning I saw her reading the Holy Quran. That meant either she was asking God to help her disguise the truth, or to make sure the hospital revealed the truth. Anyway the doctor said that there was a hole, but she couldn't tell if it had been made by a man or a finger. I should have sent her back to her family right then, and demanded the bride-price back, but she said, "They'll kill me!" – I mean really *kill* her – so instead, I hushed it up. But I found I couldn't stop thinking about it. I decided to get rid of her on some silly excuse, like waking me up.

'It's true that I took her back after a few days, but then my mother came to visit. She sensed there was bad feeling between us, and she told my wife that she ought to look after me better. My wife called her a bitch, and they had a blazing row. "You don't like me having Shukri!" my wife shouted. "You're jealous!" That was too much! "Shut up and get out!" I told her. Then she went back to her brother, who asked to see me a few days later. He said, "Shukri, you are not a man because you never revealed that my sister wasn't a virgin!" I was shocked! I had never mentioned it to anybody. How did he know? Either he had known before I married her, or she had told him later – which she said she was terrified to do because the family would kill her. Anyway, since he had brought it up, not me, I had no option but to divorce her again. Then the brother said, "All right. Now you'll have to pay me twenty thousand riyals compensation!"

'It struck me suddenly that the whole thing had been a trick. Two things were suspicious. First, why did the family send her to Saudi Arabia to get married? Secondly, why didn't her brother come the morning after our wedding night to see the blood on the sheet that proved she was a virgin? It is the custom even in Aden to do that — we call it "asking for one's *sharf*" — one's "honour" — because virginity reflects a family's "honour". Anyway I remembered thinking it funny at the time that he hadn't come for his "honour". Perhaps she'd been playing around in Aden and the parents had sent her away from wagging tongues — to make a clown of me! I felt that the brother knew all the time that she wasn't a virgin and had made the compensation clause in the contract to fiddle me, that son of a bitch! I refused to pay, so he took me to the High Court in Saudi Arabia, and he told the judge I drank alcohol and played with women and chewed qat — all enough to hang me in Saudi. I had to tell the truth — that my wife wasn't a virgin. The judge asked the brother to swear that she'd been a virgin before the wedding and he wouldn't, so he lost the case. The judge said, "It's forbidden in God's sight for you to live with this filth ever again!" and he made us marry and divorce again as a formality so that it was finished for ever. The funny thing was that by then, I loved my wife, and having the baby made it worse, of course. I wouldn't have divorced her if the brother hadn't revealed publicly that she wasn't a virgin, and forced my hand. I came home from Saudi Arabia, and explained it all to my father. I asked him, "Did I do right or wrong?" He said, "It was a mistake from the beginning. You should have acted like an Arab. Now you'll have to deal with it!'

The qat lifted me euphorically. I found myself clinging on to Shukri's story with all its twists and turns as to the most fascinating epic — it was a brilliantly illuminating window into the heart of Arab society. I could have listened all night. Outside, the landscape was pulpy gold now, the sun lowering, losing its hard edge. We passed rolling plains where the light hung on tamarisk-trees like threads of fleece. Stiff grasses puffed out of the ground like strands of smoke. Flat-capped acacias whisked in spinning vortices. The sand-and-gravel country faded, giving way to tattered hills where forts staggered on the brink of cliffs, where rock-falls littered the valleys, where the gneiss had been sculpted by time into claws and pedestals that were in the process of detaching themselves from the mother-lode. There was a muzziness in the air, sheaths of mist lurking in faery vales of palms, wadis with beds of burnished ivory pebbles, ant-heap villages of mud-block where house had been piled on house over generations, where the mud seemed to have oozed into almost every available space before setting hard. Houses with galleries of tiny windows and studded wooden doors had mushroomed organically into Gothic dream-castles. Sprouting towers evolved into spires that scratched the sky. In cramped alleys beneath them there were goats and black asses and bony oxen, tended by girls in masks like alligator heads. We followed a great trunk wadi where water trickled between plunging walls, an entire village cast in bronze on a slice of island in the stream. For me this was a new Arabia, a rich, Brothers Grimm, Lord-of-the-Rings world of phantastical geometry and faery textures.

After dark we came down to the sea, and parked for the night on a damp beach by a ruined fisherman's hut. The beach was churned up by the tracks of a million crabs, and in the moonlight I could see them – energetic spider-shapes scuttering along the edge of the surf. I spat out the last ball of qat, unrolled my sleeping-bag, and made myself as comfortable as possible in the sand. As soon as I was out of the car, Shukri locked himself inside. 'What's the matter?' I asked.

'There are Jinns in places like this,' he said through the open window. 'I don't want some ghostly hand coming in and throttling me while I'm asleep! You can sleep in the car if you want, but if you sleep outside and I see any Jinns attacking you, I'll just drive off, I warn you! There's no way you can fight Jinns!'

I remembered Shukri's withering remarks about the 'crude and superstitious' Bedu versus the 'sophisticated' townsman. Some things could not be erased in two generations, I thought.

And maybe he was right about the Jinns anyway.

★

Breakfast in Mukalla: from afar it was a crystal-white city tucked under lofty mountains – a spit of land in pellucid waters where fishing-skiffs like dark needles rode placidly at anchor. From inside, though, it was a seething mass of confusion: half-wrecked cars belching smoke, crowds spewing along deep avenues beneath crippled housing-blocks, men milling on a corner with shovels and picks, waiting for someone to offer them work. We parked the Peugeot in a rubbish-strewn back-street where boys were kicking a punctured football, and goats clambered on the bonnet of a burned-out car. We sat at a greasy table in the street, and an old man in a skullcap brought us fried eggs on flaps of bread, and sweet red tea.

Later we visited the palace of the former Qu'aiti Sultan, a ram-shackle Gormenghast of a building overlooking the deep curve of the harbour – half a dozen styles, predominantly Indian, hanging together on the edge of collapse. The place had been turned into a museum, and amidst a jumble of Indian crockery and furniture, Soviet machine-guns, pre-Islamic carvings of dolphins and sea-horses, and sepia-tinted prints of stern-looking British officials, we found a framed letter from the British government to the last Qu'aiti Sultan of Mukalla, informing His Excellency that the British would presently be pulling out of their Aden Protectorate and that they could 'no longer extend their protection to him or his heirs'. Shukri, whose English was very good, read the letter in silence. After we had set off for the Hadhramaut, though, and he had started on the second package of qat, he burst out, 'What bastards the British were, just leaving the Qu'aitis in the lurch like that! I don't mean it personally, but all the trouble we've had with the communist government was the fault of the British. They encouraged the communists because they wanted them to destabilize the region – they wanted to find themselves needed in the Gulf. My family fought against the British. My uncle shot a British soldier. He told me they were coming up in a patrol of six and he could see this soldier, who was very young. When my uncle shot him, he fell down and shouted, "I want to live!"

My uncle said he couldn't shoot him again. He hadn't the heart for it. I don't mean it personally – I think the British should pay for what they did here. God, if there were any concessions to governments for rebuilding Aden, I wouldn't let the British in!'

The Peugeot was juddering up into the Jol – the rocky region that divided the sea-coast from the Hadhramaut – twisting and turning around fearsome hairpins, with plunging arid valleys far below us, their sides brittle schist looking like liquid toffee that had run, cooled and clotted into blebs and bubbles. Sometimes the road passed within inches of a sheer drop on both sides. Shukri chewed hard in concentration, but today he chewed alone. The qat had kept me awake the previous night, and had made me shaky and washed-out all morning.

We passed a sign that read 'Beware!' in Arabic. Some witty scholar had added a feminine plural case-ending to the imperative with an ink-marker, so that the sign now implied 'Women Beware!' Shukri laughed darkly as he pointed it out to me. 'That's right,' he said. 'Women should beware. They should know their place. Take my sister, for instance – she's training to be a doctor, and she's got her nose up in the air and won't take orders. I don't speak to her any more. I told my father that when she gets married she'll have to wash and cook. She'll have to put her nose down – especially if she marries a bastard like me. How can she accept a husband as boss if she can't accept her elder brother as boss? By God, she'll be divorced in a week! I'm only doing my duty to her – I want her to be a good wife – it's *sharf* – honour – just like my wife not being a virgin. My father was right about that. If I'd done what Arab custom dictated and sent the girl home as soon as I found out she wasn't a virgin, the problem wouldn't have arisen. *Sharf* – that's the whole root of Arab society for townsmen or Bedu – the root of Islam itself. For an Arab "honour" doesn't necessarily mean fighting or courage – it's entirely to do with the purity of our women. That's why your writer Salman Rushdie got into trouble, because he suggested that the Prophet Mohammad's wife committed adultery. By God, there's a man who deserves to die! I believe in mercy, but there should be no mercy for a man who insults the honour of the Prophet Mohammad!'

Shukri seemed very steamed up, and I was surprised. Since we had left Aden he hadn't once stopped the car to perform the prayers required of a devout Muslim. The previous morning he had happily described his sexual experiences in Thailand, and even admitted to guzzling pork: 'We are Muslims like the English are Christians,' he had said. Yet here he was, a self-admitted 'joker', fuming about Salman Rushdie, an Indian-born British writer whose books he had never read. 'I don't understand,' I said. 'I mean Muslims accept that the Prophet Mohammad was just a man – not God – so surely the things that happen to other men could perfectly well happen to him?'

'No,' Shukri said. 'How could the wife of a Prophet commit adultery? If the Prophet Mohammad hadn't even got the respect of his wives, he couldn't have gained the respect of millions of followers, who all swear, "There is no God but God *and Mohammad is the Prophet of God!*" If Mohammad's wife committed adultery it would mean that he had no *sharf*, and if he had no *sharf* it would mean that God didn't care about him, and didn't care about Islam. It would mean that he wasn't a Prophet. If he had no honour then the whole of our history means nothing. Even the descendants of the Prophet are called *"The Honourable Ones"*. Honour is the root of everything – why the Bedu here would kill you at once if they thought you had insulted their honour! Honour is more important than Islam – that's the truth – because without honour Islam is meaningless. If my sister appeared in a pornographic film, for instance, I would kill her for dishonouring all the family. What would you do in the same situation?'

'Well, I'd advise her against it. I'd be very angry with the people who'd got her to do it. But in the end it would be her choice. I'd be more concerned about her than about the family, because she's an individual.'

'That's the difference between you and us, you see. It's *sharf* –

the honour of the family and the tribe – that makes us what we are. Individuals mean nothing.'

'I don't think Margaret Thatcher would have agreed with you: she said, "There is no such thing as society: there are only individuals." '

'Rubbish! Margaret Thatcher is a woman, anyway, and men shouldn't be bossed about by women! That's typical of the West! In the West today women act as if they were men. That's why so many Westerners marry Asian women. They want real women. Nature will out no matter what you do!'

I laughed, but I was still a little nonplussed. Yesterday morning I had seen Shukri the liberal, sophisticated, educated, urbanized Arab of Bedouin origin. Yesterday afternoon I had seen the Shukri who had messed up his marriage by failing to adhere to Arab tradition. Last night I had met Shukri the superstitious. Today I had Shukri the fundamentalist: we had turned full circle in less than two days. Was it a case of 'in qat veritas', I wondered?

'When you chew qat you talk more and more like a fundamentalist,' I said.

Shukri chewed silently for a moment. 'It's not the qat,' he said, 'I think it's being with you. When you meet someone from another culture – especially a strong culture – you either ape their ways and identify with them, or you fall back on your own roots and the things that make you distinct. I have just fallen back on my roots, that's all.'

As an explanation of the origins of fundamentalism in the Arab world this could hardly have been improved upon, I thought.

We halted at another open cabin at Ma'adi, high in the hills, for lunch. A few thin camels snuffled in the stunted bushes outside, and inside an old Bedui in a bright green skirt sat watching a TV set on which Umm Kalthum, the great lady of Egypt and now-deceased icon of Arab music, was warbling dementedly to the heavy brass of her orchestra. We sat on the floor and the landlord brought us roasted goat and rice with bottles of Cola. As we made ready to eat, the old Bedui watching the TV turned and stared at us. 'Don't you know a guest where you come from?' he demanded. I wasn't sure whether he was addressing Shukri or myself – or both – but I felt extremely embarrassed. We had perpetrated the ultimate Bedouin sin: even when eating in a restaurant, it was common politeness to invite others to join you. We had simply forgotten. 'Please,' I said, 'join us!' The old man considered it for a moment, then shuffled over and sat down. He was short but massively built, with enormous hands and feet, a leonine head draped in a rainbow-coloured headcloth with tassels, and a thick silver beard. His name was Hassan and he belonged to the Humum, a large Bedu tribe inhabiting the Jol and the desert beyond. 'Most of us live in mud houses now,' he told me. 'We don't use camels. When they built the road it killed all that. The Bedu used to control all the transport going into the Hadhramaut, because camels and donkeys were the only transport there was, and the Bedu owned them. They started building the road when I was a boy, and the tribes were really furious. We knew that the road would take our carrying-trade away, and we couldn't afford to buy lorries. We used to take pot-shots at them while they were working, not really to kill them, but just to frighten the workers away. Even after they finished building it, we still used to fire at trucks. It used to put the wind up them, by God! Still, it did no good – even the Bedu have lorries now.'

I asked him about the people of the Hadhramaut. 'Some are Bedu and some Hadr,' he said. 'The Hadr are divided into tribesmen and non-tribesmen. The tribesmen carry arms but the non-tribesmen – the "Weak People" – don't. They just work in the fields. In the past they were always under the protection of a tribe.'

'Then what are the Bedu?'

'The Bedu are people of the desert. They have such a hard life that they have agreed between themselves to help each other in trouble. That's what the rules are about. In the Hadhramaut or the mountains you don't need that. Everyone has his own land and his own water and outsiders are sometimes a threat – they aren't needed. Of course, the Bedu don't live such a hard life as in the past. But they are still hospitable to strangers.'

After lunch we descended into the Hadhramaut. It was an entire world hidden in a great groove in the earth, like a fabled Martian canal, its precipitous banks sometimes forty miles apart. Although only occasionally flooded – for there is no rainy season in south Arabia – the Hadhramaut was a fertile channel in the midst of near-sterility, and reminded me of nothing so much as the Nile Valley. As we motored slowly down from the Jol we began to see houses – monoliths of mud with millions of windows – scattered singly across the valley floor, each in its own small hacienda with zebra-stripes of cultivation, clusters of goats browsing on stubble, gloomy-looking camels, men clumping behind sickly donkeys, women whose faces were veiled and shadowed by huge witch-hats of straw, winnowing grain. The scattered fortress-farms became villages built amid explosions of date-palms and ploughed plots along the edges of dry-washes paved with buffed blue pebbles. The mud palazzi – many of them more than four storeys high – were precisely the same russet colour as the wadi's cliffs, as if the builders had been trying to emulate the majesty of the sweeping sandstone. There was a little of Morocco here, a bit of Nubia perhaps, but the place was truly unique. The Hadhrami people were not the scavenging Bedu tribes of the desert, but large, rich families of landowners nurtured on dates and grain and goats' milk, no cowering peasant-farmers, but strong, fierce tribesmen whose character had been moulded by generations of bitter feuding. Their militarized warren-villages reflected the wars, feuds and battles that had ebbed and flowed along the wadi since time immemorial.

Before sunset we arrived at Shibam, a ghetto of mud rearing suddenly out of the evening haze like a gargantuan termites' nest. The town was a defensive structure, ringed with a wall and entered by a single fortified gateway. Because of the restriction of space, the builders of Shibam had been obliged as they multiplied to build upwards so that the houses burgeoned till they reached their limit of stability at seven or eight storeys. The houses had to be built shoulder to shoulder, forming a labyrinth of tower-blocks reached from the rear by tortuous alleys. Some fanciful observers had called it the 'Manhattan of Arabia', though for me it resembled far more a scaled-down version of the old city of Kowloon in Hong Kong – a monstrous warren of tenements supposed to house more than 100,000 people. Kowloon was built of cement and steel, but considering that Shibam was constructed entirely of mud fortified with straw and dung, it was a very formidable accomplishment indeed.

Shukri parked the car in a side-street and we walked through the arched gateway into a small square dominated by the cigar-shaped minaret of a mosque. We wandered through the cool alleys beneath leathery walls in which shallow flutings acted as conduits for the human refuse that dribbled down from on high. The alleys were cluttered with rubble and carpeted with goat droppings. Swarms of children followed us, yelling, 'Where are you from, mister?' Women's faces appeared momentarily at high windows. Donkey-carts laden with clover creaked past. Every nook and broken corner was a roosting-place for scraggly goats, sheep or hobbled donkeys. Chickens and roosters chased each other in clucking confusion. On *mastabas* – raised step-buttresses – men in *futas* and headcloths were clattering out dice on backgammon boards, and old women in black sat silently, taking in the evening savours of goat-musk, animal dung, urine and human sweat. Some of the alleys were shaded with sacking and housed one-room shops where robust men in white dishdashas presided over sacks of grain, and tables heavy with biscuit-tins full of rice, onions, garlic, salt, cumin and red pepper. Flaps of dried shark-meat and tuna were piled up like shards of firewood, the high odours of the fish adding to the matrix of smells. One old greybeard sat contentedly cutting a well-bucket from a section of truck-tyre, the walls of his tiny shop decorated with crafted leather waterskins. Shibam was a world within a world – complete with seven mosques, many schools and several markets. You could have got lost among the twists and turns of its alleys, taken root, adopted local dress and custom, and never found your way out to the light of day. Once, under siege by the Qu'aiti family, the inhabitants had not ventured outside for sixteen years, until they were reduced to eating shoe-leather.

We took tea at a stall in the square. Piratical men sat around it smoking waterpipes made from bean-cans and old coconut shells. Others were humping rubber baskets of squashes and purple aubergines into a store. A weak old gaffer left a trail of onions behind him as he steered his heavy basket towards the gate. Below our *mastaba* men were shouting at each other over a mountain of green and yellow melons shaped like bombs. An emaciated old man with a toothbrush moustache, wearing a white skull-cap, a dirty-white jacket and chequered *futa*, shuffled up for a waterpipe, kicked off his shoes and sat down by the stall on a pad of cloth. He pulled the pipe shakily towards him, then took his own tobacco from his pocket and unwrapped it. He rubbed and rolled the stuff steadily with the ease of long practice, then lifted the pot of his pipe and filled it with unhurried grace. He sat for a moment in contemplation of it. There was all the time in the world to enjoy this pleasure. The tea-boy leaned over with pieces of glowing charcoal on a pincer. The old man planted the stem loosely in a hole drilled in the coconut-shell. He took a deep toke, coughed, spluttered, then toked again. His shrunken face lit up with pleasure as the smoke trickled back out of his mouth and nostrils. 'Where are you from?' he asked me after several more puffs. When I told him I was British, he said, 'Come up to my house when I've finished this smoke.'

The old man's name was Sheikh Moukhtar, and the room he led us to, up several narrow flights of stairs, was huge, cool, bare and spotlessly clean, lit by two brilliant electric bulbs. He opened a window from which we could see directly into the square, and across it to the sandy wadi-bed, and the rust-red cliffs on the opposite side. He had his boy bring more tea, lit another pipe, and talked about the wars between the Kathir and the Yafaʿi tribes that had shattered the peace of the Hadhramaut for generations.

The Kathir, who had spawned many of the Bedu tribes of Oman, were originally a settled people from the region of Sanaʿa, and may have begun moving east as early as AD 800. In 1494 they captured Shibam and made it the capital from which they dominated the Hadhramaut. Only eight years later, they began to import warriors from the Yafaʿi and Zeidi tribes to shore up their tottering strength. Inevitably these fighters had turned against their enfeebled masters, and the two factions had become locked in a deadly struggle which had lasted until recent times.

The Quʿaitis – eventually to become the ruling house of Mukalla – were a dominant branch of the Yafaʿis. The story of their rise began, Sheikh Moukhtar related, from an incident concerning a humble oil-lamp. 'The lamp used to hang in an old mosque in Shibam,' he said, 'and it ran on vegetable oil. Every day when the folk went for their morning prayers they found that the oil was missing. So they set a trap for the thief, filling the lamp with fish-oil instead. Sure enough, the oil was gone the following day, and they caught the head of the Quʿaiti family walking through the market stinking of fish. He was so ashamed that he fled to India, where he became famous working for the Nizam of Hyderabad. He returned from India fabulously rich, and decided to take over the Hadhramaut from the Kathirs. The British supported him, while the Kathirs were backed by the Turks. It was the foreigners who supplied them with modern rifles – and that really wrecked everything. The fighting went on for years, but neither of the families really came out on top. The Quʿaitis controlled Mukalla and the coast, and Shibam was a Quʿaiti town. But in Saiyun and Tarim, the Kathirs ruled the roost. It got so bad in the nineteen-thirties that people couldn't leave their homes – some of them never came out for twenty years! They used to dig long trenches to protect them while they went down to tend their fields. Anyway, in the end it was an Englishman who settled it. I remember him – Igna-ramis – he was the one who made the peace between the tribes.'

I took it that the old man was referring to the almost legendary Harold Ingrams, British Resident in Mukalla in the 1930s. Ingrams had seized on an incident in which a British engineer had been shot at near Tarim, to negotiate more than 1,000 three-year treaties with the autonomous villages, clans and tribes, bringing them under the aegis of the Kathiri Sultan in Saiyun. It was the first time in history that such a settlement had been brought about, though even the ponderous weight of the British Empire had not been sufficient to damp the flames of the age-old conflict for long. 'There was still fighting now and again, of course,' the old man continued, 'but life was a bit more peaceful after Igna-ramis came.'

I asked the Sheikh if there was a difference between the Hadr and the Bedu.

'The Bedu used to move about with their animals,' he said, 'and they were known for their hospitality and generosity. But they were no more courageous as fighters than the settled tribes. Of course, there were the non-tribesmen – the peasants – who didn't carry weapons – but they were always under the protection of a Sultan or a warlike tribe. In those days the Bedu used to depend on the carrying-trade with their camels, but when the Qu'aitis built the road from Mukalla it ended all that. I remember when they brought the very first motor-car here. It was right there in the square. All the people came to see it. Then they brought five aeroplanes to the airstrip, and everyone went to see them. How wonderful we thought them! I've seen everything – aeroplanes, cars, camels and donkeys – but nothing is better than an aeroplane. It used to take five days to Mukalla by camel or donkey. In an aeroplane you can do it in half an hour!'

The following day we drove through Tarim, a town of dark, dusty passageways, and out into the open country beyond. The asphalt road turned to cobble, the valley walls converging closer and closer, as we passed more isolated fortress-farms like mutilated molars, ravaged sleeping-beauty palazzi with roundhouse towers, the skeletons of very ancient villages abandoned on mounds in the wadi. We traversed lapping green water-pools, oblong roods of ploughed earth, a chaparral of mesquites ponderous with flowers, purple bougainvillaeas, pink oleanders, stands of arak whose cheesy odour hung in the air. There were packs of greyhound-slim goats in chess colours tended by witch-hatted women looking as if they belonged more to Mexico than to Arabia.

Not long before sunset we arrived at the first real Bedu camp we had seen. Four canvas marquees of foreign manufacture had been pitched near a few skeleton acacias on the banks of a wadi. Outside stood a Land-Cruiser pick-up with bald tyres, and a row of oil-drums filled with water. A bevy of Bedu women sat in the long shadows of the tents, tending a smoky fire contained in a ring of stones. Nearby, I saw a three-legged cot with a leather awning, in which a two-month-old baby slept peacefully. Behind the tents, a man and some boys were mending a chicken-wire fence that penned in a press of about thirty goats.

When we pulled up, the Arab turned towards the car suspiciously, then left what he was doing and walked over to where a Kalashnikov rifle leaned against a tree. 'I don't like the look of this!' Shukri said. 'He's going to shoot us!' The Bedui seemed menacing as he came towards us, holding his rifle in both hands, with the two boys, aged nine or ten, following at his heels. The boys wore shirts, *futas* and headcloths knotted in the Bedu style, but the man was bareheaded with a frizzle of very curly hair and a thick beard. He wore a dishdasha that was so stained, torn and tattered that it was little more than a rag. He answered our greetings with poker-faced correctness as we shook hands with him. He looked at us long and carefully, considered the car, and then, perhaps deciding that we presented no threat, said, 'Rest here with us. My house is yours!'

The Bedui's name was Suhail and he belonged to the Manahil, a tribe inhabiting the steppes between the Hadhramaut and the sands of the Empty Quarter. He called us over to sit by the fire. One of the women began to make tea, and another brought us a bowl of goats' milk. Suhail sat on his knees, nursing his rifle fondly. 'The communists took all our rifles away,' he said. 'They told us to hand them in and that they would give us new ones. It was a trick, of course. Still, we got new ones on our own. I wouldn't show it in Tarim or Saiyun, but out here in the open country who bothers?' After we had drunk tea, Suhail told his sons to load a plastic barrel into the back of the pick-up – which I noticed was carpeted with moquette – and sent them off to fill it at a local well. One of the boys launched himself happily into the driving-seat and drove the vehicle down the wadi in a slick of dust. 'Isn't he a bit young to drive that car?' Shukri asked.

'In the town he would be,' Suhail said, 'but this is the desert. Our children learn to drive cars as soon as they can touch the pedals. We are Bedu, after all.'

I asked directions to the Mahra region, and he pointed along the cobbled road. 'If you take the left-hand turning ahead you will find the road to Thamud,' he said. 'That's where the tribes live. But you will never make it in that car. You need a four-wheel-drive.'

'What about the right-hand fork?' Shukri asked.

'In that car you could probably reach the shrine of Nabi Hud. It's in a village, but nobody lives there.'

The sun surfed over the rim of the wadi behind us, and the sky turned smoky peach, then rose-pink. There was a hush in the camp. Suddenly a herd of camels peeled out of the dusk – ten or twelve animals of different sizes driven by an old man and a teen-aged boy. The camels seemed to glide across the stones, lowing gently, and Suhail ran off to help the others as they slapped the animals' shoulders to make them kneel, then hobbled their legs with strips of rope. If one forgot the presence of motor-cars here, this scene might look 'authentic', but I had long ago given up trying to decide what 'authentic' really meant. Every culture is dynamic, and the Arabs had merely acquired camel-technology at some point in their history when it suited them, and were now acquiring automotive technology which would suit them until it in turn was rendered out of date.

About 5,000 years ago, indeed, the only camels surviving in the Arabian Peninsula were wild ones grazing here in the semi-arid valleys of the Hadhramaut and the wadis of Mahra to the east. That the aboriginal peoples of south Arabia hunted these animals is clear from bones that have been found in excavated middens. Since the remains of sea-cows were found in greater abundance, though, it seems the hunters were also seafarers, who may already have been familiar with the pattern of the monsoon winds. These early peoples were confined to coastal enclaves by the vast reaches of desert which lay behind them, until they learned how to make use of an animal that could convert useless desert sedges into milk. That animal already wandered wild in the valleys of the interior, and since the aborigines relied on the sea for their main sustenance, they had both the time and the motivation to tame it. Being seamen first and landlubbers only later, it may be that they applied a familiar image to their newly acquired means of survival, naming it 'the ship of the desert'.

These prehistoric hunter-fisherman were not Arabs, nor even Semites. By the time the Semitic peoples first arrived here in 1600 BC, the aborigines had learned first to milk, then to saddle the camel. Locked behind the sand-sea of the Empty Quarter for centuries, they had not only taken their first halting steps into nomadism, but may also have begun to harness the camel's carrying power for the highly lucrative incense trade.

Their spice-caravans had eventually reached the Syrian desert, the homeland of the sheep- and goat-rearing Aribu tribes, which by the time of Shalmaneser III had acquired enough camels to threaten if not defeat the mighty Assyrians. Some of the Arabs may have followed the caravans back to their source in south Arabia and learned the secrets of the camel-trade. In the fullness of time these Arabs overwhelmed and married with the indigenes. So the 'noble camel-breeding tribes of Arabia' were born –

out of adaptability and commercial opportunism, having acquired the superior technology of an alien race.

The two newcomers joined us by the fire. The old man – Suhail's uncle – was called Sayf, and like many of the Bedu he was squat and massive, his features thick and larger than life, with a great anchor nose and an almost unbelievably long chin. The Land-Cruiser clattered back across the wadi, and the boys jumped out. Suhail helped them unload the full drum of water and poured it into one of the iron tanks. After the Bedu had performed their sunset prayer and the darkness was full, Suhail went off and returned dragging a bleating kid. 'You will eat with us!' he said, indicating that he intended to slaughter the goat for dinner. 'Yes,' I said, 'but don't slaughter the goat. It's too much. We will be happy to eat with you but don't kill it!' Shukri joined my protestations, but they fell on deaf ears. When the kid's throat had been slit with a dagger, Suhail slung the carcass from a tree and began to skin it. The boys built up the fire with faggots of acacia wood that gave out a fragrant scent. When it was blazing well they piled smooth round boulders over the flames, to roast the meat in the traditional way. Soon strips of flesh were sizzling on the red-hot stones, the delicious savoury smell of roasting meat blending with the scent of the firewood. The flesh was served on a platter, and we helped ourselves, slicing the joints with knives, stripping the bones and flinging them over our shoulders. Afterwards, tea was brewed on another fire. We sat back and looked at familiar star-patterns while the camels coughed, blubbered, and chewed the cud, occasionally squabbling and tussling heads in the shadows.

'We don't ride camels any more,' Sayf said, looking at them with some pride, 'except over short distances when they're grazing – we just hop on their backs. I don't think we even have any saddles now. I haven't seen one for years. Everything is cars and lorries – they need petrol, and petrol's expensive. Camels don't need petrol and their food is free. A camel will keep going longer than a car. A car just falls to bits in time, but a camel renews itself. You can't milk a car, can you? The Bedu will never give up camels, but I admit it's easier to travel in a car. Perhaps the oil they've found in the Hadhramaut will make us all rich.'

'I doubt it,' Suhail said. 'It will make the government rich, that's all!'

I asked Sayf about the life of the Bedu in the past.

'I'll tell you how it was in the past,' he said. 'I had seven children – three girls, four boys – praise and thanks be to God – but only two are still alive. Three of them died of sickness when they were children. One was bitten by a mating bull-camel and died of the injury, and another – a girl – died in childbirth. A Bedui's family is his life. When I was a young man – still a boy really but old enough to carry a rifle – my elder brother was shot by the Se'ar. In those days the Manahil had no tents like these – we lived in the open. My brother Sa'id was out herding camels with my cousin near Thamud when they saw a raiding-party of about twenty Se'ar racing towards them on camels. My cousin wanted to run away and get help, but my brother – God's mercy upon him – had a rifle and wanted to stay and fight. He put a shot over their heads in warning, but one man jumped from his camel and shot my brother in the hand. My cousin would have killed the Se'ari, but the rifle jammed. So they ran away to our camp, while the Se'ar took our five camels. There was only myself and my younger brother Ahmad in the camp – my father was dead by then and my uncles were away. We wrapped my brother's hand up in a head-cloth as best we could, then I said, "Sa'id, what shall we do? We are only four against them, and we have only two rifles and this useless one. And they have taken all our camels – we only have the broken old she-camel left. Shall we wait till our uncles return?" But Sa'id was angry. "No!" he said. "We shall go after them and get our camels back. God's curse on all Se'ar! Bring the old she-camel and saddle her!" We set off and followed them by moonlight all that night, and the following day, taking turns to ride the camel when we were tired. We couldn't afford to stop for rest. We were very hungry and we met no other Bedu on the way. My brother's hand was painful for him, though he refused to admit it.

We followed the Se'ar for three nights and three days. I wanted to give up, but Sa'id said, "No. We keep going!"

'Then, on the third night we saw their campfire. They didn't dream that we were following them. They had made camp in a wadi and the camels were grazing nearby. We decided to try and take the camels in the darkness, but when we moved down towards them, the Se'ar heard us and started shooting. Sa'id tried to shoot them but his hand was so badly swollen it put off his aim. My cousin had the only other good rifle and he shot at them and thought he'd hit one. Then we had to run away. "What shall we do?" I asked Sa'id. He agreed we should go back for help. I think his hand was really giving him trouble by then. The wound was black and smelt bad. So we started off back to our camp with no food and very little water and an old she-camel that was half dead. On the second day Sa'id fell down from the pain of his hand, and couldn't walk any further. We loaded him on the camel, but before long she collapsed too. We forced her on with sticks, but you could tell she was going to die. It was very hot by day and soon our water ran out. My brother was half mad, talking to himself and moaning, saying his whole arm was on fire and begging for water which we didn't have. Then the she-camel just sat down and refused to go on. Sa'id was far beyond walking, so we made a shelter out of bits of cloth slung on thorn-bushes and put him in the shade. Then we slaughtered the she-camel and slit open her belly – there was about enough liquid in it to fill a bowl – though it was dirty and stank horribly. My brother drank first, then we all had some. I was the next oldest, and I said, "Look. You two stay here with Sa'id and I'll try to get help from our people alone."

'They agreed and I set off alone with one of the rifles. What a walk that was! I saw no Bedu and no animals. After I'd walked for a day I felt I couldn't go on. I was bent over, head first – I couldn't stand upright. There was no saliva on my tongue, and my eyes felt as if they were sinking into my skull. I knew I would die if I didn't find help soon, but I tied my headcloth tight around my stomach and I found this helped a bit and let me stand upright.

'It was heaven when night came. In the distance I saw a fire – at first I thought I'd imagined it – but it was a fire. Thank God! I said. I staggered to the camp and found it was some Manahil. I was so thirsty that I couldn't speak. All I could think about was water, but they wouldn't give me any. "No," they said, "if you drink now it will kill you!"

'They moistened my lips with a wet cloth, then, bit by bit, they allowed me drops of water, until my mouth became less dry. Then, after a while, I was able to drink. I told them that I had to get back to the others. "I must borrow a camel!" I said. "But we haven't got any!" they told me. I had to go with them to a camp nearby and borrow a camel. Then we all went together – everyone who had a camel to ride – as quickly as possible. We followed my tracks to the place where I had left Sa'id and the others. Ahmad and my cousin were all right – they'd been sitting in the shade as I'd advised them to do – but we came too late for my elder brother. Sa'id was dead, may God's mercy be upon him. He died only a short time before we arrived. Ahmad said his last words were, "By God I feel hot!" '

The old man sniffed and turned away for a moment. There was silence but for the rhythmic chewing of the camels, the crackle of wood in the grate. Then Sayf drew himself up. 'You wanted to know what it was like in the Old Days,' he said. 'Well, that's what it was like!'

We stayed with the Manahil that night and in the morning Shukri refused even to attempt the road to Thamud. The wild region of Mahra would have to wait for another journey. Instead we drove to the deserted village of Nabi Hud.

The story of Hud is connected with the pre-Islamic people of 'Ad – the mythical giant race of engineers and builders, fifty cubits high, whose incredible strength enabled them to toss great stone blocks about like bricks, creating the monumental buildings whose ruins are scattered across south Arabia. Hud, himself as tall as a palm-tree, was dispatched by Allah to persuade them to renounce their veneration of the moon, but they sneered at his message and hounded him along the Wadi Hadhramaut. Mounted on his faithful white camel, Hud eluded them by riding straight into the cliff, where he was swallowed up by the rock on the very spot where this shrine was built. As a punishment for rejecting his messenger, Allah destroyed the city of ʿAd, which until now lies buried under drifting sands.

I began to climb up through the warren of blocks to the sweeping staircase that led to Hud's shrine. The eyes of the village leered down at me and the mud walls trembled with heat. On the first level, below the dome, stood an open mosque like a miniature Greek temple – rows of distempered plaster columns supporting Moorish arches, dominated by a wedge of rock which was supposed to be the petrified hump of Hud's mammoth camel. Here was a tale engraved in stone and plaster along the walls of the Wadi Hadhramaut. As I climbed up the next section of stairs, I saw the Peugeot beneath me, a fawn-coloured oblong bejewelled in light.

Inside, the domed building was starkly austere, and the shrine itself came as something of a surprise. If this was truly where Hud was buried – and opinions differ on this fact – then he must really have been as tall as a palm-tree. The shrine was at least ninety feet long.

As I hurried down the steps back to the car, I heard an unexpected noise. It sounded uncannily like a voice calling to me. I suspected at once that 'joker' Shukri was up to some trick. I looked down at the wadi: the car was still in its place. I glanced around me at the blind façades. The sound came again – a ghostly whisper like a faint echo. I strained to catch it, but heard only the creak of an unfastened gate from somewhere below. When I arrived back at the car, Shukri was sitting with his hands already on the wheel. Even before I was settled in the passenger seat, he started the vehicle, and went immediately into a racing reverse, kicking up whoffs of sand from the wadi bed. When he had pointed his bonnet down the track back to Tarim, he sighed. An expression of immense relief passed over his face.

'Anyway,' I said, 'no problem from the Jinns.'

He was quiet for a moment, then he turned his moon-shaped face towards me with a look of utter gravity. 'No?' he said. 'Then who was that old man I saw following you when you were coming down the steps?'

# 5

# The Gulf Stream
# of Wanderers

Suhail's camp was gone when I passed the spot some months later with a new driver named Faisal. It was spring, and the Manahil had taken to the high prairies of Mahra, pegging out parchment-coloured marquees around man-made lagoons and the dried-up cribs of natural lakes. Mahra was volcanic country: hills and water-basins notched and crinkled, stands of drab camel-thorn and milky-green grass on a landscape of powdered chocolate. All along the track to Thamud we could see tribesmen in luminous shirts and embroidered *futas*, egging on their camels across a sur-face coal-black with volcanic clinker, or pushing a squash of goats across ivory sand-spills in a glimmer of dust.

Our escorts – two Humumis from the village of Saum – stopped only once, to point out the twisted exclamation-mark of a *gamez*, a wild fig-tree, with its basket of shade. 'Planted by an Englishman, to rest under,' one of them said. 'There are no other trees like it between here and Thamud!'

By late afternoon, Faisal's eyes were bloodshot with thirst, and he was almost panting over the steering-wheel. It was Ramadan, and though in Islam travellers were exempt from fasting, Faisal was determined to waive this right. 'You have to make up the time afterwards,' he told me, 'and it's always harder to fast when you have to do it alone.'

We halted at Hulayya, a strip of deserted buildings with a deep well. I had been hoping to make Thamud by nightfall, but in view of Faisal's weariness, it seemed folly to go on. He protested loudly, and the Bedu sauntered over from their vehicle, Kalashnikovs bristling, to join in. 'We agreed to escort you to Thamud!' one of them – a fierce-looking Samson with African features – said. 'It would be a disgrace for us to leave you here!'

'I'll pay you what we agreed.'

'It's not the money. It's forbidden for us to abandon our travelling-companions. If anything happens to you, we will get the blame!'

I thanked them for this loyalty to tradition, conspicuously absent in my Huwaytat companion in Jordan, and gave them a note exonerating them. Honour seemed satisfied on all sides, and Faisal could rest. After dark, when the Bedu were gone, we were visited by a party of Manahil boys with an ancient, white-haired Sheikh, who joined us at our hearth for tea. The moon soared and deflated smoothly as it rose, flushing out the shadows, and immersing the landscape in satin light. 'Ah, these were the kind of nights we liked in the old days,' the Sheikh said. 'White nights we call them. You can sleep soundly on a night like this, for no enemy can take you by surprise. You can leave the camels unattended and keep your fire burning all night. There are three things the Bedouin herdsman wishes for: eternal moonlit nights, eternal green grazing, and eternal youth!'

'Yes,' Faisal said, 'the moon is a youth, who never grows old, and his wife is the sun, a dried-up old hag who is forever old and who destroys everything. The moon brings the rain, the dew and the green plants, but the sun brings only death.'

Here, wrapped in the soft fibre of Islam, were traces of the moon-worship of the ancient spice-kingdoms, which, more than 2,000 years ago, were the first bloom of civilization upon the barren landscape of Arabia.

It was on an evening a week earlier, in the office of Universal Travel, Sana'a, that I had first met Faisal. I had not given up my hope of reaching Mahra country, and this time I had decided to start from the capital of Yemen, where things were altogether more organized than in shell-shocked Aden. Even so, it had not been easy to find a driver with a Land-Cruiser ready to go into Mahra. 'Mahra is too far,' Fuad – manager of Universal – told me, lounging back suavely in his swivel-chair, 'and it is Ramadan, when all the drivers want to stay at home.' After many intense phone calls, however, Fuad had come up with the name of Faisal.

When he clumped into the office to present himself, I was struck by the contrast with the urbane, overweight Shukri. Faisal was a Bedui, proud, disdainful, acute. He wore shiny black shoes, white knee-socks under a *futa* of gilt-embroidered green, and a scarlet headcloth looped gypsy-style. His pinstripe jacket hung askew from the bottle of mineral water stuffed into the pocket, and its breast lay parted to display a hooked dagger. His cheek bulged with qat, and he clutched a bunch of green shoots in his left hand, while cupping a long cigarette in his right. Yes, he would take me to Mahra, no matter how far it was. And no, he didn't give a damn about the Jinns. He spat upon them! He would pick me up at the Taj Sheba hotel at ten, the day after next, and we would head east, first stop, Ma'rib.

I occupied the next evening wandering in Old Sana'a – once the Jewish ghetto, but now a crowded market-place. Before sundown, men were already seated at weathered rustic tables outside the gates, waiting impatiently for the time when a black thread could no longer be distinguished from a white one, and the end of another day's fasting. The money-changers were snapping shut their mock-leather briefcases with resignation. The gates were disgorging waves of bearded, kilted, turbaned figures, scuffling homeward in worn-soled shoes, their faces pinched with hunger, carrying qat under their arms in torpedo-shaped bundles. Women looking like red-and-black pears in their concealing sheets were balancing discs of hot bread on their heads as they negotiated the bottleneck of the gate. Motorcycles and scooters buzzed through the crowd like enraged bees. Inside the souq the light was already drowsy along the cobbled alleys between the perpendicular stone-built houses with their ornate glass windows. The shops were shadowy rows of pitchholes and cavities, in which ghost-figures crouched over piles of qat, dates, spices and vegetables, or sat at glass-fronted stalls stuffed with Maria Theresa silver dollars, and paper currency in dense wads of notes.

It was among the bric-à-brac on such a stall that I noticed packets of amber-coloured frankincense resin. I examined them with fascination. Frankincense – one of the gifts presented to the infant Christ by the Magi – was traditionally produced only in part of southern Arabia and the hills of Somalia. In the biblical era it was one of the most precious substances known to man, and on the fabulous profits of its trade the lost civilizations of ancient south Arabia had prospered. To the people of the ancient world the universe was populated by trickster gods and demons, which could be appeased only by the fragrant smoke of incense. Wafting up to the heavens, the sacred smoke symbolized prayer itself – a means of communicating with numinous forces beyond the veil of darkness.

Frankincense and myrrh grew in south Arabia, but it was the camel, tamed by the peoples of the arid steppe – let us call them the 'people of ʿAd' – around 2000 BC, which made the long-distance spice-trade viable. A thousand years earlier the Pharaohs of Egypt had brought back incense seedlings from the 'Land of Punt', which failed dismally to germinate in the valley of the Nile. Naval expeditions were costly and dangerous, however. The Red Sea was full of reefs, unpredictable currents and pirate bands. Beyond the Bab al Mandab – the straits dividing Arabia from Africa – ships were at the mercy of the monsoon winds, whose secrets were known only to the Arabs. The introduction of the camel rendered the overland routes quicker and safer than the troubled sea-lanes. Wonderful cities such as Maʿrib and Shabwa bloomed in the desert along the caravan-roads. The Bedu who remained in the south Arabian deserts profited by breeding the camels essential to the trade, and by pillaging spice-caravans, though unlike their cousins in north Arabia, they were never able to dominate the powerful spice-kingdoms. Instead they learned the protection strategy, and the value of extracting tolls from caravans passing through their territories.

By subtle degrees the shadows lengthened and mingled, and the gush of humanity dwindled: I followed in its wake. Raucous Arab voices grated from hidden recesses, and everywhere men could be seen packing up their wares and slamming the shop doors shut. Soon they were poised in tight circles around their Ramadan breakfast, summoning me to join them with expansive hand-signals as I passed. A moment later the muezzin's voice crashed out of hidden loudspeakers, filling the whole market with sound: 'Allah is most great! Allah is most great! I swear that there is no god but Allah . . . I swear that Mohammad is God's Prophet . . . Allah is most great! . . . There is no god but Allah!'

As soon as we had passed the police checkpoints outside the city the next morning, Faisal halted the Land-Cruiser and pulled up the front seat. There, swaddled in greased plastic, was an airborne-model Kalashnikov AK 47 with a folding butt and a curved magazine. He fitted the magazine with a smack and laid the weapon close to him on the seat. 'Are you expecting trouble?' I asked, grinning.

'If I wasn't expecting trouble, I wouldn't have got it out!' he snapped. 'I might run into someone who has a quarrel with my family. The vendetta still rules in Yemen. When you pass through a village and see everyone carrying rifles, that means a vendetta is still going on.'

It dawned on me then that travelling with the dour Faisal was going to be quite a different story from the previous experience with Shukri. 'I'm forty-five years old,' he told me, 'and, thanks be to Allah, I have five children. When I was a small child my father was shot dead near Bayda by members of another clan. I can still remember hearing the shooting. My mother snatched me out of bed, because they had murdered my father, and she was afraid they would murder me. By God's will we escaped to my uncle's place in Heraz – in the high mountains – where I grew up. It was like a fortress there – right up on the top of the hill – and you could have stayed up there all the time. We had crops on the terraces, goats and cows, and even a dam built across the wadi for water. You were completely self-sufficient and no one could approach you unawares. Anyway, the civil war came and my family fought with the Republicans. I was only a kid but they gave me a rifle and told me to kill people. I got quite good at it. Afterwards, when we had defeated the Imam, I said, "Right. I've killed people I had no grudge against, now, by God, I'm going to avenge my father!" If I hadn't retaliated, the sons of bitches would have crowed over us forever! So my cousins and I drove down there in a jeep and waited near the fields until one of them came with his sheep. Then we just stood up and shot him five or six times. He split open like a water-melon – you should have seen the look on his face, by God! We kept on pumping bullets into him till he lay still. I said, "Thank God! I've done my duty. My father is avenged!" We walked away, and nobody tried to stop us. If they had we'd have dropped the lot of them! I didn't feel bad about it – and I don't now. That was the law – a life for a life. I'd do it again tomorrow, by God! Now, of course, they're still on the lookout for me or anyone of my clan. A vendetta like this never ends. So, yes, I am expecting trouble. Trouble always comes when you expect it least.'

'But was the man you killed one of those who shot your father?'

'No. He was just one of the family – a cousin or something. I doubt if he had anything to do with my father's death. What does that matter? The important thing is that he was part of that family – it's the family, not the individual, that counts.'

'But wouldn't it have been fairer to have given him a chance?'

'Did they give my father a chance? Are you mad? It wasn't a game of cowboys and Indians we were playing! It takes enough courage just to shoot someone, without running the risk of being shot yourself!'

It took only three hours to reach Maʿrib, bowling along a road which cut through arid vineyards and fig orchards, plots of leached earth, hamlets of mud-brick houses in which old and new blended imperceptibly together, over shattered hogsback ridges on which dwellings perched like old men's bad teeth. There were ochre fields full of saplings like miniature Christmas-trees, which Faisal told me were ripening qat. 'It's the most valuable crop now,' he said. 'We used to grow a lot of coffee here. In Turkish times the Yemen was famous for coffee – Mokha, you know. But all that's gone. Qat will grow in more or less the same place as coffee, and it brings more profit these days. Wherever you see a gathering of people in the Yemen, you can be sure there's someone selling qat!'

Soon the marginal cultivation fell away and the landscape swelled into olive-sheen desert country. Maʿrib, a toytown of breeze-block and asphalt, stood in a dustbowl beyond.

In the afternoon we visited the ruins of the great Maʿrib dam, a giant's lair of masonry blocks dressed with flawless precision, stranded on a raw granite irruption, fifty feet above the stagnant pools in the Wadi Dhahna. Faisal guided me along a path that wound behind the magnificent stonework and showed me how the mountain had been shorn away to create sluices that had once carried water into an invisible catch-basin, feeding no fewer than fourteen canals. 'All this land used to be green,' he said, gesturing down the valley, 'There were green fields from here to the Hadhramaut in ancient days. Yemen was great!'

In the soft bed of the wadi below, sand-ghosts dribbled around Sodom's Apple trees with their parchment leaves and poison fruit, snaking across a great plain hazed with heat and scattered with a thousand twisted mushrooms of mud that might once have been houses. Faisal had not exaggerated in saying that Yemen had been great. Here, while Europe was still skulking in the bronze age, the Arabs had mastered the fey floodwaters of the Yemen hills, and brought agriculture to thousands of acres of sterile sands. A great and prosperous kingdom had flourished here – the biblical Sheba

– whose fame had reached the ears of Solomon, in far-off Jerusalem.

From my perch high up on the sluices, I tried to reconstruct the landscape in my imagination. Eighteen hundred feet across the wadi, the remnants of a low wall lay half buried under sand, but the central part of the structure – the pyramid-shaped barrage which had dammed up the floodwaters – was missing. According to one legend, it was torn apart by giant rats which gnawed at its wooden props and pulled away great blocks of stone that could not have been shifted by fifty men. Soon afterwards all that remained was ripped to shreds by raging torrents, and the noble city of Ma'rib flooded. Its population fled to the hills and deserts, splintering into tribes, and resuming the nomadic life they had renounced centuries before. According to Arab tradition, the Ma'rib disaster created havoc among the tribes all over Arabia. The Sultanate of Oman, for example, is supposed to have been created by a man called 'Oman bin Qahtan – the first Arab to settle in the Oman mountains after fleeing the Ma'rib flood. The famous Bedu tribe of Azd, which later occupied the deserts of the Middle East, the Bani Ghassan of the Hauran in Syria, and the Lakhm, who migrated to Egypt in the eighth century AD, are among scores of tribes that trace their origin back to the settled people of Ma'rib. The bursting of the Ma'rib dam is seen in legend as a key event in Bedu history.

No one knows for certain when the dam was built. In 1600 BC, Semitic nomads swept into Yemen from the north, and began to assimilate the natives. One tribe, the Saba'i or Shebans – perhaps the same people whose former bloodthirsty reputation as Bedu freebooters is attested in the Book of Job – settled on the plains of Ma'rib. Other tribes took root around the wadis spread across southern Arabia, in which the fabulous city-states of Arabia – Sheba, Ma'in, Qataban, Awsan, Himyar and the Hadhramaut – grew up. If legend is to be credited, though, the monumental water-harvesting technology on which these states were founded may have been developed as early as 1700 BC, by a brilliant engineer called Lukman bin ʿAd, who constructed a system of dams and canals of which Maʿrib was the *pièce de résistance*. 'As a result the arid land of Yemen was transformed into a lush green garden,' the legend goes. 'There were so many trees that travellers were never struck by the fierce sunshine and the air was so fresh . . . that people attained a very advanced age without illness.' By the time of the Greek historian Pliny, the Shebans had become the wealthiest tribe in south Arabia, 'owing to the fertility of their scent-producing forests, their gold mines, their irrigated agri-cultural lands and their production of honey and beeswax'.

As I pondered the genius of Lukman bin ʿAd, Faisal pointed out the medieval town of Maʿrib, from here a broken claw of buildings balanced on a half-moon-shaped mound above the few remain-ing patches of cultivation in the valley. Later, when we drove up to the settlement, I saw that it was a crushed shell of a place: a sym-phony in decay. It was haunted by shadows – faceless, shawled women who trod silently barefoot up steep paths carrying buckets of water, Jinn-faced urchins who raced terrified down rubble-filled alleys and spied on us from behind grilled windows. I wasn't surprised to learn that Fellini had used the old town as the setting for his film *The Arabian Nights*. Everything about the place smacked of some decadent fantasy. There were great tene-ments built of the stones the Bedu had long ago dragged out of the pre-Islamic ruins, whose walls had cracked into zigzag pat-terns and settled into unearthly contours and angles. Towers of mud and stone peeled away from the centre like giant dried banana-skins, the spaces between them blocked with dung, dust and debris. A modern water-tank – a decrepit moon-lander on stilts – threatened to topple into the streets on the merest hint of provocation.

At the base of one of the leaning towers a shrivelled man in a loincloth sat in the dust by a doorway whose original level had been so obscured by layers of detritus that one would almost have been obliged to crawl inside on hands and knees. Yet this hovel was his home. He answered my '*as salaam ʿalaykum*' gloomily, and lit a cigarette with blunt fingers. Faisal glared at him. 'Don't you know it's Holy Ramadan?' he demanded. 'Smoking is forbidden before sunset!'

The man puffed out a ring of smoke and ignored him brazenly. 'Where are all the people?' I asked him.

'Gone,' he replied mournfully. 'Gone off to every place. There's just a few of us left now to tend the crops.'

As we walked back to the Land-Cruiser, a multitude of ragged children dogged our heels shrieking, 'Money! Money!' I was about to hand out a twenty-riyal note when Faisal took it sternly, pocketed it, and brought out a wad of smaller denominations in its place. Issuing orders like a drill-sergeant, he arranged the youngsters into family groups and presented a note to the eldest child in each group with a stiff admonition that it must be equally divided. As we pulled out of the old town the children were racing gleefully back across the dung-covered square. 'Poor things!' Faisal said pityingly, as he watched them go. 'Before cars came this place used to be a really important market for the Bedu. Now it's almost dead.' At its apogee, ancient Ma'rib had been 'the Paris of Arabia', a thriving metropolis sited on the junction of the caravan-routes, an emporium of the fabulous riches of India and East Africa as well as of Arabia herself. Three thousand years ago the ancient Shebans enjoyed a standard of living undreamed of by these barefoot urchins. Even in its heyday the medieval town had occupied only a tiny corner of the ancient capital out of whose ruins it had sprung.

In the evening we visited a house in the grounds of the Jamal-ayn Hotel, to meet the Bedu who were to provide us with an escort for the next stage of our journey — across the Ramlat Sabatayn. It was dark inside the house but for spears of sodium orange that pierced the shutters from the electric lamps outside. As my eyes struggled to adapt, I saw that there were five Bedu tribesmen kneeling on the floor, each one cradling an automatic rifle across his knees. Faisal kept his own Kalashnikov braced loosely against his arm as the Bedu stood up to greet us, their faces shadowy under their tight headcloths. They were lean hawks of men with hawk noses, wearing wraparound kirtles that were weighted with heavy cartridge belts and preposterously large daggers. They moved with an abrupt assertiveness, and their manner was uneasy, suspicious, and unnecessarily forbidding.

Three millennia ago the ancestors of these ʿAbida, who bred camels for the rich spice-caravans that already plodded the length of southern Arabia, realized – like the Nabataeans – that there was more to be gained from guiding and guarding travellers than from pillaging them. It was a lesson which long outlived the caravans themselves. Now, every traveller was advised to engage a Bedu escort with its own four-wheel-drive vehicle when crossing Sabatayn sands, where unguarded foreigners had frequently been held at gunpoint by bandits, robbed of everything down to their underwear, and left stranded in the desert.

We crouched against the hard cushions they proffered, and Faisal accepted a cigarette, smoking it briskly but with dignity, sitting bolt upright with his rifle in his lap. After drawn-out introductions, he announced that we required a Bedu escort for the following day, and that our route would take us through the ruined city of Shabwa – for centuries a sanctuary forbidden to Westerners – to the Wadi Hadhramaut. The Bedu chief, Tom-Thumb-sized with the expression of an enraged penguin, received the request disdainfully. Tea was distributed and quaffed, many cigarettes sucked dry and stubbed out, and conversations yammered with hysterical speed on the flat telephone lying on the floor. Finally, the Sheikh told us: 'We will provide an escort for tomorrow to Shabwa and the Hadhramaut. The fee, non-negotiable, and payable in advance, will be two hundred and fifty American dollars.'

'Two hundred and fifty! That's a bit much isn't it? After all, it's only a day's journey!'

The Sheikh's eyes hardened. 'It's not the length of the journey, it's the danger,' he said. Only a few months ago, it seemed, two Bedu escorts had been murdered. Some bandits had held up a carload of Westerners, intending to rob them, and one of the guards – a young Bedui of the ʿAbida – had opened fire. The bandits had fired back, missing him and killing a foreigner instead. They knew that the government would punish them severely for murdering a foreign visitor, so they had decided to get rid of the witnesses. They had massacred everyone, including the Bedu guards. 'Anyway, that is what we charge,' he said. 'What is two hundred and fifty dollars against your life?'

'What if I decide to go without an escort?'

The Sheikh bared symmetrical rows of sharp teeth. 'In that case,' he said, watching me intently to make sure I caught his drift, 'you will be very unlikely to make it to the Hadhramaut.' I knew that I must either pay or drive miles out of my way, but I still resented this age-old Bedu protection racket. Camel-caravans might have been superseded by cars and spears by Kalashnikovs, I reflected, but in 3,000 years little else had changed.

When we arrived at the Bedu house the following morning, the tribesmen were still snoring under their blankets and sleeping off the Ramadan vigil. The penguin-faced Sheikh scowled at us and ordered us to rendezvous with our escort at a derelict petrol-station on the outskirts of the town in an hour's time. On the way there we passed a row of thirty-foot limestone shafts standing in lapping sands – all that remained visible of the famous Temple of Bilqis – the legendary Queen of Sheba.

The columns actually formed part of a magnificent peristyle hall containing inscriptions, bronzes and statues, now buried under dust. The hall itself was only a small section of a city-within-a-city that was once surrounded by a wall of masonry thirteen feet thick and more than 1,000 feet long. Though the temple is connected by Arab tradition with the biblical Queen of Sheba, it is actually dedicated to the Sheban moon god Ilumquh. Indeed, apart from folk-tales there is little evidence to connect antiquity's most famous queen with the ancient city of Maʿrib, where the earliest inscriptions date from about 800 BC – a century and a half after the reign of Solomon, whom she is supposed to have known.

The legends hold that Bilqis was the daughter of a female Jinn, and her ravishing beauty attracted the eye of Sharabil, King of Sheba, a monarch notorious for his drunkenness and depravity. The girl was betrothed to him, but on their wedding night evaded his amorous advances – arranging for dancing-girls to entertain him, and keeping his wine-cup judiciously filled until he passed out. Bilqis then demonstrated her wild blood by plunging a dagger into his heart, and afterwards assumed the throne in his place. Having become famous as a wise and virtuous ruler, she decided to make the seventy-day camel-trek to Solomon's court, thousands of miles away in Jerusalem, taking with her a retinue of servants, warriors and courtiers, and presents which included 1,000 carpets woven with golden thread, musk, aloe wood and ambergris.

Solomon's jealous pet demons informed him that, being half Jinn, the Queen possessed donkey's feet, and was therefore unsuitable for the marriage-alliance he was considering. The King tricked her into raising her skirts by creating the illusion of a pool of water before his throne, and observed that, far from being donkey-like, her feet and ankles were distinctly appealing. Bilqis accepted the marriage he offered, and after the wedding returned to her palace at Ma'rib, where Solomon, with the aid of a magic carpet, visited her for three days every month.

We waited in the car at the abandoned filling-station, and an hour and a half later the Bedu Land-Cruiser appeared, driven by a middle-aged Arab with a younger boy riding shotgun beside him. The driver wound the window down. 'Come on! Come on!' he shouted.

'Don't dare "come on" me!' Faisal replied like a whiplash. 'We've been waiting for you for hours!'

The cars turned off the road into creamy, jelly-roll dunes that stretched for miles, poling up to top speed, roller-coasting up the faces and bouncing over the crests like police-cars in a film chase. Faisal's face was set in a maniacal grin: 'The only way to take these dunes is at speed,' he grunted, 'otherwise you get bogged down.' On the flat plains between the undulations the Land-Cruisers played around each other like dolphins, racing abreast, circling and overtaking, falling back into file and then overtaking again. There were camel-herds in the sand-folds, grazing on low pepper-and-salt vegetation, and the animals watched us with expressions of faint disdain as we whooshed through the dunes in a frisson of dust.

Then suddenly, the Bedu car was gone.

Faisal cursed under his breath and drove up a dune covered with a billion tiny islets of yellow flowers. He halted on the crest and applied the handbrake, then we climbed out and scanned the desert in every direction. The silence hit me like a shock-wave. Travelling by camel, the desert grew upon your senses organically as you adjusted to its power. After the mad rush in a motor-vehicle, however, it was as if you had been suddenly deposited on an alien planet from space. Faisal shifted his Kalashnikov from hand to hand and cursed again. 'Fools and sons of fools,' he growled. "Escort" indeed! And they don't even know the way! I know the way better than they do!'

We waited for what seemed a very long time, listening intently. Dunes blocked the horizon in every direction. The only movement was the shimmer of heat across the slopes and the silent wave-motion of the frail grasses that covered them. A motion caught my eye in the far distance: sunlight reflected on a dust-mote drifting out of the sand. 'That must be them!' I said. But Faisal's senses were sharper, and suddenly he cocked his rifle with a mechanical 'klack!' 'That's not our car,' he said.

We could hear the purr of the engine now. The vehicle – a black Land-Cruiser – slewed towards us with the cumbrous glide of a boat cutting through surf, and halted some yards away. Inside were two black-faced men with stubbled beards, who peered at us with mocking eyes. Faisal walked slowly towards the driver's open window. The dark man made no move to get out. 'Peace be on you,' Faisal said.

'And on you. What's your business here?'

'We are waiting for our escort. They'll be along in a few minutes' time.'

The black man smiled mockingly again. 'Keep your wits about you. There are a lot of bandits around here!'

As we watched the car slide off into the distance, Faisal relaxed visibly and disengaged his magazine, ejecting a shiny cartridge into the sand. 'Well,' he said, 'we had nothing to fear from them. They were Bureikis. I could tell that by just looking at them.'

I discovered only later that the Bureikis were considered holy Sheikhs. Their role for countless generations had been to guard the sacred places of this part of south Arabia, especially the so-called 'hidden city' of Shabwa, whose ruins stood in the middle of Ramlat Sabatayn. They were probably the descendants of the tribe which had controlled Shabwa when it was an opulent trading city, commanding the caravan-roads across these sands. In the days of Pliny the town was inhabited by 4,000 sacred families, and the name 'Bureiki' itself derives from a root meaning 'sacred'. Like many of the Bedu tribes of south Arabia, they were compelled to give up the life of the town and take to the tent and the camel when the spice-trade declined in the first few centuries of our era.

Within minutes our escort vehicle appeared: 'What happened to you lot?' Faisal demanded dismissively. 'Two hundred and fifty dollars, and you get yourselves lost in the desert!' The tribesmen of the predatory ʿAbida stared back sheepishly, wilting under Faisal's scorn.

The crags of Shabwa crawled slowly into focus — cheese-wedges of rock that had pressed through the organdie-coloured surface. Here, protected on all sides by waterless sands and impenetrable hills, the city had flourished for centuries as the capital of the Hadhramaut, at one period the largest and richest of the incense-states. At its zenith Shabwa was as famous as Maʿrib and, according to Pliny, boasted no fewer than sixty temples.

While it was still cool enough, we walked about the ruins, shadowed by four or five tiny Bedu boys, sent, no doubt, to see that we didn't carry anything off. But little of the glory of the ancient days remained. Shabwa was another Arab honeycomb with the lid shaved off, a dead specimen on a dissecting-table, consisting of hundreds of roofless cells and alleyways leading nowhere. There persisted only the ruined plinths that once supported the pillars of a single temple, and bits of monumental masonry that had been used to shore up the walls of long-ruined Arab houses.

In the time of the south Arabian spice-kingdoms, the bulk of the frankincense was brought to Shabwa from the port of Qana', near modern Bir 'Ali. There were at least two major caravan-routes from the south, and another passing west through the Wadi Qalat, where all openings in the rock wall were sealed, save for a single vast gateway of masonry fifteen feet high. The priest-kings of Shabwa charged a tithe on each measure of incense brought through the town, and made it a capital offence for laden camels to turn aside from the road.

We camped under some acacias in the wadi. Faisal dragged his mattress out of the car and lay down with his Kalashnikov under his head. 'If I fall asleep, wake me up!' he ordered me. 'You have to keep your wits about you in this country!' The ruins loomed down on us, basting in the midday heat. Our escort was nowhere to be seen. Within minutes, Faisal was snoring fitfully. I hadn't the heart to wake him up.

An hour later a youth of about fourteen, with hair curling beneath his furled headcloth, came striding barefoot through the thorns and stones. Quick as a flash, Faisal rolled over, jumped up, and brought his rifle to the ready. The youth stopped abruptly, watching the older man with wide eyes. 'You shouldn't come creeping up on people like that!' Faisal growled.

I called the boy over to sit down and offered him some dates. I asked him where his people's tents and camels were. 'We haven't got any camels left,' he said. 'We are the guardians of the ruins. We get money from the government and we have our goats. I've never ridden a camel, and I don't remember seeing anybody riding one in the last few years. We haven't got any tents either –

we just live in the ruins now.' I inquired what tribe he belonged to, and when he told me 'Kurub', I recognized the name at once. Only fifty years ago, the Kurub had been one of the most feared of all the tribes of south Arabia, and were known to raid as far as Liwa oasis near the Gulf, hundreds of miles away. It seemed that the raiding spirit had departed long since: this boy's family did not even possess camels – reduced from hardy raiders to the caretakers of ruins in a single generation.

For centuries Qahtani tribes such as the Kurub had raided east into Oman, leaving pockets of their descendants scattered across the steppes. These successive waves of movement may have been set in motion by the catastrophe that had overtaken south Arabia in the first few centuries AD, symbolized in Arab annals by the bursting of the great Maʿrib dam. Actually the dam was patched up many times throughout its history. By the time it did burst finally in the sixth century – as a reference in the Quran indicates – the grandeur of the spice-kingdoms had long since waned. For centuries the sedentary farmers had been drifting away from the land and taking to the wandering life of the Bedu. Strong tribes may have displaced others and set in motion the kind of chain-reaction imagined by T. E. Lawrence in his book *Seven Pillars of Wisdom*: 'the congestion of Yemen, therefore, becoming extreme, found its only relief . . . by forcing the weaker aggregations of its borders down and down the slopes of the hills . . . Finally . . . the border people . . . were flung out of the furthest crazy oasis into the untrodden wilderness as nomads . . . There was the source of migration, the factory of nomads, the springing of the gulf-stream of desert wanderers.'

But the collapse of the dam was the symptom rather than the root of the decay. If any single event bears the blame for the decline of south Arabia, it was not the ruin of Maʿrib, but the voyage of Hippalus, a Byzantine sea-captain in the service of the Abyssinian navy. Around AD 100, he sailed his ship through the Bab al Mandab, the straits that sever Africa from Arabia, reached India, and brought a laden ship back to the Mediterranean for the first time. The Arabs had grown rich both on their home-grown aromatics, and as middlemen on the trans-shipment of Indian goods, especially cinnamon and cotton cloth. Once Hippalus had grasped the seasonal nature of the monsoon, the Romans were able to deal directly with the source, bypassing the overland routes. Thus the Arabs lost their monopoly, and the power of the caravan-states ebbed. Traders and farmers became nomads, and the elaborate water-harvesting technology that had supported their civilization for generations was no longer maintained. Dams burst and canals were buried under sand. The whole of south Arabia reverted to the desert it largely remains today.

Faisal had hoped to rest until the cool hour of the afternoon prayer, but, by way of revenge for his truculence, perhaps, the 'Abida turned up at three and churned their engine remorselessly until he clambered scowling from his bed and began to pack up. The strain of driving in the heat without a drop of water or a morsel to eat was already beginning to take its toll, but, since it was purely voluntary in his case, he choked back a bitter rejoinder and started to warm the motor.

Towards sunset we were driving across salt plains with saw-tooth plateaux in the distance – the outriders of the Wadi Hadhramaut. Faisal's eyes were swollen with thirst, hunger and fatigue, and I began to worry that he would faint or fall asleep at the wheel. 'We ought to halt and make camp,' I said.

'Not out here,' he said through cracked lips. 'Too dangerous. I have too many blood-feuds on my hands. If one of my family's enemies came on me while I was asleep, I'd be done for. And you too, probably! No, we must seek the camps of the Bedu.'

This was the age-old dilemma for desert-travellers in Arabia, I reflected. Blood-feuds and bandits made it imperative that they throw themselves on the hospitality of the Bedu.

Not long after, we spied a Bedu place, looking like a circus encampment with its bent jeeps, battle-scarred four-ton lorries, rusting water tanker and cast-off Western-made marquees. Five or six malevolent-looking Bedu with their rifles unslung and ready formed a barrier between ourselves and the camp, and a one-armed man wearing a filthy dishdasha and badly scratched dark glasses sidled up to question our escort. The left sleeve of his dish-dasha had been cut off and sewn up at the elbow, and I noticed with some surprise that he too carried a rifle on a sling. I wondered how on earth he would have been able to use it. He talked with the ʿAbida for a minute, then turned to inspect Faisal. The two Bedu shook hands, and the one-armed man peered at my companion warily.

'Aren't you from Bayda?' he inquired.

'No,' Faisal lied. 'I've never been near Bayda in my life!'

The old man showed us a place to sleep, at some distance from his tents, and after dark brought us freshly baked bread and tea. He ate sparingly, talked little, and gazed disconcertingly at Faisal's face in the moonlight. After he had taken his leave, I asked Faisal why he had lied about coming from Bayda.

'Because I recognized him,' he told me. 'He lost that arm in a gunfight with people from Bayda twenty years ago. I wasn't involved personally, but no doubt he knew me as one of the same people by my dress and accent.'

'Does that mean we're under threat?' I asked him.

'Don't worry,' he said, 'not now we have eaten bread and salt!'

But that night I noticed he kept his rifle and dagger close to him, all the same.

The next morning we parted from the ʿAbida at the first village in the Hadhramaut. As their vehicle wheeled back in its dust-shroud across Sabatayn, Faisal sheathed his rifle into its hiding-place under the front seat. We spent the day driving through the wadi and halted for a while at Shibam. At Saum, the next day, we hired an escort from the Humum to guide us out of the wadi and into Mahra country.

Wilfred Thesiger's *Arabian Sands* was my bible and guidebook on all my journeys in south Arabia. One mystery it contained was a cameo portrait of a handsome Arab with a beard and thickly matted hair. The portrait had always intrigued me, because the caption bore only the legend 'Sulaim, our rabia (companion) from the Mahra'. My objective here was to meet the Mahra, but a footnote on this journey was to find out if Sulaim was still alive.

In the 1970s, the communist government of what had then been the People's Democratic Republic of Yemen had decreed that the entire rural population should be concentrated in twenty-seven fishing centres and fifty-four agricultural ones. The nomadic Bedu – whom they considered primitive – were to become settled farmers. Thamud had been one of the sites of this failed experiment in social engineering. In earlier days a watering-place for the Manahil and 'Awamir tribes, it was now a clot of crumbling Stalinist terraces along streets paved with squashed drinks cans and the oxidized rubble of scores of broken motor-cars. There was no sign of the well at which Thesiger and his Bedu had watered their camels on their trek here from Oman in 1946. Instead, life revolved around the petrol-pump, where a young Bedu called 'Amr was filling up a Land-Cruiser. He studied the photograph of Sulaim from Thesiger's book and said, 'I'm not certain. That picture is very old, but I think it is Sulaim bin Dughshayn – a Mahri who lives near Armah.' He agreed to guide us as far as Armah in place of our escort from the Hadhramaut. First, though, he took us to the house of a very ancient Bedui, who he believed might remember Thesiger's companion.

The old man lay on a vermin-infested mattress in the corner of an airless, lightless room, evidently near to death. His son – himself well past middle-age – helped him to sit up and as he did so an enormous red cockroach scuttled out of the Bedui's ragged robe and dashed through the open door. The old man watched it in horror and let out a whimper of disgust like a child. I shuddered involuntarily. The young man thrust the photo of Sulaim in front of his elder's nose. 'This Englishman has come to ask if this picture is of Sulaim bin Dughshayn of the Mahra!' he shouted, almost in the old man's ear. 'The companion of a Christian who came here with the Bedu years ago. Do you remember?'

The old man stared at the photo with eyes starting out of his head. 'Christian?' he slurred, swaying so heavily to one side that 'Amr had to catch him and hold him upright, 'I don't remember any Christian.'

'But is this Sulaim bin Dughshayn?' the boy insisted.

The old man's eyes focused on me for a moment. 'Sulaim?' he croaked. 'Why do you want him? What has he done?'

'Nothing. I just want to talk to him.'

He clung desperately to 'Amr's arms. 'Water!' he sobbed, 'bring me water! I don't know anything about Christians!'

I muttered my apologies and left, and later the man's son came and squatted with us outside the house, where naked children were playing amid flanges of rusted car. 'Do you have any medicine to cure my father?' he asked.

'I'm sorry. It seems that he's had a stroke of some kind.'

'He used to be a very strong man. When I was young we 'Awamir used to take our camels right into the Sands in the cool season, and stay there perhaps half the year. We used to take the women and children riding in litters. It was a good life. Then the government made us settle here. Living in houses like this gets to be a habit, but to me they have always seemed like a prison. In the old days there were no houses and no cars, but you were free from outside interference. We were better off then in my opinion. Living in houses has reduced my father to this!'

Later we drove towards Armah across a table-land of leopard-skin colours – beige, black and yellow – through stunted hills, past rubble screes and wadis winding through parched acacias. The white trapezoids of Manahil tents stood all around us. In the early afternoon we arrived in a grove of nabak trees, where 'Amr had pitched his tent. In contrast with the others we had seen, this was a traditional Bedu tent of black goats' hair. We drank tea while his children frolicked around us, and I asked him if his womenfolk had woven the tent in the traditional way. 'No,' he said, 'they wouldn't know how to. We never had tents in the past. We got this one sent ready-made from Abu Dhabi!'

At Armah, another desert eyesore where acres of axles and engine-blocks festered in the sun, we approached a crowd of tribesmen from the Mahra who were repairing a water-tanker. They passed round Thesiger's photograph of Sulaim, squinting at it, alternately shading it with their hands and angling it into the light, bantering in Mahra: 'I know that man!' one of them declared. 'It is bin Dumaysh. He's the Sheikh of the Amerjid section of the Mahra. His tents are pitched not far away.'

'Never,' another cried. 'That is not bin Dumaysh. It is bin Dughshayn!'

'No, by the Prophet!' a third cut in. 'That is nothing like bin Dughshayn!'

I took back the picture, confused. The first Mahri, a weazen-faced man with a pointed beard, said: 'This is Sulaim bin Dumaysh, by God! His tents are nearby. If you pay me money I can take you there!'

We passed out of Armah with the Mahri in the front seat, clutching his AK 47 firmly between his knees. He guided us beneath fractured knolls of metamorphic slag, through copses of *ithil* and *merkh*, across soft-bedded wadis and plains of coarse grass. After we had been driving for an hour and a half, Faisal began to look thirsty and pained. 'Didn't you say the tents were near?' he demanded.

'Not much farther!' the Mahri said.

I began to wonder if we were on a wild goose chase, or worse: this Mahra country was well beyond the reach of any government authority. I started to feel very glad of Faisal and his Kalashnikov. Presently, though, we came to a group of tents oriented along a wall of knotted sandstone, in which a wide cave had been fenced off as a refuge for sheep and goats. A bevy of unveiled Mahra ladies were working around a fire outside, one of them tending a baby in a three-legged cot, and another perched over a sewing-machine.

As we halted, three Bedu men in blood-coloured headcloths, all carrying rifles, came riding up the wadi on magnificent-

looking she-camels. These were almost the first camel-riders I
had seen in the Yemen, and though they had no proper saddles –
only pads behind the hump – the three of them rode with the
ease of long practice. They couched the animals in the sand and
came to shake hands, genial, self-contained men, whose flint-
coloured eyes sparkled through lids made slits from gazing into
the sun. The eldest of them showed us a stony shelf across a wadi
where we could park the car and spend the night. A hour before
sunset, when we had set out our small camp by the vehicle, the
men came over to join us, bringing glasses and a pot of tea. I asked
after Sulaim, and passed round the black-and-white picture.
'These are the tents of Sulaim bin Dumaysh, my cousin,' the
oldest man said. 'But Sulaim has gone off with his goats to the
Wadi Mahrat.'

I pressed him over the photograph, and he examined it carefully. 'I couldn't say that it is my cousin,' he said. 'It is a very old
picture. I remember stories about an Englishman – Mbarak bin
Landan – who travelled with the tribes, but his friends were from
the Bayt Imani. The Bayt Imani were neighbours of ours, and used
to water their goats not far away at Sanaw, but most of them went
to Saudi Arabia or Oman when the communists came. Their territory is Mahra country now. Sulaim will be with his goats in the
Mahrat. If you are going that way you might find him.'

Defeated, I put the book away. 'Who are the Mahra?' I asked.
'Are they Bedu?'

'The Mahra are Bedu. There is no distinction between the
Mahra and other Bedu, except that we have our own language.
This is all Mahra country, from the hills of Dhofar to the Wadi
Hadhramaut.'

The Mahra may be the descendants of the Himyarites, who
founded the last great spice-kingdom of south Arabia. Bred in the
tumbling, terraced hillsides behind the western toe of the Yemen,
they conquered Sheba, occupied Ma'rib, took control of the spice-
port at Mokha, and became the most powerful and famous people

of their time. By then, though, the golden age was past, and the
strife between Persia and Byzantium had created a slump in the
spice-market. Roman merchant-ships now plied the Indian
Ocean, and the Axumites from Abyssinia had secured a major
share of the incense-trade. The Ma'rib dam was already tottering
through lack of maintenance, and the spice-realms of ancient
times had begun to break up. In the third century AD, the Axumites seized much of south-west Yemen, bringing with them
their Christian faith. Syrian missionaries, fleeing persecution in
their own land, had introduced Christianity to the Yemen long
before, though the first Christian embassy was established here by
the Byzantine Bishop Theophilos Indus after the Axumite invasion. The power of the old gods – the sun and the moon – had
declined as the flow of wealth dwindled, and Theophilos was able
to take advantage of this vacuum to establish a church at Aden,
and two more in the Himyarite country. Within four years he had
received Tha'ran, King of Himyar, into the Faith. Forty years on,
though, Tha'ran's grandson turned his back on the church when
he visited Yathrib in the Hejaz, and there became a Jew. Afterwards, the Himyarites who remained Christian were systematic-
ally hunted down and persecuted. The last King of Himyar, Dhu
Huwas, massacred 20,000 of them at Najran. The Christians called
on the Byzantine Emperor for help, and he dispatched his proxies,
the Christian Axumites – who had withdrawn across the Bab al
Mandab decades earlier – to the succour of their religious breth-
ren. They re-invaded the Yemen and remained as rulers until they
were defeated by the Persian King, Chosroes, a few years after the
birth of the Prophet Mohammad. A century later, elements of the
Himyar – by then Muslims and nomadic Bedu – migrated to
Egypt, and planted their genes among the Egyptian Fellahin.
Writing in the fourteenth century, Ibn Khaldun recorded – with
more than a touch of condescension – that the Himyar were one
of the tribes which 'lived in the hills and the sources of plentiful
living . . . Their lineages were mixed up, and their groups inter-
mingled . . . as a result of intermixture with non-Arabs.'

I asked the Mahra why they were living so far from the government centres in Thamud and Armah. 'The government tried to make us stay in one place,' the old man said. 'They told us that all our children must go to school. If you refused to let your children go, they'd shoot you and take them, people said! They told us that we were backward, and that we ought to become farmers. All right, I said, we have nothing against farming, but you show me some good land that I can cultivate at the same time as I herd camels and goats! They couldn't, of course. If you stay always in one place you can't keep large flocks of goats or herds of camels. Well, why not just move with them, like we've always done? Maybe that's what they call being "backward", but it makes sense to me!'

I reflected again that it was an Arab – Ibn Khaldun – who was ultimately to blame for such folly. It was he who first held that the Bedu were 'more primitive' than sedentary people, not in the sense that they lived materially simpler lives – which was self-evidently true – but meaning that they had been stranded in a 'backward' state, from which the rest of mankind had long since progressed. This view would probably be echoed even today by most sophisticated lay observers – Westerners or Arabs. It was precisely the view that had led governments to condemn the nomadic life as an anachronism from which its victims must be rescued, and made to settle as farmers – that is, to catch up culturally with the rest of the population. Even those who argued against the settlement of the Bedu generally based their case on Ibn Khaldun's premise of Bedu moral purity, as if the Bedu were a rare and exotic species which should be preserved in its natural habitat for the benefit of others.

Archaeological evidence has exploded Ibn Khaldun's argument. We now know that agriculture and pastoral nomadism developed concurrently from hunting and gathering, as a result of the 'Neolithic food-producing revolution'. If both ways of life appeared at the same time, neither can be considered 'the final stage' of human development. In chronological terms, camel-pastoralism, supposedly the 'purest' form of nomadism – with a history that can scarcely be traced back earlier than 2000 BC – developed long after the ancient Egyptians and Mesopotamians had become urbanized in cities. Emanuel Marx has pointed out that, far from being 'primitive', the 'pure' camel-nomads could never have existed other than in connection with a complex urban civilization, because their high degree of specialization rendered them exceptionally dependent on agricultural products, and highly vulnerable to the vagaries of the market.

The following day, when we had dropped our guide back in Armah, we drove towards Sanaw, where Thesiger's favourite tribe, the Bayt Imani, had once watered their flocks. We halted at the Mahra tent to ask directions, and an aggressive-looking Bedui appeared with his rifle. 'Why are you going to Sanaw?' he demanded, nastily.

'Because I want to see it.'

'Have you got your papers?'

'Yes, thanks.'

'Let me see them.'

'No.'

The Bedui scowled at me and showed rotted teeth. 'You shouldn't go to Sanaw. That is near the border with Saudi Arabia. Perhaps you are a spy!'

'Thanks. Let's go, Faisal!'

Before we pulled away, though, the Bedui shouted: 'If you go to Sanaw you will both be killed!'

I brooded over this disturbing incident for several hours as we bounced under blocks of black stone, across rubble floors and long sweeps of valley, past bundles of grass like helmets and scratchy thorn. The day was very hot, and Faisal looked increasingly annoyed as he wrestled with the wheel. Eventually he gave me a look so hard and venomous that I was taken aback. 'Is something wrong?' I inquired.

'That man,' he burst out. 'You should have showed him your

papers. You shouldn't have been rude to him. You foreigners! Coming here and being rude to people. I don't want any trouble!'

'He had no right to ask for my passport. He wasn't the police!'

'How do you know? He could have been a government officer!'

'If he was, he should have said so!'

'Who are you to say that? This is our country!'

'I've got a right to be here. I've got my visa and I have hired you and your car through the most reputable company in the Yemen. That man made me feel I was doing something wrong, which he had absolutely no call to do . . .'

Faisal's reaction was shocking in its suddenness. He screeched to a halt, switched off the engine and instinctively reached for his Kalashnikov with blazing eyes. 'Who are you to say what people have and haven't got the right to do in our country?' he screamed.

I was taken off guard. Faisal had been stern and robust from the beginning, but always reliable and fair. I watched his hand as it tightened around the stock of the rifle, and it occurred to me that I was in the remotest corner of Yemen, alone in the middle of the desert, with a man who had already murdered at least one person in cold blood. I tried to keep my voice calm when I said, 'I'm sorry you feel like this, Faisal, but I think we'd better turn round and go back to Sana'a. I'm a stranger in your country; I have hired your car in good faith, and you have your hand on a loaded rifle.'

I kept my gaze steady, staring straight into his eyes. He looked away abruptly and relaxed his hold on the weapon. 'I'm sorry,' he said, suddenly. 'It's the fasting. Driving in this heat without eating and drinking makes you go crazy! It's the first time I've been to Sanaw, and there may be army and police there. I don't want any trouble, that's all.'

'Look, I'm sorry too. We can turn back if you want.'

'No, no! We'll go on!'

When we arrived in Sanaw half an hour later, it was something of an anti-climax: all we found were three wells stinking of sulphur, a deserted police sangar, and a pile of rubble which had once been a British base.

Next day we crossed the switchback pass into the Mahrat – the wadi which formed the heartland of Mahra country. I had never read any detailed description of the Mahrat, and its lushness came as a complete surprise. Here, hidden in the steppe-land beyond the Hadhramaut, was a second great water-system, where cool streams babbled across graded stones, marbled by light strained through the leaves of tangled palm-trees. Here was a tropical forest in the midst of nowhere. There were Bedu tents in the palmeries, but as we moved south, we sighted block-house castles rising from the stepped buttresses of the valley walls, overseeing with multiple eyes the running water, the knots of camels, the cultivated gardens and the date-groves. Evidently the Mahra here were unaccustomed to visitors, for a grown woman carrying firewood pelted away from the car, splashing wildly through the stream, losing both her plastic shoes but retaining the bundle on her head. Further on, two boys eyed us mistrustfully from the branches of a tree and one of them dropped down and rushed towards the nearest tower.

At sunset we made camp in sand on a curve in the wadi between deep groves of arak trees. A thickset old Mahri whose face resembled a weathered granite boulder, with crows' feet puddling in concentric rings from the corners of his eyes, approached us on foot, and willingly partook of our evening pasta. 'This part of the wadi is called the Kidyat,' he said, 'and it's divided between the Bayt Imani and the Mahra. They are mostly farmers. I've lived here and cultivated date-palms all my life.' I suddenly remembered the photo of Sulaim, and showed it to the Mahri, asking if it was indeed Sulaim bin Dumaysh, and whether he knew where to find the man. 'I know bin Dumaysh,' he told me. 'He was here in Kidyat only a few days ago, but he's gone to Oman. The border is closed, but that doesn't bother the Bedu. We put on Omani dish-dashas and just walk to Salalah, and say we're from Oman!'

'Do you think I will find bin Dumaysh in Salalah?' I inquired.

The old man beamed. 'God knows, you might,' he said, 'but it won't do you any good!'

'Why?'

'Because the man in the picture is not bin Dumaysh. That is a man called Sulaim bin Mayza. And he's been dead for twenty years!'

# 6

# Another Country,
# Long Ago

Salalah lies no more than 130 kilometres east of the Mahrat, on the shores of the Indian Ocean. The town is encircled by a hot, pebbled plain, and a little way inland the landscape buckles suddenly into a coronet of hills that, in summer, stand under a perpetual quilt of mist. It is only the mid-section of the range that draws this vital moisture, for the Dhofar mountains are fashioned like a saddle between two pommels, angled in such a way as to channel the monsoon directly to their centre point. The hills are rumpled gently like English downs, dun-coloured, sap-green, verdigris, a-bristle with grass, wrapped in jungle-thick thorn-bush, from which the trunks of monstrous fig-trees protrude like lengths of plaited cable. Between bights that interlock like soft, giant knuckles, canyons are incised sharply through strata of fluted files.

On a day near the end of the summer wet, a Bedui called Mohammad bin Saʿid and I picked our way down the side of one of these canyons. It was a time of milk and honey for the Bedu, and nomads of the seashores, the mountains, and the deserts had gathered in the gorges to feast their flocks on the last fruits of the monsoon. Below us, the farms of the mountain people, squatting low and flat against the rain, were encompassed by masses of dwarf cattle — dun-and-white, black-and-white, strawberry roan. Mohammad, wearing silver-rimmed spectacles and a studious look, climbed with surprising confidence into the abyss, with the hem of his dishdasha pulled up to reveal muscular legs. He was carrying a bundle of bedsheets tied to the stock of a heavy but beautifully made rifle, yoked across his shoulders like a stick. The track was very narrow – a ladder of boulders on a hillside of thick *macchia*, pitching along the side of the ravine. Where the *macchia* had not penetrated, there were stands of juniper and *tishga* scrub, and mats of mosses and wild yellow flowers. Mellow smells, monsoon smells, cattle smells, drifted up from the humid cleft below. On a clear day you could see the ocean from here, but now the sky was a rinse of vapour, soaking up the last pale fuel of the sun.

Mohammad halted at a flat place and sat down on his bundle. While we shared a cup of water, I inquired why he was carrying his rifle. 'First, because it's a tradition of the Bedu,' he said, 'and second because of the wild animals – leopards, hyenas, wolves, and foxes. Actually, there are hardly any wolves, hyenas, or leopards – it's the foxes I worry about, because they have rabies. We never had rabies here in the past – it arrived recently. When I was a boy I used to look after my family's goats in these valleys, and the thought of wolves and leopards used to frighten me to death. Well, there I was one day, six years old, and a wolf *did* carry off one of our kids. I shouted to my uncle, who was within hearing distance, 'A wolf is carrying off one of the kids!' and he shouted back, 'Chase it! Don't let it get away!' I thought the wolf would eat me, so do you know what I did? I just ran round and round a tree, yelling 'Stop! Stop!' so that my uncle would think I was chasing the wolf! In the end he fired a shot at it and it dropped the goat, which was injured in the throat. Another time, I can clearly remember my father shooting a leopard. He took the skin to the Wali in Salalah and got a reward.'

Mohammad had volunteered to act as my guide in the Dhofar hills, where I was searching not only for the Bedu, but also for the frankincense or *mughur* trees, which had once made Dhofar legendary. He had proved a charming, remarkably intelligent, and unusual companion: 'When things change, something is lost and something is gained,' he was fond of saying. 'Take me, for instance. I am a Bedui born in the desert. I speak both Arabic and the Jabali language as mother-tongues. For the first six years of my life I knew nothing but the desert and herding goats. Then there was the war here in Dhofar and my father was shot dead by the British forces – wrongly, because he wasn't even involved with the guerrillas. Afterwards, my uncle sent me to school. I did well, and ended up going to the University of Arizona to study electronic engineering. Now I'm due to study for my PhD. If the war in Dhofar hadn't happened – if no one had rebelled against Sultan Bin Taimur – then what would I have been? Still illiterate, herding goats in the desert?'

Mohammad's dignity and generosity gave the lie to any misplaced idea that education had somehow 'spoiled' the Bedu. And he himself was under no illusions about the traditional way of life: 'In some ways, perhaps, the lives of our forefathers were happier,' he told me, 'because although they were poor, they knew nothing else. But it was a happiness that came from ignorance, and there is no real nobility in ignorance, or poverty, or disease. Think of the human potential you lose when people can't read or write: when children die as babies, when people's life expectancy is only thirty-eight years!'

'Yes,' I answered, 'but isn't it more important to live those years intensely rather than to live twice as long in boredom?'

I recounted a story I had once heard, in which a pilot had landed his aircraft in the desert to take his lunch. As he was eating, a caravan of nomads had ridden past, and he discovered that both he and they were going to the same place. 'How long will it take you to get there?' he asked them. 'Seven days,' they replied, 'how long will it take you?' 'About half an hour!' 'Great God,' they said, 'but what on earth will you do with all the spare time?'

Mohammad laughed at the story, and then said without animosity, 'That story is nonsense, of course. It implies that the nomads were inferior to the pilot because they would have had less idea of what to do with their leisure than he did.'

'Well, wouldn't they?'

'Do you think we are less intelligent than Westerners? Having more leisure is an important thing because it frees people to use new bits of their mind – to study, to read, to create things, to develop themselves, to see other countries and other peoples. All the great inventions of the past – like cultivation and livestock-rearing – were made because people had the leisure to do it. People who are struggling to survive don't have the time to experiment with new ways. Western technology – the basis of Western supremacy – was only possible because people had the leisure to develop it. Again, it's human potential that is lost when people are condemned to struggle for their entire lives.'

After dark, the humid scents were replaced by the smell of woodsmoke, and campfires were bracelets of light spanning the hillsides. We strayed from the track and approached a fire where a Jehovah of a man with a shaggy grey beard, naked but for his loincloth, sat with his two children by a cattle-fold. The darkness held the odours of sour milk and manure. From some distance away Mohammad called out a greeting in Arabic, and the Jabali shouted back: 'What kind of people are you, that you don't come by the track?'

'We are strangers who don't know the way!' Mohammad said, as we emerged from the shadows. He began to speak in Qara – the ancient mountain language of south Arabia – an ooze of odd sibilants and emphatics. The old man led us on a little way in the darkness, ambling barefoot, and soon after we heard the moan of camels, the glimmer of several campfires, the sound of voices. We broke out of the darkness, and suddenly we were among a crowd of friendly, bearded men, clasping and releasing our hands, and passing us bowls of frothy camels' milk.

They sat us down on fibre mats in the midst of a great circle of camels. A wood fire crackled in the hearth, and the camels' heads bobbed around us like jack-in-the-boxes. The Bedu were wearing loincloths and *ghutras* and all of them had rifles and daggers. They rolled cigarettes of bitter tobacco, constantly replenishing the milk-bowls from milk-skins, everyone talking at the same time. Mohammad's elder brother, Mabruk, a narrow-faced man with a crop of stubble in place of a beard, hailed me in impeccable English: 'I used to work in a helicopter crew,' he said. 'Radio-operator. I was good – very good. I got commended for my work, and they even had me down for training as a pilot. But then I had a row with my boss. I suppose I have hot blood. Anyway, I couldn't see the point in it all. Money – big house, a nice car: what did it mean anyway? So I quit. They were really surprised when I left. "What are you going to do?" they asked me. "I am a Bedui," I said, "I'm going to herd my camels in the hills!" So here I am with my ten camels – this is me!'

'Do you think there's a future in herding camels?'

'Yes, but only if we diversify with sheep and goats and cultivation. In the past you were lucky if you had a camel. Now, everyone has hundreds, and it's a buyer's market, because we are overproducing. Nobody rides camels – except in the races – and people like mutton better than camel's meat. I don't see why the Bedu way of life should die out – I don't think it ever will, while there are animals to be herded. But like everything else, it's bound to change.'

Just then there was a commotion in the bushes, and some of the Bedu jumped up, flashing torches in whose beams, just for a moment, I glimpsed the glittering eyes of foxes. 'Shoot them! Shoot them!' someone yelled, but already the animals had disappeared into the night. Mohammad said that rabid foxes were emboldened by the disease, and had attacked several herders recently. The Bedu kept their eyes peeled and their rifles and torches close as they gathered once again around the fire. There were still a few leopards in these hills, they said, but not enough to pose a threat to their herds. It was difficult to be certain that they were really talking about leopards, though, for while Arabic possesses more than a hundred synonyms for 'lion', most of the lesser species of cat are lumped under the title *nimr* – literally 'leopard', but in practice anything from a cheetah to a caracal. The true leopard, *Panthera pardus*, is certainly to be found in the hills of Yemen and until recently ranged through the whole of western and southern Arabia.

A shy young man called Musallim sat down beside us and announced, to my amusement, that he was Mohammad's uncle, though he was evidently years younger. He added that he had just returned from Britain, where he had graduated in mechanical engineering from the University of Leeds: 'I liked Leeds,' he said, 'I was happy in England. I wouldn't mind going back there. The thing is that the Sultan's Special Forces sponsored me for a degree. The CO promised me that I wouldn't have to do the full selection-course – after all I would only be working in the workshop: I needed to know how to march and salute, perhaps, but not all that special training. Well, when I got back, I found that there was a new CO and the policy had changed. He wants me to do the full thing – running across the desert with a rucksack! I said, "No, by God! I'm not doing that: I'm an engineer! My father was killed in the Dhofar war, as a soldier of the government. He was searching a cave, when a booby-trap went off and blew him up. So much for being a foot-soldier! I don't want any of that, so I thought I'd herd my few camels up here until I find another job. But God, I feel homesick for England!'

It was pondering this totally unexpected expression of sentiment from a Bedui that I retired to my sleeping-bag.

At sunrise on a day two weeks earlier I had awoken on the express bus as it pulled into Salalah, with Muscat lying twelve hours behind me, across a thousand kilometres of desert steppe. A taxi had taken me to the Redan – a hotel on a busy thoroughfare, run by an efficient team of Indian Muslims from the Malabar coast. The town was very different from the ruined village set around a crumbling palace which the explorers Bertram Thomas and Wilfred Thesiger had found here in the 1930s and 40s – a geometry of right-angles in queues of flat-blocks, cinemas, supermarkets, ice-cream parlours and Coca-Cola bars. Yet the old Salalah lay like a phantom among the blocks. At the produce market – an octagon of shade under high arches – men were filling plastic bags with blade-shaped sardines straight out of the net, and bargaining over sharks, dogfish, catfish, squid, mullet and tuna. Women wearing unexpectedly vivid dresses and gold nose-rings were selling bottles of liquid butter, terracotta incense-burners, bags of frank-incense, varnished camel-sticks and balls of black goats' hair. Mahra tribesmen were sitting in the sun with headcloths tied around their knees, stroking Lee-Enfield rifles of 1940s vintage, wearing hooked daggers. There had been peace in Salalah since the civil war ended in 1976, but every tribesman still carried a rifle as a matter of course. Around the market there were light trucks full of strangely bald goats, and pick-ups laden with old she-camels bound for the butcher's block.

Despite the roar and honk of gleaming Land-Cruisers, Mit-subishis and BMWs that filled the streets in the afternoon, there remained along the Corniche an almost mesmeric sense of calm: coconut palms with heads like water cascading in the sunlight, cows and bullocks tethered in the shade, waterlogged fishing canoes hauled up out of the surf. As I walked there near sunset I saw whorls of blue cloud over the ocean, pricked by spalls of light igniting volcanic colours across the sky. An ancient Bedui with a beard like steel wire and a scrap of cloth around his head was walking through the wet sand at the sea's edge, balancing a rifle muzzle-forwards on his shoulder, towards a new palace of pol-ished marble walls and Moghul domes, where armed tribesmen in khaki dishdashas guarded the studded doors. The Bedui left a trail of perfect footprints behind him, but soon the old sea lobbed its rollers ever higher up the beach, erasing them for ever.

It was through the intervention of John Crowther – British Council representative in Salalah – that I was introduced to Mohammad bin Sa'id, who, over tea in the Redan, had told me the story of his life. I was concerned to know if he harboured any grudge against the British for the death of his father. 'It wasn't actually the British who murdered him,' he said, 'it was Baluch troops under British command. I still remember the day it happened. Some Baluch stopped my father and told him to leave his rifle and come towards them. As he did so they just shot him in cold blood. My uncle ran to help him and the soldiers ran away. My father was dead, of course. I have never liked the Baluch since then, but after all it was an individual, not a tribe or a people who killed him.'

'Isn't it the tribe that matters?'

'Of course. In the old days there would have been a blood-feud. But that's considered uncivilized now.'

I inquired how he had enjoyed his time in Arizona. 'I liked it,' he said. 'It's desert country similar to Dhofar, so in a way I felt at home. I didn't experience any real prejudice in America. People were friendly. I had more trouble from the Iranian Muslims than anyone else. I remember one Iranian student asking me if I believed in the Ayatollah Khomeini. "What do you mean, 'believe'?" I asked him. "That he is the Imam," he said. I told him that to me an Imam was just someone who led the prayers in any mosque. "Then you are not a Muslim!" he said. Can you imagine how angry that made me?'

Mohammad told me that he admired the West, but pitied Westerners for their spiritual poverty: 'There's no religion, really,' he said, 'there's a big religious gap in people's lives. The West needs something to fill this spiritual vacuum, and I think that Islam will eventually fill it.'

The following day, Mohammad had taken me in his Land-Cruiser to see an agricultural project created by his tribe, the famous Bayt Kathir. All morning we cruised on through the monotonously flat salt-plains of Jiddat al Harasis, a landscape of utter bleakness, unrelieved by trees, rocks or even sand-dunes. Shortly before noon, though, we saw patches of green standing out like an archipelago of islands in the emptiness. Here, at a watering-place known to the Bedu for 400 years, notorious for its remoteness, the wilderness had been turned green by giant water-screws that sprayed acres of wheat and clover and whole fields of water-melons. Pencil-cedars had been planted in interlocking squares as a shelter-belt, and within the perimeter were pens holding spare Dhofari cattle and slim white goats. A covey of hobbled camels moved haltingly through the stubble of a clover-field, and new incense-trees – brought as saplings from the Dhofar hills and carefully nurtured – were in full royal leaf. Pakistani, Egyptian and Indian workers were everywhere, moving amid coils of hose and stand-pipes like strange totems in the desert. A surprisingly tall and stringy Bedui called 'Ali spread a carpet for us by the cattle-pen and brought us buttermilk in enamel mugs, and a plate of fresh water-melon. He wore a ragged dishdasha, smoked cigarettes perpetually, and spoke with an abrupt, abrasive manner. 'You've got better cows than this in your country, I know,' he snapped. 'Yours bring you twenty-five litres of milk a day. These are poor things as far as milk goes, but your great clumping buffaloes would never stand the climate here! I know. I've tried them!'

I asked them if it wasn't something of a come-down for a Bedui to turn settled farmer. 'That's nonsense,' he said, shrugging with exaggerated irritation. 'This is the future for us. Diversification. We've got cattle, goats, camels, cash-crops and fodder. We're not waiting for the rains like they used to in the old days. We're not going to go hungry either – if God wills!'

On the way back to Salalah, we visited the ruin of Khor Ruri. It lay on a bay of black basalt boulders, enclosing mobile turquoise waters and shallow marshland where long-beaked terns and waders were basking in the sun. The ruins appeared to be no more than a formless pile of stones, the same size and colour as the basalt blocks around them, but closer up you could see the remains of standing walls which dated back to the time when this fortress, Sumhuram, guarded the harbour of Moscha, one of the richest and most significant incense-ports on the south Arabian coast.

Samhuram came to prominence late in the history of the spice-trade. An inscription discovered in the ruins reveals that it was built as a colony by King Ilazz of the Hadhramaut – almost 400 miles away – not much earlier than AD 100. Frankincense had flourished in large forests on the northern side of the Dhofar hills, and the settlement had been built as a handling depot for the spice. The spice-mongers of Moscha traded directly with merchant vessels which put in to the harbour, but also floated a large proportion of the crop on rafts made of inflated skins down the coast to Qanaᶜ – near modern Bir ᶜAli, in Yemen. From there it was shifted overland by camel-caravan to the key distribution-point at Shabwa. Some have surmised that, many centuries earlier, Dhofar was already trading with Solomon's legendary 'navy of Tharshish' – a fleet built for him by Hiram of Tyre – which returned from the fabled 'Land of Ophir' laden with 'gold and silver, ivory, apes and peacocks', after a voyage lasting eighteen months.

In the Redan that night, Mohammad suggested a trek in the Dhofar hills to find what remained of the sacred incense-trees on which the fame of legendary Ophir had been based.

The morning was a tumult of camels grunting and snarling among the trees, a honey-coloured sun rising over the crest of the forested spurs, and Mohammad's brother Mabruk – once a radio-operator – standing on one strut-like leg at the udder of a she-camel, spurting milk into a bowl in time-hallowed Bedu style. He offered the milk to me first: 'We get three litres from each camel morning and evening,' he said. 'Six litres a day. We hardly know what to do with it!'

The day was clear and as Mohammad and I climbed back up the valley we could see camel-herds fanning out across the lush green mountainside – rich mobs of four or five hundred fat beasts tended by walking Bedu, many shoeless, naked but for loincloths. As we crested the escarpment, a Qara tribesman called us over to drink milk. He was very dark, almost Ethiopian-looking, with grey, curled hair that hung in ringlets from beneath a headband of plaited leather. His loincloth was of a deep, rich purple, and he wore a very ornate, filigreed dagger in the folds of a shawl tied around his waist like a cummerbund. He selected a camel-mare with a bulging udder, strapped with cloth, and a calf a couple of weeks old. 'This is my best milker,' he commented. 'She gives me twenty-five litres a day sometimes, but I have to keep the calf near, or she won't let down her milk!' The she-camel squared up aggressively and growled like a male as the Bedui tried to move the calf. When the bowl was full, he presented it to Mohammad, who took it with both hands and crouched down to drink, following Bedouin etiquette.

By mid-morning the monsoon cloud had lifted and sunlight rolled down the valleys, ejecting the lees of mist from the ravines. As we trudged up the steep track we paused often to take in the miracle of this haven in the barren heart of Arabia. Farther on we halted at some corrugated-iron outbuildings, set in a mush of mud. This was a Bayt Kathir place, and we were greeted by yet another of Mohammad's relatives, a young man with a crop of curls and cow-dung behind his toes. An unveiled woman wearing a nose-ring was making buttermilk – shaking a great goatskin to and fro on a wooden tripod. A little boy with goblin features and large ears looked fearfully at my face and began to cry. The man milked a dwarf cow and brought two bowls of cows' milk, then stoked up the fire and placed several large pebbles in the ashes. When the stones were red-hot, he picked them up deftly with a makeshift pincer of sticks, and dropped them one by one into the first bowl of milk. He then poured half of the bubbling milk into the second bowl and beat it with a stick, whipping up a head of froth. He passed the first bowl to us and we drank in turn – the milk tasted slightly toasted, but delicious. The second bowl tasted of vanilla ice-cream – even better than the first. The woman watched us drinking and said something to Mohammad in Qara. He laughed and said in English: 'You know what she said? She asked me how I could drink from the same bowl as a Christian!'

'But surely that's not a problem, is it?'

'No, Muslims are permitted to eat or drink with Christians or Jews – and most of the Bedu wouldn't bother even to ask about religion. But some of these Jabalis – mountain people – are ignorant. I say that, even though they belong to my tribe, the Bayt

Kathir. Most of the Bayt Kathir live in the desert, but a few of them live in the mountains.'

I wondered how the Bayt Kathir would fare in Glubb's paradigm of the Bedu as the 'noble, camel-rearing tribes', for here was a people who reared more goats than camels, who ranged from the sands of the Empty Quarter to the hills of Dhofar, where some of them herded cattle. No one in Oman would dispute that they were 'true' Bedu, though.

Before we left our host made up for the woman's remark by giving us a bag of *janbet* – root-plants which looked like the wizened meat of large walnuts. The tribesman peeled several and handed them to me one by one. They tasted like a rather mature, nutty cheese.

It was already afternoon when we reached the northern side of the mountains where the monsoon-raised vegetation gave way to the raw carapace of the rock. There was no sudden transition from hill to desert: the limestone knolls grew smaller by degrees; deep fissures became shallow washes with frail walls; trees became sparse until there remained only isolated copses of stunted thorn. The Dhofar range began to unhinge in geometrical buttes – pyramids, cusps, and polygons. The *mughur* trees stood on a shallow dry-wash, talons of branches six metres high with tiny scrolled leaves and silvery trunks. Mohammad told me that the Bayt Kathir still culled the incense from them, and that the spice had a small market in Yemen and Oman. 'They only collect from a few of the best trees,' he said, 'and only in the hot season, when the sap flows best.' He ran his hand over the healed wounds on a horny trunk: 'They make an incision here,' he said, 'and peel back a bit of the bark. Then they come back in a week and there is a blob of *luban* (frankincense resin) on the bark, as big as a golf ball. It's still mostly the Bayt Kathir who harvest the *luban*, but the trees are owned by the Qara and a few by the Mahra.'

It was once believed that Dhofar had been the only source of frankincense in south Arabia, though a more careful reading of the classical geographers has revealed that trees of varying quality grew all the way between here and the Hadhramaut. The relatively late foundation of the spice-handling colony of Samhuram may suggest that the Hadhramis were scouring the land farther and farther east as demand outstripped supply. If so, then it may be that they had saved the best until last. The unique geographical conditions of the Dhofar range, with its moist-arid oscillation, its altitude, and its limestone soil, combined to make the frankincense of Dhofar – the so-called 'Sakhalitic incense' – among the most prized of all. In the time of Pliny the incense was produced here by a few families whose members were considered holy. The harvesting of the sacred gum was shrouded in ritual and taboo. While making the incisions, for instance, the harvesters were forbidden either to meet women or to take part in funeral processions. The frankincense was stored in caves in the Qara hills during the rainy season, when the south-west monsoon winds prevented any vessel from leaving the harbours, then shipped by camel down to the coast, where much of it was purchased wholesale by Indian merchants. India remained a substantial market for the spice up until recent times.

Next day we motored to Shisur, a line of neat miniature castles around a spring in a deep cleft in the rock. These bungalows – only recently completed and fitted with globe-lamps, flush toilets and air-coolers – were stranded in the midst of grey stone desert, the homes of the Bayt Musan, a Bedu tribe who drove their camels deep into the Empty Quarter in winter. We were invited to stay by a mischievous-looking man called Salih, who showed us a bed of soft sand outside his house, where we could sleep for the night, and after dark slaughtered two small goats for us.

After we had eaten, we were joined by six or seven Bedu, one of them an old man who recalled meeting Wilfred Thesiger on his first crossing of the Empty Quarter in 1946. 'They watered their camels here,' he told me. 'In those days it was hard work indeed to water your camels at Shisur, but it was necessary, because there was no other good water between here and Mugh-

shin.' In those days the Bedu had been obliged to crawl down between the sand and the overhanging rock, enter a cave, fill their
skins and drag them back thirty feet up to the surface. It had un-
doubtedly been back-breaking work. Now the sandbank had
been cleared away, revealing ancient cave-paintings of gazelles and
antelopes, and a few years earlier the government had built a
flight of steps down to the cave. More recently they had installed
an electric pump, which drew the water out at the touch of a
button to feed a small but promising garden of date-palms nearby.
'We still move into the Sands,' Salih said, 'but we use motor-
vehicles now. There's plenty of grazing in the Sands – much more
than there is here.'

I asked about the possibility of hiring some camels to make a
trek from here to Mughshin along the Umm al Hayt – the trunk
wadi which channelled the washes coming off the Dhofar mountains to the edge of the Sands. 'I'm ready to take you,' Salih said,
'but I will have to get time off from my job.'

'What *is* your job?'

'The *Firqat* – the militia. I don't actually have anything to do,
but I'm on call. I have to get permission for time off.'

'How much would you charge?'

'Fifty riyals a day,' Salih said.

'That's more than I'd pay for a motor-car and driver!'

'Well, you need at least three camels, and two Bedu. It's dangerous to make a journey by camel with less than three men.'

'And then there's the camel-feed,' a younger Bedui added.
'You would need a car to bring food and water for the camels.'

'The camels can live off the land, as they did in the old days,' I
said.

'That was the old days. The camels aren't used to it any more.
They are accustomed to drinking every day and eating properly.'

'Even so, a camel is a camel.'

'But we don't want them to lose condition. We like them fat!'

By now everyone was joining in excitedly. The idea seemed to
have whetted their imagination, engaging Bedu rhetoric to the

full, if only as a mental exercise. One old man began to take my part, pleading for me like an advocate: 'This is a poor man,' he said. 'He's got nothing. How can you charge so much? Come down a little!'

'No, I can't,' Salih said. 'It's the effort he has to pay for. I mean, we're not used to riding camels any longer. Why go anywhere by camel when you can go by car? We are accustomed to air-conditioning and cool drinks – no one wants to bother with riding camels these days. We don't see the point in it!'

I divined that Salih was not serious about a camel-trek, and even if he had been, what, indeed, would be the point of travelling by camel with a car to bring fodder and water every night?

'But isn't there a challenge in travelling by camel – I mean, without motor-cars?' I asked.

Salih looked at me for an instant with what I took to be in-comprehension, then a young, extraordinarily strong-looking Bedui with a thick black beard piped up. 'I know what he means,' he said. 'Remember when three of us set off from Thumrait to ride to Shisur on camels just to see what it was like? That's what he means!'

'Yes, that's exactly what I mean! How was it?'

'Terrible! We took only a small skin of water with us. It was summer and very very hot, and we finished the water quickly. Then we cursed our stupidity. Our fathers would have known, but we didn't. We came to a Bayt Musan tent where they fed us and gave us water and we forgot the problem of thirst. We set off again into the heat and within half an hour we were craving water again. At the tent they had given us a leg of goat, but we were so thirsty we couldn't eat it. We just threw it away into the sand. Then, of course, when we found water, we felt hungry, and we said, "By God, I wish we hadn't thrown that leg of goat away in the sand!" I suppose we thought riding camels would be like driv-ing a car – you'd just get on them and whoooosh – you'd be there! By the time we got to Shisur we were hungry, thirsty and so sore from riding we could hardly stand. I said, "Well, if that's what the lives of our fathers were like, you can keep it! From now on I go by car!"'

I joined the rest of them in their mirth, but I could not suppress a sense of sadness. The passing of old ways, old skills, was inevitably deplorable in hindsight, especially to those, like myself, who did not have to live by them for ever. 'You are no longer Bedu,' I said, laughing. 'You can't ride camels any more!'

'You're right,' the young man said. 'Many of the Bedu live in the city now – in Salalah or Thumrait, or they've gone to Abu Dhabi or Dubai. They get jobs, their children go to school. Already the Bedu are few. Soon they will disappear!'

'Rubbish!' Salih said. 'We are still camel-herders, and besides, it's not going to school or getting a job that makes you what you are.' He placed a hand over his heart. 'Being a Bedui is what you feel here!'

Salih invited me to visit his camels, and we drove out to Umm al Hayt, across grey gypsum flats and salt-licks that stained the smooth desert skin with crystalline white. Sand-coils of orange, several hundred feet high, were levitating above the skyline in platinum wrappers – the outer skirts of the Empty Quarter. The camel-herds were gathering in Umm al Hayt among broken tree-stumps and roots. Two Baluch herdsmen had made their beds inside a wire compound, where two week-old camel-calves – one black, the other white – were tethered to poles. A litter of squashed sardine-cans surrounded the ashes of a fire. One of the Baluch herders – who spoke passable Arabic, and was friendly to the point of obsequiousness – brought us camel's milk. His companion, a dark, silent man, observed us with hostile eyes. The previous night Salih had said, 'We are still herdsmen,' I reflected, but even this was not strictly true: the Bayt Musan had once been camel-herders, but were now camel-owners: the Baluch were, in a sense, the new 'Bedu' of Oman.

Salih insisted on taking us to a Bayt Musan tent, and we followed his Land-Cruiser down the soft wadi bed, passing a procession of camels marching in review order in search of grazing.

There were sand-plants in plenty here, and though the vegetation appeared long dead to me, Salih reported that it was acceptable pasture. Later, he showed us the smudged tracks of a Land-Cruiser straining suicidally to the summit of a sheer dune. 'That was me!' he declared smugly. 'Only the Bedu can drive in sand!'

The tent had been pitched on the salt-flats, outside the wadi. It was almost identical to the black tents of Syria and Jordan, divided by a screen into women's and men's sections, and surrounded by a barbed-wire fence. A small, canvas-covered 'kitchen-tent' stood outside. Inside there were rich carpets, piles of steel trunks, a huge radio/cassette-player, and a TV set attached to two twelve-volt car-batteries. It was occupied only by two women in black robes and purple masks — an old lady, and a plump, chirpy girl, who offered us cans of warm lemonade instead of camels' milk. 'English?' the old lady said, when Salih had introduced me properly. 'I remember the first Englishman who ever came here: Thomas. I was a little girl then. No such things as tents in those days, no, by Allah!' She broke off to ask me the time, then said excitedly to the younger woman: 'Switch the TV on! It's the racing!'

The girl flicked the switch and the screen blinked into life, filling the tent with images of dashing camels ridden by tiny boys in helmets and scarlet livery. The Bedu watched enthralled: 'They tie those boys on with rope,' the old lady said, 'and if the camel falls they often get killed!'

A fire was smouldering outside in the broken lid of a tin box filled with sand. Baluch herdsmen in knee-length shirts were feeding knots of camels, slitting open pink sacks of fodder manufactured in the town. Others were watering camels from a mobile tanker. Despite camel-racing on TV, despite motor-cars, despite affluence, these Bayt Musan were, at the very least, still here in the desert. There was, perhaps, no necessity for them to live this life: for the first time in their history, perhaps, they truly did so out of choice.

The bus to Muscat was full of Indians and Pakistani workers with cardboard suitcases tied up with string. The driver was a Filipino and the conductor Sudanese. An undernourished-looking Pakistani counted out his money into the hand of the Sudanese conductor, blinking hopelessly in the light. The Sudanese shook his head: the money was two riyals short. A tall young Omani in a spotlessly clean dishdasha, sitting next to me, delved into his pocket and handed the two riyals out languidly with scarcely a word. I was deeply touched by this simple act of generosity to a stranger.

The Dhofar hills passed behind us, then Thumrait. The solitary Jiddat al Harasis was a void of desert until we reached Izki, hours later, where the walls of the Akhdar range rose with unexpected grandeur out of the plains like tongues of blazing fire. Muscat was a battalion of halogen lights floating on a pool of darkness. From the bus-station at Qurn, I made my way to the Mina Hotel, near the waterfront at Muttrah.

Muscat is the most beautiful town on the Gulf. Its harbour is an almost perfect crescent under a fraternity of mountains as cold and arid as icebergs. On the Corniche restored Portuguese houses with windtraps and ornate balustrades harmonize with the contemporary architecture: a blend of Arab and Andalusian styles – Moresco arches, *mashrubat* windows, slit openings, white stucco. Everywhere water-wealth is flaunted with conspicuous boldness: water foaming out of giant tilted coffee-pots, tumbling out of water-jars, squirting out of fountain-jets, sizzling out of sprinklers on green lawns. Walking along the waterfront at Muttrah, I saw wooden sailing-vessels like caravels at anchor, and a shattered dhow half drowned in the shallows. Motor-vehicles hummed past, hooting at a Bedui in a shredded dishdasha who was riding a donkey defiantly along the Corniche, his head thrown back in proud disdain, white fingers of beard fluttering against his breast.

At the office of a hire-car company, I met an Anglo-Indian called Gerry, who was to motor me around northern Oman. Like thousands of other Asians, he had come to the Sultanate to make his fortune. He had been a professional musician in India, but had managed to scratch no more than a bare living. When he first arrived in Oman he had known nothing of driving. He had failed his driving test half a dozen times before obtaining his licence. Then he had worked as a van-driver, delivering frozen chickens for a cool-storage company, until – through someone else's perfidy – a load of chickens had gone missing, and he had taken the blame. Nevertheless, I liked Gerry. He was a pleasant man, full of preposterous claims and unexpected sensibilities. I explained that my plan was to cross the small coastal desert called the Wahiba Sands, and inquired if he had had any experience of desert driving. 'Oh yes, Sah,' he assured me, 'I am having plenty of experience of driving in the desert. I am driving many, many people in the desert. Don't you worry, Sah, I am knowing the desert very, very well.'

The next day we motored down to Minterib in the eastern part of the Sultanate, a sleepy town where palms bent the light into dapples, and blue water gurgled along the roadside in shallow troughs. Houses with walls the texture of cheese leaned on each other like exhausted combatants, and a broken water-pitcher lay in the street. A toothless old man was sitting in the dust in the shade of his wall: 'Eh? What's that?' he demanded when I asked him for directions. 'Going to the sands? Yes – just take this track – you'll get into the sands!'

We motored through a half-deserted village of scrapwood cabins, with camels and goats in pens of rusted wire, and women striding about in black robes and hawk masks. A sand-blasted two-seater Toyota pick-up passed us, coming in the opposite direction, driven by a black-bearded Arab who peered at us as he zoomed by. Within half an hour we were enclosed in swales of 100-foot jaguar-coloured dunes, riveted together by a rash of low scrub. A well-defined motor-track wove between the high sands for a while, but no sooner had it petered out than Gerry began to look worried. He edged the speed to 100 kph as if hoping to catch up with the lost track, and the vehicle began to bounce dangerously over ruts and slide unnervingly sideways on the flat.

'Gerry, please slow down!' I told him. 'Shouldn't you let some air out of the tyres?'

'Oh no, Sah! Quite unnecessary!' he said.

Gerry had brought a stock of cassette-tapes with him, and I quickly discovered that his idea of music was hardly sitars and classical Indian fugues: 'Cliff Richard, Engelbert Humperdinck – both Anglo-Indians!' he announced proudly. 'We've got music in the blood!' His tapes were lambada, country-and-western, slow rock. When we halted for an hour or so to investigate an interesting dune, I could hear the car stereo caterwauling at full volume from my place on its summit:

It's four in the morning and what's more the dawning
Just woke up a warning in me-eeee . . .

We trawled along for an hour or two until suddenly, ascending a sand-slope, the wheels started to spin. Gerry revved the engine recklessly, but let it stall. He twisted the starter, and the motor spluttered weakly and died. He twisted again. this time there wasn't even a splutter.

For a moment there was complete silence. Finally, he said, 'This should not have happened, Sah! But I'll get it fixed, Sah, I guarantee!'

He jumped out, lit a Gold Flake cigarette, and propped up the bonnet. I watched him tinkering with screws and cables.

'It is the clutch, Sah,' he declared at last. 'Something is wrong with the clutch.'

'Can you fix it?'

'Oh yes, Sah, I can fix it, I guarantee!'

He strode back and forth purposefully from cabin to engine for ten minutes, while I watched, impressed. Finally he paused, leaned on the front wing lighting another cigarette, and said, 'It is not the clutch, Sah.'

'What is it then?'

'It is the dynamo!'

But it wasn't the dynamo, either.

And already the sun was sinking behind the dunes, casting orbs of shadow into the narrow valleys between them. 'Why don't we try to bump-start it?' I suggested, digging into my poor store of strategies for stranded vehicles. 'Where's your shovel? We'll dig out the wheels!'

Gerry wagged his head sadly from side to side. 'I am not having a shovel, Sah,' he said.

'No one goes into the desert without a shovel,' I said. 'Didn't you tell me you'd driven plenty of people in this desert?'

'Not exactly *this* desert, Sah.'

'Which desert, then?'

'Well, actually, I am preferring to stay on the roads.'

'You mean you've never driven in the desert before?'

'Well, not exactly, Sah, no.'

To give Gerry his due, he did volunteer to walk off and look for help, though to me it seemed unwise to leave the vehicle. Instead we made camp, cooked up our supper, and waited for the morning.

Most of the night I lay awake straining for the sound of an engine. This desert might have been no more than a blot on the map of Arabia's Empty Quarter, which itself would have been swallowed whole, many times over, by the immensity of the Sahara. Yet the Wahiba Sands was still as large as Wales, and a dangerous enough wilderness to be stranded in with a useless motorcar. At first light I sat up to see the dune-crests peeking through gossamer mist that eddied around them like liquid. My sleeping-bag was so wet that the sand clung to it in globules. Light sliced through the ground-mist, carving it into smaller and smaller fragments until it disappeared and revealed the true contours of the dunes. For an hour afterwards it remained bitterly cold, then, all at once, the heat throbbed like timpani out of a sky whetted a perfect cobalt-blue.

Suddenly, I was certain I could hear something. At first it was no louder than the whine of a mosquito. I strained my ears again.

The whine was persistent, and it was growing perceptibly louder. I jumped to my feet and scanned the valley. Far in the distance a black comma was clearly visible under a tailback of dust.

The vehicle came directly towards us. When it was a stone's throw away, I recognized it as the same antique, sand-scarred Land-Cruiser pick-up that had passed us the day before, just after we had left Minterib. At the wheel was the same gnarled, black-bearded Bedui. The Toyota creaked to a halt and the Bedui leaned casually out at us. 'All is well, *Inshallah*?' he said.

'Yes, all is well, except our car won't start. Could you help us?'

The man stepped out of his vehicle. He was about my own age, a jaunty figure in a stained mustard-toned dishdasha, with hands and feet that looked over-large for the body, like a Mannerist sculpture. His nose was long and hooked at the end and his eyes were very alert. He shook hands and told us that he was Zaayid of the Wahiba, the largest and most famous Bedu tribe in eastern Oman. He opened up the bonnet of our car, inspected the engine, then leapt into the driver's seat and tried to start it. 'The battery is flat,' he declared. 'Someone must have left the key switched to ignition while the car was at a standstill!'

Within minutes Zaayid had expertly changed his battery for ours, and at the first turn the engine exploded magically into life again. The Bedui trotted around the vehicle letting squits of air out of each tyre. Then he took the wheel while Gerry and I heaved the motor-car out of its pit of sand. Afterwards Zaayid said, 'You have been lucky. Very few cars use this route. And praise be to God you didn't start walking – there is no village in that direction for a hundred and fifty kilometres. My place lies an hour away, over there,' he pointed, using both hands. 'You are welcome to come to my tent, rest, eat and stay with us – just follow me!'

For sixty minutes Zaayid handled his car with the consummate skill of a rally-driver, picking invisible paths through the dunes, vaulting over sand-humps, wrestling with drum-sand. Often he had to wait for us to catch up, and several times he took the wheel from Gerry when our car became bogged down. As he scurried

back to his own vehicle, Gerry would gaze after him in ad-
miration.

'This man is Bedu, Sah,' he said. 'They are very famous for
their driving in the desert!'

Only a generation ago, I reflected, the Wahiba had known
nothing but camels, and for centuries they had been distinguished
by their camel-skills. Yet within only a few decades they had
adapted to the motor-car and become equally distinguished for
their desert driving. One technology had merely given way to
another here, but the new technology had not destroyed them:
the Bedu continued to be defined by this wild landscape of which
they remained the masters.

Soon we halted outside a 'tent' which stood on a sandy stump
among a seam of *ghaf* and arak trees. I had been expecting the
traditional black tent of the Arabian Bedu: instead, I found a
shanty timber shelter with a canvas roof surrounded by a heavy
iron fence with a hinged gate. Outside, long-haired goats snuffled
among the *ghaf* bushes and there was a single bull-camel, foot-
hobbled and tethered to a tree. On a breeze-block platform stood
a massive water-tank with a rubber hose, and nearby three or four
oil-drums containing petrol. The sand around the camp was littered with the familiar crushed soft-drinks cans, discarded oil-tins,
plastic wrappers, bits of engines, perforated cylinders and a rusty
giant gas-ring from a cooker.

Under the canvas awning, though, it was cool and pleasant.
Light filtered in through coloured cloth that had been stretched
across the back of the tent, and we sat on a hand-woven rug
against embroidered cushions. A mirror hung on one cloth wall,
next to hand-tooled saddlebags of leather. Zaayid introduced us
to his wife, a buxom woman, wearing a *burqa* with a curious ridge
dividing the face. Two little boys clung to her skirts, staring at us
with large brown eyes ringed with kohl. They were dressed in
tiny dishdashas, and wore amulets against the evil eye around their
necks in cube-shaped pouches.

Zaayid's wife brought in a mass of sticky dates, a giant vacuum

flask of tea, and a pot of coffee. Zaayid poured the coffee, a spoon-
ful at a time, in the traditional egg-cup-shaped bowls. It was
strong and bitter and spiced with ginger. He continued to refill
our cups until we shook them from side to side to signify that we
were satisfied. Afterwards he asked if I would like a ride on his
camel, and when I agreed he began rummaging about in the recesses of the tent for the necessary gear. 'I'm sure I had an old
riding-saddle here,' he said. 'We do ride camels from time to time,
but only for short journeys. For any important journey we go by
car. When I passed you yesterday I was on my way to Minterib to
get some medicine for my wife. That journey would have taken
about four days by camel.'

Later, Zaayid couched his bull-camel next to his Land-Cruiser.
As he went about strapping the saddle to the camel's rear, I asked
him how the Wahiba derived their income.

'The work of the Bedu is rearing goats and camels, just as it was
for our fathers and grandfathers,' he said.

'So the Bedu aren't only those who rear camels?'

'Maybe they say that in Saudi Arabia, but not here. Anyway, we
could have houses in the town, but we decided to stay in the
desert with our goats and a few camels. Now, when you get old,
or if you are sick, the government gives you money, but not if you
are young and strong. I worked for five years in Dubai as a soldier
in the Defence Force, and another five years in Abu Dhabi. They
are good countries, but not as good as Oman.'

The work of saddling was over in a moment: the saddle was, in
fact, not the double-poled saddle of Jordan and Syria, but the
more primitive south Arabian saddle, the *rahl* – the simple pad
fixed behind the camel's hump. I sprang aboard and the camel
gurgled in annoyance and rose to its feet. It was evidently unaccustomed to being ridden, for it twisted and wormed its head as
I took the headrope. Finally, I jumped down into the sand. 'I think
I'll walk!' I said.

A sweeping valley opened before us – flat, hard sand rising
slowly up to low folds of dunes, pocked with calf-high vegetation

and the occasional grove of trees outlined against the sky like parasols. We passed a well, where salty water was being pumped up by an electric motor. Zaayid pointed proudly at the green strips the Bedu had planted with melons and cucumbers.

A little farther on he halted abruptly and called me over to look at a series of sliver-marks in the sand. 'Don't move,' he ordered me. 'Hold the camel!' I watched him as he followed the tracks for a few yards with extreme caution, holding his stick ready. He raised the club slowly, then with incredible speed and force he smashed down at something hidden behind a hump of sand. He took a step closer and whacked down just twice more. Then he looked up triumphantly and beckoned me forward to see the mutilated coils of a puff-adder. 'Very dangerous!' he said. 'You can tell an adder from its tracks, just as you can tell a scorpion.' As we walked on, he drew my attention to some asymmetrical puncture-marks in the sand. 'That is a scorpion,' he said. 'His track is ragged, not clean like a beetle. Scorpions are very dangerous too. Sometimes their sting is fatal, sometimes not.'

Soon we came to another scrapwood and canvas shelter, where an old man with a face like a gargoyle was sitting in the shade of a tree. He was as thin as a cadaver, his features accentuated by their angularity. Pure grey locks fell from beneath his tight headcloth, and a spiral of beard sprang from his chin. He rose to greet us, his eyes glinting almost demonically in the sun, and tattled with laughter as I spoke to him in Arabic. He was wearing thick, ankle-length socks, almost as stiff as boots, woven from layers of black goats' hair. He noticed my interest in them: 'They stop the scorpions and the snakes,' he said, 'and they're good in the hot sand.'

Presently two youths appeared, wearing rust-coloured dishdashas. One of them carried a heavy air-rifle, the other a platter of chicken and rice, which he set before us. 'Come on!' the old man said. 'Eat! Eat!' And we crouched around the platter in the sand. The eating was a serious business, during which conversation was suspended. Afterwards, as the Bedu cleaned their hands in the sand, I asked the old man if times were better before there were cars. 'Ah!' he replied. 'Cars are so good! There's nothing like a car!' He pointed to the steel water-tank that stood next to his tent. 'We have drinking-water now, brought by car. Nothing like that in the old days. We had to bring it by camel, and it was always salty.' He nodded at two youths, busy cleaning the air-rifle. 'They go to school, now,' he said. 'They can read and write. Not like us. They go to school in Minterib. Couldn't do it if we had no cars. If one of us is sick, we can get medicine from the town. Couldn't do that in the past. All we had to cure sickness was camel's urine or a branding-iron. All nonsense! Children used to die and women used to die in childbirth. Now we can take them to hospital in a car. Camels are fine for riding short distances or for racing or for milk. Cars are wonderful. There is nothing like a car!'

Next morning Zaayid guided us across a sweeping sea of sand washing against purple table-tops, across acres of sand-scoops with thick veins of panicum grass and *ghaf* trees. Wahiba camps were sited on the dune-crests, flat-topped shelters of cotton spaced out one or two kilometres apart, surrounded by oil-drums and parades of sheep and goats. There were about 3,000 of the Wahiba living in these sands, making this tribe a tiny one in comparison with the vast tribes of Syria and the Nejd. In south Arabia, it has probably never been true that the Bedu tribes dominated the settled people, for they were always too small and weak. In north-eastern Oman, power lay in the mountains, which until the Islamic invasions were inhabited by Persians. Soon the dunes merged with hard shoulders of gravel boiling beneath the tyres and smoking behind the vehicle in trails of fine dust. Once, Zaayid waved excitedly and pointed north. Leaping through the low scrub were the lithe outlines of three Dorcas gazelles.

Zaayid parted from us at Hajjar, and for several days we pressed on across the stark Jiddat al Harasis. While the Wahiba had elected to remain in their fertile desert, the Harasis had withdrawn from these raw salt-plains for richer climes. I had searched southern Arabia for the spirit of the Bedu that had once lit the landscape like a flame, and everywhere I had encountered change. In places that spirit still hung on tenaciously, despite everything, but not here in the Jiddat al Harasis. Here the landscape was vacant, naked, meaningless, bereft of the people who had survived upon its scant resources for generations. True, there is no nobility in ignorance, poverty or disease. And yet those people – irrational, and superstitious perhaps – had had a sense of belonging in this unfathomed universe which we rational people will never know. At Marmul, I saw half a hundred steel pumps, like horse-flies, bleeding crude oil from the desert, acrid gas-flares trailing smoke from their chimneys like flags. Once, where these oil-rigs now stood, the Bedu had stayed alive by squeezing the dew out of rags left on bushes overnight. But that was in another country, long ago.

# 7

# Miracles and Wonders

Our caravan departed at first light from a stony place near Mersa Matruh on the sea the ancient Egyptians called the 'Great Green': five camels – three male, two female – a Bedouin called Selmi, and myself, an Englishman. It was a crisp winter morning. The camels shivered as they marched, and their nostrils steamed like steam trains. They picked their way painfully through the stones, occasionally gasping as a sharp one prodded their soft-shod hooves. The smells were of camels, sea-salt, and the chalk and dust scent of the desert. Matruh – Paraetonium to the ancient Greeks – stood like a single whitewashed citadel on the edge of the plain, below a great slice of turquoise sea. The sky was heavy with foam-heads that waltzed across the horizon like dancing dwarfs and anthropomorphic elephants puffing smoke.

The landscape warped into deep gorges, where the local Bedu had built water-terraces to harvest the winter rains. Fig-trees and olives bristled there like green islands in a pastel sea of stone. The Bedu farms were dotted across the plain, flat-roofed dwellings of white gypsum blocks with fluffball sheep in pens of rusty oil-drums, and bony cattle tied to stakes outside. The ground was prickled with calf-high brush, and littered with mother-of-pearl snail-shells. This was the plateau of Marmarica or Al Duffa – a grey isthmus dividing the Great Sand Sea from the Mediterranean. Eight days' march before us lay Siwa oasis, standing at the foot of the plateau, the gateway to an alien world.

It is the very alienness of this desert that thrills me. I might have been born too early to explore Mars or Venus, but travelling on foot in this part of Sahara is an acceptable substitute. It has the loneliness of a primeval planet, where the very remoteness imposes a self-reliance meaningless in our automated landscape. For me, born on an overcrowded island on an overcrowded planet, where most life is sucked into the pullulating cities, the feeling of being able to walk for thirty days – even fifty days – without encountering a soul, a track or even a motor-car is a very special privilege indeed.

The desert may not constitute what northern Europeans have come to regard as beauty. But those who have known it have rarely returned untouched by its magic. Veteran explorer James Wellard wrote of 'An awareness of silence such as is never heard outside the real desert, neither in the mountains nor in the sea; a sense of timelessness that transcends even the sense of mortality; and a glimpse of the mystery of life in its most primeval form.'

To the earth's young civilizations the desert's great silence was awe-ful. The ancient Egyptians feared the Sahara. Their universe was a balance of matching opposites – life and death, night and day, light and darkness, the homely Black Land of the Nile Valley against the sinister Red Land of the desert. The Red Land was Ament – the country of the Dead. Out there lurked the unspeakable evil – the aardvark-headed demon Set, who ripped himself out of the belly of the great Sky-Cow Nut. It was Set who murdered his brother, Osiris, tearing his body into many pieces and scattering them through Egypt. It was Set who raped his nephew, the falcon-headed Horus. Set rode astride the desert's elemental forces, brewing up monstrous typhoons in the earth's bowels, sending the pestilence, drought, famine, the thunder, the lightning, the dust-choked wind.

The ancient Greeks, who made their first landfall in North Africa on Seal Island in 639 BC, regarded the desert as the den of the dreadful gorgon Medusa, whose look turned everything to stone. Perhaps this belief was nurtured by tales of petrified trees and fossilized animals. Medusa was a dark female entity from a lost era – one of a race of stone-age Old Gods that in Greek mythology were to be banished by iron-wielding heroes like Perseus. The Greeks were a sea-roving folk who had little interest in the desert's interior, inhabited as it was by savage tribes they called 'Libyans'.

To these ancient Libyans, Medusa was a symbol of the creative and destructive powers of the earth. She was the Earth Mother, possessing the undying power of the serpent that was able to slough its skin and continually renew itself. Far earlier, in the mists of prehistory, the Libyan tribes had conceived of nature's unifying spirit as a ram or cow holding the sun between its horns. Adopted later by the ancient Egyptians, the solar disc assumed profound significance as an image of the wholeness of life. For the Libyans each feature of the earth, each tree, spring, well, hill, wadi, stone or stream had its hidden spirit – each an aspect of the Earth Mother's power. It is these spirits which linger on in the deserts of the Middle East and North Africa as Jinns. Jinns may enter a man's head and possess him permanently. Their voices may be heard in the howling of the wind, the rumbling of the sands, the rasping of stones. A Jinn may call to you from behind a rock: if you answer you will be dead within a year. A Jinn may properly be seen only in a dream, unless it assumes the form of a ghoul – half human, half animal, with donkey's feet.

The Fellahin of the Nile Valley have inherited their ancestors' fears of the desert and its Jinns. W. S. Blackman has written: 'The vast solitudes of the deserts are terrifying to the country folk, most of whom, up to the present day, cannot be induced to traverse even the lower fringes of these wastes after sunset. Fear of hyenas and still more, fear of ʿAfarit (Jinns), forbids any man to venture beyond the cultivation at night.'

Below us a chasm loomed unexpectedly – steep sides lined with pointed stones like gorgon's teeth. I held the camels while Selmi shimmied among the slabs and pinnacles in search of a way down.

I waited, and my smoky breath mingled with that of the camels which were shifting and nuzzling each other's noses. Soon Selmi reappeared, a slim, graceful figure in his flowing jallabiyya. 'What do you think?' I asked.

'If God wills, we'll get down.'

We manoeuvred the snorting, trembling camels down, and suddenly a bloated sun plopped up miraculously from beneath the skyline, spreading a layer of molten light among the rain-heads. I saw the strange reptile crania of the camels outlined in a sheen of light, and then the sun vaulted into the saddle of my lead camel, Shaylan. For a split second it seemed to balance there, the animal bracing himself against its weight. Ancient Libyan rams had carried it, the Egyptian bull had worn it between its horns. Now it was the camel's turn. Down in the desert's depths, there still resonated the gorgon's song: 'I am the Sun that rose from the Primeval water. My Soul is God. I am creator of the Word.' Selmi followed my eye to the camel's back and for an instant his face was illuminated in wonder as Shaylan carried down his titanic burden.

For eight days Selmi and I marched across an endless flat black plain, where the horizons never flinched or flickered. The camels dragged their feet through crops of angular stones that glittered like rubies in the light of the lowering sun. The sky was leaden with moisture and the clouds furled and billowed like the sails of schooners. Each night we borrowed a piece of the earth – a little bit of Gaia – and furnished it with our familiar surroundings – saddles, jerrycans, panniers and firehearth, and for a few hours it became our own place, a cell of life on the eternal plains. Walking away from this spot at night, it appeared no more than a blemish on the earth's face, and farther away still it was swallowed by the darkness. Then for a moment I could savour the desert's vast silence, truly alone.

In the morning, when we had hoisted our mobile world once more on camel-back, the place reverted to the wilderness it always was. Only a hearth and ashes would tell of our passing.

For the first fresh hours we would walk, leading the camels or letting them wander before us. Walking at camel's pace, occasionally exchanging a few words, more often drinking in the emptiness of the surroundings, we could read the planet's surface like musical notation. Here were the traces of a shepherd's nightly camp: the scuff of sheep-tracks, the shallow depression where the man had lain down, the stumps of the roots he had used for fire. There were the tracks of a renegade she-camel, and there the dog-like prints of a Ruppell's sand fox. There were the tail-slithers of a sand fish, and the crisp nicks of an Anderson's gerbil. There were whole galaxies of the mother-of-pearl shells belonging to the unique edible snail of Marmarica that Bedu children had once collected by the bucketful.

Occasionally we crossed alkali-flats, ovoids of scarlet earth fractured into an intricate tortoiseshell pattern that appeared to glisten with a film of moisture. Once, I reached down to touch the liquid, but like much else in the desert it was an illusion, created by the play of sunbeams on a trillion trillion salt crystals that laminated its surface. Selmi chuckled as he watched me. 'The Devil's mirror!' he said.

To live and survive in the desert, one has to learn the desert's grammar – the syntax of the wind, stones, plants and animals. It is the language of thirst, and all around you see the pressures of moisture conservation. Plants mostly hug the ground and have contrived various tricks for cutting down transpiration. Their leaves are small and sometimes waxy, often able to curl up in the heat to reduce the surface area. They are widely scattered and push down long roots towards the water-table. Some of them – like the desert melon – store up water in succulent organs.

The Great Egyptian jerboa – *Jaculus orientalis* – is an essay in the literature of water-stress. Kangaroo-shaped with huge eyes and ears and sand-coloured fur, it can clear six feet at a bound, reducing contact with the burning sand. It is mostly nocturnal, though, curling up under its long ears during the day in a cool subterranean nest stoppered with sand. *Jaculus* never drinks, but can metabolize liquid from dry plant matter. In 1930, explorer Ralph Bagnold encountered a *Jaculus* colony in the Egyptian Sahara, in a region as lifeless as the moon. 'No vegetation, dead or alive, had been met for the last 220 miles,' he wrote, 'nor was any seen until we reached ['Uwaynat] 200 miles further on. Yet a colony of jerboa kept us awake by hopping over our faces at night . . . What do they live on? Surely nothing but sand!'

The camel itself is a seminar in the process of water-conservation. It does not store water in its hump, of course, but rather uses its reserves with extreme parsimony. Under normal circumstances – when not being ridden fast or heavily laden – it will not begin to sweat at temperatures less than 40°C. It excretes very concentrated urine – less than a litre per day. Its large body – relatively fatless but for the hump – is a natural radiator that dispels excess body heat without losing water. The Bedu cannot do this, but instead they use the camel's unique qualities to export the water they need into the emptiness in skins or jerrycans. Waterskins are artefacts of great antiquity in the deserts of the Middle East and the Sahara. They have stood the test of time. They keep the water cool by evaporation but lose it by the same process. In this moistureless desert, the advance of the dreaded Ghibli can deplete waterskins with awesome speed. Selmi's Bedu still carried a few skins for the sake of coolness, but several near-encounters with death by thirst had led them to adopt the plastic jerrycan. They used the ten-litre jerrycan, which was easier to carry than larger ones and lost only a trifling amount if smashed by accident. Each of our camels carried four of them and we had our two skins as well. This 200-odd litres would keep us going for at least two weeks.

On the bed of another alkali–flat, Selmi discovered some heavy pieces of red pottery – clumsy sherds that looked as if they had been modelled by hand. He fitted together the two halves of a handle thoughtfully. 'Not the kind of pottery the Bedu use,' he said. 'It probably belonged to the Romans. We find their old houses sometimes.' 'Romans' was Selmi's codeword for the great blank page of the past. For him there was no distant past, only a hodge-podge of tribal legends and stories of raids and heroes. G. W. Murray wrote perceptively that 'The Arab looks at the desert much as the mathematician looks at his space-time continuum.' This is a view with much to be said for it. Often I felt we were not really alone here, but part of a continuing migration of souls across millennia. There were others walking beside us, divided from us only by the flimsy membranes of created time – an invention of civilization. Sometimes, walking silently in desert like this, I actually sensed the presence of someone else. I imagined footfalls behind me, mournful voices aching across the emptiness. Jinns, perhaps, but I was reminded of Eliot's famous lines from *The Waste Land* – the ones about the hooded figure in brown who is always walking alongside.

The Bedu are figures out of myth and folklore for Westerners, but in reality they are no more than ordinary men and women who have learned the lessons of the desert. These lessons are open to anyone with the humility to learn. People of almost every variety of race have adapted to the desert's harsh ministry, and enough adventurous Westerners – ordinary men and women – have survived T. E. Lawrence's 'death in life' to prove his statement mistaken. The Awlad ʿAli – the Bedu of this plateau – for instance, reckon part of their ancestry back to a Greek sailor who was cast up like Robinson Crusoe on the Mediterranean shore. If Selmi and I had walked here only thirty years ago, we would have seen their camels' hair tents pitched in basins around the deep rock cisterns the Romans built. We would have seen whole families on the move – convoys of camels carrying stowed-down tents, bloated waterbags, packs of firewood, braziers and cauldrons, urns and skillets, bedrolls, bundles, scrips and coffers, ropes, hobbles, bridles and halters, and women and infants rolling with the pitch of their litters. We would have seen tailbacks of dust trailing after mobs of loose camels and clowders of goats and sheep, driven by men riding lean stallions, cowled against the dust and carrying spears and antique rifles across their pommels. These were the

Bedu Lawrence Durrell described as 'tall, lean men, made of brown paper, whose voices cracked at the edges of meaning with thirst, and whose laughter was like fury unleashed'.

They hustled their livestock from the green hills of Cyrenaica to the gates of Alexandria – which until 1843 were shut nightly against them – straddling the caravan route that hugged the sea-coast. They scoured a living from the bitter soil, yoking their camels to the plough and sowing barley in the clay hollows in autumn, from which they reaped a good crop once every five or six years. Much of the crop – incidentally – ended up in the brew-eries of Burton-on-Trent, where it became English ale. They buried their seeds for the following year in secret caches and bar-tered the remainder for maize, honey, and dried dates in the Delta. In winter they netted quail on the beaches, and tracked down fennecs, jerboas, and sand fish in the desert. Women and children collected snails and sniffed out truffles to vary their diet of cheese, milk and unleavened bread. They also plundered caravans and robbed travellers, and had built up a profitable trade running hash-ish. Always feared by the Delta Fellahin, they were described in 1929 by G. E. Simpson: 'The presence of these desert wanderers near a village was always a source of anxiety as they may be hostile or more probably robbers . . . They pitch their tents where they choose, and at no time will they submit to any laws except their own.'

Though the Bedu of Marmarica once sneered at those who took up settled farming, 'losing caste among their kind for giving up the free, lawless life of the desert', as Simpson put it, the grand-children of these same wanderers were now settled in the gypsum-block farms we had seen around Mersa Matruh. The few shepherds we had met marshalling woolly sheep on the edges of the coastal plain were the remnants of a people whose way of life was gone for ever. But their spirits lingered.

One evening, not long before sunset, we sighted a steel skeleton in the far distance, with a winking red eye. It was evidently miles away, yet our gaze was drawn to it. For days, since leaving the coastal plain, we had been entirely alone. Now there was a different focus of life on the bleak landscape, and our perspective was turned inside out. But the desert was too vast to be dwarfed by a steel mosquito, and the surreal, timeless feeling I had acquired on the journey remained. It was as if we were part of a science-fiction scenario. It was an oil-derrick — a tiny colony on a hostile planet, in which there would be crewmen in hard hats drinking beer in a thermostatically controlled environment, with freezers and moisture-seals, and all the paraphernalia of an outstation on Mars. We were the Martians — primitive beings stalking the lifeless peneplains with our pack-animals, suspiciously skirting these visitors from the stars.

The desert here was suddenly churned up by caterpillar tracks that looked as alien as if they had been made by robot-remotes. There were inexplicable impressions of oblongs and squares. Neither Selmi nor I could figure out what had made them. There were roadways marked out by wooden pegs, which with the disregard of barbarians we collected as priceless firewood. The downing sun illuminated a caravan of smoky clouds that migrated across the horizon. We stopped and unloaded the camels, heaving the panniers into a protective wall, setting out our rugs, saddles and jerrycans. Each item had its own prearranged place, and we laboured in silence. A few days had been all it took to work out roles. Selmi doled out grain in the camels' nose-bags, and I stood on guard with my stick as the hobbled animals made grasshopper lurches towards him. With the nose-bags hanging from their snouts they looked like weird Bosch monsters with truncated heads. Selmi lit the fire. I cooked pasta with bully-beef washed down with tea. Afterwards there were our pipes: the comforting gurgle of Selmi's portable hubble-bubble, the scent of honey-tobacco.

It was pitch dark but for that intrusive winking red eye, ruining our sense of aloneness. 'I don't like those things,' I said.

'Why not?'

'They destroy what you feel in the desert.'

'They don't destroy what I feel. They're only doing what my people do. We collect rock-salt. They drill for oil. What's the difference?'

There was justice in his argument. It was only a question of degree. Selmi's Bedu might quarry rock-salt for millennia and not appreciably change the face of the earth. But oil spelt cars and engines, roadways, asphalt and effluent: it meant snarling up the wilderness with human imprints, turning a pristine landscape into a building-site. Roads and engines brought sprawling breeze-block civilization into the last wild lands. But it was futile to argue about change. Change was the only constant in this universe. And the very ground we were sitting on, this desert where the units of history seemed to have no meaning, had been a vital proving-ground for the human race, a veritable laboratory of change.

It is clear now that the ghosts which inhabit this desert land-scape are very ancient ones indeed, yet the antiquity of human activity here was hardly even suspected until, in 1930, prehistorian Gertrude Caton-Thompson and her geologist colleague Elinor Gardner began their excavations in Kharja. On the floor of the oasis depression they noticed a number of crater-like mounds with concave tops, packed by three-foot-thick plugs of sand-rock. Neither Caton-Thompson nor Gardner had ever come across their like before.

Slicing into one of the mounds to a depth of twenty-five feet, they were confronted by yet another geological enigma. The intestines of the mound were layered with alternate strata of clay, loam and silver-grey sand that appeared to have been violently disturbed and faulted. Yet the mounds stood high above the oasis bed and still higher above the water-bearing bedrock. 'By degrees,' Caton-Thompson recalled, 'it became clear that the [deposits] had been laid down by a spring of remote age, long ago dead or "fossil".' Slowly, the excavators began to grasp the monumental significance of their discovery. The layers of loam and clay had been built up during periods when the Sahara was far wetter and greener than it is today and the sand deposits marked the hyper-arid eras that had separated them. The Sahara had been green, not just once, but a number of times. In between the wet periods, drifting dunes had covered the valley, and the desert winds had scoured down the surface like an abrasive brush, leaving the spring deposits high and dry. Here, in the bowels of these curious mounds, written in dust and dirt, the biography of a living desert was laid bare.

Between 1930 and 1932, Caton-Thompson and Gardner eviscerated six such fossil springs, making a series of exciting finds. Cemented into the sediments, they discovered very ancient stone tools of the type known as 'Acheulean' – dating back at least 200,000 years. During a rainy period called the 'Abbassia Pluvial', the makers of these stone tools – not yet modern humans but a transitional phase between Neanderthals and *Homo erectus* – had wandered the prairies of the Sahara hunting big game animals such as elephant and buffalo. In the summer months they had retired to the lush verdancy of the oasis, subsisting on wild fruits, roots and berries.

The Acheuleans' art of hand-axe making was a technique that had survived unchanged for more than a million years. When you hold such a hand-axe in your palm, feeling the fine symmetry of its opposing convex faces and the intricacy of its knuckled surface, you suddenly become aware of the sense of beauty, balance and proportion that existed in an almost-human mind perhaps 2,000 centuries ago. Taking a hunk of chert or sandstone, the toolmaker would strike flakes from it with a stone hammer. When the core assumed roughly the right size and shape, he would trim round the edges with a piece of horn or bone, knapping off ever smaller flakes until he had produced a boat-shaped core with a long axis. The hand-axe, also called the biface, represents a combination of several ideas, and is a triumph of technical achievement. The Acheulean peoples of the Sahara also produced fine cleavers, choppers and scrapers; lacking the arrow and the stone-tipped spear, though, they probably drove or lured their prey into game-pits, where they slaughtered it with fire-hardened sticks. That they were efficient hunters is apparent from the vast period over which their tools remained unchanged. In the Sahara, though, about 90,000 years ago, they disappeared.

They were replaced by new men with a new technology which at the time was as superior to theirs as the helicopter gun-ship to the club. While the old Acheuleans had merely sculpted their stone cores into the required shape, these new men – the Aterians – learned to use the flakes struck off the core. This method – a small step in retrospect, but a giant leap for human culture – enabled them to produce light, sharp blades of predictable size. So light and finely tanged were they, the Aterians discovered, that they could be gummed or lashed to a wooden shaft. So the arrow and the stone-tipped spear were born.

It took a million years for the Acheulean hand-axe to become the Aterian spear-point, but technical evolution now seems to rush beyond our understanding at the speed of light, leaving us without anchor in a malevolent cosmos. To deal with this Niagara of change, we must develop a time-sense beyond our immediate perspective – we must be aware that tomorrow's history is today. Our industrial age is nothing, not even a blip on the screen of time – 70,000 million hunter-gatherers walked the earth before our era. And the Acheuleans were late-comers on the scene. There are campsites of *Homo habilis* in the Sahara desert which may be as much as 2 million years old. The great civilizations of the past – the Egyptians, the Persians, the Carthaginians, the Greeks, the Romans, the Arabs, the Turks, the British, the French – are mere flotsam in the tide, of no more significance than an Acheulean hand-axe lying on the desert surface. This oil-well was technology in direct line of descent from that hand-axe. Already there are museums for veteran cars and obsolete aircraft. One day this derrick would be shreds of twisted metal, and oil itself a fossil of a vanished age. And always the landscape remained, the raw fact of the desert before you, as Lawrence Durrell put it, 'the nakedness of space, pure as a theorem, stretching away to a sky drenched in all its own silence and majesty, untenanted except by such figures as the imagination of man has invented to people the landscapes which are inimical to his passions, and whose purity flays the mind'.

Near dawn on the eighth day we came to the place where the world ended. The flat plateau we had been crossing suddenly disappeared over the lip of an abyss in which whalebacks of basalt wallowed in a steam-bath of haze. The landscape shattered like a glacier into icebergs. The rock was sliced into sections to reveal bands of butter and cream, like the layers of a great gâteau. Stone icicles overhung and in places had fallen away, now lying in the chasm beneath like the skulls of tyrannosaurs. There was a subtle change in the air, sea-moisture giving way to the overbearing, spicy scent of sand. This was where the true desert began.

We heard rather than saw the sunrise. Vibrations of light and colour beat bars across the spectrum, a gush of curried gold rose in crescendo then fell away to the low harmonics of the desert. Half a sun, like an upended boat, irradiated in the valley the green promise of palm-groves, olive orchards and vineyards. Siwa oasis, a miniature paradise in the most hostile landscape on earth, sat like an emerald in the silver frame of its salt-lakes. After eight days' march across the wilderness with camels, no sight could have been more refreshing. We led the camels down a sand-slide to the oasis of Amun.

We marched past tilting palms, water gardens, palm-frond fences, soda-encrusted patches, gypsum-block houses, mangy military barracks with models of tanks outside. There was the sound of water purling in the gardens, water spilling out of iron spouts, small fountains playing sparkling colours like diamond prisms across the road. There was the moss smell of rankness, scents of humidity and humus.

Most of us recall childhood illustrations of oases – a few palms in the desert grouped around a neat pool among the dunes. Certainly there are oases in the eastern Sahara almost like that, but Siwa is ten times larger than Manhattan island and contains a quarter of a million palm-trees, over 1,000 springs, and is hemmed in only by salt-lakes that have steadily encroached since classical times on the good earth of the cultivated land. Close up, the oasis resembled an encampment in tropical jungle, chlorophyll-green against the desert pastel, with crusts of hills jutting from its canopy. The Old Town was a derelict tenement – salt-brick masonry being honed down by wind into wolf-fangs bared at the desert sky. To the east was the hill of Aghurmi, where the god Amun's temple had once stood, and in the distance the double plinth of Dakrur hill, where Siwans used to hold their annual orgy of garlic-eating.

The place was dominated, above all, by the bulging dunes of the Great Sand Sea – layer upon layer of carmine and amber sand, seething visibly to the tune of the wind and lazily a-boil with dust-smoke and the wild, shimmering colours of the new sun.

Buildings grew out of the desert and soon we were enclosed in unfamiliar corridors of brick and stone. We passed greasy petrol-pumps, a hotel, flat-blocks, gloomy civic buildings, a flyblown handicraft shop, a market sprawl of shanties, stalls displaying squashy tomatoes and green onions, flaps of bread, pressed squares of Siwan dates. Western tourists freewheeled past on rented bicycles, weaving among flat-bedded donkey-carts, driven by bearded men, and carrying cargoes of women bundled up in grey and black striped sheets from which, cyclops-like, a single eye pro-truded. Urchins chased behind us, poking at the camels, and a gaping youth drummed on our panniers, babbling in his ancient Berber tongue. 'What's the matter?' Selmi demanded in Arabic. 'Haven't you seen a camel-caravan before?'

'Only in books!' grinned the boy, and I was struck by the un-expected paradox of a Saharan oasis where only a Westerner and his companion would arrive on camels.

We passed gratefully out of the market scramble, into a cool tunnel cut die-straight through palm colonnades. Serrated fronds drooped low enough to touch, intertwining with the silver blade-lets of olive trees, the fat fingers of figs, the shiny leaflings of oranges and limes. Sunlight spilt through the gaps and lay in liquid dapples beneath our feet. Green water bubbled along feeder-channels at the forest edge, and if you halted for a moment you could hear again the sacred sound of running water. The smell of it was everywhere. Suddenly, after eight days in desolation, we were assaulted on all sides by life that pressed with vibrant audacity through the palm-fibre fences.

We halted the camels in an abandoned garden, half enclosed by an unkempt mud wall. While Selmi attended to watering our caravan, I hired a donkey-cart, to have a look round the oasis. My guide and driver, a bark-faced old Siwan called Ibrahim, spurred on his bony donkey with judicious kicks from his bare feet, chanting, 'Get on, or I'll sell you to the knacker!' each time the animal paused. As we swayed through the latticework of light and shade among the palmeries, the old man waved his hand expansively at the trees. 'That's the real wealth of Siwa,' he said. 'They talk about tourists – but tourists aren't dependable like dates! When I was a boy the Bedu used to come and help with the date harvest – they would bring their camels and pitch their tents around the gardens, and there was always singing and dancing. I've seen caravans of three or four hundred camels leaving Siwa loaded with dates for Cairo, Alexandria and even Tripoli! That's all gone, of course. They send the dates in lorries now.'

Our first stop was the village of Aghurmi – once the main settlement of Siwa – where mud-brick hovels crouched among the ruins of one of the most famous sanctuaries of the ancient world. Little was left of the temple of Amun but a gateway, a façade and a tangle of blocks and broken pillars standing on an unstable outcrop high above the palms. Yet in the days of ancient Greece and Rome, this place was sought by all the great and noble of the world. Amun was the god of prophecy, and squatting here on his desert promontory, sampling the pure desert wind, he peered across the frontiers of time as a Bedui peers at sand-tracks in the desert: tracks from the past, tracks into the future.

To glimpse the shape of things to come – what fabulous power it implied! So valued was the prescience of the Siwan oracle that the Athenians – a major power of the day – kept a special galley on permanent standby to take their messengers across the sea to Paraetonium – the modern Mersa Matruh. Alexander the Great broke off from his campaign against the Persian king Darius to encounter the oracle personally: Cimon of Athens, laying siege to Cyprus in 445 BC, sent a delegation here to whom the oracle predicted Cimon's own death; Queen Cleopatra came here; Hannibal sent a deputation; the Greek athlete Eubotas was so assured by the oracle's prediction of his success in the 93rd Olympiad that he ordered a victor's statue of himself before the race (and duly won).

The oracle was not a man, but a shapeless peduncle of plaster, probably representing a human body shrouded for burial in the upright manner favoured by the ancient Libyans. Before the consultation a throng of priests would parade it through the palmeries on a silver barque, followed by a procession of maidens singing hymns intended to induce a favourable prophecy. The petitioner would then be called into the secret crypts of the temple, where the god's prophecies were relayed to him by the corps of priests.

The fame of the oracle lasted for almost 1,000 years – suggesting that enough of its prophecies were efficacious to allow it continuing credibility. The last classical traveller of note – the Greek Pausanias, who visited the place in the second century AD – discovered here a stela half buried in the sand, which bore a hymn of praise to the oracle. The poem had been penned by the lyric poet Pindar nearly 600 years before.

Did the oracle predict its own demise, I wonder? A later traveller, in the time of Plutarch, reported that there was nothing left at Siwa of importance but an oil-lamp that was kept burning the whole year – demonstrating, at least, the Siwans' continuing obsession with time. The priests told him that the lamp required less oil from year to year – proving, they said, that the years were becoming shorter.

Ibrahim drove me through tight streets of mud-brick and gypsum-block, looming canyons of buildings in lopsided galleries of pigeon-hole windows and doors like deep throats. Children tumbled in the dust, dogs yapped at us, chickens clucked, geese cackled, men leered out of open windows, women glanced at us slyly from under their shapeless sheets. We arrived back in the bustling market-square, where, leaving the cart, we scrambled up a steep alley. A studded palm-wood door swung open to admit us to the belly of the Old Town – Shali – into which almost the entire population of the oasis had once disappeared like clock-work every sunset. According to the *Anonymous History of Siwa* – a medieval manuscript still held by one of the old Siwan families – the oasis people moved here from Aghurmi in AD 1203. The oasis had fallen into a dark age since the oracle's decline – the Muslims had arrived. 'This famous abode of idolators met with complete destruction at the hands of God,' the manuscript runs, 'in storms and raging tempests of such a force as to overthrow the temples and their statues.' Of more concern to the Siwans of those times were the human tempests – hordes of desert Bedu – who hurled themselves annually on this green haven. The nomads continued to plague the oasis right up until modern times. 'Bedu from Libya used to come here to water their camels,' Ibrahim said. 'No one was safe until they got up into the cliff and locked their doors.' Until 1820, when the Khedive of Egypt took over the oasis and provided a measure of security, few Siwans dared build their houses outside Shali's walls.

The honeycomb of ruined houses resembled a Chinese puzzle of shapes, textures and angles. Floors had collapsed one upon the other, plunging holes had appeared in the centre of the winding streets, frayed and twisted beams hung out of the distorted walls like severed blood vessels. For generations, Siwa families had built upwards inside the girdle wall of this fortress, each family expanding slowly into the limits of its space, until the hollowed-out hill became a warren of pinched alleys and tilting tunnels, so narrow that two donkeys could not pass. In this almost rainless land, a rare downpour could wreak more havoc than an army of raiders. 'We used to live here when I was young,' Ibrahim told me, 'but then a great shower of rain came that lasted three days. It only rains here once every forty years or so, but when it rains these mud houses fold up like paper. There were even people trapped inside, by God! The government declared it was forbidden to live here after that.'

'It must have been very hot and stuffy in here, anyway.'

'Never! These old mud houses were the coolest houses you could imagine. Not like the concrete ovens they build now. The high windows used to trap the desert air and send it down through the streets. That's why people went on living here even though they knew it was dangerous. Give me the Old Town any time!'

Desirable these close-packed homes might have been, but the claustrophobic conditions bred some dire internal pressures. Within these restricting walls, thick with the musks of men and animals, there festered two cliques of deadly enemies – the 'Easterners' and the 'Westerners' – who slugged out their differences in gun-duels on the wasteland beneath, exchanging shots round by round until one side gave way and the victors rushed into their houses, ravishing their women and stealing their chattels. When the British explorer W. G. Browne arrived here disguised as a Muslim in 1792, he was told, 'on the slightest grounds arms are taken up; and the hostile families fire at each other in the streets and from the houses'.

Later Ibrahim took me to a salt-island, about three miles from the oasis centre, across a slippery causeway through a snow-white lake of shimmering salt. The island was a jungle of palms and olives, where bronze doves crooned in the fronds, and wagtails skittered noisily from branch to branch. Within these groves was a cool glade containing a spring of crystal-clear water, gently shimmering up from about ten feet. Ibrahim showed me how the water was channelled into feeders that gridded the whole island. 'Every piece of land is granted so many hours of water according to its size,' he explained, 'and when each man has had his share, his feeder is closed off with a big stone and another opened.' The

crucial distribution of water-flow was supervised by a man holding the ancient office of 'Water Bailiff', who was paid a tree's
worth of dates or olives from each garden supervised.

Siwa was dependent for existence on its springs, but traditionally the Siwans had a superstitious fear of these doorways to the
unknown. Al Maqrizi, the Arab historian who passed through the
oasis in the fourteenth century, remarked that the oasis people
were plagued by Jinns, who they believed lived in the springs and
emerged each night in the forms of dripping devil-horses, ghost-
donkeys and vampire-goats. The Siwans also believed that Jinns
floated around in the atmosphere, and held to the supernatural
power of the Ghibli – the south wind – which had, they claimed,
saved them from invasion on more than one occasion.

As we rattled back towards the oasis proper, I decided to try
Ibrahim on the delicate question on the *Zaggalah*. They had been
bands of young men working as guards and labourers who were
obliged to sleep outside the walls of the Old Town, and who had
become notorious for their homosexual practices, including male
marriage. 'They were just youths,' Ibrahim told me, 'the younger
sons of Siwan families who were forbidden to marry. They lived
outside in the hills and gardens and filled the nights drinking
palm-spirit, smoking hashish, dancing . . . and you know. Of
course, there's none of that left now.'

It was sunset by the time I returned to camp. Selmi had filled all
our jerrycans, which stood in files like guardsmen on parade. 'The
camels hardly drank anything,' he said. 'No God but God, what
an animal! Eight days without water, marching every day, and still
they won't drink!' We loaded up and moved out along the tunnels between the groves. The last of the light fell in heavy slats
through the greenery and boiled molten on the surface of catch-
basins half hidden in the trees. We passed the remains of Umm
'Ubaydhah, Amun's second temple, a nest of stone blocks scattered
around a single standing wall inscribed with hieroglyph figures –
men with Egyptian crowns, ram-headed gods, serpent-women
carrying sun discs. This temple had been discovered by W. G.

Browne on his 1792 visit, but was probably a great deal more interesting in his day. In 1897 an Egyptian administrator had it blown up with gunpowder to provide stones for his office.

Further on, in the grey light of dusk, we came to the glade containing 'Cleopatra's Bath' – a famous spring of bubbling water which had been used as a bath by supplicants to the Siwan oracle – among them Queen Cleopatra, last of the Ptolemies. As we led the camels past, Selmi nudged me urgently, his eyes almost starting from his head. Floating in the water, face-up, was the gently paddling body of a completely naked girl.

'Is that human or Jinn, Omar?' he demanded breathlessly.

'Perhaps it's the ghost of Cleopatra!'

A little further on we discovered a bicycle of the type rented out to tourists, propped up against a palm-fibre fence.

'Omar,' asked Selmi, solemnly, 'did Cleopatra come here on a bike?'

# 8

# The Opposition Stone

We camped for the night beneath the double cone of Dakrur, on the shore of the Great Sand Sea, and awoke in the freezing pre-dawn gloom to find the entire horizon dominated by yellow ochre dunes with domes and crests shadowed in limestone mauve. Yardangs of abraded rock poked through the sand-skin like lone teeth. There was no real sunrise, only a sabre-slash of crimson through the mainsheet of the cloud, then lasers of light cutting a trail of colours across the sand-slides. The low cloud had sealed in the heat, and soon the dunes were steaming with heat-devils. Before leading our camels off, we spared a moment's awe for the majesty of the sands. Here was Gaia's quintessential desert, not the largest sand-sea in the world – that honour belonged to Arabia's Empty Quarter – but certainly the most dangerous. This was a region that was at least partly unexplored. 'The easy bit is over,' Selmi said. 'This is where the journey really starts.'

We marched briskly up towards the towering crests, trying to get the blood circulating in our shivering bodies. Soft slopes folded around us and soon the bights and buttes of sand were manoeuvring like the limbs of giant amoebas to engulf us entirely. Suddenly we were in the zoophage's belly. No human mind could have conceived this fantastic architecture of planes and curves and angles. The dunes were spongy cell walls around us, flowing forwards, bellying out in bays and inlets, building up like globs of amino acids along a double helix. Without warning the camels began to flounder in soft sand, groaning and honking, picking their legs up as if trying to extract them from liquid toffee. Selmi and I rushed to jerk their headropes, plunging up to our knees in sand and wildly shoving them out. We moved up the dune in fits and starts, for the whole windward slope was booby-trapped with these sand-pools, some of them large enough to swallow a tank. You could not distinguish them from the solid going. We were so preoccupied with this drum-sand that we did not see the sharp fall of 200 feet that suddenly gaped at us from below. 'God curse the father of all dunes!' Selmi grunted, pulling back hard on the lead-rope, 'You can't see the drops. It's like walking in the dark!'

As soon we had the animals on the flat sand below, we squatted down for a cup of water. 'I can't believe anyone has crossed these sands by camel,' Selmi said. 'It's impossible going. If the dunes were spaced out with gaps between them it would be easy, but here one dune just opens into another. The camels will be shattered after a day of this, and so will we. And what about the direction? You say you can navigate in a straight line with your compass, but not here. We are wandering all over the place!' This was uncharacteristically pessimistic of Selmi, but I knew what he said was influenced by his experience. All his life he had been trekking through the relatively flat sand-sheets of the desert further south, with only the occasional dune. He had never even imagined dunes like this. And neither had I.

The Sand Sea was like the mythical labyrinth that led to the underworld – a maze of mirrors where every tangent, line and level was out of true. There seemed to be no perceptible pattern to these dunes, no recognizable system from which we could construct a mental map. So strange were the shapes and textures that you could really believe you had entered another dimension. As we trekked, the labyrinth symbolism kept coming into my head. The islanders of the New Hebrides had a myth that after death the soul sought out the gates of the underworld, where a female guardian sat with a labyrinth design in the dust before her. As the spirit approached she would erase half of the design, and the spirit had to restore it accurately to be admitted. Those who failed were summarily torn to pieces.

I knew that if we could not supply the missing half of the labyrinth map, then we too would be torn to pieces by the raw forces of the desert. In the Sand Sea we had no thread to follow but the ordinary human penchant for seeking out patterns. Nothing here was as it seemed. In the high sun the sand burned with a white glare, and there were no shadows to give dimension to the sand-shapes. Instead, our eyes mistook faint colour bands in the sand for non-existent contours. Impossibly acute inclines suddenly became gentle dips when we stepped on them. Bottomless shafts yawned like dragon-maws in apparently continuous sand. Blown sand cannot, in fact, assume an angle of more than 33° before it avalanches, but my eyes were telling me that these gradients were twice as sharp, and I had to force myself down against instinct.

For two days we laboured on through the labyrinth trying to discover its secret rhythms. Locked within the dunes, already as far from the outside world as was Hades, everything seemed larger than life, and I was seeing images of Selmi and the camels blown up as if on a cinema screen. When Selmi spoke, the words came out in big, bright bubbles, like cartoon captions. We crossed drum-sand that boomed like timpani when we broached it, walking on eggshells waiting for the next liquid cave-in. Sand crevasses were hidden behind soft sand-bars. Dunes were joined by narrow necks only knife-blade thick. The entire edifice of the Sand Sea was slowly changing form all day, moving like a rotating stage as the sun waxed and waned, obscuring shapes already familiar and highlighting strange new geometries ahead.

Actually, there *was* a pattern in these sands. The prevailing wind blew from the north-west, and the dunes further south had arranged themselves in chains along its axis. Here around Siwa, though, the pattern had been obscured by the greater depth of the sand and the local vagaries of the wind-currents. Oil company bores show that the sand here is up to 900 feet thick, the dunes overriding an enormous wedge of it that peters out to the south.

No one knows for certain where the dunes came from. For centuries it was believed that they had once been the floor of an ocean which had long since disappeared. In 1981, however, the space-shuttle Columbia, on its second mission, overflew the Egyptian Sahara. On its payload was a radar camera, SIR-A, which produced geological images by bouncing radar signals off the earth. Part of SIR's kilometre-long film was passed to geologist Carol S. Breed of the US Geological Survey, who was astounded to see that the radar had probed sixteen feet below the surface of the sand, to reveal the unmistakable pattern of a very ancient drainage system. A whole network of rivers had flowed in this hyper-arid desert more than 17 million years ago, a few of them passing beneath the dune-chains of the Sand Sea. When these rivers dried up in more arid times, their sandy beds may have been mobilized into the pattern of dunes that exists today.

To the explorer Ralph Bagnold, the dunes seemed to have a secret life of their own: 'some unexplained principle was at work, analagous to life itself,' he wrote, 'capable of doing repetition work on a colossal scale, or organizing innumerable tiny grains of silica into a family of vast creeping forms identical in shape and detail.' The dune-chains are ranks of ancient whaleback plinths, upon the shoulders of which sharp crests form out of the mobile sand blown up the dune face. The crests are the living spirits of the Sand Sea – they may ride forever on their parents' backs or streak across the erg alone, covering 300 feet a year.

We crept up yet another crest and flung ourselves down on a mattress of rippled sand, exhausted. The old camel we called Ghaffir – 'The Caretaker' – promptly slumped down next to us. 'I don't like the look of him,' Selmi said. 'There's something wrong. His eyes are dull, and he's panting too much.' I watched Ghaffir gloomily. We had carefully worked out our requirements in water, food and camel-feed with an ample margin of error – the one thing we could not have allowed for was foundering camels. Unlike Theseus on his search for the Minotaur, we had no un-reeling line to follow back out of this maze. We could only go on.

Selmi led the camels off while I drove from behind, through quilts of saffron sand that split open to reveal strawberry sand beneath. Winds stirred ominously in the cauldron of the Sand Sea. The dunes began to quiver and wobble in anger. There was the rasp and buzz of sand-sheets grinding against each other, chattering and rumbling with the voices of the Jinns. We bent double into the surging stream of dust, tightening our headcloths around our heads, stomping on half blind through soft sand up to our knees. Mile after mile we plodded until my calf-muscles screamed with strain from the deep sand. Then suddenly, through a momentary gap in the dust-cloud, we glimpsed an inselberg of black rock winking over the dunes like a mirage – the only suggestion of solidity in the entire landscape. Selmi pointed to it, his motions as slow and ponderous as those of a diver. 'Let's get them over there, Omar!' he bawled. Reluctantly, I gave up all hope of following a compass bearing. Now, getting to that hill became our obsession.

Each time I imagined we had crossed the last barrier dividing us from the plateau there was another waiting, hidden by the phosphorescent skirts of the dunes. The sun grew hotter and hotter and my mouth became gritty and dry. Yet we dared not stop to think. The battle with the sand was sheer will-power, fighting with tortured calf-muscles and straining thighs. This was the hardest day's trek I remembered in almost 15,000 miles by camel. I tried to stop myself wondering what would happen if the camels collapsed. We worked our way up to the top of a candyfloss-pink dune, and the black crag of rock appeared before us. 'This must be the last one,' I told myself. 'We've almost made it!' We began to zigzag the camels down as the wind seethed in our faces. Ghaffir was the last animal on the string. Suddenly he pulled back on the rope and snapped it. He stumbled, hit the steep slope and rolled, twisting madly in a spin of head, feet, panniers and saddle, until he came to rest at the base of the dune and lay there, still.

We brought the rest of the caravan down, then ran over to the motionless Ghaffir. He was still breathing and there was a weak light in his eyes. Selmi pulled off the remains of the saddle and panniers sadly. 'It's over,' he said. 'He will never get up. We can do what we like, but he'll never again move from this spot.' I was tempted to disagree, to try anything, even lighting a fire under him as Arabs were said to do to revive foundered camels. But I realized that Selmi had seen this condition many times. There was no doubt at all in his voice. There was nothing we could do.

'Just leave him,' Selmi said. 'For us he's as good as dead anyway!'

I hesitated, shocked by the suddenness of death in the desert. Already the wind was building up seams of sand against the camel's flanks. This was, I thought, a terribly lonely place to die.

We dragged the remaining camels on, advancing with gritted teeth through the sand-spills and the abrasive wind towards the rocks. Occasionally we turned for a last glimpse of Ghaffir, his useless saddle and panniers piled neatly next to him like a monument. 'See, Omar,' Selmi said, 'camels will do almost anything to keep up with their companions, but he hasn't even moved!'

Soon Ghaffir was out of sight, concealed by the Sand Sea until some other foolhardy traveller – in God knew how many years – might happen on his bones.

The sand-storm had blown itself out on the last embers of sunset. We offloaded the camels and set up our comforting little cell in the emptiness. The camp felt a shade smaller without Ghaffir and we ate silently, nursing our apprehensions about the way ahead. The night sky was clear, but the temperature had dropped near to freezing. The camels were shivering under the old sacks we used to cover their backs. After the meal we smoked our pipes, Selmi wrapped in his home-woven rugs and myself in my sleeping-bag.

'It's my fault,' I said, breaking the silence. 'I could have stopped the fall. I was too slow.'

'It wasn't the fall that killed him, Omar,' Selmi said. 'It wasn't fatigue, either. This sand is hard going, but the camels have only been travelling for ten days, which is nothing for trained animals. The beast had something inside him – you could tell that from his eyes and his rotten breath. I think it was the sleeping-sickness.'

The words exploded in my head: sleeping-sickness – tripanoso-miasis – trips – a flyborne disease prevalent in the Nile Valley and the Delta, that sometimes infected large numbers among the camel-herds being brought to Egypt from the Sudan. Its presence didn't matter to the merchants as long as they got the camels to market, for most of the camels at Imbaba were sold for meat.

'It comes so quickly,' Selmi went on, 'and you can't tell if the animal's got it before it comes.'

'Then the others might have it too?'

'Yes. They might.'

For the first time, Selmi looked really worried. 'I've seen it happen in the caravans,' he said. 'You can have five or six camels with the sleeping-sickness and they all go down. But on the salt-run we know every inch of the way because we've done it since we were children, and we leave caches of food and water for the way back. Here we're in strange country – we have no secret caches and no camels to spare. These dunes make my head spin. You said that you could find the way with your compass – but now you have no idea where we are!'

I had to admit that Selmi was right – indeed, had been right all the time. I *had* boasted about my ability to navigate using the compass, but I had never expected the dunes to be so incredibly dense and irregular. All the reports I had read suggested that they were arranged in 'avenues' and that one could easily travel between them. I knew that for two days we had not been travelling on a direct bearing, but wandering in a series of squiggles. I looked around desperately, and felt panic welling up inside me.

We were trapped in the labyrinth with a caravan of potentially sick and dying camels, completely lost.

Later I managed to get the panic under control, and examined the map carefully by torchlight. I picked up Bahrein, a small oasis somewhere to the east of us, where at least there would be water. The problem was that, since I didn't know exactly where we were, I should have to guess our position, with the possibility of missing the oasis entirely and ending up even more lost than before. 'I can find the way to Bahrein with the compass,' I told Selmi, with much more confidence than I felt. 'We'll be all right as long as the camels keep going.'

Selmi looked at me doubtfully. 'What's Written cannot be unwritten anyhow,' he said. 'All of us die – men and camels – when it's time for us to die. The name of every human being is written on a leaf that grows on the Tree of Life. When your time comes, the leaf with your name on it withers and falls. Then you die.'

I thought of a story told by Professor C. Vance Haynes, the leading authority on the eastern Sahara. Motoring in the desert west of Dakhla, Haynes had come across the heat-mummified remains of a camel. There was nothing particularly odd about this, except, he noted, that one of the camel's legs had been cut off, and was missing. A little further east he discovered the missing leg, and further on still he found the corpse of a man. The cadaver's skin was intact enough for Haynes to identify him as a Tubu or Tuareg rather than an Arab, and even the man's tattered clothes still clung to his bones. Since the man had been heading east, he had probably been fleeing from Libya or northern Chad, across unknown country, when his camel died. He had cut off and taken the camel's leg as food, but had soon succumbed to thirst. In the pocket of his rags, Haynes found a leather purse containing silver coins used in Libya during Turkish times – perhaps 100 years ago. The man had died a miserable death in country so hostile that even the vultures scorned it – no one had even laid eyes on his corpse until Haynes and his team had happened by, decades later.

Next morning Selmi told me he had been dreaming. 'I dreamed there were no more dunes,' he said. We marched along the edge of the rock wall, leading the four camels beneath crooked crags and pinnacles of ebony stone that seemed to have been stained by generations of soot. Soon, we found a tapering pass that led us straight up into the dunes. 'So much for your dream!' I commented drily. We plunged into the sand, which stung like freezing water. Gasping, we struggled up to the crest, to see an endless grey-black plain covered in sharp particles. The pinkish coxcombs of the dunes curved far to the south. Selmi regarded me with silent triumph. 'All right,' I admitted at last. 'Your dream was right after all.'

Things were looking up. For the first time since leaving Siwa we were able to mount our camels. As the sun seamed through the clouds, roasting the black spall beneath us, we slipped into the saddle by mutual consent. 'Aaah!' grunted Selmi. 'How good to ride after walking so far! Like water to a thirsty man!' We settled down to the pounding rhythms of the camels. The day was utterly still, and there was no sound but the slapping of water in our jerrycans, the creak of saddle-frames and the crunch of camels' feet on the stones. The percussion of their pace lulled me into a trance. I was absorbed into the timeless continuum of the desert.

Selmi hooted suddenly, snapping me out of my daydream. The plain had ruptured into a moonscape of black ridges, and on one of them, standing out distinctly, was a tooth-shaped mound – a pile of stones, the first sign of human existence we had seen for days. After being lost in the ageless dunes of the Sand Sea, it was almost like finding traces of human presence on the moon. For generations Arabs had left these road signs all over the Sahara. A pile of rocks maybe, but a cairn could give directions, warn, advise and even tell jokes. Coming across it like this you felt no time-barrier between yourselves and those who had made it: they were merely ahead of you – an hour, a year, 100 years.

Half a mile away was another cairn, then a whole parade of them, attracting the attention like a deafening shout in the silence.

Soon we came across camel-grooves, shallow, straggling curves that meandered gracefully between the ridges. Camels never travel in straight lines, but oscillate left and right, giving their grooves a serpentine beauty that bears no relation to the stark symmetry of a road. 'These tracks were made by many, many camels,' Selmi said, 'and not in a day or a year – in many years. They were probably made by the date-caravans from Siwa in the old days.'

Further on we found flat places where camels had knelt down on the sooty ground – the shape of their folded legs and chest-pads deeply engraved in the earth. On gravel serir centuries of desert winds could not erase a single track. Even the grooves made by Roman chariots were – until they were destroyed recently by rally-drivers – clearly visible in parts of the Egyptian desert. The minutiae of history were scratched in the desert surface as on a vinyl gramophone record. Each step of the way was imprinted with memories, and man was the needle that played them. The camel might have been superseded, but for us these camel-tracks were as significant as they were for the Arabs who made them long ago. The grooves sometimes passed through double cairns – stones piled four feet high, standing several yards apart. 'We call them "doorways",' Selmi said. 'They mark the edge of the way.' We both burst out laughing at this Bedu joke: doorways in an infinity of space – doorways into nowhere.

We arrived at the head of an abyss, where a camel-skeleton lay, a bag of barbed-wire bones and hard leather ligaments. A clear alphabet of signs led us down on to the valley floor, into a boxed arroyo whose walls had been weathered into bell-jar shapes. The valley opened out slowly, and our grooves drifted along the line of the scarp until they were absorbed by the sand. Selmi trod a wide crescent around us but came back crestfallen. 'Only God knows which way now,' he said.

'Look. These caravan tracks behind us – thousands of camels over hundreds of years – *must* have been going somewhere, and it

can only have been Bahrein oasis. There's no other place the caravans could have found water and grazing!'

'How do you know? There *may* be other watering-places. The
caravans may not have watered at all! And even if it's true, we can't
follow the tracks. They've been eaten up by the sand.'

'Yes, but if I set my compass in the same direction, we are
bound to see Bahrein sooner or later.'

Selmi gulped. He knew how questionable my decision was.
'You're the guide, Omar!' he said, at last.

We spent a restless night, both silently nursing our fears. The
caravan-tracks had seemed a boon, but had they really been leading us towards Bahrein? If not, then my solution of setting a compass bearing on the direction of the tracks would only take us
deeper into unmapped desert, where we would eventually flounder madly around in circles until our water ran out or the camels
died, and we expired on the sand. I thought of the mummified
corpse Haynes had found east of Dakhla, of Selmi's relative who
had been so sure he knew the way, but had never returned, of
Selmi's companion who had dropped dead while cooking a meal.
I shivered. Once again, I felt panic hovering on the edge of my
consciousness. I knew that in a totally alien landscape like this, the
worst danger could come from inside oneself. Not only Westerners, but Arabs too, had succumbed to the terrors of this void.
Even the seasoned Bagnold had described how easily one could
be seized by the impulse to rush in any direction in a frenzied
effort to escape from the soul-flaying nothingness, like a drowning man gasping for air. The most horrific story I had heard of the
power of such terrors concerned three British soldiers in the
1914–18 war, who had strayed from their column in the desert
south of Mersa Matruh when their light car had broken down.
Having fixed the fault, they drove very fast in the wake of the
convoy, only to find after several hours that they were without
water and hopelessly lost. Then the terror had struck. Accelerat-
ing in panic, the sergeant-driver had crashed the car into a rock.
The three men had begun the long walk back to the coast, but

depressed by his failure or demented by a combination of sun, thirst, shock, and the terrifying sterility around him, the sergeant had drawn his pistol and shot himself in the head. Unfortunately, he had only succeeded in maiming himself, leaving the two privates to finish him off with their bayonets. Some time later the two soldiers were discovered by a British patrol, half dead and ranting, crawling on their hands and knees towards Mersa Matruh. Their water-bottles had been filled with the sergeant's blood.

Next morning was still and clear. We marched for four hours without a break, until we sighted grey cliffs on the horizon, and beneath them upright totem-pole figures wrapped in cocoons of shadow. We stared and squinted and shaded our eyes, thinking we could see palm-trees and even the outline of houses. 'Are those real, or just an illusion?' Selmi asked. It took more hours of agonized marching before the vertical shadows resolved clearly into palm-trees. This might or might not be Bahrein, but it was certainly an oasis. As we drew nearer still, Selmi observed that there were no signs of human beings – no litter, no power-lines, no sound of engines – just a ragged mess of trees, pieces of palm-fronds, old trunks, fibrous ribs scattered in velveteen sand. What we had thought were houses, indeed, were no more than the reflection of the sun on sandstone crags.

The final 100 feet seemed to last a lifetime, and then suddenly we were into the trees and leaping from our camels. We shuffled up a sand-ridge among the jungle of palms. There below us was a stunning sight – a lake of bluer-than-blue rippling water surrounded by reeds and palms and tamarisk-trees. On the surface of the lake, there were flocks of pink roosting flamingos. Selmi gasped, then held up his stick with two hands, as if it was a rifle, pointing it at them. 'We could have had one of those for dinner!' he said.

Later we hobbled the camels in thick 'agul bush, and Selmi smashed his way enthusiastically through reeds to get at the lake. He hurled himself in, jallabiyya and all, and found suddenly that the water was only up to his ankles. Recovering from this surprise, he lifted a handful of the liquid to his lips with an expression of rapture – open water in the desert was a Bedui's dream. At once an intense look of disgust crossed his features. He spat the water out with a long 'Yuuuuuk!' looking at me with wide eyes. 'God's curse on it!' he said. 'This water is brackish!'

Afterwards we spread our rugs beneath the palms, unwrapping our pipes and settling down to enjoy this respite from the terrible Sand Sea. Watching the camels shuffling happily from bush to bush, I felt as if I was gazing back into history. Although date-caravans had not been here for thirty years, it was still possible to maintain the illusion that nothing had changed for centuries. 'You can tell from the state of the palm-trees that nobody lives here,' Selmi commented. 'There are still old dates on the trees. Nobody has harvested them for ages. Are you sure this is Bahrein oasis?'

'Where else could it be?'

'God knows, Omar,' he said, laughing. 'It could be Zerzura!'

I laughed with him, thinking of the abortive journey I had once made with a Bedui companion years ago, in search of Zerzura – the legendary lost oasis of the eastern Sahara. Supposed by the Arabs to contain fabulous treasures, Zerzura was a myth that reflected the peculiar Bedouin view of the desert. While ancient Egyptians, Greeks and Romans had feared those wastes, the Bedu always believed that wealth awaited them in the wilderness for the picking of the wise. There was wealth in the form of rich grazing at the desert's edges for their goats and camels, wealth in the form of trans-Saharan trade of which they became the masters, wealth in the form of salt which cost nothing, yet which in the heyday of the old caravans could be bartered weight for weight in gold. And if precious salt could be found lying in the sands, a bequest of some forgotten age, then why not treasure itself? Tales of lost oases and treasure-cities in the desert can be traced in the *Arabian Nights* and even in the Holy Quran.

'What do you know about Zerzura?' I asked Selmi.

'My father told me about it. A Bedui from Dakhla once tracked a lost camel-calf into the desert and found it in a green valley full of palm-trees and lakes, just like this. He roped the camel, and before he left he cut down a bunch of dates from one of the palms and tasted them. They were the best dates he had ever eaten in his life. He drove the animal back to Dakhla, eating the dates and dropping the stones on the sand, so that he'd be able to follow them back. He got all his brothers and cousins together and they saddled their camels and set off to find the place again. They never found the oasis or even one of the date-stones he'd scattered. My father said that Zerzura only opens up at certain times, which is why it can never be found twice, but if you know the right spells and if you make a sacrifice – preferably human – it will open up to you!'

The idea of a lost city in the desert that can never be found twice is a very ancient one in North Africa, and probably even predates the arrival of the Arabs. Writing in the first century AD, Strabo repeats a legend common in ancient Libya of a city of Dionysus lost in the desert sands that might be happened upon by travellers, yet which they could never find again. The *Anonymous History of Siwa* elaborates on this theme, recounting the tale of a group of men who fled from the Nile Valley and who were led by a wild ram to an oasis blooming with orchards and vines. The fugitives remained there happily for years, but yearned to make a last visit to their homes on the Nile before returning to live out the rest of their lives in the oasis. After visiting the river, they set out once again into the desert, but found no trace of the fabulous valley.

The lost oasis might have remained no more than an eccentric reflection of Bedu culture had it not been for the interference of foreigners. The story of the quest for Zerzura really began with a British traveller, Sir J. Gardiner Wilkinson, who visited Dakhla oasis in the 1830s and inquired of the natives what places lay in the unexplored desert to the west. Surprisingly, they listed two places called 'Wadee Zerzoora' – one of them five days' journey away, the other three. The latter was the first of a trinity of wadis in one

18. Husn al Ghuwayzi, Mukalla, Yemen. Constructed on a perilously overhanging rock, this fortress dates from 1884, when the Hadhramaut and its coast were in the throes of a struggle between the Kathir and Qu'aiti families for control of the region.

19. Sultan's Palace, Saiyun. Built in Indonesian style, the palace was the hub of Kathiri power in the Hadhramaut until 1967.

20. Ruins of old Ma'rib. This medieval town was built on the ruins of a much older and larger city which flourished in the time of the legendary Queen of Sheba. Once a flourishing caravan centre for the Bedu, Ma'rib is now all but abandoned.

21. Sunset on the beach at Salalah, Dhofar, Sultanate of Oman.

22. The wadi at Bahlah, Oman. This fortress town in the Oman mountains
was once a great centre of commerce and industry, serving Bedouin tribes as far north as
the coast of the United Arab Emirates.

23. Bedouin boy, Wahiba Sands, Oman. This boy belongs to the
Al Wahiba, a Bedouin tribe who have elected to remain in their tiny coastal desert rather
than settle in town.

24. Old man of the Al Wahiba,
Oman, still living in a tent in the
Wahiba Sands. His Bedouin's
features reflect the great poverty
and hardship of his youth, when
motor-cars and hospitals were
undreamed of.

25. Bedouin women, Dhofar, Oman. Photographed at Bithna, near the Yemen border, these women belong to the Rawashid (Rashid), a famous Bedouin tribe who still graze their camels in the Empty Quarter.

26. Boys at Birkat al Mauz, Oman. The people of this fortified hill town in the Oman mountains may be descended partly from Bedu tribes which occupied the hill after the collapse of the dam at Ma'rib.

27. Nubian house, Belly of Stone, Sudan. An example of the unique
mud-brick architecture of the Nubian region, this doorway is decorated with the
skull of a crocodile to guard against evil spirits. Crocodiles became
extinct here only recently.

28. Jibrin wad ʿAli. Jibrin, my Kababish companion on the
journey to Selima oasis, works on his saddle-pad as we camp with a camel-herd
bound for Egypt.

29. Old man of the Bishariyyin, Sudan. Occupying the Red Sea hills in the
eastern Sudan, the Bishariyyin are of mixed Bedouin and Beja ancestry. They still live in
palm-fibre tents and wooden huts like this one.

30. Bishariyyin woman serving coffee, Sudan.

of which grazed many cattle. Beyond these three wadis, farther west still, lay oases called 'Gebabo', 'Tazerbo', 'Wadi Rebiana' and 'Aujela'.

Of these four places listed by Wilkinson, only Aujela was then known to exist – a major caravan-centre in Libya's Jalo oasis, which had been visited by Friedrich Horneman in 1789. Almost a century later, though, in 1878, Gerhard Rohlfs discovered that Gebabo and Tazerbo were parts of the vast Libyan oasis of Kufra. In 1922, Ahmad Hassanein Bey and Rosita Forbes confirmed that a group of oases called Rebiana stood beyond Kufra to the west. Zerzura remained the only missing part of the puzzle. If all the other oases mentioned to Wilkinson by the Dakhla people existed, why not Zerzura?

The hunt for the lost oasis fired Western imagination. *Murray's Guide to Egypt* of 1896 mentioned four different possible locations for Zerzura, all of them elicited from the statements of Bedu. One story, reported by the explorer H. W. Harding-King, was that buried in a secret place near Dakhla were a mirror and a manuscript. The manuscript gave directions to Zerzura, and when one looked in the mirror the oasis would appear. In fact, there *was* a book containing directions to Zerzura which required no secret directions or digging. This was a fifteenth-century guide to Egyptian treasure-troves called *The Book of Hidden Pearls*, published in French, but originally written in Arabic. The book listed 400 sites in Egypt that could be discovered by spells and incantations, many of them believed to be mines of precious metals and minerals once used by the ancient Egyptians or the Romans, but long since forgotten. The book's reference to Zerzura as a white city with the effigy of a bird on its gate, in which a king and queen were asleep on a hoard of treasure, was to provide a tantalizing image to later explorers.

The quest gathered momentum between the wars, when Egypt became the backdrop for a cast of wealthy colonial dreamers, adventurers, scholars, surveyors, diplomats and royal princes which would not have been ill at home in the pages of Hergé's

*Adventures of Tin-Tin*. For this desert-venturing jet-set, Zerzura had become the *raison d'être* of their sometimes frivolous endeavours. Even the level-headed Ralph Bagnold was caught up in the romance. In 1930, over a few cold beers in a Greek bar in old Wadi Halfa – a town now lost under the waters of Lake Nasser – he and his colleagues founded the 'Zerzura Club' – an association that would flourish mainly over good dinners in exclusive London clubs during the Indian summer of that decade.

One of the most intriguing of the Hergé-esque characters of the 'Zerzura Club' was the self-styled 'Count' Ladislas Almasy, a Hungarian pilot who turned up in Egypt in the entourage of the Crown Prince of Liechtenstein. In 1932, Almasy re-examined Wilkinson's original account of the Zerzura story. Four of the oases mentioned there had been discovered since Wilkinson's day – only Zerzura itself remained an enigma. He perused the map with a pilot's attention to detail. If one were setting off in a straight line from Dakhla to the oases in Libya named by Wilkinson, he reasoned, one would almost certainly have to pass through or round the massif of Jilf Kebir – an island-sized inselberg in lifeless desert where archaeologists had found rock-paintings and pottery belonging to the forgotten peoples of the Sahara. The Jilf was not an oasis of the artesian type – it was not near the water-table – but Almasy learned that there were fertile wadis inside the massif, fed by the occasional rains. A reconnaissance flight over the plateau confirmed that there *was* rich vegetation there, and later he managed to enter the massif on foot, discovering two wadis full of blossoming acacia trees. Wilkinson's account had mentioned three wadis, however, and Almasy's conclusions looked doubtful until an old Tubu guide told him that a third wadi did indeed exist, and that the Tubu – black Saharan nomads – had grazed their cattle there for centuries. Since the wadis were rain-fed, rather than depending on groundwater, Almasy thought, the vegetation would persist for only a few years after a big rain and then, perhaps, die out. This would explain the disappearance and appearance of the Zerzura legend – the 'lost and found' motif.

It was on this uncertain note that the affair ended. Almasy assured himself that he had found the lost oasis – albeit a far cry from the white city and treasure-hoard of *The Book of Hidden Pearls*. Ralph Bagnold, master of the 'Zerzura Club', was less convinced, however. 'Assuming that Zerzura does not now exist,' he wrote, 'it may have done so once . . . at a time when rain fell more frequently than it does now, or it may have a foundation in reality, being the exaggeration of some small inconspicuous water-hole, difficult to find, but still existing; or again it may exist entirely in the Bedouin mind.'

Ironically for Bagnold, perhaps, the 'Bedouin mind' proved the cryptic clue which brought about the revival of the Zerzura question, long after he himself had left the Sahara forever. In his day it was well known that Bedu from Egypt – Selmi's people – hauled rock-salt from the Sudan. As early as 1909 customs officer Andre von Dumreicher had noticed the tracks of salt-caravans entering Kharja from the south, and had proposed to stop the salt-smuggling by reporting the Bedu to the Salt Monopoly. Dumreicher, like most of those after him, assumed that the salt came from 'Bir as Sultan' – one of the wells in Al 'Atrun, which was the Sudan's major source of the mineral. Yet he was wrong. The Bedu had kept the whereabouts of the salt-oasis a closely guarded secret for generations.

In 1980, when Bagnold was in his eighties and most of the old 'Zerzura Club' long dead, C. Vance Haynes, Professor of Earth Sciences at the University of Arizona, made a surprising discovery. Exploring the desert north of Merga, in the Sudan, he picked up some unexpected camel-tracks. Following them for several miles, he and his Bedouin guide found themselves in a deep depression, whose floor sparkled with rock-salt crystals. In the depression they saw a well, and a caravan of black nomads digging rock-salt. The nomads told them that the depression was called 'Oyo'. Haynes realized quickly that this was where the Egyptian Bedu had quarried their salt, undiscovered for so long. The only vegetation to be found there was some coarse esparto grass, though a number of toppled and sand-blasted palm-trunks revealed to Haynes that the oasis had been more fertile in times past. Was Oyo – the last oasis to be discovered in the eastern Sahara – also Zerzura? Or were there other Zerzuras left to be found, one of them containing a white city with a king and queen asleep on a mass of gold, as the legend specified?

Haynes, one of a new generation of explorers for whom science and legend were merely data to be used to the same end, gathered up the scattered clues of the Zerzura story to create an overview that in its way was far more fascinating than the dream of a white city in the sands. Oases, Haynes said, were no more static than any other living structure – no more fixed than the desert itself. Like stars, bacteria, oysters and human beings, they had a life-cycle of their own. The oases of the eastern Sahara, he explained, were the remnants of an age in which this desert was a rich savannah roamed by giraffes, elephants, buffaloes, and many other creatures of the open veldt. The animals had watered at shallow lakes and water-bearing depressions, which had become the last centres of life as the Sahara unravelled into sand. 'As these [lakes] began to dry up with the expansion of the Sahara,' Haynes wrote, 'they passed through stages of lakes or open pools to marshes, to places where water could only be had by digging shallow wells, finally to complete dessication. After the final stage is reached the depression becomes a lost oasis, known only to tribal elders until it becomes lost altogether to human memory and is relegated to legend. Thus between 3000 BC and AD 1500 there were many potential Zerzuras in the eastern Sahara.'

Later, Selmi knocked some dates down from the trees above us, and we sat down to taste them. They looked dry and desiccated and dissolved into sawdust at the first bite. Selmi spat out the lees noisily. 'No, this can't be Zerzura,' he said. 'The dates there were supposed to be wonderful, but these are the most horrible dates I've ever tasted in my life!'

In the morning we led the camels up a red sand-hill to a sky skeined in salmon-pink wisps of cloud. All the way along the sand-folds, there were souvenirs left by previous visitors – shreds of camel-bone like polished teeth, an old tin trunk full of sand, a dead quail, and even the tracks of a gazelle. From the crests we looked over a landscape of luxuriant curves, tumbling in every direction. Gazing back down the dunes we could see now that there were two distinct lakes at Bahrein – two separate circlets of vegetation like dark scuffs on the virgin plain. Within the haloes of the trees, water flashed electric-blue in the sun. What we were seeing was almost a miracle, for in this desert-of-deserts the sun is so merciless that liquid is transformed into vapour at a phenomenal rate. The relative humidity in this part of the Sahara is reckoned at less than 2.5 per cent – which gave human water-pots like me and Selmi about forty-eight hours without recharge to be burned to a frazzle. How, then, could such lakes exist? The answer lay in the Great Invisible River – the water-bearing aquifers that underlie the vast area of the eastern Sahara, which are almost everywhere the same height above sea-level. Bahrein, like Siwa, is one of a string of oases sprawling along the northern rim of the Great Sand Sea on a fault-line where the aquifers surface. Qattara – the Sahara's greatest depression – is also part of this feature. Once a vast lake, it is now a salt-marsh in the process of maturing into a desert *sebkha*. Open water could exist at Bahrein, despite the terrific evaporation rate, because of the awesome volume of underground water recharging it.

The going remained too soft and steep for riding, but as we trawled steadily along the dunes, we were able to talk. I asked Selmi what he would do with the money I was paying him. 'I'm going to buy the concessions on some land,' he answered. 'I'm going to become a landowner – there's profit and security in land. There's profit in salt too, of course, but I've tired myself out with salt-caravans and camels. My family came from Sohaj in Upper Egypt. My forefathers lived in black tents and herded goats and sheep and a few camels on the edges of the desert, outside the cultivation in the Nile Valley. In the old days, before I was born, the Bedu used to move up and down the river. They didn't stay in one place, so they weren't subject to taxes or military service. Then the government said, "Fine. You want to keep moving, then keep moving!" and they refused to let the Bedu pitch their tents anywhere. They had to keep wandering all the time. The women and children slept in litters on the move, and they used a special brazier so that they could cook food on the camels' backs – that's my father's story, anyway. In the end, of course, they had to settle in one place. The government was able to grab them for military service and taxes. In those days, a lot of the land on the Nile was owned by a few rich families. Jamal Abdal Nasser ended all that by putting a limit on the number of *feddans* any one person could own, and that made land available for the poor. He started a big agricultural project at Kharja and Dakhla, which he called 'The New Valley', and the concessions on the land were going cheap. My father bought some and we moved to Kharja when I was still a baby. At first we lived in some mud houses right out in the desert, but when they built the new road from Kharja, they moved us to Baghdad.'

I had heard about the 'New Valley' Project. Dreamed up by Nasser in 1958, its prodigious aim was literally to create a second river Nile across the Western Desert, branching out from Lake Nasser and flowing into the Qattara Depression. The scheme had probably been inspired by the myth of the Bahr Bela Ma – the 'River without Water' – which since Persian times was rumoured to exist out here in the western wastes.

Herodotus had called Egypt 'the gift of the Nile', and only by traversing the vast empty landscape of the Western Desert, perhaps, is it possible fully to appreciate that fact. A mere 11 per cent of Egypt's total area is agricultural land, most of it situated along the Nile Valley. Nasser's vision was simply a new incarnation of an obsession with which all recent Egyptian leaders had been concerned – how to increase the agricultural potential of a country that was 89 per cent desert.

Nasser did not succeed in creating 'The New Valley' – the geographical obstacles proved insurmountable, and the visionary project had to be abandoned. Though large numbers of settlers – among them Selmi's family – were moved to the oases of Kharja and Dakhla, and new areas cultivated there, the pioneers had to depend on the faithful water–table that had sustained the population since the Acheulean hand–axe makers had moved into the oasis 200,000 years ago.

'Now, of course, the land in Kharja has become expensive,' Selmi told me, 'and a lot of the springs have given out, because there are too many people using the water. I'm not looking for land at Kharja, but at the new project at ʿUwaynat, where it's much cheaper.'

I gaped at my companion as I digested the irony of this fact. ʿUwaynat, an oasis lying 400 miles south–south–west of Kharja, had been abandoned by cattle–nomads of the C–Group 5,000 years ago, when the Sahara's latest arid spell matured. Now Selmi, the settled Bedui whose family were among the hopeful pioneers of Nasser's 'New Valley' Project, would play a part in reclaiming that long–isolated corner of the Sahara. The wheel turned once more.

ʿUwaynat remained unknown to history until 1923. It was in that year that Ahmad (later Sir Ahmad) Mohammad Hassanein Bey, with four Bedu companions, left the Mediterranean coast at Solloum to begin a journey that would take him 2,000 miles through unexplored territory, and turn into one of the epic camel–treks of all time.

Hassanein, an Anglophone Egyptian, graduate of Balliol, Oxford, fencing blue, boxer, friend and tutor of Egyptian monarchs, a 'gentleman of quality by the highest standards of any nation or time' – as one obituarist put it – might have come out of the pages of Lawrence Durrell's *Justine*. Before discovering ʿUwaynat in 1923, he had already won distinction as an explorer by reaching Kufra with Mrs Rosita Forbes two years earlier. On that journey he had come across the remains of a caravan that had perished, half buried in sand. A human hand, the colour of parchment, had stuck out of the sand, and as Hassanein's caravan passed, one of his men had reverently hidden it again. It had been a grisly reminder of the hazards of desert travel, and – like Selmi – Hassanein had sworn that this first desert trek would be his last. But the call of the unknown had proved too strong. Within a year he had been planning a journey into the *terra ignota* beyond Kufra.

The region through which he intended to march was a blank in space as well as time. It had been unknown to the classical geographers – Strabo, Heredotus and Pliny – and largely avoided by earlier explorers. No motor-car had ever penetrated it and no aeroplane flown over it. He had had little more to guide him than the assertions of his Bedu camel-men and a collection of folk memories. Hassanein was aware of the vague but persistent rumours of fertile lands hidden in the great desert west of the Nile, of the legends of Zerzura and the mythical Bahr Bela Ma. On his first visit to Kufra he had heard tales of 'lost oases' in the desert beyond – places which the local people knew only by tradition and hearsay. Two unnamed and apparently uninhabitable oases had been placed on the map – from the same hearsay evidence – by Justus Perthes of Gotha in 1892.

Hassanein sighted the hills of Arkenu – the first of these two oases – in the early hours of 23 April. Racked by exhaustion after an almost sleepless eight-day march from Kufra, his Bedu were driving the camels through a warren of plunging dunes when the mountains suddenly sprang up before them out of the dust-haze like a vision of enchanted Gothic castles. For Hassanein, this was the outstanding moment of the journey: 'I let the caravan go on,' he wrote, 'and for half an hour I sat on a sand-dune and let the sight of these legendary mountains do its will on my mind and heart. I had found what I came to seek.'

Within the rock walls he found a lush green valley, where his men made camp. As they sat down to eat, a party of Tubu nomads slipped out from among the boulders. Far from being hostile, they gave the explorer ample information on the second oasis – ʿUwaynat – where, they said, Jinns had left strange animal drawings on the rocks – 'Writings and drawings of all the animals living,' they told him, 'and nobody knows what sort of pens they used for they wrote very deeply on the stones, and Time has not been able to efface the writings.' Hassanein could hardly contain his excitement. After a crippling all-night march his caravan reached the hills of 'Uwaynat, and within forty-eight hours he had located the unique rock-pictures.

At this time no other explorer in history had laid eyes on such pictures in the Egyptian desert. There, careening over the rocks, like a shower of stars, were the shapes of wild animals no longer found within hundreds of miles of 'Uwaynat. There were troupes of giraffe with shimmering reticulate coats, prides of lion, scuttling ostrich, phlegmatic cattle, gambolling gazelle of many species. Skilfully etched on to the stone, a quarter to half an inch deep, the animals were so weathered in places that Hassanein could easily scratch off their lines with a fingernail. As he studied them, he was struck by two things. First, whoever had made these engravings had had no interest in – and therefore probably no knowledge of – the camel. Second, an animal which could not today survive in this hyper-arid country – the giraffe – was the creature most commonly depicted there, suggesting that it had once been plentiful. The only date which Hassanein had to work with was that of the camel's supposed introduction into northern Africa by the Persians in 524 BC. He concluded that not only must these pictures be at least 2,500 years old, but the environment here had been dramatically different before that time. Hassanein's discovery was startling. It was to be another ten years before Caton-Thompson and Gardner would investigate their fossil springs at Kharja, and give scale to the breathtaking antiquity of the Sahara's past. Hassanein had unearthed something of more lasting consequence than a lost oasis or a hoard of treasure – incontrovertible evidence that the most sterile desert on earth had once been green.

And if it had been green once, surely it could be made green again. The Suez Canal and the Aswan Dam had already begun to impress upon the Egyptians the regenerative power of twentieth-century technology. Unfortunately, it was soon realized that ʿUwaynat was not an artesian oasis like Siwa, but merely a hump of mountain high enough to trap the Sahara's rain-bearing winds. It was not until decades after Hassanein's death – in a motor accident in Cairo – that space-shuttle Columbia's state-of-the-art radar photography revealed reservoirs of groundwater in the desert to the east of ʿUwaynat. The water was of the 'fossil' type – the harvest of rains that had fallen here in prehistoric times – and was not subject to recharge from the water-table. This meant that, like Arabia's oil, it was a finite resource – if tapped, it would possibly last 100 years. Against the advice of some geologists, the Egyptian government – desperate for land as always – decided to go ahead with the plan to turn the desert into a new agricultural scheme.

'When I get my concessions at ʿUwaynat, I'm going to get married again,' Selmi said. 'My wife isn't interested in having any more children. She was very upset when one of our children died, but it didn't bother me. I said, "Don't worry, I can easily just ride you again and get another one!" I want to marry a girl like one of those we saw in Cairo. I've already told my wife that I want to marry again. It's good to have two wives – one working in the house and one always pregnant – that's how it should be!'

'Wasn't she angry when you told her?'

'No. I think she was pleased. We didn't get married for love, you see. We got married out of duty to the family. It didn't seem to bother her at all when I told her – but it's true that some women really go crazy with jealousy when their husbands re-marry. There was a Fellah in Baghdad whose second wife died only a few weeks after he married – everyone said the first wife had poisoned her. I don't know if it's true, but women are perfectly capable of it. They haven't got the sense that men have, that's why they need to be kept in their place. There was a girl-relative of mine, for instance, who did very well at school and wanted to study at the university as a teacher. Then she would have lorded it over us, because we can't even read and write. Her cousin, who had first refusal on marrying her, was a tough man, and decided to take her for a wife. "I'll soon put a stop to this studying nonsense!" he said – and he did. Now she's a good wife with three children.'

'Why do you always marry your cousins?'

'Well, for one thing, the girl inherits some of the land and animals of her father – so if she married outside, the wealth would go to another family. Our women are very special to us. They are Bedu women – they wear the veil, dress in black, and can dance like Bedu. The women are ours – our property. I don't say I love my wife strongly, but if she did it with anyone else, by God I'd kill her, then I'd lure whoever it was out into the desert and slit his throat! The women are our honour. There are Bedu who take Fellah women as wives – usually second wives – but we would never, never give away one of our girls to a Fellah!'

I reflected that it was the Bedu passion for blood-lines, the endogamy which gave every man the right to marry his first cousin, the preservation of 'pure' genetic strains – which had so endeared them to Western aristocracies, for whom they represented the 'purest race on earth'. The *crème de la crème* of the Bedu were those tribes which were dominant, and whose members could recite their genealogies back in a direct line to a noble ancestor. That line had, they claimed, been preserved by continual interbreeding between first cousins. In fact, the genealogies themselves were in essence fictitious, and would be altered frequently to admit individuals and groups who had no blood-ties at all with the rest of the tribe – just as Selmi's people married Fellahin women. These groups and individuals would, of course, eventually intermarry with members of other households and so introduce new strains into the genetic pool.

The tribal genealogies were actually a political weapon. They were supposed to define the relationships between tribes – that is, which were 'superior' and which 'inferior' according to purity of blood – but were in fact constantly reconstructed to suit the power-relationships that existed at any given time. As one tribe or lineage grew more powerful, for example, the genealogy might be altered to show that it was in direct line of descent. If it grew weaker it would be moved to a peripheral place on the tree, and might eventually be dropped from it altogether.

A classic example of the process of rewriting genealogies can be seen in the Quda'a, an Ishmaelite tribe who fought with the Qahtanis in the civil war in Arabia in AD 680–84. As a result of their alliance with the Qahtan, they were magically switched from the Ishmaeli to the Qahtani side of the tree.

Far from displaying actual genetic purity, the genealogy was a diagram of those who acted together and felt themselves close, no matter what backgrounds they might originally have come from – it was a metaphor for the *de facto* situation. Glubb's edifice of Bedouin 'nobility' comes crashing down on this point. Such a quality can be assigned neither to 'pure' breeding, nor even to morally superior behaviour. It is simply an acknowledgement of wealth, prestige and political power.

'The family comes before everything to the Bedu,' Selmi continued. 'Whatever we earn – whether from the land or from the caravans – we give to my father, and he gives us back according to our needs. He'd be very angry if we held on to it. Only my brother Mohammad is outside the family, because he's such a spendthrift and he does no work. With this money you're paying me, though, I want to get the concessions on my own land, so that I can set myself up. I don't want to go on giving my father money for ever. The only time I did anything that wasn't for the family was during my military service. My father didn't like it, of course. He said my duty was to the family, not to the government, but there was nothing he could do. It was quite a good life – I got about a bit, saw different places, and we ate well. I was in the Border Police, so a lot of the time I was on guard duty in the desert. When the officers – university boys from Cairo – used to lord it over us and treat us as if we were complete fools, I used to pretend to be a bumpkin and half-wit who knew nothing – so as not to attract attention. They don't like Bedu – they know we look down on them – so I kept quiet. I smiled and nodded, and said, 'Yes, Sir!' but I knew there wasn't a single one of them I couldn't have left behind in the desert if I'd wanted to!'

I asked him if he really meant to give up the salt-caravans that had been part of his life for so long. He considered the question for a moment, then said, 'Only God knows, Omar. It's good to have land, but I doubt if the Bedu will ever give up camels. It's a question of balance. The Bedu in the eastern Sudan – our relations – have a great many more camels than us, but when there's a drought and famine, they might lose them all. It's better to have a balance between livestock and land, then you are more secure. The same applies with everything else. It's good to have motor-vehicles when you need them. They aren't good for everything, of course, but you'd look a bit silly going to the shops in Cairo on a camel. I admire modern things, but it doesn't mean I despise camels. Those Saudis we talked to in Cairo had all the money in the world, but they still love their camels. All my children will go to school – even the girls – because, while we are proud of our customs, there has to be a balance between the old and the new. The future belongs to the children. It's not my job to make a life for them, but it is my job to make sure they have a chance. It would be wrong to tell them, "No need for reading and writing," when every poor Fellah's kid can read and write. Only God knows what the world will be like tomorrow. Perhaps we'll be going to the moon, or perhaps all the oil will run out, and we'll be going back to camels again! Everything that has been or will be is Fate. I don't even know if I'll survive to get the concessions I'm after. Only Allah knows that!'

All morning we trudged, and the streaks of cloud that had decorated the cold dawn were licked down into a sink-hole hidden in the sands. The sun was left unshrouded and its fire blazed along the crests, shaking out heat-devils that smouldered all around us. Selmi was tirelessly magnificent, always jogging ahead, undeterred by sinking sand, ferreting out the safe ground, gauging the steepness of the slopes, tracing an easier path down the sand-slides. In the valleys between the dunes there were limestone blocks lying smashed like giant crabs scuttled on a beach. Along the dunes there were milk-white streaks – deposits of calcium flakes the size and shape of penny coins There were trillions of them, some lying flat on the ground, others arranged in groups with their edges uppermost like strange razor-blade plants. I picked up one of the larger plaques. On its upper side was etched the perfect four-petalled pattern of a flower. 'Beautiful!' Selmi commented.

They were fossilized spatangid sea-urchins. In a sea that ceased to exist here long before these dunes were formed – the Tethys Sea – this tiny creature had filtered limestone out of the water to construct its shell. Somewhere on neighbouring land, the roots of a tree had dissolved the limestone in the rock beneath it, and the rain had washed the solution down to the sea. Sunlight to plant to sea-urchin to ocean to desert floor. The spirit of Gaia wandered its unceasing migration between life and non-life and back again. 'A question of balance,' Selmi had said, and, handling this shred of the planet's history, who could doubt it? Life is a cybernetic system, a process of feedback, a question of balance. No one knows exactly why this desert has switched back and forth from green to arid over the ages, but the frequency of the change suggests that some vast regulating system is at work. Milutin Milankovich, a Serbian mathematician, believes that every 40,000 years or so the earth wobbles on its axis, changing the amount of heat the planet absorbs from the sun. The change is small, but enough to trigger off an expansion of the ice-caps: a new ice-age is born. Glaciers begin to move south, their glittering spines reflecting the sun's heat back into space like giant mirrors. This reflection continues the cooling process, and the colder it becomes, the further south the glaciers push. So much water is locked up in the ice that the sea-levels fall, reducing rainfall in some areas. The Sahara reverts to desert. Only after the feedback switch is tripped – perhaps by concentrations of carbon dioxide in the atmosphere, which tends to heat the earth – does the ice melt, and, for a time, rain falls afresh on the desert plains.

This happened last in about 10,000 BC, when the great Wurm glaciers that had covered Europe for millennia began finally to recede. Rain fell again on the sizzling plains west of the Nile, and enterprising pioneers – Selmi's spiritual if not genetic forebears – moved out to colonize the new lands. The shapes of these men and the world they knew – changing, always changing – appear on the rocks like Chinese shadow-puppets. For thousands of years pluvial periods alternated with arid ones. Somewhere, lost in the tempest of these fluctuations, hunter-gatherers became cattle-nomads. The Sahara's great lakes expanded and contracted as the warm-weather regime stabilized in other parts of the world. Finally, by about the third millennium before Christ, it was all over.

The anvil on which the most adaptive of creatures – man – had beaten out his skills of cultivation and pastoralism was lost, its ancient tracks forgotten. The tribes and cultures which once mingled in the desert were scattered and divided, the old contacts severed. The Sahara became a sea of stone and sand, its inhabitants stranded across it on islands called oases. Where elephants and giraffes had browsed in green forests, the Ghibli wind now spun drifts of sand. Where hippos had basked in mud, families of bar-chan dunes took root. Where cattle had mooched across grass-lands, men now measured out their water cup by cup. Millennia later, paper-dry, wind-gnarled men with hawkish eyes and wizened faces would come dashing across the sands on strange beasts called camels. Robed and muffled, obsessed by the need for water, they would know nothing of the green world that had once teemed beneath their feet. The strange pictures they would find on the rocks – messages from a forgotten time – would always remain for them the work of Jinns.

Selmi and I were perhaps among the last of these sand-riders, as we kicked up plumes of dust down the dune-slopes. We halted between them to eat our midday meal – tins of sardines, hunks of dried bread green with harmless mould – and afterwards Selmi broke out his pipe. He was about to light it when he stopped, sniffed, put down the mouthpiece, and hopped to his feet. 'Look at that!' he cried, gesturing to the horizon. Pillars of dark smoke were moving across our flank like a forest fire. Pricks of grit struck our faces. The desert trembled as if a vast cart was rolling over its surface. 'This could kill us!' Selmi shouted. 'Let's get the camels moving!' Before we had finished packing, sand was screeching down on us like waves of harpies. We wrapped up our faces. Both of us were wearing three jallabiyyas apiece and woollen jerseys, but still we shivered from the cold. We stalked out into the clouds of sand like a jungle of reeds around us. Visibility was down to a few metres already. The whole desert was alive with a malevolent force. We dropped down from the dunes on to a flat serir, but still the dust-demons chased us, hacking at our heads, searing at the camels, rasping into our eyes, noses and ears. Underfoot the sand-billows were thicker and in places they moved in particles like huge armies of ants. We stumbled into soft sand and stumbled out, tripped over sharp rocks, cursing and shouting. Swell upon swell of middle-sand slapped against our heads. The wind was so strong that even the camels turned their heads away. For hours, all afternoon, we pressed through the storm. Suddenly Selmi yelled to me to stop. I looked round to see that the male camel we called 'Umda – 'The Mayor' – was sitting down.

'It's the sickness!' Selmi shouted. 'He won't budge!'

We kicked and pummelled to no avail. The earth belly-growled, the sand slashed at our ears.

'Either we stop here, or we leave him!' Selmi croaked through his muffling headcloth. 'There's no way he's going on while the storm lasts.'

'All right. We'll stay here until the morning.'

Tonight there was no shelter behind our panniers. The wind whipped through them and around them, and we had to sling a rug from the backs of two camels to keep the sand out of our eyes. For almost an hour we struggled to light the fire before giving up.

As we scrambled into our covers and went to earth hungry, Selmi said, 'This is really the work of men, isn't it, Omar? Just think, if we'd stayed at home we'd have missed all this!'

The raw energy of this wind was terrifying, and I began to understand the power it had exerted on the minds of those who lived around this desert. For the ancient Egyptians it was pure evil – the spawn of Set – but the people of Siwa believed that the south wind had been their saviour several times, spectacularly in the case of Cambyses' army.

Cambyses II of Persia conquered Egypt in 524 BC, and in the same year sent an army of 50,000 soldiers across the Western Desert, on what was probably the first Saharan expedition ever to be equipped with camels. The force had been detached from the main column at Thebes, near modern Luxor, with orders to attack the Siwans, reduce them to slavery, and burn the oracle: 'The force can be traced as far as the town of Oasis, seven days' journey across the sand from Thebes,' the historian Herodotus wrote. 'General report has it that the army got as far as this, but of its subsequent fate there is no news whatever.'

The 'town of Oasis' – a week's trek across the desert from Thebes–Luxor – can only have been Kharja. From there, the troops might have marched straight across the desert to Siwa, or chosen the more logical route through the chain of oases that spans the Western Desert – from Dakhla to Farafra and into Siwan territory. 'When the men had left Oasis, and in their march across the desert had reached a point about mid-way between the town and the Ammonian border,' Herodotus noted, 'a southerly wind of extreme violence drove the sand over them in heaps as they were taking their mid-day meal, so that they disappeared for ever.'

In the morning we awoke to a cold, eerie silence. The sky was still glowering grey, but the storm had passed over, leaving its legacy of dust in everything. 'Umda was still alive, and after we had reduced his load to nothing, he stood up groaning. We strung the camels together and advanced over pasteboard-blue rock and pockets of soft sand. We lurched into another range of dunes washed clean by the storm, and Selmi pointed out something glowing brilliantly in the middle of the valley. From a distance it looked almost like a concrete bollard – but how could such an object have come to be in the sands? Selmi walked up to investigate it. He turned it over easily and then lifted it up for me to see. 'A pot!' he said in surprise. 'Who would bring a pot out here?'

I hobbled the camels and walked over to examine the object. It was a perfect amphora, pale cream in colour, standing almost a metre high with a narrow neck and side-handles – a water-jar, but certainly not a modern one. Its base was pitted and scored by wind, sand and time. It could quite easily have been here for millennia. Could it have been dropped by Cambyses' army, I wondered, when it passed here in 524 BC? Could the bones of Cambyses' soldiers lie under these dunes? The geography seemed about right. Assuming that the Persians took the logical route, it is likely that they met their fate somewhere between Farafra and Bahrein – somewhere around here.

Selmi called to me excitedly and pointed out the flash of white bones – hundreds upon hundreds of them – lying half buried in sand under a nearby ridge. The bones were clearly very old, for they were no more than slivers of polished enamel scattered for a great distance along the valley floor. It was impossible to tell whether they belonged to humans or animals. Selmi began digging in the sand with his stick, however, and soon pulled up a thigh-bone like a giant's clenched fist. 'Camel!' he declared. We hunted among the sands further, finding skulls, leg-bones and rib-cages that were clearly those of camels. Selmi pointed mutely to another nest of finds further on still – a galaxy of blackened hearthstones arranged in the triangular pattern used by the Bedu, and scattered around them the butt-ends of sooty sticks, a bent enamel drinking-mug with a hole in it, a pair of sun-browned sardine-cans, a twisted oil-can, even the heat-crushed corner of an old waterskin, and a fibre camel-hobble that fell to pieces at the touch. 'This is Bedu stuff!' he said.

On the way back to the camels, I examined the almost intact

amphora once more. Clearly, the Bedu camel-men had not brought such a thing with them. How old was this vessel? And again – how did it get here? Dumps containing pottery ranging in age from modern to classical have been found in other places in the Western Desert. In 1917 the geologist John Ball, on a military reconnaissance about 120 miles west of Dakhla, sighted a fin-shaped hill, around which he found dozens and dozens of earth-enware pots, all but a few of them smashed. Some were of the style still used in the oases, while others were of ancient Greek origin. Why should so many water-pots be lying here in open desert, he wondered? Inquiring about this place at Dakhla, he was given an answer.

Ever since the dawn of history, Dakhla and her sister oases had been plagued by attacks from scavenging black nomads out of the desert to the west. One such raid had taken place on Farafra around 1770, when the bandits had carried off women and chil-dren. Another one had occurred around 1850, and on this occa-sion the Dakhla people had chased the raiders far out into the desert, tracking them to the place Bell named 'Pottery Hill', and discovering the cache of water-jars. They had smashed most of the pots, believing that they were used by the raiders for storing water. Since the presence of Greek amphorae suggested great an-tiquity, Ball was inclined to think that this water-store had been used by raiders since ancient times, and was itself the origin of the Zerzura legend.

I wanted to take the amphora with me, but, knowing that I would inevitably be accused of 'grave-robbing', and considering the state of our camels, I reluctantly settled for a photograph. Then we quickly roused the caravan and stepped out into the desert. Our stopping-place soon blended into the background as if it had never existed. Had we found a souvenir of Cambyses' army? Was there ever an army in the first place? Why should Cambyses, one of the world's most powerful kings, have con-cerned himself with an unimportant desert oasis such as Siwa, which posed not the slightest military threat to his forces? The

Victorian traveller Vivian St Martin suggested that Herodotus or his informants had been mistaken. He believed that Cambyses' real objective had been not Siwa, but rather the oasis of Dakhla, a reasonable ten days' direct march across the desert from Thebes. Dakhla had also had a temple of Amun, he explained, so the 'Ammonites' mentioned by Herodotus could equally have been the people of Dakhla. Other scholars quickly pointed out that, even if Dakhla had been a town of any importance in Cambyses' day – which it had not – its Ammonian temple dated only from the later, Roman, period.

Fifty thousand men with camels and all the panoply of war would have been a difficult skeleton even for desert as lonely as this to conceal over two and a half millennia, always supposing that there had ever existed a sandstorm powerful enough to bury an army, as Herodotus described. Historian Oric Bates suggested that an ordinary sandstorm had blown up and the Persians had panicked, killing their local guides and wandering around aimlessly until they died of thirst. Others have surmised that the guides were local partisans who had deliberately lured the column into the desert in order to abandon it there. Perhaps the whole story was concocted by the Siwans themselves as a warning to anyone who threatened their oracle. We shall never know for certain, until bones, armour and weapons are recovered from their putative resting-place under the desert sands.

For a while we trekked through a region where table-top plateaux succeeded one another in serried ranks, their walls in places gnawed out by erosion into fantastic pillars and dolmens like the relics of grotesque stonehenge temples, built by a race of giants. Soon, though, the plateaux fell away and we found ourselves in infinite black plains, unchanging mile after mile, hour after hour, day after day, inducing the familiar feeling that we were not travelling through space at all, but merely marking time on the same spot. On these plains there was not a single snail-shell, leaf or blade of grass. There was nothing to indicate that we were in Egypt or, indeed, on planet earth at all. Not only was there no life here, there was no indication that life had ever existed – no camel-grooves, no hearth-bricks, no droppings, no car-tracks. Instead there were stones, stones and more stones – stones like old apples with the cores cut out; stones like squids and sponges; stones like cast-off bits of iron in a welder's yard; stones laid out in patterns as if by children; stones like black and red billiard balls lying on mats of velvet sand. Then, abruptly one evening, a week after the storm, we were dropping down through carved and moulded sugar-loaves, beneath hills like wine-pitchers without handles, to an-other flat valley floor. In the morning we saw the wall of Jabal Quss Abu Sa'id, a forbidding 1,000-foot high amalgam of sheer rock and sand-slope, arching out of the newborn light. This was the landmark we had been searching for – the only recognizable feature in the whole lifeless desert.

It was at precisely this moment that 'Umda collapsed. Selmi managed to coax him up, but after a few minutes of staggering he went down again. This time, even I could observe the ragged panting and the glazed eyes that were symptoms of the disease. We settled him in a patch of sand, and Selmi doled out some grain and – as a desperate emergency measure – a little water in our cooking-pot. Finally we induced him to march again, and reached the base of the inselberg, turning east and trekking along its shadow.

For the first time in days we saw the evidence of rain – channels the water had carved out of the rock and patches of sand with sparse *khurayt* bushes. Selmi told me that it often rained in this area – once every few years at least! The sand turned to brown chalky soil, and there were low plinths of white plaster scattered across the valley like fungi. Unexpectedly, there were camel-tracks – not the grooves of ancient caravans, but fresh tracks and droppings made only a few hours ago. Selmi squeezed a black ball of dung between finger and thumb. 'Eating greens, these camels,' he said. 'Must be camels from Farafra!'

The ground underfoot became softer and softer. In the distance we sighted lines of pencil-cedars like smoke. Then there was the flash and sparkle of light on a stream of liquid coiling across the brown silt. I stopped and peered at it with shaded eyes, thinking that it must be a mirage. But further on there were knots of tamarisk-bush, and a great tract of marshland in a tangle of phragmites reeds. It was no mirage, I realized, but water, running in the desert. No sooner had the camels sniffed it than their heads jerked up and they were pounding towards it, pulling against the headropes for the first time since we had started. We had to run to keep up with them. 'Slowly! Slowly!' Selmi roared. 'Be careful here!' But it was too late. Already the camels were floundering up to their hocks in mud, slipping and sliding in the undreamed-of wetness. Three of them managed to romp through it to a drier patch, but 'Umda's strength deserted him. He lost his footing and plumped over, up to his armpits in the squishy soil. Selmi and I rushed to help him. 'Umda turned on to his side, struggled ineffectually, then lay still, whimpering. We began frantically to dig out the buried limbs which his struggles had only embedded more deeply in the mud. We dug down, and heaved on his back. 'Umda made one last tremendous rally and we heaved again. In a moment he had dragged his legs clear and half-leapt, half-slithered out of the quagmire to join the others on the solid ground. He looked a sorry sight, caked in sulphur-yellow mud up to his shoulders. 'It's criminal!' Selmi said. 'They make a bore and they're supposed to keep the water in a tank with mud walls, but the walls burst and they just leave the water running in the desert like that! There was a Bedui in Baghdad who got twenty-five camels bogged down in the mud in one day. He had to get a tractor to pull them out, but two of them died. Mud is worse than anything for camels, by God! Even the dunes weren't as bad as that!'

Soon we found a pool of open water with more stable banks, where the camels could drink with ease. The water, pumped from another deep bore, was clean and good, lapping around tamarisk and phragmites reeds, from which came the cries of water-birds. The camels lowered their great heads like cranes and drank – for the first time since we had left Imbaba, twenty-three days before.

Selmi filled a bowl and, as we took turns to drink, I watched a black moorhen gliding serenely across the pellucid surface.

Not long before sunset we came to a spin-off from Nasser's 'New Valley' scheme. It was an agro-project outlying the village of Farafra – a huge tract of whiffling green wheat contained in a basin like a giant bathtub, surrounded by a rampart of earth on top which an asphalt road had been laid. All around its rim soft limestone hills had been bulldozed and flattened. Inside the tub, jets of water foamed into the wheat from stand-pipes like huge maggots, and there was the constant burr of tractor-engines. As we led the camels along the base of the earth wall, a man came along the road above us, riding a bicycle. He did not wave or acknowledge our presence in any way. We had not seen a living soul since leaving Siwa, twelve days before, yet the first human being we encountered ignored us completely – it was almost as if we had become invisible.

We reached the corner of the agro-basin, where a gothic-looking pipe protruded from above, decorated with taps and stop-cocks from which water, dripping into the desert beneath, had produced a miniature salt-lick edged with reeds and a few stunted tamarisk-bushes. 'Umda chose this damp place for his demise. His eyes, inflamed now, were almost closed. He slumped down into the salty sand. Both Selmi and I knew this was the end. The sleeping-sickness, the cold, the heat, the hunger and the thirst, had finally finished him. He had already made a heroic effort. 'Pity,' Selmi said. 'It's only one more day to Abu Mingar. If he could just have made it there, he might have been saved!'

On the morning after the following day, we arrived at Abu Mingar, the settlement near Farafra oasis where Selmi's family owned houses and land. Ahmad, Selmi's elder brother, a slight man with an irrepressible smile, stood outside the house watching us descend from the plateau with our three surviving camels. He waited, grinning but composed, as we marched along the dusty track through squares of green wheat and *fuul*-beans, basking suddenly in the smell of rich earth, the trill of birds, the scent of water. Girls in brilliant red and yellow dresses came racing across the cultivation towards us. A Massey-Ferguson tractor, magnificent in scarlet livery, thudded to a halt, and the driver leaned out of the cab to shout a welcome. An escort of youths trailed after us on white donkeys. At Ahmad's house seven or eight Arabs were waiting to greet us. They helped us to couch and unload the camels, gathering close around us, shaking hands, greeting us with the double cheek kiss, exuding relief and palpable warmth. From the background, invisible women loo-loolooed shrilly and small, peanut-faced children peered around doors with saucer-eyes, crying, 'Selmi! Selmi is back with the foreigner!'

'I dreamed Selmi would come today,' said Hiroun, Selmi's uncle, a Bedui with a maudlin face and gold teeth. 'You are heroes, by God!' Selmi swelled with barely contained pride at this compliment, and I felt happy for him. 'But tell me,' Ahmad said, as he ushered us into the shade, and brought water, 'where are the other two camels?'

'How did you know there were two more camels?'

Ahmad grinned again, showing gleaming teeth. 'I got all the news at Imbaba. I arrived there the day after you left and 'Alaysh told me you'd taken five camels. Now I see only three!'

We sank gratefully on to the rugs he had spread for us, and watched Selmi's younger brother, Salim, leading the weary camels off towards some mesquite bushes. Later Salim returned with a cartload of clover which the animals fell on ravenously – the first fresh fodder they had found for many days. Another Arab brought us glasses of scalding tea. As we sipped, Selmi explained how we had left Ghaffir in the Sand Sea, and how, only a day and two nights ago, at sunset, 'Umda's strength had finally given out.

Abu Mingar was the end of the first stage of our journey. From here, we would trek across the open desert to Kharja, and then traverse the limestone plateau that divided the Western Desert oases from the Nile. Ahmad examined Zamzam, our grey she-camel, and announced, 'She's mangy. If you take her much farther, she'll flounder too!' Luckily there was a vet in the village, a young man called Salama who sported Levi jeans and a mock-leather jacket like a city tough but who was nevertheless politely deferent to the Bedu and their knowledge of camels. He puffed Cleopatras from the side of his mouth cowboy-style as he inspected the animal. 'Don't worry,' he said. 'It's not trips in her case. It's just a blood-parasite – oh, and quite a serious attack of mange as well!'

He produced a doctor's black bag and brought out of it a colossal hypodermic like something bought in a joke-shop. While Selmi, Ahmad and I held Zamzam's head, he speared her in the neck, puffing his cigarette and talking: 'Mange isn't a fatal disease. It's really a skin parasite – a sort of fungus that exists in the air and can strike at any time. It causes very bad irritation, though, and can drive the camel so crazy that it can't go on. Then it will die of thirst.' Afterwards he brought out three paper sachets marked 'Naganol', for the blood-parasite. 'I'll have to inject them all,' he said, 'because the parasite is highly contagious.' He asked for three tea-glasses, dissolved a packet of white powder in each, then filled the mammoth syringe and injected the camels in the jugular. Afterwards, as we relaxed over tea, Selmi and the doctor got into a heated argument about camel-ticks, which Salama said developed from eggs laid in the camel's hair, but Selmi asserted formed spontaneously from the camel's blood when it was exhausted.

Selmi's uncle Hiroun slaughtered a sheep for lunch, and we sat in the shade of the *mejlis* on rope-beds as we waited for the women to prepare it, smoking, talking and drinking tea. Mohammad, Selmi's eldest brother – the most experienced caravaneer of the family – was a mildly spoken, almost apologetic man, who seemed fascinated by Zerzura and *The Book of Hidden Pearls*. 'Yes, by God,' he said, 'the treasure of the Romans and the Pharaohs is still there. You only have to know where to look. I've heard about a well near Kharja, for example, in which, if you descend right into its depths, you will find a door. If you open the door you will find yourself in an old town, full of treasure. I know where the well is, but it's very deep and I've never been able to go down it.'

After lunch, he asked me to walk a little way into the desert with him and we sat on rocks warming ourselves with cigarettes in the freezing wind. He was a charming companion, and I wondered why Selmi had said that he was 'outside the family'. When I asked him about this, he was not at all abashed. 'I don't share with the rest of the family, because I found that I was doing all the work – I've been to the salt-place far more than anyone, for example – and I was getting no benefit. I'm hard up. Next time, you should take me on a camel-journey instead of Selmi. Do you know, I've got six daughters and no sons? It's all Fate, of course. I did have a son, but he died when he was four years old.'

'That's hard!'

To my surprise, he actually laughed. I could not make out whether it was to cover his deep anguish, or genuine amusement at my concern.

'It's not hard,' he said, 'it's the Will of God. It's no good getting upset about it. You've got to accept it. It's Fate. It's best just to say, "God have mercy," and accept it rather than crying and beating the wall like some do. We're all going to be dead as doornails soon enough – none of us knows when!'

We sat in silence for a few moments, then finally Mohammad came up with the subject that I suspected had been on his mind from the beginning. 'Omar,' he said, 'next time you come, could you bring me a copy of that book about buried treasure, *The Book of Hidden Pearls*? I'd really appreciate it.'

From Abu Mingar, we made a wide loop through the southern part of the sand-sea, skirting Dakhla oasis, far out in the desert. We trekked through the very heart of Set's country – through Daliesque rocks shaped like sharks and flying swans, fragments of human limbs, butchers-block leftovers, scraps of rusted steel, wafer biscuits, Henry Moore sculptures, wet-look leather coats. It was as if some great and terrible holocaust had swept through this place aeons ago. Were these stones the crashed fallout of some fantastic galactic star-wars; or dragon-bones; or the relics of dino-saurs, I wondered?

The cold never let up now. The days were the coldest I had ever known in the desert, so cold that my hands would tremble as I laced up my saddle, and Selmi would stand quaking helplessly for minutes after getting up, as if paralysed, holding a sack over his hands, moaning, 'It burns! It burns!' until I shouted, 'Get moving, for God's sake or you'll freeze to death!' We learned later that this had been the coldest winter in the Middle East for forty years.

We passed through a region of petrified trees – great gnarled and fluted trunks lying where they had fallen in the sand ages ago, looking precisely like sun-pickled wood, until you ran your fingers along their grain and felt the polished wood surface of old stone. As we walked among them I closed my eyes for a moment and imagined a forest in this lifeless spot. Trees with green canopies quivering above me, humidity, wet ground, insects, animals – it was all here but a moment ago, a heartbeat ago on the scale of the universe. The desert is a space-time continuum – time present and time past, present in time future, and time future in time past. There is no real difference between 1,000 years and 10,000 years, between a million years and a second. I imagined a hunter stalking in a forest here, my ancestor, carrying my seed in his loins. I opened my eyes and saw trees become rock, lying toppled in the sand. What would this place be like tomorrow, in a million years' time? Would there still be a creature called man, or would all his sound and fury have been burned out at the flick of a finger? If I closed my eyes again I could feel the planet's engines rumbling under me, feel the reflexes in my legs tense and relax, feel the earth's electric pulse moving in them, and the universe sizzling in and out of my head like magnetic power. I staggered on with these images spurling through my mind like water, aware of the desert and the camels' pounding feet, but at the same time only dimly aware. Slowly the vision faded and was carried off, leaving imperfect shadows on the shores of my consciousness. The desert did this. The desert restored equilibrium. For the 'Black Land' of the Nile to exist, it was also necessary to have the 'Red Land' of the desert. The existence of the wilderness is essential to the human sense of balance, for only in the wilderness can we truly appreciate who we are, how far we have come and how far we have yet to go. Red Land and Black Land – Horus and Set – desert and sown – wilderness and civilization – each was inconceivable without the other. 'We have long been ill-disposed towards deserts and expanses of tundra and ice,' Barry Lopez has written. 'They have been wastelands for us; historically we have not cared at all what happened in them or to them. I am inclined to think, however, that their value will one day prove inestimable to us.'

As for the Bedu, they are the supreme example of man's ability to adapt to a hostile environment without destroying himself. They are not separate, but merely ourselves in another guise. By living and travelling with them, we urban men can see ourselves more clearly – what we have gained, what we have lost, what we have yet to gain. No longer to be able to do so may be a tragedy for us, but not necessarily for the Bedu. They too must have the knowledge that there exists the possibility of an alternative life. The idea that development provides the answer to all problems – the myth of progress – is as inadequate as all other myths, but a ceaseless trend towards greater and greater technical sophistication is the hominid way. 'Nearly all of us have been told more than once by our tribal elders that things were better in the "good old days",' James Lovelock has written. 'So ingrained is this habit of thought that it is almost automatic to assume that early man was in total harmony with the rest of Gaia . . . [in fact w]hen primates . . . first formed an intelligent nest, its potential for changing the face of the Earth was as revolutionary as that of the photosynthetic oxygen producers when they first appeared aeons before. From the very beginning this organization had the capacity to modify the environment on a global scale.' To yearn for the past is futile, for the past is an illusion – no one knows in which direction it lies. And besides, while the desert exists, and while people herd livestock within it, there will always be Bedu. They may not ride camels or live in tents, they may not even be related to the Bedu of the past, but they will still be Bedu. For the Bedu are not ideal beings, noble people, elves or fairies. The Bedu are people of the desert.

After many days' march we turned due east, and, slugging on through the wastes south of Kharja, we climbed up into the limestone plateau at the pass of Dush. Old 'Eid, Selmi's father, who had made this part of the journey many times, had described the route to us: 'Beyond the pass of Dush, you will find two dead calves,' he had told us. 'Then you will find, next to the camel-tracks, a great stone, called the "Opposition Stone". In the old days caravaneers had to move the stone from one side of the tracks to the opposite side to show that they had passed. It was a kind of test of strength, because the stone is a very heavy one, and shaped so that only one man can lift it. After that you will come to a cairn that divides the way, left to Isna, right to Idfu.' We followed 'Eid's directions exactly, tramping past the skeletons of the two dead calves, and coming shortly afterwards to a single pumpkin-sized stone standing by the side of age-old camel-grooves – the Opposition Stone. I slipped down from my camel and lifted the thing, grunting with effort as I just managed to shift it from the northern side of the grooves to the southern side. Not to be outdone, Selmi jumped down and shifted it back. 'I wonder how long it has been since anyone moved it!' Selmi said, jogging back to his camel. And I realized that this was yet another time-capsule the Bedu employed to communicate across the hidden dimension. I wondered how long it would be till someone moved it again.

After almost a week's marching we descended a steep defile into a sheer-sided gorge axed out by water, aeons ago, which widened gradually into the rocky hammada that verged on the Nile Valley. One morning, just as we were leading the camels off from our camp in sight of the plateau, we heard the sound of engines. Selmi hesitated and stared south. I followed his gaze, and saw, racing across the hard gravel, the shapes of Land-Cruisers –

eight or nine of them – black and silver in the new sun, buzzing towards us in the heat, like flies. 'Those aren't army or police,' Selmi said, his eyes searching wildly around for non-existent cover. 'I don't like the look of it, Omar. They're coming straight towards us.' The drone of the engines was nearer now, and with an ominous appearance of purpose the vehicles sluiced out of the desert in their shrouds of dust, coming to rest in a rough semi-circle around us. There were ten Land-Cruisers, new-looking, each containing one or two hatchet-faced men in long jalab-biyyas, tight turbans or woolly hats and sunglasses. Doors creaked open, and the men began to get out. As they did so, I saw that several of them were armed with Kalashnikov rifles. They watched us with the forbidding countenances of hawks. For a second no one spoke, then Selmi said, without any noticeable nervousness, 'Peace be on you!' The men replied in a grumble with a telling lack of enthusiasm, then one of them, a robust man with a dark face, like a Sudanese, waddled towards us, balancing his Kalash-nikov. The others remained where they were.

'Where are you coming from?' the fat man demanded.

'From Kharja,' Selmi replied.

'What is your tribe?'

'"Awazim.'

'And that man there,' he nodded towards me. 'Who is he?'

'He's an Englishman and he doesn't speak Arabic.'

'I see. What are you carrying?'

'Nothing, only camel-food. The Englishman is on a journey. The *Mukhabaraat* – the Intelligence Service – have given him permission. These are his camels.'

The dark man tensed at the mention of the Intelligence Service. He rubbed his chin with a bulbous paw. For a moment the tension was palpable. Then he snapped, 'Move on, and don't look at the cars. If anyone asks, you haven't seen us!'

'Of course,' Selmi replied, as we started the camels moving. 'It's not our business. Come on, Omar!'

We marched way from the semicircle of cars briskly but not as briskly as to suggest fear, putting a hundred, two hundred, three hundred yards between ourselves and them. 'Don't look back!' Selmi whispered urgently. At last we heard the sound of engines gunning and gears grating. Only after another interval did we glance behind to see the cars searing off into the haze of the desert. 'Who on earth were they?' I asked.

'They were 'Ababda, Arabs from the eastern desert,' Selmi said. 'I know them. I could tell by their accent. Thank God you were with me, Omar! Only the fact that you were a foreigner and had the permission of the *Mukhabaraat* saved us. That's why I said you didn't know Arabic. Thank God, you didn't speak! If I'd been on my own, they would probably have shot me! The only people who drive through the desert like that are smugglers, and they think nothing of silencing witnesses. Who would ever know out here, so far from the Nile? Pray God they don't change their minds and come back!'

Selmi looked genuinely frightened, and I felt a thrill of adrenalin, followed by the sinking sensation that came with the knowledge that we had no weapons, and not the least chance of defending ourselves if they happened to change their minds. I thought again of the corpse found by Vance Haynes – so many secrets concealed in the desert.

'What do you think they were smuggling?' I asked.

'I reckon it was fish.'

Despite my apprehension, I burst into loud giggles, at which Selmi looked seriously offended. 'Good God!' I said. 'Tell me it was rifles or heroin or opium or anything, but don't tell me we stood to lose our lives for a few smelly boxes of fish!'

The minutes passed, the hours passed, and we heard no growl of engines. By afternoon we had drifted under great electricity lines crackling with power generated by the Nile in Aswan, on its way to light up Cairo. The camels mounted hard gravel shoals from which the earth opened to reveal the Nile Valley below us. 'There it is, Omar!' Selmi said. 'God is generous. When those cars pulled up this morning I thought we'd never make it!'

There were acres of green such as we had not seen in the two months of our journey, peat-brown mud villages, factories belching smoke, and, to the south, the river was a snake of quicksilver meandering around a leaf-shaped island. From this height, with the weight of 1,000 camel-miles of Red Land behind us, I could see the valley as it really was – a fragile strip of fertility in the most sterile desert on earth.

We passed out of the Red Land, following car-tracks, bulldozer-tracks, camel-tracks down towards the asphalt road that outlay the Nile, but before we had come within a few hundred yards of it, a decrepit pick-up screeched to a halt, and out dived five or six soldiers in battledress, led by an officer. They lined up outside the jalopy, rifles at the ready, with what seemed exaggerated drama. But I could see triumph on their faces – they had caught us red-handed, they were thinking, two ragged Bedouin smugglers with laden camels in the very act of reaching the Nile. The soldiers advanced on us. '*As salaam 'alaykum!*' I said. No one replied.

One of them – a heavy man with eyes of Afrangi green and a gingery complexion rarely seen in Egyptians – halted impertinently close to me, and shook a hairy, freckled fist under my chin, eyes flaming with righteousness. 'What have you got in those panniers?' he wanted to know.

'Listen,' I said, fixing my eyes on his, 'I am an Englishman and a guest in your country. I have permission from the *Mukhabaraat* for this journey, so I will thank you to speak to me with a little more respect!' The soldier's eyes registered disappointment. The fire slowly died within them. It had all seemed so obvious. The officer gave him a scowl and shoved him away. 'Your permission, please?' he said. I produced my carefully preserved piece of paper and he scrutinized it, then handed it ruefully back. 'There are a lot of smugglers about,' he said, half in apology, half in explanation for the rough treatment. 'Did you see any cars out there?'

'No,' Selmi cut in. 'We saw nothing.'

The officer directed us grudgingly towards Bimban, the

famous ferry-point on the west bank where camel-herds were transported across the Nile after their forty-five-day journey from the Sudan, to the camel-market at Daraw. We were in Upper Egypt, where the Nile Valley was wilder and less populated than further north, and where the river meandered through narrows dominated by palmeries, acacia-woods, and terraced limestone cliffs. We hauled the camels across the asphalt road, past a field where a phalanx of Fellahin with troglodyte faces and flowerpot hats were slashing down sugar-cane with bush-knives that glittered and brilled like swords as they advanced. Other men were hefting loads of cane on to the back of a four-ton truck. 'Where are you coming from?' someone shouted. 'From the Oases!' Selmi shouted back.

The men looked blankly. 'Where's that?' one asked. 'Is it in the Sudan?'

'No, no!' someone else answered him. 'The Oases are a long way. Near Libya. Libya itself, really!'

Selmi smirked. 'These Nile Fellahs only know the Sudan,' he said. 'They don't even know where the Oases are!' We followed the crags along the river, where a path had been beaten in the dust by the tracks of scores of camels going to the ferry-point at Bimban. Below us the sunlight formed a million gold dewdrops that rode like stars on the deep, sombre stream. We descended to a road that wound through more green fields – banana trees with their leaves burned copper-brown – trenches full of stagnant green water – palms with rustling feather heads.

We found a deserted place close to the riverbank to make camp. The acacias here were in bloom, and their caramel perfume mingled with the smells of humidity, dust and sweet earth. 'Every time I smell that smell – the scent of the Nile Valley – I feel drunk!' Selmi said. We unloaded near some trees on a shelf from which we could see the river scything east around the hull of the island. After we had hobbled the camels so that they could browse leisurely, we sat by the phragmites reeds that shrouded the shore, smoking our pipes, and listening to the glugging of water against

the banks, like music. The sunlight fell in silk bars across the rip-
ples. A felucca glided past under sail, like a floating flower. A bum-
boat breasted the current, laden with stones, shirts flapping like
signal-flags from a line across its deck. Squads of cormorants with
sheeny black feathers preened themselves on limestone steeples
high above the trees. A black and white kingfisher, perched on an
overhanging branch, made a headlong dive, splashing into the
stream, and reappeared carrying a small silver fish. Suddenly a
great pleasure-boat chugged into view, a floating white tourist-
palace on whose decks sprawled men in shorts and women in
bikinis. They saw us sitting there and waved and pointed cameras
at the camels. Selmi and I shouted and waved back, rolling with
laughter.

As the sun sank into an aurora behind us, the phragmites reeds
were inflamed. The river sucked and lapped at the shore. From
somewhere upstream came the poignant fugue of the Call to
Prayers. To know fully the beauty of the Black Land, one must
also know the hardship of the Red – it had been worth marching
1,000 miles across the most arid part of the earth, just to absorb
that fact. The sun-disc was a delicate hyacinth-coloured ball spinning on the edge of eternity, its day's journey done. For a
moment the great theatre of the world halted to watch its fall into
Ament, the Country of the Dead.

# 9

# Voyage into Nubia

Souq sounds washed through the window of my room in Aswan like a dawn chorus – the braying of a donkey, the rumble of carts wheeling down the narrow street, the constant gurning of voices. I awoke with the rags of a dream in my head, and for a moment I was disoriented. I recalled the streets of the bazaar the previous evening, the light slumping along them like liquid lead, the drift of blown sand in the gutters, the skirl of Arab music, baskets of dates, rolls of carpet, the smells of coffee and spices, a boy riding pell-mell on a donkey, yelling '*Baalak!*', an angular Sudanese camel-man still wearing the desert's dust, shouting at a shop-keeper.

I had to crank my memory backwards, pausing at each signifi-cant node – yesterday afternoon I had parted with Selmi at Daraw; yesterday morning we had sold the camels; the night before, we had slept in the palm-groves outside the market, and the night before that, on the riverbank. While waiting for the pick-up to take him back to Kharja, I remembered, Selmi had asked me a question, that, he said, had puzzled him for some time. 'How was it,' he asked, 'that you knew where to find us? I mean, we were the only people in Egypt who could have helped you on that journey, and yet you knew exactly where to come. How did you know?' There had been no time to tell him the full story then, but now, as I lay in bed, drinking in the sounds of the street, my thoughts returned to the Sudan, the country that, over a period of almost ten years, had become my home. I recalled that last journey I had made with Jibrin to Selima oasis, a journey that, in a sense, had begun here in Aswan, on a crisp winter morning like this one, when I had boarded the Lake Nasser ferry, bound for Wadi Halfa.

After breakfast I took the train to the High Dam. The morning sun was already burning the colours out of the sallow sky, purging the dam's long shelf of shrinking shadows. Seagulls were riding the thermals above the smoke-blue waters, and the wakes of giant catfish were circling along the hull of the steamer *Sinai*. The ferry was already at the quay with its barges lashed alongside, looking as if they might have graced a gunboat in the days of General Gordon. The Sudanese were massed to take occupation, a wild army of tall, dark men in gleaming white robes and turbans, standing amid humps of luggage. Egyptian officers in tight uniforms and peaked caps were strutting about with hands on hips, or posing to tilt bottles of 7-Up to their mouths with self-conscious nonchalance. The ramp crashed down on the quayside, and the signal to embark was given. The Sudanese struggled, twisted, elbowed, cursed, and thrust themselves into a crazy dogs-leg of a line, as if gathering for an assault. Already you could taste the wildness of the Sudan, a thrilling, otherwordly sense of the exotic that belonged to no other country.

By the time I reached the third class quarters – the deck – the passengers had already crammed themselves into almost every available nook and cranny, and many were already crouching around white enamel bowls, dipping their hands into Egyptian *fuul* and white cheese. I made my way up to the roof of the crew's cabins where an incredibly weedy, bronze-skinned young man in European clothes was already sitting. I took him to be Sudanese, but he introduced himself as Abdu, a Somali with Kenyan citizenship. 'It will be cold up here at night,' he told me in English, 'but for now it is better than being stuck down on deck!' Abdu's only baggage was a blanket and a black briefcase, which he opened to reveal, among other papers, a neat wad of air-tickets – perhaps eight or ten of them. My curiosity was engaged. It was impossible to say whether or not the tickets were used, but if they were not, why was this young Somali travelling third class on the Lake Nasser ferry? If they were used, why was he carrying them, neatly banded, in his briefcase? He plucked a address-card from the case and snapped it shut. The card read: '*Abdal Gadir: Khadija Islamic University of Angola*'. 'That is my work,' he said, 'I am founding an Islamic University in Angola.'

'But why Angola? It's hardly an Islamic country!'

'That's the reason I chose it. It is a communist country. There are no Muslims, but I hope we will make converts. We will teach all subjects, especially Islamic subjects, and all students will be welcome. I have been working on this project for four years, with only God's backing. I made a request for 150 million dollars from the Islamic Development Bank in Saudi Arabia, and from the Al Saud. They have promised to help. I am also expecting support from the Gulf countries – Kuwait, Bahrein, Qatar, and the others!'

I wasn't quite sure what to make of this. There was a fanatic, almost hypnotic gleam in Abdu's eyes which made me feel slightly uneasy. Were these delusions of grandeur, or a calculated confidence trick on the grand scale?

We watched the final passengers picking their way through the crowds on deck: two colossal women in pink *taubs*, their faces deeply etched with vertical Nubian tribal scars, exuding the fragrance of smoked sandalwood; some stick-dry camel-men from the Red Sea coast, who had just driven camels all the way from the Sudan; a tribe of dark-faced Nubians, carrying canteens of aluminium vessels fitting neatly inside each other like Russian dolls; a trickle of waxen-faced farmers wearing woollen hats, yakking incessantly over the price of dates.

At last the ramp was shut with a bang. The screw churned. A wet breeze snaked amid the tight-wedged passengers. A youth began to play an accordion, pumping out base tones – and a hum of repetitive bars spiralled around the deck in a swelling vortex. *Sinai* shook and rocked like an old motor-wagon out into the lake.

This lake – 'Nasser' to the Egyptians and 'Nubia' to the Sudanese – had grown out of the eternal Egyptian dream of controlling the restless waters of the Nile, on which the country's life depended. The ancient Egyptians had never discovered the source of the Nile, nor understood why the inundations came during the hottest part of the summer. They knew only that in the years when the floods did not arrive they faced starvation, and if the waters failed for successive years the entire edifice of their civilization might topple. From time immemorial they had sought to appease the Nile gods, but in the industrial era their successors aspired to conquer them through the miracles of technology. By the turn of this century, the demography of Egypt had altered little since Pharaonic times – its population stable at about 10 million. By mid century, however, the population had doubled, and would very soon be trebling. Egypt ceased to be the exporter of foodstuffs it had been for millennia: it needed desperately to cultivate new land. The solution was the High Dam at Aswan. Completed in 1960, the dam created a reservoir – the lake – which extends 500 kilometres south, covers an area of 5,000 square kilometres, and has brought 2 million acres of new land under tillage.

Abdu and I arranged our baggage, and looked at the baked-crust edges of the hills with their shaded terraces and flat tops, almost fluorescent in the high sun. The waters were curls of steel-blue, creamed along the surface with runnels of spume. Abdu told me he was on his way back from Saudi Arabia. 'When I got there the Saudis arrested me because I didn't have a visa,' he said. 'I told them I had come to perform the 'Umra – the Minor Pilgrimage – not to try and get a job. They sent me to Riyadh, but they gave my passport to an air-stewardess with instructions to see that I reported to the authorities there. I managed to give her the slip at Riyadh airport and got away.'

'How did you manage that?'

'Easy. I have the power to make myself invisible.'

'Really!'

'Yes. When you reach such a high level of Quranic study as I have, you develop special powers. You see that this life and all the world are nothing. You should not fear any government – they are nothing. Only God is Great!'

'So you escaped by becoming invisible?'

'Yes, but after a while it wore off. I was arrested by the police and held in prison for nine days. I decided then that if God did not help me perform the Minor Pilgrimage I would resign from Islam. Then the Prophet sent me a message – it was brought by some pigeons which I saw from the window. The message said that I would be taken to Jeddah, and once I arrived I should say, "I'm going to Mecca. Goodbye!" and walk out. Well, the next day they took me to Jeddah in a prison-bus – it was a long journey, I was handcuffed, and the bus had no air-conditioning. But we had hardly got out of Riyadh when it broke down – this was a sign that invisible forces were working for me. At Jeddah prison I was surrounded by soldiers, but the moment they unlocked the cuffs, I said: "I'm going to Mecca. Goodbye!" and I simply walked out. No one lifted a finger to stop me! In the end I had an interview with the Sharif of Medina, who promised to supply me with twenty thousand copies of the Holy Quran!'

All this was related with a dead-pan face, burning eyes, and the perfect appearance of sincerity. Abdu fumbled in his briefcase again, and came up with another address-card. This time it read: 'Abdal Gadir: President: The World Security Council of Islam'. Delusions of grandeur indeed!

By now it was midday, and the sun was a savage overlord in a sky unblunted with cloud. The heat reverberated back from the steel decks. I suggested a trip to the first class saloon – the only place where decent meals were served. We sat at a square wooden table covered in a plastic tablecloth bearing poor reproductions of Pharaonic tomb-paintings. The steward brought us omelettes,

Egyptian *fuul*, cheese, jam, fresh bread and coffee. As we were tucking in, Abdu asked: 'Why are you travelling to the Sudan?'

I explained that my interest was principally in the Bedu.

'That's interesting,' he said. 'I am a Bedui myself – almost every Somali is a Bedui!'

There was truth in this: though the Somalis were not Arab, and did not speak Arabic as their mother-tongue, they did fit into at least one definition of the Bedu – as nomads who lived in the desert. Even in south Arabia, Somalis were considered tribesmen and counted as being on a par with the noble Bedu tribes. And Somalia was the world's leading producer of camels – with 3 million head, it outstripped even the Sudan. 'I was a camel-boy until I was eleven years old,' Abdu went on. 'I was born the last child of a woman called Halima. She had produced four children before me – three boys and a girl – but the boys all died, so my father divorced her while she was pregnant with me, and married a woman called Hawa. When I was small my sister and I were sent to live with Hawa, who had children of her own. They were younger than us, but bigger and stronger, so they used to beat us. Hawa used to water down our camel's milk so that we would always be weak. When I was about seven, I rebelled, and of course Hawa had been waiting for this excuse to attack me. She choked me until I wet myself and fainted. But my sister ran to call a neighbour – an old man – who stopped her going further, otherwise she would surely have killed me! Later, my mother, Halima, arrived at our camp, and heard the story, but said nothing. The same day we were moving pasture, and she packed her camels and moved out with us. Out in the bush, mother stopped and tied her camels to a tree. Then she thrashed the living daylights out of Hawa with her fists and feet. "That's a lesson to you for beating my children!" she said. Hawa couldn't resist her, because my mother was big and very strong, and Hawa was afraid of getting a worse beating. Mother just laid her on the back of one of the camels and led them to a new camp, where my father was to be found. She told him what had happened and that she was taking my sister and me with her: "If you want to fight, I'm ready to take you on," she told him, but my father was aware of her strength and of the shame of being beaten by a woman, and let us go. After that we went to live with my grandfather at Al Wak.'

Later, we were invited to the crew's quarters below decks by a galley-mate with one blind eye, who claimed to have served with the British army. He brought us tea, while five men in sneakers and torn trousers, crammed around a tiny table, played dominoes, shuffling and reshuffling the plastic pieces, creating ever new configurations on the table, slapping them down with terrific force as if trying to intimidate each other into submission, keeping up an endless current of banter as they played. Near sunset we were back on our perch, as the steamer approached Abu Simbel – a great protrusion of rock from which the famous temple of Amun-Ra emerged, its vast statues of Ramses II staring with blind eyes and self-satisfied expressions through the sea-damp aura. Centuries after these colossi had first been hauled into place by the Pharaoh's slaves, parties of men whose tribes and tongues had not even existed in Ramses' day had sawed the old temple to pieces, moved the pieces with machines, and glued the entire structure together only 200 feet from where it had always stood.

Before the 1960s, the long stretch of river between Aswan and Wadi Halfa, now uninhabited, had been a living, flourishing land of palm-groves and mud-built villages, the homeland of more than 100,000 Nubian Fellahin. Half of them were officially Egyptian, half Sudanese, but they shared languages and a culture which had survived the ragbag of races – including the Arabs – they had absorbed from the outside world. The villages and palm-groves had been drowned by the waters of the lake and the tribesmen transplanted, the Egyptians to Kom Ombo, north of Aswan, and the Sudanese to New Halfa, in the semi-arid plains of the eastern Sudan.

The sky was painted suddenly with clouds like bats' wings, and a thousand little rivulets of fire slipped along the darkening waters. As the day melted into methyl orange along the banks, I reflected that it was on this route that Bedu warriors first entered the Sudan, soon after they had conquered Egypt in AD 642. In Nubia they encountered a very different enemy from the enfeebled Byzantine regiments they had so recently defeated in the Delta. In Egypt, the Byzantine rulers had lacked the vital support of the Christian natives, some of whom welcomed the Arabs as their deliverers. The Christian kingdoms of Nubia, however, were indigenous and well organized, accustomed to defending their borders against Egyptian incursions. Their bowmen – the famed 'Nubian archers' – proved doughty foes, as the Arab historian Al Baladhuri recalled: 'I saw one of them [a Nubian] saying to a Muslim, "where would you like me to place my arrow in you?" and when the Muslim replied "in such-and-such a place," he would not miss.' As a result of such haughty skill, the Arabs returned 'with many injured and blinded eyes, so that the Nubians were called "the pupil smiters".'

In time, the Arabs had abandoned the idea of conquering the *Bilad as Sudan* – the 'Land of the Blacks' – and instead concluded a treaty with the Christian king whose capital lay at Old Dongola, on the east bank of the Nile. The Nubians agreed to pay a number of slaves annually to the Arabs, and to allow Muslim traders access to their markets without hindrance, in return for immunity from attack, and quantities of grain, wine and horses. This treaty – *al Baqt* – defined relations between Muslim Egypt and Christian Nubia for 600 years.

During those centuries the Bedu achieved by infiltration what they had failed to achieve by military conquest. Following the Muslim invasion of Egypt, each new governor brought his own private contingent of Bedu troops, swelling the numbers of restless warriors moving up the Valley of the Nile. In 834 all Bedu fighters in Egypt had their salaries and pensions struck off. Many returned to the life of pastoralists, driving their herds ever farther year by year, until they reached the rich ranges of the Sudan. By the fourteenth century, the Juhayna – a tribe which had migrated to Egypt in 732 – were established on the Butana plain between the Atbara and the Blue Nile. Bedu families also drifted down the west bank of the Nile, and by 1300 they had formed a rough confederation across the desert marches of Kordofan and Darfur. This assortment of nomads raised camels and sheep, and since they were of both Qahtanite and Ishmaelite origin, they named themselves *Kababish*, after the Arabic word *kabsh* – meaning a ram. Today, the Kababish remain the largest group of camel-herding Bedu in the Sudan.

After dark, Abdu continued with his autobiography, holding me spellbound with his mesmeric tale. 'When I was eleven, I went to school in Nairobi,' he said. 'I didn't distinguish myself there. But my uncle, who was working in America, arranged for me to go to Newark County College in Washington State. At first the USA amazed me, but the shine soon wore off. I found the Americans uncivilized and racist, and I was glad to get back to Kenya at the end of the year. My uncle had a transport business, shipping coffee from Uganda – a very profitable business – and he gave me a lorry. In a few years I had a fleet of lorries of my own and I was making more money than my uncle. The trouble was that I was living a wild life – spending too much on women and qat and entertaining – and soon I had no money to pay any hire-purchase debts. The finance company repossessed my vehicles and I was indicted on a charge of forgery and corruption. I never maintained that I was innocent – I admitted I was guilty – but I told the judge that I had no fear of the government, because my government was God, and I only feared Him. This made a great impression on the Muslims and was reported in the press. I received a message from the Prophet that I would not be punished severely. Everyone was saying I would get thirty years in prison, but as it turned out I only got two years' probation. No one could believe it! I still had the problem of bankruptcy, though. My uncle told me that no one in the family would help me, because I had rejected the advice of my elders and lived a wild life. I told him I didn't need his help: I needed only the help of God. Well, the next day I got the bus to Nairobi and I found a sack on the seat next to me. Inside it there was almost one million Kenyan shillings! I went to the finance company and got one of my lorries out of hock, and I was soon in business again!'

I felt like commenting that I wished all *my* problems could be answered with such prompt manna from Heaven, but Abdu told his stories with a 'disbelieve-it-if-you-dare' attitude that defied mockery. These might be delusions, but if so they were tales constructed with loving detail. Instead, I asked why God should have rewarded him for such evident wrong-doing. 'Faith in God will always be rewarded,' he answered, without a moment's hesitation. 'We should not fear anyone or anything but God.'

The steamer docked at Wadi Halfa at about ten in the morning, and the crowds erupted into a frenetic madness, screaming and tearing their way to the ramp. Abdu and I waited, leaning on the rails and watching a troop of Sudanese longshoremen unloading sacks of onions and sheafs of aluminium buckets from the vessel's hold. Before the creation of the Nubian Lake, Wadi Halfa had been a fine old river-town of noble buildings, housing more than 40,000 people. The new Wadi Halfa, which stood several kilometres from the docks, though, was a shanty railhead of buildings constructed partly of mud and partly of sleepers and rails taken from the railway which Kitchener's army had built along the Nile in 1898. The shacks were spreadeagled over a treeless yellow plain, whose pale foundations fell into the dazzling blue and silver waters of the lake. On two sides the town was contained in an amphitheatre of weathered sandstone crags sculpted by the chafing sands of the Nubian desert.

We joined the queue of Sudanese being marshalled by immigration officials in uniforms of grey dacron. A hollow-cheeked old sergeant examined my passport and said: 'Your visa has expired!'

I looked at him in astonishment and began to protest, when he held up the document with a languid expression. 'Expired yesterday!'

'What can I do?'

'We can do it here, but for a price – let's say fifty Sudanese pounds?'

'That seems a bit stiff!'

'You think that's stiff? I'll tell you, fifty is nothing! I have been working here for thirty-three years, and I still don't have the price of my own coffin!'

Afterwards we made for the station, where the Khartoum train was standing ready. Donkey-powered carts were creaking into the yard carrying loads of custard-powder and Chinese lamps, and traders were setting out piles of Egyptian goods on fibre sheets to tempt the passing travellers: monstrous platform-soled shoes, synthetic textiles in the most sickeningly gaudy colours, aluminium cooking-pots and woollen shawls. On the platform I parted with Abdu, whose destination was Khartoum, and set off to find a lorry heading down the Nile.

There was no proper road along the east bank of the Nile, only a crude track that alternately followed the river or threaded out between the sandstone buttes of the Nubian desert. Along the alluvial terraces big, spare men with faces of acacia bark, as brown as the soil, were at work on the rich earth, following the wizened haunches of oxen trundling ploughs. We bounced through strings of villages, glimpsing the flash of the Nile through acacia-jungles, sleeping at night on the floor of one-roomed inns, eating bread still warm from the baker, and drinking many glasses of tea. We passed through Akasha, Abri, Delgo, Kerma and Seleim. On the fourth day from Wadi Halfa, I was stepping off a lorry at the town of Ed Debba.

# 10

# *To the Last Oasis*

Ed Debba was a rural market which for generations had served the desert nomads. It was here that the Wadi al Milik, a seasonal watercourse, in places thickly forested, in others a stagger of thorn-trees across sterile desert, drained into the Nile. The Wadi al Milik was the watering-place for almost four-fifths of the Kababish, yet in prehistoric times, when the Sahara was greener than it is today, it was a perennial river and an important artery of movement. It was probably along Milik that the mysterious cattle-people known to archaeologists simply as the C-Group colonized the Nile, migrating from the plains of the Sahara, as it turned barren year by year. In time, these cattle-people would be succeeded by camel-rearing men.

I had come to Ed Debba to find a companion for a long camel journey. Ever since my first visit to the Sudan, years ago, it had been an ambition of mine to reach Selima, a tiny oasis near the Sudanese–Egyptian border, once a station on the ancient caravan-route known as the Forty Days Road.

In the souq I was introduced to a Bedui from the Kababish, called Jibrin. About thirty-five years old, he was small and lean as a gazelle, beardless except for a toothbrush fuzz of whisker on his firm chin, his eyes the smoke-grey shade that some Kababish had, his features hard and angular like interlocking blades. His body might have belonged to an athlete or a swimmer – broad shoulders, rope-like pectorals, muscular thighs, clearly defined calves. He moved with a curious spring-like quality that I had only seen among nomads. Jibrin was modest, reserved, and mindful of his dignity. He was a man who saw all and said little: his speech clipped, gruff, considered, and to the point.

Jibrin had pitched his camels'-hair tent squarely in the middle of the market-place, as if in protest against the terrible drought that had shorn his family of their animals and their livelihood. 'All my life I've lived in the desert,' he told me, 'and I've seen plenty of bad years, but never one as bad as this. In the desert, if it doesn't rain in one place you can pack your tent on your camels and move to the place where it has rained. But this year we had no-where to move to. The rains usually come during the hot season, and as soon as the news breaks we move south. Then we follow the clouds – women, children, tents and everything, halting for a few days wherever there's pasture. In a good year we would go right into the Great ʿAtmur and the men and boys would stay there for weeks sleeping on the ground and drinking only camel's milk. When the grazing is over, and the days get hotter, we retire to the wells in the Wadi al Milik with our families.'

This year, as they sweltered out the summer in the wadi, news of the rains had never come. Jibrin's family, like many others, had decided that they had no alternative but to trust themselves to the safekeeping of God and move to the Nile. Though Jibrin had visited Ed Debba once or twice before to sell animals, the river remained for him a foreign land. 'We always dislike the towns and villages, and always distrusted the townspeople,' he said. 'Some of them are good and some bad, of course, but most of them are out to take your money or cheat you in one way or another. In the desert we were free. Our law was the law of the tribe. It's true that the tribes were always fighting, and there were camel-raids and blood-feuds, but at least you knew who the enemy was. In the towns we are subject to the police and the government, who always demand money and treat us badly. The government is just a trick to steal money from poor people. The merchants, the

police, the army – they're all in on it! And if they are the government, why didn't they help us in the drought? Why did they leave
us to starve, when they've got plenty?'

Now, stranded in the town without his animals, Jibrin had
begun to wonder if he would ever escape. 'The towns are dirty
places,' he commented. 'Even the air is full of fevers. We hadn't
been in Debba for more than a week when my nephew and my
wife went down with the sickness.' He had been obliged to take
on work for a wealthy townsman, watering the trees in his palm-
groves. This was better than starving, though it was demanding
work for a Bedui. If the palms had been his own, he would have had
no such reservations, but the work was hard and the man paid him
a pittance, because he knew Jibrin had no choice. 'How I hate the
town!' Jibrin said. 'You can't see the sky there like you can in the
desert. You feel shut in. You can't read the tracks because there are
so many, all crossing each other and fouling each other up. You
can't trust your senses because there are so many smells and noises
and sights to contend with. In the desert you know every tribe,
and even if you don't know the individual by sight, you can soon
tell who he is and where he belongs. In the towns people are all
mixed up and you don't know who is who.'

Despite the suspicion the Bedu reserved for the settled places
along the river, there had always been an intimate relationship between the desert and the sown. They were not separate but like a
pair of scales constantly shifting in balance. Since the earliest times
nomads had been spilling out of the Sahara as its climate fluctu-
ated from fertile to arid, finding a niche among the villagers and
eventually merging with them. It was interesting to note that in
times of hardship the Kababish automatically moved east to the
Nile rather than west to the hills of Chad, almost as if they had a
traditional memory of the safe havens to be found there. Their
dialect words for 'north' and 'south' mean 'down' and 'up' re-
spectively, which suggested a long-standing orientation along the
direction of the river. Among the original population of the river-
banks – the Nubians – who had retained their own languages,

there were pockets of Arabs who had kept their old tribal names and spoke Arabic, yet who had been farmers for generations. Obversely, there were fully nomadic Kababish clans who had almost certainly, at one time or another, been settled along the Nile. Bedu to Hadr to Bedu – nomad to farmer to nomad – it was a reversible system in ceaseless motion, and as Jibrin and I rode north along the Nile's banks from Ed Debba, I found striking evidence of it.

Along the stark gravel shoulders of the desert, outside the palm-groves and farthest from the river, stood the tents of new arrivals – Bedu displaced by the recent drought, as Jibrin's family had been. They were shelters of the most temporary nature – often no more than a ragged piece of woven camels' hair draped over a frame of sticks – that could be loaded on a camel within moments. The Bedu had not bothered to take pains over pitching their tents properly, as if to say, 'We're not staying long!' Further in, on the plain between the cliffs and the palm-groves, were straw dwellings, extended with bits of tent, sometimes surrounded by wire pens containing knots of goats or a brace of hobbled camels. These were more permanent, but could still be packed up and moved if circumstances changed. In the next rank of houses, though, straw walls were being replaced by mud-brick, and further in still were Arab huts built entirely of mud. Their owners were in transition from Bedu to Fellahin – they had come to stay. Beyond them, among the verdant foliage of the palm-groves, stood only the mud forts of the Nubians and the tribes who claimed Kababish ancestry, but were no longer counted among the nineteen sections of the desert Kababish.

I recalled how, on my last journey in the Sudanese desert, I had picked up a small, blue stone shaped like a bivalve, polished on both sides, with a keen cutting edge. I had known at once, having seen many like it, that it was a stone celt or hand-axe of the type made by nomads of the C-Group perhaps 5,000 years ago. I handled the smooth stone, feeling how perfectly it fitted into my palm, how painstakingly it had been shaped and sharpened all those centuries ago. Primitive beside a smart bomb, perhaps, but in its time the ultimate state-of-the-art precision engineering. Who were the engineers, I had wondered, whose humanity was hidden under the remorseless term 'C-Group'? What was their story?

Between 1929 and 1934, a prehistorian called Oliver Myers, who was excavating at Armant, in Upper Egypt, had unearthed some curious potsherds. Quite unlike any other ancient Egyptian pottery, they proved to be identical to sherds found in several sites across the Sahara – the nearest at the oasis of Bilma, 1,500 miles away. Myers realized with mounting excitement that he had happened on the remains of a lost Saharan culture that had once stretched from the Atlantic to the Nile.

Myers's first objective was to establish the age of this pottery. Sifting through the dust in the excavation-site, his team found evidence that suggested a connection with the VIth Dynasty, beginning with the Pharaoh Unas in 2400 BC. Myers began a careful study of ancient Pharaonic texts from the period, and came across a reference to a tribe of cattle-breeding nomads – the Temehu – who had first been sighted in Egyptian territory at this time. Could the Armant pottery-makers and the Temehu be one and the same? As Myers reconstructed some almost complete vessels, he noticed that they were strikingly similar to others belonging to the people prehistorians already knew as the C-Group – named after their C-shaped hieroglyph – who had arrived on the Nile in Nubia around the same time. He divined that C-Group and Temehu were branches of a related culture, a cattle-herding people which had migrated out of the desert in mass exodus in the third millennium BC. In that era, quite suddenly, the once-fertile Sahara had become inhospitable to cattle-rearing men.

For the story of the C-Group, I realized, I had no further to look than to Jibrin, to his people the Kababish, to the changing texture of the Bedu dwellings along the hard shoulder of the Nile. The time had been different, the details varied, but the story was essentially the same. A nomadic people, whose appearance and language we do not know, had been driven out of the desert by climatic changes still not fully understood. Their cattle-culture had eventually been replaced by one more adapted to the severe conditions of the desert – the camel-culture. Now, 5,000 years on, the wheel turned again, and those same camel-breeders, once the 'new men' of the desert, were being driven out by precisely the same inexorable forces.

On our first evening, near Al Ghaba, we halted at one of the mud-brick houses built outside the palm-groves, occupied by the family of Hamid, a cousin of Jibrin's. Lean and lithe like Jibrin, Hamid was dressed in a long, townsman's jallabiyya and a white skull-cap. He welcomed us with the profuse, lingering greeting of the Bedu, clasping our hands over and over again, repeating, 'God greet you! God's blessing upon you! Your coming is blessed! God give you peace!' Hamid and his son unsaddled our camels with their own hands and laid our equipment neatly along the wall of their house. Later, they dragged out their own *angarebs* – beds of heavy wood upholstered with string, like Indian charpoys – and insisted that we slept on them, though I knew that this meant they themselves would be sleeping on the ground.

They brought armfuls of sorghum-stalks for our camels and adamantly refused to take money for it, though I guessed that Hamid had had to buy it himself. After dark our host laid before us a bowl of goat stew with fresh salad and quarters of home-made bread, apologizing repeatedly that there was no fresh goats' milk. 'What could we wish for more than this?' Jibrin countered. 'God requite you! May your bounty increase!'

Hamid had been living on the Nile for a couple of years, and his talk was of date-farming, crop-growing and the price of cattle. 'It's not a bad life in the village,' he said. 'In the desert it's so pre-carious – you live close to the margin, and if a bad year comes you go over and everything you have is gone. Here things are more re-liable, because we've got the one thing that the Sons of Adam must have to survive – water. That makes all the difference. The people of the Nile are more "civilized" than those of the desert. They wear clean clothes, they wash, they have decent food to eat. A lot of them can read and write. I want my children to go to school, and maybe – God is all-knowing – to university and to become important people. Here, everything is possible.' Jibrin remained unconvinced, however. 'It's green here, I'll grant you,' he said, 'and there's water. You have to say it's more fertile than the desert. But you feel confined here by walls, and houses and people. It's like being in prison. Give me the open country any time!'

After we had eaten and drunk several glasses of very sweet tea, Hamid fetched his prize possession – a Japanese radio/cassette-player – something I had never seen among the desert Kababish. 'Listen to this!' he said, proudly, as he snapped into place a cassette of modern Sudanese music and turned up the volume. Jibrin smiled appreciatively, but my heart sank. I knew that Hamid had brought out the cassette-player for our entertainment, but as the singer's voice squawked and trembled to the crash of the band, I longed for the silence of the desert.

The next morning Hamid walked us out of the village, as Bedu politeness demanded. Then we trekked along the desert road. On our left the Sahara stretched away west, flat and sparkling like a sheet of white ice. To our right we saw the fluffed heads of date- and dom-palms, as dense as rainforest along the river, punctuated by Nile acacias in winter bloom, their saffron-petalled flowers giving out a heady perfume. There were squares of cultivation – green wheat and clover – fed by thumping irrigation-pumps which sent clear, cool water down narrow channels. Villagers in shirts and tight white turbans laboured in the fields with hoes and curved knives. Women in *taubs* of pink, saffron and lime-green rode side-saddle on muscular white donkeys.

The sand was soft and deep and the going hard. Once, a Fiat lorry rumbled past, startling the camels, and the two black lorry-boys perched on the cab jeered at us. Later, though, we found the lorry stuck in the sand, its engine screaming in rage, its great wheels spinning impotently, lashing the lorry-boys with dust as they toiled with shovels and sand-boards. Jibrin chuckled. 'That's what you get when you go by lorry!' he commented as we rode past. 'A camel is better any day!' The youths scowled at him and turned away. However, we soon had a problem of our own to contend with: there was no clover to be had for our camels. Each time we halted to ask the villagers working in clover-fields, they answered rudely, 'It's not for sale!'

By sunset that evening we had found neither clover for our camels, nor the firewood we needed to cook our evening meal. Firewood was at a premium along the Nile, and most of the villagers cooked with charcoal, which was of little use without a brazier. The sun was firing the desert with pumpkin-toned streaks, and the first electric lights, powered by private generators, came up among the palm-groves like baubles hung on their fronds. Cicadas began their rasping sunset chorus in the cultivation, and from the direction of the river came the honk of frogs. Just before dark we heard the grumble of an engine and saw an immensely broad-shouldered man in an elaborate turban at the wheel of a Massey-Ferguson tractor, with a fitted disc-plough. This was a rare sight, even for the affluent Nile, and Jibrin and I stopped to watch as he shunted back and forth, turning over the sod in a wide field. Beyond the field, sheltered by *nim* trees, stood a rambling house of mud with buttressed walls and moulded steps, partly encircled by high walls, from which time and the occasional rain had bitten substantial chunks. Through one such breach I spotted a cluster of big-boned cows tucking into a bale of clover.

'We can't go on in darkness, anyway,' Jibrin said, following my eyes. 'This is a good place to stop. Perhaps these people would sell us some clover. As for dinner,' he nodded towards the tractor, 'they won't turn away a guest.' We did just as we would have done had we come to a Bedu tent. We couched the camels at a respectable distance from the house, and began unloading, expecting our host to come and greet us warmly. As we laid out our saddlery, the man driving the tractor cut the engine, jumped down and walked over to us. Compared with the diminutive Jibrin he was a giant – six feet three if an inch, and towering over us in his dung-splattered jallabiyya. His face was dark, bullish and broad, with low brow-ridges. Before we could wish peace upon him, he said: 'You can't stop there!'

'Why not?' Jibrin inquired. 'Is it your land?'

'No,' the giant replied. 'It's the graveyard!'

Only then did I notice the dozens of shaped stones underfoot, some of them scrawled with Arabic writing. We muttered apologies and moved camels and equipment to the edge of the plot. The big man disappeared inside the house, without, we both noticed, inviting us to dinner. 'I've never seen anything like that in my life!' Jibrin fumed. 'They talk about the meanness of the village people. That man must be rolling in money, but he didn't even invite us to spend the night in his yard. By God, what a miser! If anyone did that among the Bedu he'd never live it down!'

'Well. Perhaps he'll invite us to dinner later. Anyway, we'll have to go and ask him to sell us some clover.'

We climbed the shallow steps and battered on the door, shouting out a greeting. After a while the tractor-driver appeared, scowling, and answered our '*as salaam 'alaykum*' with a grunt. I explained that we had no clover for our camels and concluded, 'I thought we could buy some from you.' The man's eyes bulged at me. 'We have no clover here.'

Jibrin and I exchanged glances. I was about to protest, when the giant was abruptly replaced by another man, clad in the same kind of dirty jallabiyya, and if anything even taller and broader than the first. 'What is it?' he asked. I repeated my request to buy fodder. The second giant, older and more weathered-looking, shifted uneasily and then, looking at me pointedly, said, 'Come inside. Just you, not the Arab.'

Jibrin's eyes flared with anger at this incredible rudeness. 'We go everywhere together,' I said.

'No, that's all right, Omar,' Jibrin said. 'You go in. One of us should keep an eye on the camels.'

The room was oddly shaped and full of shadows from the thick mud columns whose presence made it surprisingly small. Two string-beds with mattresses stood side by side at one end, next to a chair with a hole in the seat. A oil-lamp, smoking in an embrasure in the stucco wall, had left soot-coloured streaks on the plaster. A faded old mirror and an assortment of shirts hung precariously from nails. A palm-fibre mat had been spread on the floor, and the men sat down heavily on it. I kicked off my sandals and joined them. They asked questions about who I was, where I was going, and why. 'What's your name?' the younger one inquired.

'Omar.'

'No, I mean your *real* name. That's an Arab name. What's your English name?'

'All right. Michael.'

The big man's eyes lit up in recognition. 'Oh!' he said, seesawing his massive arms in a parody of dancing. 'Like Michael Jackson!'

'Yes,' I said, determined to get the conversation back to clover. When I mentioned it again, the old man said, 'We haven't got any clover for sale, but there are some old melon shoots you could have. We don't need those. Cows won't eat them. I'll let you have them for five pounds! I'll come over and sort it out later.'

'Thanks,' I said, and, thinking that it would be too much to mention the firewood, I rose to my feet. 'Wait,' the older giant said. 'Surely we can offer you something before you go!' He had been wrestling with a deep pocket, from which he brought out a small brown chemist's bottle. He unscrewed the top and held it out to me. The bottle contained small white pills. '*Valium*,' the man said, smiling. 'Have one!'

I muttered no thanks, slipped on my sandals and walked out, but not before I had seen both giants swallow a small white pill each, with evident satisfaction.

'Animals, not people!' Jibrin said later, as we lay on the hard ground with rumbling bellies. 'They are . . . they are blacksmiths – that's what they are!' This was about the most withering insult an Arab could think of – blacksmiths being universally detested as uncouth and untrustworthy in the Sudan, as in most Arab countries. These men had flunked the absolute Bedouin litmus test of humanity – they were worthy only of disdain. 'Curse their fathers!' Jibrin continued. 'To let us go to sleep on empty stomachs! The worst thing one can ever say about a man is that he did not know a guest!' We slept fitfully, and in the morning awoke to find that while we had lain there starving, the local termites had made a great feast on chunks of our blankets and saddle-gear.

For days we wandered north through Nubian villages of houses like cream-cake slices – cubes and rhomboids of painted alabaster with oval doorways, elaborate stairways and stepped *mastabas*. Often we discovered earthenware pots of ice-cool water on iron stands nestled in the shade of *nim* trees, each with its own steel cup on a chain – an offering to passing travellers like ourselves. 'They always keep the pots full,' Jibrin said, 'because they believe that if they run dry then the river will dry up too.'

Sometimes we were able to follow the Nile itself. Its waters were either serene and beryl-blue, a-glitter with stars, or, when the wind whipped up from the desert, swelling sea-green, furious with waves and seamed with froth. In places the stream was cleft by blade-shaped islands top-heavy with jungles of date-palms. The islands could be reached only by barges under crackling butterfly-wing sails, steered by old men with melting ceramic faces, heaving on rudders like giant halberds. We wandered in and out of palm-groves, hearing the wind soughing in the palm-heads, and emerged again into the pack-ice infinity of the desert, where dunes had piled over broken walls and wormed their substance to the very water's edge. Chattering children played on donkeys at the well-heads, and Nubian ladies, giggling under soft *taubs*, called us to eat bread and tomatoes in the shade of tamarisk-trees. Often we met wayfarers coming in the opposite direction – a file of walking men, perspiring under heavy sacks, who answered our greeting with grimaces; an Arab in a greatcoat leading a camel-caravan laden with firewood for sale in the town; two Nubians clicking along on donkeys behind a drove of mottled sheep; two riders on swift dromedaries, their faces white-bandaged and inscrutable, who waved to us and were gone. Nowhere did we encounter the lack of hospitality we had met at the 'House of the Giants': almost every time we halted someone would scurry out from the nearest house to welcome us, and return later with fresh bread and stew, or a plate of griddle-cakes.

On the outskirts of Dongola al Urdi, the capital of the Sudan's Northern Province, some boys, their jallabiyyas tucked into baggy trousers, were playing football in a square. As we passed through them we met some Arabs whom Jibrin knew by sight. We halted to greet them with the drawn-out greeting of the desert, our camels shifting nervously as the boys hooted, shrieked and scuffled around us, chasing their plastic ball through the dust, oblivious of all but their game. The Arabs advised us to spend the night in the local mosque, for, in the Sudan as in many Islamic countries, mosques also doubled as inns for poor travellers.

We found the mosque nearby. It was small and square, enclosed by a low wall in which a row of taps for ritual ablutions were shaded under a narrow roof. The Imam, a stocky man as fair as an Egyptian, with a neatly cropped silver beard, welcomed us at the gate, and helped us to unload and hobble our camels outside. He allotted us a place to sleep, in the shelter of the wall, and later we were joined by some displaced Kababish who were looking for work along the Nile. After sunset, local villagers arrived with a tray laden with dishes – Egyptian *fuul* in a sauce of onions, crumbled white cheese, beef stew, sardines, fresh radishes and tomatoes, flat griddle-cakes and loaves of leavened brown bread still warm from the oven. The Kababish, small, bird-like men with bearded faces and sand-coloured shirts, wearing their rosary beads around their necks in Bedu style, told us that they, like Jibrin, had lost all their animals in the drought. 'Those who still have their camels have moved far south to places no Arabs have ever been before,' one of them explained. 'Right up to the Jonglei river. But we heard that some of them had been attacked by blacks and shot dead. Those infidels are scoundrels, by God! The Arabs went to their country in time of need and that was the kind of welcome they were given!'

It was tragic, but easy to forget that in the old days the Arabs had built up a profitable trade, burning the villages of those same southerners, killing the old and useless and leading off the rest in chains. 'The blacks should be taught a lesson,' the Imam cut in. 'The government should send the army down there and wipe them out!' This seemed a singularly uncharitable opinion for an elder whose God was deemed 'The Compassionate, The Merciful', yet certainly if a southerner should walk in here and now, he would have been made comfortable just as I had been. Later, as the wind blustered against the mosque wall and our camels rumbled contentedly outside, I basked happily in the glow of Muslim hospitality. Whatever the savage sentiments expressed, I thought, where else at the end of the twentieth century but in the Sudan could an Englishman dressed as an Arab and riding a camel find welcome in a mosque, and be treated as just another human being in need of food and shelter?

One morning, as we awoke on a sandy shelf by the river, Jibrin told me that a camel-herd had passed our camp during the night. 'Must be a herd going to Egypt,' he went on. 'If we catch up, we might be able to travel with them for a while.' By mid-morning we had sighted them, about 100 animals as tightly packed as a school of fish streaming along in a current. Balanced upon the humps of several camels were white Nile egrets, their heads and beaks buried in their breast-feathers, looking like miniature hitchhikers cadging an easy passage to Egypt. The camels were being driven by four Arab drovers dressed in overcoats, turbans and woollen shawls, who chanted camel-cries as they wheeled their riding-beasts and cracked their hippo-hide whips to keep the herd in line. At midday, the drovers pushed the beasts into a grove of tattered tamarisk and unloaded their saddles and firewood. The guide was an oldish man named Shawish, whose parched face was a long tale of wind, sun and deprivation, and who was wearing around his neck a pair of antediluvian motorcycle goggles. He invited us to share their lunch – a half-football of polenta, served with spiced gravy.

Afterwards, when we had scrubbed our scorched fingers in the sand and drunk tea, Shawish began to fill a biscuit-tin with the moist black tobacco that the Bedu used orally and only very occasionally smoked. He took a pinch of tobacco and placed it tenderly between his teeth and lower lip. He spat out the excess and arranged himself comfortably in the sand, his chin bulging. 'Good stuff,' he sighed happily. 'The good tobacco can only be found on the Nile!'

He told us that there were scores of camel-herds moving downriver behind them, and dozens more in front. 'Like an invasion!' he said. 'The Bedu are selling their camels in thousands because of the drought. It's either that or let them die, or move south to the Jonglei, where the blacks are waiting. They're going dirt cheap and all the merchants are trying to make a few pounds. Even the settled people of the Nile are taking herds to Egypt now!' When he discovered I was British, he gave me a grin restrained by his wad of tobacco. 'I know the British!' he said. 'I was a gunner in the Sudan Defence Force during the war – a sergeant, that's why they call me 'Shawish'. It was an air-defence battery, with Bofors guns. I fought at Jalo in Libya. What a fight! Shot down a lot of Italian planes.' He grinned twistedly again, and added in tortured English, '*Bloody fools! Bloody stupid fools! Bloody man!*'

I suppose it was only the English he knew.

We travelled north with the herd for several days, passing from the teeming Dongola reach and into the wilder, more remote region known as the 'Belly of Stone', where the broad swaths of cultivation were replaced by blue volcanic magma, crushed and pounded and layered into strange formations. At the village of

Oki, a clot of square buildings on a rocky shelf which overlooked a plunging ravine, the drovers ran their camels into a copse of acacia-trees. I walked to the edge of the ravine to see the Nile, glinting metallic-blue below. Suddenly there was a shout, and I looked up to see a little old lady in a pure black *taub*, her witch face a mask of hatred, hurtling towards me flailing a flexible palm-rib and shrieking, 'Eeeh! You dogs! Eeeh! You sons of the forbidden!' Only at the last moment did I realize that she was on a collision course, and take evasive action, dodging a slashing blow from the palm-rib. The old woman was no higher than my shoulder, as thin and frail-looking as brown paper, yet she was astonishingly agile. She gave me a whack on the shin before I managed to get hold of the stick, and as I tried to wrest it away she clung on with surprising tenacity, her face knotted with effort. 'Get your camels off our land!' she spat. 'These trees are for our donkeys! We've had enough of the likes of you Egyptians stealing our browse!'

We were doing a sort of precarious tango around the edge of the ravine, with the old lady cursing and myself laughing and protesting: 'These camels aren't mine! They're nothing to do with me!' and trying to prevent any more blows from connecting, when Jibrin and Shawish appeared and managed to pull her away.

'These aren't his camels!' the guide said. 'Only one of them is his!'

'Whose are they then?'

'I'm the guide,' Shawish said, and he was obliged to leap ungracefully sideways to avoid a swipe of the palm-rib. 'You stupid woman!' he gasped. 'You'll be lucky if we don't beat you black and blue!' I guessed it was pride more than intention talking. The old woman backed away among the camels and began to belabour left and right with the rib, still crying, 'Eeeh! Eeeh! Drive them out!' as the animals bucked and snorted in their rush to get away.

Shawish made a move towards her, but as he stepped out a sharp stone hit him squarely on the cheek with an audible crump. He rubbed his cheek, examined a trace of blood on his fingers, laughed to maintain face, and then noticed, as we all did, that dozens of other villagers, men, women and children, were pouring out of the houses, waving sticks, picking up stones and shaking home-made rattles of pebble-filled steel jugs, which were extraordinarily effective in scaring the camels. Another volley of sharp stones spattered in the sand near us, and as I jumped back quickly to get out of range, I tripped over a boulder and twisted my ankle. 'All right! All right!' Shawish was shouting to the villagers. 'That's enough, by God! Drive them out, boys!' As we slunk away in the wake of the camels, I turned to see the little old lady standing on the rock platform outside the village, swinging the palm-rib in ferocious triumph, with her family gathered around her.

In the morning my ankle was badly swollen, and I had to lean on my stick as I walked. To my relief no one commented. Trailing behind the herd, I came alongside one of the camels which was, like me, hobbling painfully and lurching from side to side. An Arab ran back and walloped the beast once or twice with his whip, with no appreciable effect. There was a dull glaze in its eyes, I noticed. The herder stopped his walloping and said, 'It's no good. His nerves are completely shot. Hunger has pierced his heart!' Soon after, Shawish halted the herd and the animal was led off to its execution. The Bedu couched the camel and hobbled it, then one of them doubled its head backwards and down into the sand. Shawish took out his razor-sharp dagger from its arm-sheath and plunged it into the beast's carotid artery, just below the neck. Blood sparged the sand. The camel gave one pathetic snort, and the light in its eyes was switched off for ever. The Arabs hustled around with their daggers ready, excited by the prospect of meat. They skinned it expertly, severing the neck, ripping out the entrails, slicing off the muscle. Within minutes, two leather saddlebags were brimming with wet meat, and we were crouching around a bowlful of raw liver that was still warm. 'Eat!' Shawish shouted. 'You don't get liver as fresh as this every day!'

The hollow carcass of the camel still knelt among the rocks in precisely the position in which it had met its death, a giant blood-spattered insect, already surrounded at a respectable distance by a gang of black Nubian vultures, roosting truculently on the teeth of the rocks, waiting patiently for our departure. The herd was one camel less, but the deficit was made up – if only momentarily – before we had even got the camels moving again, when a pregnant she-camel gave birth to a foal. The foal lay in the sand, a whimpering, wriggling rag-doll wearing a slimy membrane like a jacket. The she-camel stood over her baby, directing a deep-throated warning roar towards the vultures, which turned their gaze on the foal with malevolent interest. Another pair came gliding in with a snap of wing-feathers, and on the opposite side there gathered a back-up shift of smaller Egyptian vultures with white feathers and sulphur-yellow heads. A third contingent was made up of piebald crows which croaked, cawed and fluttered with an impatience that seemed vulgar beside the massive imperturbability of the vulture tribe. I knew that as soon as we moved away the scavengers would tear the living foal to shreds, eyes first. 'We can't take it with us,' Shawish said, 'and we can't wait for it to walk. It'll be dead soon anyway. Tonight Hassan the Jackal will be out to do his work!'

As the Bedu moved the herd off, the mother howled pitifully. More than once she turned back to the helpless foal, but the herders caught her and forced her on, keening. Before we had gone 300 feet, the big vultures were hopping clumsily towards the rag-doll in the sand, circling it like a death-squad. The last time I looked, one of them was pecking out its eye.

In the evening we made camp under a rocky overhang. The drovers piled their equipment along the base of the rocks and laid out their blankets. Someone made a fire and began cooking camel-meat. Others twisted hobbles out of fibre they had brought with them, and the guide, sucking tobacco, occupied himself in cutting out leather patches from a cow-skin and dunking them in a bowl of water. Afterwards he stitched the patches to the camels' hooves with a packing-needle and leather thread. 'These camels are accustomed to the soft sand of Kordofan,' he said. 'They're not used to rocky ground and sometimes the skin wears right off their hooves. We have to stitch these patches on like shoes, or they'll never make it to Egypt.' Thinking of the beast slaughtered that morning, I asked him how many camels he generally expected to lose on the forty-five-day trek. 'Only God is all-knowing,' he answered. 'Perhaps five, maybe ten. It depends on the state of the camels to start with and what you find to eat on the way. I once lost forty-three camels from a single herd – almost half of it – on the way to Egypt.'

After we had eaten roast camel-meat and drunk tea, the Bedu sat up, talking and telling stories. Nursing my swollen ankle, I retired to my bed in the shelter of a rock. Venus came up like a fireball gleaming yellow, and shortly a full moon rose over the desert, so bright and personal that I was immediately transported beyond myself, beyond the individual units of life, beyond birth, death and predation, into a vision of a vast, eternal process in which everything, both organic and inorganic, played a part.

Jibrin left the company and settled down next to me, staring at the moon. 'You know,' he said, 'the Arabs say that the moon is the husband of the sun, and twice a month they have intercourse. She is so insatiable that the moon is weakened and grows thin. Once, when he refused to sleep with her, they had a fight and each knocked out the other's eye – that's why there is that dark patch on the moon – you can see it – where his lost eye should be.'

'Some people – Christians – have already walked on the moon, but they didn't find a blind eye!'

'Walked on the moon! That's just nonsense!'

'All right. Perhaps it is.'

The she-camel was still howling, bemoaning her lost foal. Later, in the moonlight, Hassan the Jackal came out to do his work on the leftovers of our dinner. He passed so close to my bed that I could almost touch him.

It was in the desert west of the Nile, several days after we had parted from Shawish and his herd, that we sighted the mysterious footprints. A seething wind had seared our bodies all morning as we drifted on behind our camels, hoping their bulky frames would give us some protection from the cold. Jibrin shivered as he marched. Both of us had snuffling colds, and I was limping from my sprained ankle. Jibrin's camel – already weak when we had started the trek thirteen days before – was now exhausted, its eyes glazed with a sinister mist whose meaning Jibrin knew only too well. 'Look at him,' he said fretfully. 'Look at the way he holds his head!' He was obliged to walk to preserve his camel's strength, and I felt obliged to walk too, out of solidarity. The pain in my ankle was excruciating and I would have given almost anything for a few moments in the saddle, but pride prevented me from mounting up. Each time Jibrin prompted me to 'Ride! Ride!' I always answered, 'No. Not until you do!' And of course he never did.

By midday the wind had mercifully blown itself out and the desert was still and featureless except for the crags which lay directly in our path. Though Jibrin had never been in this region before, he had made inquiries from the caravaneers at Saqiyyat al ʿAbd, and told me that these crags marked the second of three stages in the journey from the Nile. Once a year a caravan would set out from Saqiyya to collect salt from the oasis of Selima, taking three days each way. The caravaneers, who had once been nomads but were now settled on the Nile, halted in precisely the same places on each journey. As we approached, the crags gradually solidifed into crusty basalt blocks, growing like alien fungi on the pale sand-and-gravel desert floor. It was here that Jibrin spied the footprints weaving drunkenly from side to side as they approached the rocks. He knelt down to examine them and looked up, mystified. 'These tracks are only a few hours old,' he said. 'They've been made since the wind dropped, which means that whoever made them is not far ahead. But there is no sign of a camel! No God but God, this is strange! Who would travel in this wilderness without a camel?'

'Perhaps his camel has been stolen.'

'No. There are no thieves in empty desert. The camel-raiders live on the fringes of the desert where there's plenty of move-ment. Here, a bandit would have to wait weeks – maybe months – without water to come across a single camel. It wouldn't be worth his while. No, this is strange, very strange indeed!'

We followed the tracks for a while until they disappeared into a patch of hard gravel almost surrounded by a wide circus of rock. On one side the basalt had been eaten away to form a perfect overhang. Beneath it were the remains of old cooking-fires. Spread out at the base of the rock wall lay a carpet of dried grass – the remnants of bales of hay the caravaneers had carried months ago from the Nile to feed their camels. Jibrin brightened visibly. We had been feeding our camels on sorghum-grain, but his mount was constantly jibbing – it pined for grass.

While the camels grazed, however, I looked around the circle of rock, and felt suddenly depressed. In the basalt I saw the gro-tesque figures of dragons and griffins. The sky was momentarily dark. The rock overhangs and the remains of old fires produced an inexplicable sense of gloom. Panic oozed up inside me, and then something happened that I have never experienced before or since. Suddenly, it was as if a voice was screaming inside my head, sobbing, *'Oh God! There's a dead man here!'*

At sunrise we saw a broken hill scarring the horizon, which I took to be Selima mountain. Jibrin reserved judgement. We packed up and set out grimly into a polar wind that rendered the desert ghostly and insubstantial. The sun hovered reluctantly above the fuzzy skyline, colouring the sands raw sienna and salmon-pink. Jibrin's camel still wobbled unsteadily, but no more unsteadily than myself – my ankle was softball-size after the pre-vious day's hard trek, and it was all I could do to limp. To cap it all, my snuffle had worked itself up into full-blown fever. My tem-perature was 39.5. 'I can't understand it,' I told Jibrin. 'This is the worst I've ever been in my years of travelling by camel!'

'I don't know why you do it! You could have got here in a day by car. Why go through all this when you have the choice?'

As we shuffled along in silence behind the camels, I wondered what answer I should give. I might have said that it took a Western genius like Einstein to formulate a simple truth that should have been obvious to any traveller – namely, that the speed of the observer changes his perception, squashing and distorting the landscape. When Westerners first began to explore this desert with motor-cars in the 1920s, they found their Bedu guides useless. 'They have no idea of distance in a car,' wrote Ralph Bagnold, '. . . accustomed to reckoning distances by the time of camels' movement . . . they are many miles past a landmark before they think of looking for it.' If I had travelled here by car, my experience would have been a blurred confusion of images with only highpoints standing out, like a videotape on fast-rewind. Walking along at camel's pace allows you to perceive the environment as it unfurls in its full royal glory. James Lovelock has written: 'the simplest way to explore Gaia is on foot. How else can you easily be part of her ambience? How else can you reach out to her with all your senses?'

This drifted through my mind as I limped on feverishly, but by the time I had thought it out, Jibrin had long ago given up waiting for my answer, if indeed he had ever wanted one. We climbed the spur, dragging the camels by their headropes across a surface littered with flat shards of basalt which chinked like steel under their feet. The ascent was agonizing, but I was driven on by the thought that from the summit we were certain to see Selima below us. From the top, though, we saw nothing but sand-devils playing over empty desert and another ridge of rock in the distance. We inched painfully down the perilous slope into a gully where the stones were gnarled and twisted. Beneath them were a few red sherds of broken pottery, decorated with rough but intricate striations. I picked up one of the sherds. It was a relic, perhaps, of Oliver Myers's C-Group nomads, whose cows had tramped through the golden savannahs that covered this desert 5,000 years ago.

In 1938 Myers joined the motor-explorer Ralph Bagnold on

an expedition deep into the *terra ignota* of the eastern Sahara. Rattling out of Kharja oasis in their 'flying bedsteads' – Model 'T' Fords – his team's objectives were the remote oasis of 'Uwaynat and the plateau of Jilf Kebir, standing near the Libyan border, where earlier explorers had found fascinating drawings etched into the rock. It was Myers's hope that these rock-pictures could be connected in some way with his Armant pottery – that they would provide a direct window into the world of the C-Group nomads.

At Jilf Kebir – a sandstone massif almost as large as Sicily – he investigated two wadis where there was evidence that prehistoric lakes had formed behind sand-bars that blocked their upper reaches from wall to wall. Stone-age peoples had camped around the lakes, and the presence of grinders and milling-stones suggested that these nomads had planted barley in the wadis. Myers also found pottery, stone tools and ostrich-shell beads, and stone rings that had probably been laid around nomads' tents of hide or straw. The pottery was different from that of his Armant invaders, but further south, at 'Uwaynat, he found sherds that were identical.

While Myers had been searching for potsherds, his colleague, Hans Winkler, a Swiss art-historian, had spent two weeks wandering the arid valleys of 'Uwaynat and Jilf Kebir, examining boulders, scrambling over screes, and peering into dim caves, recording the mass of rock-art to be found there. He discovered an entire literature of engravings and paintings that told the saga of Saharan prehistory from as far back as Paleolithic times. The pictures showed human figures – some of them lumpen matchstick men who lassoed dinosaur-necked giraffes or swayed hand in hand around some sinister masked shaman in a hypnotic dervish-dance. Others were more finely drawn figures painted yellow, white and red: men with triangular trunks and waspish waists, loping off with bows and arrows in pursuit of gazelles: figures in penis-sheaths jerking with skirt-clad women in a rhythmic mazurka. There were globe-skulled warriors with devils' horns and feathers guarding herds of mottled cattle, and couples lounging like pashas in caves and grass huts with milk-pots suspended from the roofs. Among the animals Winkler found, there were plump ostriches, stumpy elephants, pooch-like lions, cows with swollen udders and bent horns, dogs on leashes, spider-legged camels, skeletal horses, and antelopes with comb-like limbs. There were abstract shapes that might have been filched from surrealist art – Catherine-wheel spirals, rippling serpentine strings, fishbone trees, blots and blips on legs, the outlines of hands, clusters of toadstools, clumps of interlocking honeycombs and lizards with human heads.

The story these pictures told was of far greater import than that of a single exodus of cattle-people out of the Sahara. The displacement of the C-Group was but one chapter in a vast cycle of change – of successive waves of peoples that moved back and forth across the Sahara as it expanded and contracted, now rich and fertile, now dissolving into sand. The earliest pictures, Winkler thought, had been made by hunter-gatherers: 'Animals, footprints of game, geometrical designs, occupy the mind of these men. They had little interest in the portrayal of human beings. In the moment of first discovery of these drawings and again after having studied them week after week, I feel they are expressions of quite a foreign mentality . . . the same genius which inspired artists of other primitive hunters – in Australia and North America . . .'

The waspy-waisted men in penis-sheaths, more numerous than the matchstick hunters, were always found in association with herds of cattle. It was among them, Winkler surmised, that the C-Group belonged. Cattle were everything to these men, and their beasts were often decorated with amulets, suggesting a cult significance. Carefully drawn udders denoted the importance they had attached to milk. Here, he felt, was something extraordinary. These men had somehow discovered the secret of taming wild cattle, and probably plant cultivation too. They had 'broken the eternal flow of Paleolithic times and started the explosion of a new era in humanity's life'.

In more recent pictures, the cattle-people had disappeared. Their vivacious portraits of men and cattle had given way to poorly drawn horses and riders, then to pipe-cleaner camels with over-large humps. Evidently, these pictures belonged to a later period when conditions in the Sahara had changed. One final picture that intrigued the metaphysically inclined Winkler was of a British soldier seated in a tent, with an eccentric-looking locomotive puffing by. He wrote: 'We may look at our material from the desert, a material beginning with hunters and with an early mentality which is to us incomprehensible, and ending with our day of railways and guns. The main acquisitions not only of these desert peoples, but of humanity, have appeared beneath our eyes: the domestication of cattle, the discovery of plant cultivation, and the taming of horses and camels.'

As we moved, four tiny living creatures in the vast cathedral of the desert, I felt humbled by the knowledge of this breathtaking epic that had lasted hundreds of thousands of years. Beside that, the wails of Western romantics – myself included – over the Bedu becoming settled, or adopting motor-cars and machines, seemed as insignificant as a whirling dust-devil on the desert sands. The saga on the rocks was the saga of endless diversity – of humanity thirsting and thrusting to adapt and to improve. The machine-age – represented in Winkler's rock-art by a single picture – was simply the latest stage in a journey that had begun with the crudest stone tools, and has never ceased. On the stage of eternity it would be over in the winking of an eye, and something yet undreamed-of would take its place.

Suddenly Jibrin pointed to a long shadow on the desert floor. It was made by a rough cairn, and no sooner had we come abreast of it than a wonderful sight met our eyes. There, in a saucer-shaped depression, invisible from afar, lay a garden of palm-trees, tamarisk and esparto grass, like a vision in a fairy-tale picture book. Selima was the perfect oasis of myth and legend – a small, compact, bloom of palms heavy with unpicked dates, its greener-than-green grasses blossoming around pools of open water. It seemed incredible to find it here.

We drove the camels into the luxury of its dappled shade, unsaddled them and sent them off into the tamarisk and the esparto grass. We laid out our blankets under the palms, and while Jibrin sauntered off gleefully to knock down the ripe dates with stones, I lay back, resting my swollen ankle, and enjoying the immaculate peace and harmony of this tiny paradise that seemed to belong to a different age – far beyond roads and cars and aircraft. My movements were heavy, my eyelids weighted with lead. My eyes closed. I drifted off on a gently undulating wave of tranquillity.

And then an engine growled.

It was so totally unexpected that I jerked up in fright. Jibrin stopped his date-bashing and stared into the desert beyond the trees. About 300 metres away, a heavy truck that had been converted into a bus had just materialized out of the dust-sheen, and was grinding to a halt. Even before it stopped, something told me it was a tourist vehicle. And this was unbelievable, because in my time in the Sudan I had only occasionally met a tourist, and never an organized group. Sure enough, the doors snapped open, and out came a score of pale-faced Europeans, elderly men and women in safari pants, T-shirts and sun-hats, who lurched across the sand towards us with the determination of disturbed bees. Almost all of them were carrying cameras or camcorders with microphones, and they jostled each other to get at us, jabbering in French. They surrounded us, pointing their cameras, poking microphones and zoom lenses into our faces. Jibrin, who had never seen a camera before – or a European other than myself – blanched with fear and looked around for escape. 'These are hyenas!' he said. I could smell the sun-screen, the deodorant and the insect-repellent, and as they pushed nearer, I found myself thinking: 'So this is what it's like to be photographed by tourists!'

I flattered myself that they had taken me for an Arab, and when the initial excitement had worn off, I began to explain who I was in English to the tour-guide, a dark, confident-looking Frenchman called Jean-Yves. 'I know who you are,' he said, deflatingly, 'because the police on the river told us you had left for Selima. Actually we have been following your tracks. The reason these people are so excited is because they think you might have had something to do with the dead man.'

'Dead man!'

'Yes. This morning we found a dead body only a few metres from the place with the rock overhang. We found your tracks there. You must have seen it, surely! One of these men is a doctor. He said the man hadn't been dead for more than a day. Probably died of thirst, because he had with him an empty gallon jerrycan with a missing top.'

I thought of the mysterious tracks we had found in the desert the previous day, the place with the rock overhang, the feeling of depression, the momentary panic I had felt – the voice that had screamed inside my head: *There's a dead man here!* I had never believed in premonition or any kind of ESP, and I had to rack my brains to be certain I actually heard that voice: there was absolutely no doubt in my mind.

I had hardly recovered from my surprise when Jean-Yves hit me with another: 'Did you see the salt-caravan?' he asked.

'Salt-caravan? But the caravans from the Nile only come once a year.'

'This one wasn't coming from the Nile. It was coming from the south – from the desert!'

He had hardly finished speaking when a train of about forty camels suddenly uncoiled out of the desert, led by four walking men in jallabiyyas with unfamiliar wide sleeves and white turbans. One of the men was limping badly, I noticed. Each camel carried two cylinder-shaped baskets packed with rock-salt. Jibrin stared at them as they couched the camels some distance away. They unloaded quickly, and turned their camels out to join ours among the tamarisk. Suddenly this remote spot in the desert, only a few minutes ago the most tranquil haven imaginable, was as busy as Piccadilly Circus.

'Those aren't Kababish,' Jibrin said. 'I never saw any Bedu who used baskets. From their dress you'd say they were villagers. I thought I knew all the tribes in the desert, but they don't belong to any tribe that I know!'

The French tourists immediately lost interest in us and scurried off to photograph the newcomers. We hung back until the tourists had gone off to make camp, then we approached the caravaneers. They had stripped off their jallabiyyas and turbans, and were wearing only woollen long-johns and singlets. They were certainly Arabs, not Sudanese townsmen, but their features were different from those of the Kababish. As we sat down among them, though, I could hear the accent of southern Egypt. They were Egyptian caravaneers on Sudanese territory – one of the most unexpected sights I had met with in all my travels in the Sudan. One of them, a shrivelled old man, told us: 'We are ʿAwazim – Bedu from the Kharja oasis in Egypt. We travel into the Sudan to get rock-salt from Al ʿAtrun.'

'I've been to Al ʿAtrun, but I've never seen or heard about Bedu from Egypt!'

'Ah, you've been to the Sudanese ʿAtrun. Our ʿAtrun is in a different place. No Sudanese know about it. It's beyond the oasis of Laqiyya, and beyond Merga, but its exact location is our secret. From Laqiyya we follow the old route called the Forty Days Road.'

The situation grew more intriguing by the minute. For years I had been searching for Bedouin who knew the Forty Days Road, the ancient caravan road that for millennia had joined Egypt to the Sudan. I had believed that the route was disused and forgotten since the British had halted the slave-trade along it a century ago. Even the veteran Ralph Bagnold – doyen of motor-explorers in the eastern Sahara – wrote: 'There is probably no one left alive who remembers the old trade along the "Forty Days Road".' Now, quite unexpectedly, I had discovered that the secret of the old route had been kept alive by the Egyptians. I did not dream then that in due course I would come to know some of these Egyptian Bedu almost as intimately as I knew the Kababish.

The ʿAwazim brought us tea in large enamel mugs and offered us packets of Cleopatra cigarettes, of which they had enormous quantities in their saddlebags. Cigarette-smoking was almost unknown among the Kababish, and Jibrin raised an eyebrow at their obvious affluence. He ran his practised desert eye over their camel-gear – their cylindrical baskets, now standing in ranks on flat bases, and their curious saddles – no more than a V-shaped wooden frame on a huge pad of sacking and palm-fibre. The old man showed us how the ensemble worked – the baskets were so tall that they stood higher than the camel's back, and were held in place by two pegs. As the camel rose it took the strain of the baskets, and when it was couched their flat bases simply rested on the ground. 'No lifting or lowering,' the old man said proudly. 'No ropes. Not a single knot to tie. One man can load and unload fifty camels without any trouble. We have these baskets made to our pattern by artisans, but we make the saddles ourselves!'

I asked if the ʿAwazim were still nomads.

'A generation ago there were those among us who lived in tents,' the old man said, 'but now the government has settled us into houses. We grow our own crops as well as having goats and cattle. We don't breed camels because there is little grazing in Kharja – we usually buy them in the market at Daraw. We are still Bedu, though.'

By now, the French had erected a line of two-man bivouac tents in the belly of the oasis, and Jibrin, never having seen such things before, was intrigued. He inspected one of them, felt the lightness of the material, and as a professional tent-dweller pronounced them 'suitable'. I was wondering what scathing remarks he would make about Christian meanness if they failed to offer us hospitality, but to my relief Jean-Yves invited us both to dinner after dark.

As we walked back to our camp afterwards, the normally silent Jibrin was full of talk: 'Did you see that, Omar? Every one of them had his own stool that could be folded up and put away. No sitting in the sand for them! Men and women eating together, but instead of eating with their hands out of a dish, everyone had his own plate – made of paper! And they changed the plate every time they changed the food. They ate with tools that I've never seen before – forks or whatever you call them. What that stuff was we ate only God knows – it looked like a lot of worms – it was quite disgusting, and I had to force myself to eat it. But that horrible yellow thing they gave us afterwards, with the bad smell, was too much. I just couldn't eat that.' He was referring to a very expensive variety of French cheese.

'At least you can't say they didn't know a guest!'

'No, they didn't fall short. But I've never seen women like those, showing their hair and their legs. Don't they feel ashamed?'

'What did you think of them?'

'Well, some of the women were quite nice, but the men looked like hyenas. So ugly! I can't understand how the women can sleep with them!'

The Bedu caravan set out at first light, and the tourists soon after, both heading for the Eyptian border. We let our camels graze while Jibrin filled half a sack with dates from the palm-trees, then began to saddle up. Before we left, Jibrin inspected the tourists' campsite and called me over, chuckling, to look at something they had left in the sand. It was a very large, black, leathery turd, smothered in ream upon ream of supersoft toilet paper. Jibrin was staring at it in wonder. 'Paper! No God but God, now I've seen everything!' he said.

As we tramped back across the lonely desert in our own footsteps, heading for the Nile, Jibrin told me, 'I think one day soon the Kababish will be like those Egyptian Bedu. Perhaps we'll start to grow crops and live in houses, and just keep a few camels to bring salt and water, and a handful of goats. Did you see how rich they were? They had everything, by God!' I could hear the envy in his voice. 'Perhaps we will go back to our lands if the rains come. Perhaps we will remain in the towns. Only God is all-knowing, but for the Bedu nothing will ever be the same again.'

It was tragic to witness the end of an era, I thought. But the wheel of change turned ineluctably, crushing all who would stand in its path. Man is an adaptive animal – he had adapted to this most extreme of environments. With his technical ingenuity even the elderly Westerners we had met at Selima, who knew virtually nothing about the desert, could survive here. The true threat to existence lies not in change, but in becoming entrenched in a rigid response to a universe which is itself always changing. No matter how successful such a response may be, time and change will ultimately render it worthless. The Bedu are perhaps history's most brilliant example of man's ability to adapt. They have endured precisely because their ways were not immutable – because they have always been able to ride and roll with the waves of change. In shifting to cultivation and motor-cars they were merely doing what they had always done, using the same penchant for adaptation they had employed for 4,000 years.

The dead man lay precisely where Jean-Yves had said, his skin parchment-yellow and stretched tight over his skull, lying in a foetal crouch under his ragged jallabiyya. He was partially covered with stones from the half-hearted effort the French had made to bury him on the hard ground. Jibrin took a long look at the taut, lifeless face and exclaimed, 'By God, I know that man! That is Falih of the Kababish! God have mercy upon him!' This far from the Nile there were no vultures, and his eyes were mercifully intact, but I shall never forget the rictus of suffering on his features as a terrible warning of the agonies of death by thirst. Near to him we found an empty plastic can that had once held motor-oil, and an army-surplus haversack containing some sorghum-flour and a pair of new leather shoes. Knowing we should have to report his death to the police on the river, we searched his pockets, hoping for some documents. Instead, we found them stuffed with refuse – a page of algebra torn from a child's exercise-book, a piece of a cigarette packet, part of a plastic bag, a sweet-wrapper, a ragged ribbon, a bit of newspaper. Jibrin grasped all these trifles in his hand and shook his head sadly as he examined them. 'I remember seeing him in Ed Debba,' he said. 'He was crazy even then. They say he was once a Sheikh, a rich man with fifty camels and a huge flock of sheep, famous for his hospitality. Then the drought came, and most of his animals died. He gave away the rest out of compassion for the suffering of others. Then he moved to the town, where his four children and his wife were taken by the sickness. He was left a beggar. I suppose his mind couldn't stand it. He took to wandering up and down the Nile as a madman, talking to himself and collecting this kind of rubbish. Falih was a Bedui. None knew better than him the dangers of walking out here without a camel. He must have realized his time was finished, and returned to the desert to die!'

We left Falih buried under a cairn of stones, another monument to the history of a landscape. Here, I thought, lay the last of the Bedu. Yet I knew deep down that I was mistaken: that in my search for the last of the Bedu, I had been hunting the snark. There are no last things. Individuals die, cultures change, life evolves, flowing always against the direction of time. In several billion years our sun, whose heat had flayed Falih to death, will burn out, and this planet will be no more. Yet those billions of years give life an almost infinite chance of survival. The adventure is only just beginning. Time present and time past are present in time future – the lessons life has learned through the Bedu will never be lost. As entities we wither, but as a process we continue. We shall change, but we shall survive. We shall survive.

# BIBLIOGRAPHY

Abu Lughod, Lila, *Veiled Sentiments: Honor and Poetry in a Bedouin Society*, California, 1986.

Adams, William, *Nubia – Corridor to Africa*, London, 1977.

Al Baz, Farouk, and Maxwell, Ted, *Desert Landforms of SW Egypt: a Basis for Comparison with Mars*, Washington, 1982.

Al Faruqi, Ismael, and Lamya, Lois, *The Cultural Atlas of Islam*, 1986.

Armour, Robert, *Gods and Myths of Ancient Egypt*, Cairo, 1986.

Asad, Talal, *The Kababish Arabs – Authority and Consent in a Nomadic Tribe*, London, 1969.

Asher, Michael, *In Search of the Forty Days Road*, London, 1984.

Asher, Michael, *A Desert Dies*, London, 1986.

Asher, Michael, *Impossible Journey*, London, 1988.

Bagnold, Raph, 'Journeys in the Libyan Desert in 1929 and 1931', *Geographical Journal*, 1930.

Bagnold, Ralph, 'A Further Journey through the Libyan Desert', *Geographical Journal*, 1935.

Bagnold, Ralph, *Libyan Sands*, London, 1935.

Bagnold, Ralph, 'An Expedition to Gilf Kebir and Uwainat in 1938', *Geographical Journal*, 1938.

Bailey, Clinton, *Bedouin Poetry from Sinai and the Negev*, Oxford, 1991.

Barakat, Halim, *The Arab World – Society, Culture and State*, London, 1993.

Bates, Oric, *The Eastern Libyans*, London, 1914.

Beadnell, H., *An Egyptian Oasis: Kharga*, London, 1909.

Blackman, W. S., *The Fellahin of Upper Egypt*, London, 1927.

Browne, W. G., *Travels in Africa*, London, 1797.

Browning, Iain, *Palmyra*, London, 1979.

Browning, Iain, *Petra*, London, 1982.

Bulliet, Richard, *The Camel and the Wheel*, Cambridge, Mass., 1977.

Burckhardt, J. L., *Notes on Bedouins and Wahabys*, London, 1831.

Campbell, Joseph, *The Masks of God: Primitive Mythology*, London, 1959.

Caton-Thompson, G., and Gardner, E., 'The Prehistoric Geography of Kharja Oasis', *Geographical Journal*, 80, 1932.

Clark, J. Desmond (ed.), *Cambridge History of Africa: Volume 1*, Cambridge, 1982.

Cole, Donald Powell, *Nomads of the Nomads. The Al Murrah Bedouin of the Empty Quarter*, Chicago, 1979.

Cribb, Roger, *Nomads in Archaeology*, London, 1991.

Deledale-Rhodes, Janice, 'The True Nature of Doughty's Relationship with the Arabs', in *Explorations in Doughty's 'Arabia Deserta'*, ed. Steven E. Tabachnick, Georgia, 1987.

Dickson, H. R. P., *The Arab of the Desert*, London, 1948.

Doe, Brian, *Southern Arabia*, London, 1971.

Donner, Fred M., *The Early Islamic Conquests*, New York, 1981.

Doughty, Charles, *Travels in Arabia Deserta*, London, 1885.

Durrell, Lawrence, *The Alexandria Quartet*, London, 1968.

Eliot, T. S., *Collected Poems 1909*, London, 1966.

Fakhry, Ahmed, *Siwa Oasis*, Cairo, 1974.

Fedden, Robin, *Lebanon and Syria*, London, 1946.

Fiennes, Ranulph, *Atlantis of the Sands*, London, 1992.

Gabrieli, Francesco, *Mohammad and the Conquests of Islam*, 1968.

Glubb, John Bagot, 'The Bedouins of Northern Iraq', *Journal of the Royal Central Asian Society*, 1935.

Glubb, John Bagot, 'Arab Chivalry', *Journal of the Royal Central Asian Society*, 1937.

Groom, Nigel, *Frankincense and Myrrh*, London, 1983.

Harding-King, H. W., *Mysteries of the Libyan Desert*, London, 1925.

Hassanein, A. M., *Lost Oases*, London, 1925.

Haynes, C. Vance, *et al.*, 'Holocene Palaeontology of the Eastern Sahara: Selima Oasis', *Quaternary Science Review*, 1989.

Haynes, C. Vance, 'Oyo: a "Lost Oasis" of the Southern Libyan Desert', *Geographical Journal*, 155, 1989.

Helms, I., *Early Islamic Architecture of the Desert*, London, 1990.

Herodotus, *The Histories*, trans. A. de Selincourt, London, 1954.

Hitti, Philip, *History of the Arabs*, London, 1937.

Holt, P. M., Lambton, A. K. S., and Lewis, B. (eds.), *Cambridge History of Islam: Volume 1*, Cambridge, 1970.

Hourani, Albert, *A History of the Arab Peoples*, London, 1991.

Ingrams, Harold, *Arabia and the Isles*, London, 1952.

Janzen, Jorg, *Nomads of the Sultanate of Oman: Tradition and Development in Dhofar*, London, 1980.

Jarvis, Claude S., *Yesterday and Today in Sinai*, London, 1931.

Jarvis, Claude S., *Three Deserts*, London, 1936.

Johnson, Douglas L., *The Nature of Nomadism*, Chicago, 1974.

Kabbani, Rana, *Imperial Fictions*, London, 1986.

Kay, Shirley, *The Bedouin*, London, 1978.

Lancaster, William, *The Rwala Bedouin Today*, Cambridge, 1981.

Lawrence, T. E., *Seven Pillars of Wisdom*, London, 1935.

Lopez, Barry, *Arctic Dreams*, London, 1986.

Marx, Emanuel, *Bedouin of the Negev*, Manchester, 1967.

Marx, Emanuel, 'Are There Pastoral Nomads in the Middle East?', in *Pastoralism in the Levant*, 1992.

Murray, G. W., *The Sons of Ishmael*, London, 1935.

Musil, Alois, *The Manners and Customs of the Rwala Bedouin*, New York, 1928.

Palmer, E. H., *The Desert of the Exodus*, London, 1871.

Rodinson, Maxine, *The Arabs*, London, 1981.

Russell, Kenneth, W., *Ethnohistory of the Bedul Bedouin of Petra*, Jordan, Amman, 1993.

Shoup, J. A., *The Bedouin of Jordan: History and Sedentarisation*, MA thesis, unpublished, Utah, 1980.

Simpson, G. E., *The Heart of Libya: The Siwa Oasis, Its People, Customs and Sport*, London, 1929.

Sitwell, N. H. H., *The World the Romans Knew*, London, 1984.

Stookey, Robert W., *South Yemen: A Marxist Republic in Arabia*, London, 1982.

Sweet, Louise E., 'Camel Raiding of North Arabian Bedouin: a Mechanism of Ecological Evolution', *American Anthropologist*, 1965.

Thesiger, Wilfred, *Arabian Sands*, London, 1959.

Thomas, Bertram, *Arabia Felix*, London, 1932.

Thurman, Sybil, *Rivers of Sand*, 1984.

Tidrick, Kathryn, *Heart-Beguiling Araby: The English Romance with Arabia* (revised edition), London, 1989.

Vatikiotis, P. J., *The History of Egypt*, London, 1969.

Weir, Shelagh, *The Bedouin*, London, 1990.

Wellard, James, *The Great Sahara*, London, 1964.

# INDEX

Proper names are indexed alphabetically according to the commonly used element in the names, and where they are prefixed with al, Ibn or bin, these words remain as prefixes but are ignored for purposes of alphabeticization, thus Ibn Khaldun is indexed under K.

289

# READ MORE IN PENGUIN

In every corner of the world, on every subject under the sun, Penguin represents quality and variety – the very best in publishing today.

For complete information about books available from Penguin – including Puffins, Penguin Classics and Arkana – and how to order them, write to us at the appropriate address below. Please note that for copyright reasons the selection of books varies from country to country.

**In the United Kingdom**: Please write to *Dept. EP, Penguin Books Ltd, Bath Road, Harmondsworth, West Drayton, Middlesex UB7 0DA*

**In the United States**: Please write to *Consumer Sales, Penguin USA, P.O. Box 999, Dept. 17109, Bergenfield, New Jersey 07621-0120*. VISA and MasterCard holders call 1-800-253-6476 to order Penguin titles

**In Canada**: Please write to *Penguin Books Canada Ltd, 10 Alcorn Avenue, Suite 300, Toronto, Ontario M4V 3B2*

**In Australia**: Please write to *Penguin Books Australia Ltd, P.O. Box 257, Ringwood, Victoria 3134*

**In New Zealand**: Please write to *Penguin Books (NZ) Ltd, Private Bag 102902, North Shore Mail Centre, Auckland 10*

**In India**: Please write to *Penguin Books India Pvt Ltd, 706 Eros Apartments, 56 Nehru Place, New Delhi 110 019*

**In the Netherlands**: Please write to *Penguin Books Netherlands bv, Postbus 3507, NL-1001 AH Amsterdam*

**In Germany**: Please write to *Penguin Books Deutschland GmbH, Metzlerstrasse 26, 60594 Frankfurt am Main*

**In Spain**: Please write to *Penguin Books S. A., Bravo Murillo 19, 1° B, 28015 Madrid*

**In Italy**: Please write to *Penguin Italia s.r.l., Via Felice Casati 20, I-20124 Milano*

**In France**: Please write to *Penguin France S. A., 17 rue Lejeune, F-31000 Toulouse*

**In Japan**: Please write to *Penguin Books Japan, Ishikiribashi Building, 2 5 4, Suido, Bunkyo-ku, Tokyo 112*

**In South Africa**: Please write to *Longman Penguin Southern Africa (Pty) Ltd, Private Bag X08, Bertsham 2013*

# BY THE SAME AUTHOR

**Thesiger**

'A superbly penetrating study of the last primitive figure left alive in our national mythology ... a magnificent biography' – Geoffrey Moorhouse in the *Daily Telegraph*

'It is Asher's achievement to have diagnosed both the complexity and naïvety in Thesiger, yet to have evoked his hero's intransigent grandeur ... A work of unmistakable stature and commitment ... it is hard to see how it will be superseded' – Colin Thubron in the *Independent on Sunday*

'Compiled from lengthy interviews with the man himself, meticulous pilgrimages over the same ground, and conversations with his surviving travelling companions, the book both celebrates Thesiger and incorporates what you might call the case against' – Francis Spufford in the *Guardian*

**Shoot to Kill**
A Soldier's Journey through Violence

Michael Asher was eighteen years old when he joined the Parachute Regiment of the British army in 1971. For the next eight years he experienced at first hand the harsh realities of life in the élite fighting units. His journey led him to patrols on the streets of Belfast, to the agonies of selection for the SAS, and to the search for 'an honourable death' in Ulster – under the guise of a Special Patrol Group officer.

'Gripping narrative ... This is a tale of physical endurance, endless drudgery and frequent humiliation. It will bring home to many what life in our armed forces is actually like ... Michael Asher has a fine, observant eye and a keen writing style' – Paddy Ashdown in the *Scotsman*